Shiloh's
True Nature
— D.W. Raleigh —

Shiloh's
True Nature
D.W. Raleigh

Hobbes End Publishing, LLC

Shiloh's True Nature
by D.W. Raleigh
Published by Hobbes End Publishing, LLC, a division of Hobbes End Entertainment, LLC

1st Printing
Hobbes End Publishing: trade paperback, 2014
Printed in the United States of America

ISBN: 978-0-9859110-7-2
Library of Congress Control Number: 2014902190

Cover and internal design: Jordan Benoit

For information, contact:
Hobbes End Entertainment, LLC
PO Box 193
Aubrey, TX 76227
www.hobbesendpublishing.com

Acknowledgments

This book is dedicated to my grandfather, Charles S. Raleigh Jr.,
my father, Charles S. Raleigh III, and my uncle, Steven Carl Raleigh;
none of whom made it to see me published . . . and to my uncle,
H. Ron Raleigh, who thankfully did.

Thank you to my 'first-readers' – Jason Cameron, Mary Fischer-Wood,
Cheryl Cassidy, Judy Mahaffey, Blaine Burns, Lori Raleigh-Sopher,
and Allison Burt.

And finally, a special thanks to my number one reader and fan,
Judy Fischer.

July 20th

Shiloh Williams walked along in the late-afternoon heat, on his way home from the town of Salem. The lanky twelve-year-old brushed his sweat-soaked, brown hair away from his blue eyes with one hand while trying to finish the ice-cream cone he carried in the other. His bare feet were relieved to step off the asphalt main road and onto the narrow, shady dirt path leading to his home.

The dusty, dirt lane was flanked by a vast cornfield to one side and towering black willow trees and intertwined brush on the other. Shiloh inhaled the sweet scent of honeysuckle as he licked the cone, gazing toward the two-story, white Victorian house in the distance. The house was his home, and the cornfield part of his family's farm. One of the few farms left in the area, his father always liked to mention.

Shiloh was in a good mood: partly because he had spent the day in town playing with some friends, but mostly because this was his first actual vacation day of the summer. Until today, he had been working on the farm all day every

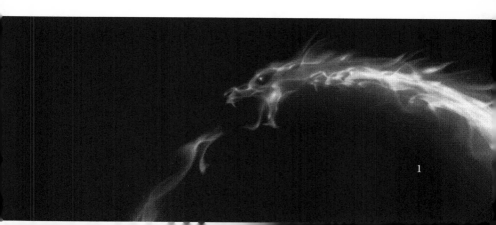

1

Shiloh's True Nature

day, since school ended. When his father told him he was receiving a two-week break, Shiloh decided he was going to make the most of it and be thankful he didn't have to work another day in the brutal July heat.

As he strolled along the dusty path, Shiloh heard something rustling in the brush beside him. He turned his head and saw two large black birds only a couple of feet away. The birds cawed as they boldly jumped from branch to branch trying to keep pace with him. He assumed it was the ice cream they were after, so Shiloh tossed the remainder of the cone toward the brush and watched as the birds descended upon it.

Farther along, Shiloh spotted an expensive-looking, black car in front of the house. It was parked next to his father's battered, old pickup truck, which made any other vehicle look nice. There was a man leaning against the rear of the car wearing a black suit and cap. Shiloh found that strange, considering he was dressed in a white T-shirt and shorts and had been sweating since he stepped outside that morning.

As he drew closer to the house, Shiloh realized his hands were sticky with ice-cream residue. He wasn't supposed to be eating sweets this close to his suppertime, and knew his mother would scold him if she found out. So he slipped into the cornfield to let the giant stalks conceal his five-foot frame until he could reach the back of the house to wash off undetected.

He quietly snuck through the field and came up behind the giant stack of hay bales perpetually piled at the rear of the house. After glancing around to make sure it was clear, he crept up to the porch and over to the rusty, old spigot. He winced as he slowly turned the squeaky faucet handle, hoping the noise didn't make it through the kitchen screen door just a few feet away.

As Shiloh cleaned his hands, the aroma of his mother's cooking filled his nostrils, while the sound of arguing voices filled his ears. When his hands were no longer sticky, he quietly moved over to the back door, and stopped when he could hear the discussion in the kitchen. He immediately recognized one voice as his father's, but there was another, unfamiliar, rough-sounding man's voice. It must have been whoever came in the black car, he thought.

Listening intently, Shiloh was startled when something rubbed against his leg. It was one of his cats, Lovie. The gray and black tabby mix rubbed her face against his anklebones as she walked figure eights between his legs. Shiloh knew if Lovie was around, his other feline, Cheepie, couldn't be far behind. He looked over his shoulder toward the faucet and found the other gray tabby, one that looked like a miniature tiger, entranced by the remaining water droplets dribbling from the nozzle.

His attention returned to the kitchen door when the rough voice said, "I don't know how you're keeping this farm productive when all the others in this area have gone under, but whatever you're doing is going to fail eventually. So you might as well sell it to me before I decide to withdraw my more than generous offer."

Shiloh imagined the scowl on his father's face as he heard him answer, "You've been trying to get your hands on this property for years, but I'm not going to give it to you. Not now. Not ever. Not at any price. And if there are problems with the soil around here, you need only look in the mirror for the cause."

"I'll not be insulted by the likes of you, Joseph Williams. Good day," the man huffed.

Shiloh heard footsteps, followed by the front door slamming. He was curious about this unfamiliar man, so he leapt off the porch and ran up along the side of the house. In his haste to see the stranger, Shiloh slipped on some pebbles and fell just as he reached the front corner of the house. The man immediately turned toward Shiloh scowling. Shiloh looked up at the stranger, but the bright sunshine kept him from distinguishing any of his features. The one thing Shiloh did notice was, like his driver, the man was dressed all in black, except for a hideously bright orange tie.

The man's gaze was broken as two black birds descended and began attacking him. The man quickly ducked into the rear of the car, the birds turning their attention to his driver, who ran around to the other side to enter. As the car pulled away, Shiloh noticed it had a peculiar, black license plate with orange lettering reading HAINES.

When the vehicle left his sight, Shiloh returned to the back door, but again paused by the screen door when he heard his father's agitated voice. "The crops looked a little off today. We definitely need to get some cash together for fertilizer. They could use a dusting too. And on top of that, I haven't paid Rikki and Peco for a couple weeks. I'm glad I agreed to let them stay in the old barn. Otherwise they might've left by now. I'll need to find a way to make it up to them."

Shiloh heard the oven door open and close, followed by his mother's voice, "Are you having second thoughts about Haines' offer, Joe?"

"What? No! I'll work the fields alone and eat dirt before I let that man get his hands on this land, Mary," Joe stubbornly declared.

Mary scoffed. "Okay. Well, I'll see if I can round up some recipes for dirt . . . just in case."

Joe chuckled slightly and Shiloh smiled to himself, thinking about the easy way his mother was always able to diffuse his father's anger.

Joe then noted, "By the way, I spoke to Doc and he said it would be all right. In fact, he suggested it before I even asked."

"He's not going to be happy about it," Mary sighed.

Shiloh frowned, wondering what they were talking about, as Joe continued, "Well, that's too bad. A vacation is a vacation. He's almost a man now, and he needs to learn that part of being a man is having to do stuff you don't want to do."

Mary snorted sarcastically. "Say it just like that, Joe. That'll make him feel better about it."

Joe chuckled again and said, "Give me a break, Mary."

"I won't give you a break, but I will give you dinner. Go wash up," Mary replied with a giggle.

Shiloh heard a chair slide across the kitchen floor and waited until the footsteps faded before opening the screen door. When he stepped through the doorway onto the black and white tile, he found his mother's tall and slender frame

Shiloh's True Nature

at the sink. As Mary washed her hands, her long sandy-blond hair was illuminated by the sun shining in from the window above the sink.

After she dried her hands, Mary turned to open one of the nearby wooden cabinets and said, "No ..." pointing in Shiloh's direction and downward. Shiloh looked around in confusion. "... I'm making dinner and those two are not coming in here," she finished.

Shiloh looked down and realized she was referring to the cats lingering in the doorway.

"One keeps trying to drag dead mice in the house. And the other keeps eating bugs, which wouldn't be so bad if he wasn't throwing them up all over the place afterward," she continued.

A tight-lipped smile rolled across Shiloh's face as he turned to shoo the cats back out the door.

When he turned back around, Shiloh found himself face-to-face with his mother. Her chestnut-colored eyes stared straight into his baby blues with a smirk. "What's this?" she asked, pointing to his chest. "Ice cream?"

Shiloh looked down at his T-shirt to see a couple of stains from his earlier treat. "Oh ... that was from earlier this afternoon," he replied with a wide grin.

"Really? Because it still looks wet," Mary noted, returning his smile with a shake of her head. "Go wash up. Dinner is almost ready."

The family dinner was relatively quiet. Shiloh tried to stuff himself so he wouldn't be lectured by his mother about eating ice cream before supper. He avoided eye contact with his father, because after hearing Joe grumble about all of the farm's problems, he feared he might lose his time off.

When he finished, Shiloh took his plate to the sink and tried to make a hasty retreat out the back door without saying a word. However, it wasn't to be. "Hey . . . take a seat," Joe called, pointing to Shiloh's empty chair at the dinner table.

Shiloh walked back to the chair feeling certain his father was about to revoke his vacation time "for the good of the farm." He looked up to see his father leaning forward with his elbows on the table and his large callused hands folded. Joe was a tall, muscular man with perpetually unkempt, light-brown hair, piercing blue eyes, and his face always appeared to need a shave.

Joe stared at Shiloh for a moment before asking, "How would feel you about spending some time with your grandfather?"

He was taken off guard by the question, but shrugged and answered, "Okay, I guess."

"Good," Joe smiled. "He'll be by to pick you up tomorrow."

"What?" Shiloh responded in shock.

"You're going to spend a couple weeks with your grandfather," Joe answered pointedly.

Shiloh's disbelief and agitation spilled out of his mouth in rapid succession. "A couple weeks? Why? I'm supposed to go swimming at the pond tomorrow! The carnival is in town next week! My birthday is in two weeks! I don't want to go!"

Joe leaned back in his chair, shaking his head, "You've been complaining about having to work the fields all sum-

Shiloh's True Nature

mer. I'd think you'd be glad to get a break from it."

"Yeah, I wanted a break to have some fun with my friends. Not a break where I'm sent away to some strange place . . . I'm not going!" Shiloh's voice shook with anger.

Joe, not the kind of man to listen to long protestations, replied, "You are going. End of discussion." He returned to his meal.

Slamming his hands on the table, Shiloh rose from his chair, and walked toward the back door. "Get back here," Joe called, as Shiloh forcefully pushed open the screen door.

He heard his father yell, "Shiloh!" but he ignored him and ran into the immense cornfield. He ran through the field until he grew so tired he had to walk. He continued walking until he found himself on the far edge of the field, where he stepped out onto a narrow dirt trail that surrounded it.

Shiloh looked back to see how far he had come and the farm's old horse barn caught his eye. The faded, maroon monstrosity had fallen into disrepair, but the barn's current residents, Rikki and Peco, loved it for some reason. It was their big, red dilapidated mansion.

When his gaze drifted across the field, Shiloh saw his home in the distance. The towering cornstalks obscured all but the top half of the house. Taking a couple of steps backward, trying to find a better view, he suddenly lost his balance. He began tumbling down a slick embankment covered with reeds and into the swampy marsh that separated his family's property from the Delahanna River.

Shiloh was uninjured by the fall, but landed on his backside in the mud. He sat for a moment to catch his breath, gazing toward the river stretching out in front of him. He saw some Great Blue Herons standing nearby in the marsh. The large gray birds were motionless, with their S-shaped necks pointing up into the distance.

Following the herons' gaze, Shiloh saw the large factory to the south. He knew the factory was there, but never paid it much attention. It was practically invisible due to the thick cluster of hickory trees lining the rear of the farm. The factory's most distinguishing feature was an enormous cylindrical brick smokestack with a giant, orange H on its side. The huge tower emitted a perpetual gray smoke that seemed to linger in the air.

Hearing voices in the distance, Shiloh turned back toward the river. An old fishing boat was anchored just offshore with some young people frolicking around the deck. He watched as a young man jumped from the deck into the river. "It's freezing!" the young man hollered, emerging from the water.

Shiloh smiled, remembering how he used to love the crisp bite of the river water on a hot summer afternoon. His parents wouldn't allow him to swim in the river anymore. They said it was too polluted and dirty.

Straight across the river were some lights from the town of Old New Castle. Just beyond that was Pike Creek, where his grandfather lived and where he would apparently be going the next day. This made him think of the things he'd be missing in the next two weeks: going swimming, the carnival, spending time with his friends.

Thoughts of his impending departure made Shiloh feel sick to his stomach, so he tried thinking of something else.

Shiloh's True Nature

He looked around and noticed several gray puddles of water with a number of long-stemmed, gray wildflowers growing out of them. He frowned because he couldn't recall ever seeing a gray flower before. He plucked the closest one and thought it was a wild daisy of some kind.

Another flower grew out of the puddle right before his eyes, taking the place of the one he picked. This second flower was not gray, but golden yellow with a black center. Though startled, Shiloh scowled and dismissed the peculiar occurrence, recalling how he'd seen colorful mushrooms grow right before his eyes while working very early in the morning on the farm.

As the sun began to set, Shiloh climbed the embankment, deciding he had better return to the house. He chose to walk back through the cornfield instead of the path along the edge of the field, because it was shorter. He came to regret that decision when the sunlight faded and the tall cornstalks blocked out what little light was left in the sky. To make matters worse, it was a new moon, so there was no heavenly light to guide him.

In the darkness, the size of the farm became more apparent than ever. Shiloh walked and walked, seeing only dark rows of corn ahead of him. He knew he would escape them eventually, but not knowing exactly where he was made him uncomfortable. The odd collection of noises echoing out of the darkness only added to his discomfort.

Shiloh dismissed some fluttering and flapping sounds, thinking it was probably one of the Great Blue Herons he saw earlier in the marsh. He then heard an odd, thumping sound, as if something was running around. He tried to dismiss that as well, remembering his father had mentioned seeing red foxes in the fields. Shiloh had never seen a fox on the farm, but supposed one could be the source of the noise.

The thumping sound seemed to grow closer and closer, but every time Shiloh stopped to listen, it would cease. The louder the noise grew, the more Shiloh's heart raced. He tried to ignore the sound, focusing into the distance to locate his house. When the thumping became so loud it seemed just a step away, Shiloh panicked, breaking into a run.

He sprinted along until he tripped, falling forward onto the ground. Shiloh remained still and listened for a moment, but the only sound he could hear was his pounding heart. Looking behind him, down the corn row, he saw an indistinct dark mass just a few feet away.

Fear gripped Shiloh, who now thought only of escape. He turned his head around, thinking if he could just stand he might be able to outrun whatever was back there. He was shocked to discover a second dark figure blocking his path. The second shape was lower to the ground, with glowing eyes, and it was growling.

Shiloh didn't know what to do, but figured whatever it was would have to start with him being on his feet. He took a deep breath and readied himself to stand, but before he could, the second dark figure charged him. He placed his hands over his head, preparing for an attack. However, no attack came. The figure leapt over him, chasing whatever was behind him down the corn row. Shiloh stood and sprinted away as fast as he could.

Shiloh's True Nature

As he neared the edge of the field, he could hear a loud, fierce growling and tussling behind him. Resisting the temptation to look back, he broke through the edge of the cornfield and ran straight into the house.

July 21ˢᵗ

Shiloh woke in his powder-blue bedroom to the low whir and soft breeze from the spinning blades of his ceiling fan. He rubbed his eyes, guessing it was late morning by the brightness of the room. His late start was the result of recounting the previous night's happenings multiple times to his parents.

Shaking off his slumber, Shiloh gazed around the room and found his cats lying nearby. Cheepie was in his usual spot, sunning himself in an old armchair beneath an open window. Lovie was at the foot of the bed purring loudly and proudly as she gnawed away on something Shiloh didn't recognize. It resembled a large, chalky, dark-brown feather.

"Did you get a bird, girl?" Shiloh asked, sitting up, trying to identify what she had in her clutches. He leaned forward to take a better look, but Lovie pulled away, quickly jumping out the window with her prize before he could examine it.

With his stomach growling, Shiloh threw his covers off and left the bed. As he walked down the stairs, he overheard

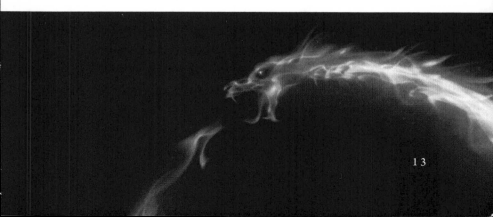

his parents talking in the kitchen.

"I'm telling you, he made the whole thing up to get out of going, Mary," Joe said, certain Shiloh had fabricated the prior night's events.

Mary seemed less skeptical. "He seemed pretty shook up for a made-up story, Joe."

"Maybe it happened. Maybe it didn't. The only thing I found were those sneaky cats lurking around," Joe replied.

Searching for reasons to believe her son, Mary asked, "What about Rikki and Peco? Did they find anything?"

"They're out right now driving around the perimeter of the field looking for anything out of the ordinary . . . but I'm telling you they aren't going to find anything," Joe said, shaking his head.

"Then why are you having them drive around if you're so sure?" Mary questioned.

Joe smiled and said, "They love riding around in that old truck. So I thought I'd give them a thrill and maybe they'd forget about the fact that they haven't been paid in weeks."

Irritated with his father's skepticism, Shiloh pushed open the kitchen door and said, "I did not make it up. There has to be tracks or prints or something."

Mary shook her head and said, "It rained overnight, honey. Any tracks were washed away."

"Convenient, huh?" Joe said, lifting an eyebrow.

"What about the corn? There must to be some broken stalks or something," Shiloh said, defending himself.

Joe shook his head, saying, "There are acres and acres of corn out there, Shiloh. I'm not going to walk through all that looking for a few broken stalks."

Shiloh protested, "It happened right out there. I'll show you where."

Joe smirked again. "I don't need to see some broken cornstalks to know that you don't want to go to your grandfather's."

Shiloh raised his voice. "I'm not making it up! There was something out there!"

"Fine. We'll keep an eye out and take care of any pests while you're gone," Joe added.

Shiloh shook his head at his father's stubbornness. There was no middle ground with Joe. He believed Shiloh had made the whole thing up to avoid going to his grandfather's, and no amount of evidence would convince him otherwise.

Being reminded of his pending trip spoiled Shiloh's appetite, so he walked out of the kitchen and started back to his bedroom.

"Don't you want something to eat?" Mary asked, calling after him.

"I'm not hungry," Shiloh replied, stomping up the stairs.

He returned to his room and immediately went to the window. He peered out into the seemingly endless cornfield wondering what was out there. What were those things that boxed him in? Had he been in serious danger? Shiloh sighed. Because of his father's unwillingness to investigate further, he would never know the answers to those questions.

Shiloh glanced downward to find Lovie lying outside, underneath the windowsill. She was still clinging to that chalky, dark-brown thing. He leaned out of the window to try to

Shiloh's True Nature

grab it from her, but a voice from inside stopped him.

"What are you doing?" Mary asked.

Shiloh looked over his shoulder and saw his mother standing in the doorway holding a tray of food. He withdrew from the window, walking over and sitting on the bed. Mary took a seat next to him, placing the tray on her lap.

"Eat something, honey," she said with a comforting smile.

Shiloh wrinkled his nose and shook his head. "I'm not hungry."

Mary sighed and said, "I know it's not how you wanted to spend your two weeks off, but it might be fun. You haven't seen your grandfather in quite a while. I think it would be nice for you to get to know him a little bit."

Shiloh looked out the window, shaking his head.

As she did with his father, Mary always knew what to say to make Shiloh feel better. "Well, think about it like this. How much fun do you think it's going to be around here with your father if you don't go?" she asked with a smirk.

Beginning to smile, Shiloh asked, "Can I take the cats with me?"

Mary grimaced and said, "You know I'd love to be rid of them for a while. But I don't think it's a good idea. Cats are very territorial, and they don't take well to being uprooted."

"Mary?" Joe yelled from the foot of the stairs.

She rolled her eyes, placed the tray in Shiloh's lap, and said, "Eat." She gave Shiloh a kiss on his forehead and then rose from the bed, adding, "You might want to start packing once you finish."

As he ate, Shiloh began haphazardly throwing things into

an old green duffel bag. He wasn't really sure what to take, so between bites he scanned the room for items he thought he might need. By the time he finished eating he had stuffed the bag full of T-shirts, shorts, socks, and underwear. He took one last look around the room and saw a pair of blue swim trunks lying on the back of a chair. He frowned undecidedly to himself, but then grabbed the trunks and pushed them into the bag, just in case.

The rest of the afternoon Shiloh milled about his bedroom, doing nothing in particular until he heard faint voices outside. He looked out of the window and saw Joe talking to two dark-skinned men with long, black hair peeking out from under their straw cowboy hats. The shorter of the two men stood nodding with an armful of broken cornstalks, while the taller, thinner man spoke and gestured toward the field. It was Rikki and Peco.

Shiloh smiled to himself as Joe quizzically examined the stalks. As Peco continued to talk, Joe turned toward the house and saw Shiloh grinning down at him. Joe scowled, but then something drew his attention toward the front of the house and he left Rikki and Peco behind to investigate.

Shiloh watched his father walk out of sight and felt slightly vindicated by the discovery of the broken stalks. He started to turn away from the open window, but spun back around when he heard an odd clip-clop sound. The noise grew louder and louder, but then abruptly stopped. A moment later, the front porch door creaked open and some greetings commenced. He realized his grandfather had arrived.

Shiloh was in no hurry to go downstairs. He paced back

Shiloh's True Nature

and forth, thinking about the unfairness of his predicament. His contemplation was brought to an end when his mother appeared in the doorway, saying, "Shiloh, your grandfather is here. Come down and say hello."

He grabbed the green duffel bag from his bed and reluctantly walked toward the door. Mary stopped him in the doorway and gave him another kiss on the forehead. "It'll be all right, honey. I'll bet after a couple of days you won't want to come home." Shiloh shook his head, finding that hard to believe.

When Shiloh swung open the kitchen door, the two men were sitting at the kitchen table. His father was in his usual place, facing the doorway. Sitting on the opposite side of the table was a man with shoulder-length, salt-and-pepper hair. Joe reached for his cup of coffee, but paused when he realized Shiloh was standing there. The man glanced over his shoulder toward Shiloh and his face lit up with a wide smile.

It had been so long since Shiloh had seen his grandfather that he had almost forgotten what the man looked like. Other than being older, his features weren't all that different from Joe's. He was tall and muscular, and he too always looked like he needed to shave. His most distinguishing feature was his eyes. He had one blue eye and one brown eye. He was the only person Shiloh had ever seen with two different colored eyes.

Maintaining his ear-to-ear grin, his grandfather said, "Hey, Shiloh. Long time, no see."

Shiloh gave him a reluctant smile and took a seat in one of the empty chairs at the table.

"I hear you had a bit of a scare last night," his grandfather announced.

Joe snorted and shook his head. Shiloh frowned at his father, replying, "Yeah . . . not that anyone believes me."

"I believe you," his grandfather said with a wink.

Joe frowned and was about to speak when Mary bumped into him as she picked up the coffee pot off the table. Mary extended the pot across the table and said, "We believe you, Shiloh. Can I top you off, Doc?"

"Yes, thank you," his grandfather replied.

Shiloh thought for a moment and then remembered Mary always called his grandfather "Doc." He never understood why. To his knowledge, his grandfather was not a physician.

Doc took a long sip from his coffee cup and then looked at Joe. "I understand you had a visitor yesterday?" he asked.

"Yeah? How do you know about that?" Joe asked, a frustrated look on his face.

"Oh . . . I hear things," Doc said, smiling at Shiloh while tugging on his earlobe.

Joe's face contorted into a cocky smile as he said, "Then you'll hear me when I say never you mind about my visitor yesterday. I sent him on his way."

"Just like that?" Doc asked.

"Just like that," Joe quickly replied.

Shiloh looked back and forth between Joe and Doc, watching the uncomfortable tension between them. He recalled the two men never seemed to relate well, but it mostly seemed one-sided from his perspective. Joe always took exception to everything Doc said and could be downright hos-

Shiloh's True Nature

tile toward the man at times.

Joe's irritation manifested itself through his fingers, which tapped the table from pinkie to index over and over. "I'm curious as to how you're able to get into my business from way across the river," Joe blurted out.

Doc looked down into his coffee cup and, with a tight-lipped smile, said, "I'm not getting into your business, son. I just wanted to let you know that if you need some help or advice, all you have to do is ask."

Shiloh's eyes widened at his grandfather's remarks and waited for the explosive response his father would no doubt give. He knew if there was one thing Joe prided himself on, it was self-sufficiency. Joe would rather fail alone than succeed with someone else's help. He was the definition of stubborn.

"Well, I have no need for your help or advice, Dad. I've been running this farm just fine without it for years," Joe sneered.

Doc kept smiling as he said, "Yes you have, son. It's amazing how you've been able to make this place thrive over the last twelve years or so. I never would have thought it could be so productive."

"Amazed, are you?" Joe raised his voice, his irritation clearly mounting.

Doc rose from his chair, prompting Joe to do the same. Doc looked toward Shiloh and said, "We have a long trip ahead of us. We should probably get going."

Shiloh frowned, confused by the "long trip" comment, but he assumed their abrupt departure was simply his grandfather's way of avoiding further confrontation.

"Are you sure you won't stay for dinner?" Mary asked, trying to calm the situation.

Doc smiled at the offer, but said, "No. We should be going."

Shiloh grabbed his duffel bag and followed Doc out the front door into the late-afternoon sunshine. A light breeze washed over him, and he thought maybe the drive to his grandfather's wouldn't be so bad. However, he was stunned to learn how they would be traveling. Right next to his father's pickup truck sat a horse-drawn cart.

The cart itself was made of beautiful, glossy wood that had unique symbols carved into it. The long bed was covered with a shiny sheet of black canvas and supported by huge, black rubber wheels. Shiny, gold-trimmed black leather covered the seating area. Its means of locomotion was two of the largest horses Shiloh had ever seen. The two chestnut mares had to be over twenty hands high and had gigantic blankets covering their enormously wide frames.

Despite the beauty of the cart, Shiloh saw little more than an embarrassing ride through town. He turned to his mother behind him, a look of disbelief on his face. Mary leaned over with a smile and said, "When you get back on your birthday, I'll have a wonderful party for you."

Mary then turned to Doc and gave him a hug, saying, "Doc, it was wonderful to see you."

Doc gave her a kiss on the cheek and replied, "It was nice to see you too."

Joe knew Shiloh was annoyed with him, so he bent down to look Shiloh in the eye and whispered, "I'll make it up to you on your birthday. I promise." Joe smiled slightly at Shiloh then returned to his usual stern look, nodding in Doc's direction and added, "Dad."

Doc returned the nod and said, "Son."

As Shiloh began to climb up into the cart, he noticed Lovie and Cheepie were standing side by side at the rear of the cart-bed. He hesitated, looking at them curiously. He didn't know how it could be, but he could have sworn they were smiling at him.

"Climb on up," Doc said, drawing Shiloh's attention.

He tossed his duffel bag on to the seat and stepped up into the cart.

Once he was seated, Doc asked, "Ready?"

Shiloh nodded to Doc and then looked back over his shoulder to find the cats had disappeared.

Initially, Shiloh found riding in the cart tolerable, even a little fun. He had a much better view of the surroundings than he would in his father's pickup truck. However, the farther along they went, the more embarrassed he felt to be traveling that way. By the time they reached the center of town, Shiloh found himself trying to hide his face from anyone familiar. He kept his hand on his forehead with his head tilted down and inward toward Doc. His view now consisted of the right side of Doc's torso and the top of the canvas covering the bed.

It soon became evident to Shiloh that the roads of Salem didn't have the smoothest pavement. An automobile passenger may have barely noticed anything, but riding in the cart revealed every minor imperfection in the road. Every time they hit a bump the entire cart bounced up and down.

Shiloh watched the canvas flap with each bump and thought he saw movement underneath. He squinted and watched for his next opportunity to see something. When the next bump hit and the canvas bounced up, Shiloh was surprised to see Lovie's head pop out from under the sheet. She briefly looked at him before sliding her head back under, like she was playing peek-a-boo. Shiloh smiled and wondered to himself if Cheepie was back there as well.

His answer came at the next bump when Cheepie's head popped up in place of Lovie's. Shiloh tried not to laugh as only Cheepie's nose and mouth stayed visible when the canvas flopped back down. Cheepie wriggled his little nose, sniffing the air while the canvas pulled on his whiskers revealing his teeth. Shiloh found it amusing to see what looked like a tiny smile in the darkness under the sheet.

Once they were through the town Doc turned to Shiloh and remarked, "I understand you weren't too happy about coming for a visit."

Shiloh shrugged his shoulders, feeling a little embarrassed that Doc knew this.

"I promise you will change your mind once we get there," Doc added with a smile.

Shiloh wondered what at his grandfather's could possibly make him feel better about missing the town carnival or not being able to go swimming with his friends. He then realized he had never actually been to his grandfather's home. The few times he had seen Doc were either back at the farm or they met him somewhere.

Shiloh's True Nature

When Shiloh returned to sitting normally, his angst was renewed as they approached the bridge to take them across the river. He didn't like heights and the bridge arced high above the river to allow ships to pass underneath. Whenever he would cross the bridge with his parents, he would just slide down in the seat and close his eyes until they were on the other side. He couldn't do that in the cart.

Shiloh then remembered what his mother always told him, which was to focus on something else. So, to take his mind off it, Shiloh blurted out the first thing that came to mind, "Why don't you drive a car like everyone else?"

Shocked by the sudden question, Doc chuckled and asked, "Oh, so you've finally decided to speak to me?"

Shiloh again had a feeling of embarrassment, realizing he hadn't spoken to his grandfather until then.

"There are a lot of reasons I don't drive a car . . ." Doc said, as a large, noisy truck passed them. " . . . That's one of them . . ." Doc continued, pointing to the black smoke spewing from the truck's exhaust stack. Doc motioned over his shoulder back toward Salem and said, " . . . Over there is another reason."

Shiloh turned and looked, but wasn't sure what he was supposed to see. There were sparse patches of tall trees, some of which didn't look very green considering it was mid-summer. So Shiloh asked, "What do you mean?"

Doc nodded toward Salem again and asked, "You see that big brick tower with all the smoke pouring out of it?"

Shiloh looked again and realized Doc was referring to the large factory next to his family's farm. He saw the tall brick smokestack with the big, orange H on the side spewing smoke in the distance.

"Yes. I see it," Shiloh confirmed.

Doc added, "Well, it's bad."

"What do you mean, it's bad?" Shiloh inquired, looking back at the smokestack again.

"You wouldn't want to breathe that, would you?" Doc asked.

Shiloh shrugged his shoulders. "No . . . I guess not."

"Believe me, you don't. And you see how the smoke comes out and drifts higher until you can't see it anymore?" Doc pointed into the distance.

"Uh-huh," Shiloh said, watching the dissipating smoke.

"Well, even though it looks gone, the smoke is still there. It's just mixed in with the clean air. That factory pumps out smoke all day, every day. And even when you can't see it, the smoke is still there."

Shiloh thought for a moment, and then asked, "So what does that have to do with you not driving a car?"

Doc paused as some passing cars honked their horns in frustration because they had to go around the slow-moving cart. Doc just smiled and nodded at them as they passed before continuing. "All these cars passing by us, they are doing pretty much the same thing. The motors that power them are giving off exhaust and it's going right into the air, just like that factory. It's not as much, and might be something a little different than the factory smoke, but it's still not something you want to breathe. So, it's bad, Shiloh. It's bad for you. It's bad for me. It's bad for the birds. It's bad for the fish."

Shiloh's True Nature

Shiloh frowned quizzically. "It's bad for the fish?"

"Yes. That smoky junk floats up into the clouds and combines with the water vapor there. Then when it rains and the water drops or flows into the river, the fish swim in it and they breathe through it, which is bad for them. And then people eat the fish. And it's the same thing with fruits and vegetables. So people are breathing and eating it too," Doc said with a disgusted look.

"So why doesn't anyone stop it?" Shiloh inquired.

"Well, some people don't believe it's bad. They think that there's so much air in the world that pumping the smoke into it won't hurt anything. And then there's money, of course," Doc added.

"Money?" Shiloh questioned.

"The man who owns that factory is named Haines and he makes money from what is produced there. So, just telling him it's bad won't stop him, Shiloh."

Shiloh looked back at the factory again and said, "That factory is pretty close to our farm."

"Yes, it is," Doc replied.

"Is that why you said you were surprised my father was able to keep the farm going? Because that factory is nearby?" Shiloh asked.

Doc smiled. "You're a smart young man, Shiloh."

Shiloh smiled back at Doc.

When they finally crossed the bridge, Doc took the cart in a direction unfamiliar to Shiloh. There was a large sign by the side of the road that read WELCOME TO OLD NEW CASTLE. Curious about their route, Shiloh asked, "Why are we going this way?"

Doc mumbled something about saving time and then asked, "Hey, you've got a birthday coming up, don't you?"

Shiloh nodded affirmatively.

"It's your thirteenth birthday, isn't it?"

Shiloh nodded again and Doc added, "Thirteen . . . that's a special birthday."

Without thinking, Shiloh asked, "Special enough for you to get me a present this year?"

Doc squinted and smiled, "Maybe." He grimaced for a moment before saying, "I know I've missed a few of your birthdays and I'm sorry for that. But I could never think of what to get you."

Shiloh rolled his eyes, thinking it was more like all of his birthdays Doc had missed.

Doc continued, "The thing about presents is, you always think you want something and you're excited about it . . . then you're happy when you get it . . . and you play with it every day, at first . . . but then you play with it less and less over time, until one day you don't play with it at all. I don't like to give presents like that."

Doc could tell Shiloh was confused by the look on his face. So he added, "A true gift is something that is enjoyed every day." Doc paused for a moment and then asked, "Can you think of any gift you've ever received that you enjoy every day?"

Shiloh thought for a moment and shrugged his shoulders.

Doc smiled and asked, "Are you sure?"

Shiloh confirmed, "I can't think of anything."

Shiloh's True Nature

With a wide grin, Doc reached back, lifted up the tarp from the bed and asked, "What about these two? Do you enjoy having them around every day?"

Shiloh looked back realizing Doc was referring to the cats and explained, "I didn't know they were back there until after we left! I swear!"

Doc raised a calming hand and said, "It's okay, but you still haven't answered my question."

Shiloh looked back toward the tarp and smiled, "Yes, I enjoy having them around every day."

"Then I think the only two birthday presents I ever gave you were pretty good gifts," Doc added.

Shiloh had forgotten it was Doc who gave him Cheepie and Lovie. He couldn't remember exactly when he received them, but he knew the cats were always there when he went to bed and always there when he woke up. On bad days their antics could always make him smile, and on good days their presence was just icing on the cake. He loved them and they were, by Doc's definition, "true gifts."

After they passed through Old New Castle, the paved street turned to a dirt road as they entered a farming area. The area seemed familiar to Shiloh, but he soon realized that was only because it had similarities to his farm. It had reeds bordering the river on one side and a cornfield on the other. However, the cornfield there didn't look nearly as healthy as the one on his farm. The cornstalks were tall and overgrown, but they weren't uniform. They had grown together, bending in strange directions, and the leaves appeared to be growing upside down.

The farther along the cornfield they went, the more un-comfortable Shiloh felt. The sun was beginning to set and it felt like the road had narrowed and the dense cornfield was closing in on them. Shiloh's anxiety eased slightly as they came upon a small opening in the field. It was little more than a half-circle indentation in the field that contained a scarecrow.

The scarecrow had hay sticking out of the leg openings of its overalls and the arms of its old flannel shirt. Its head was a pumpkin, carved with a scary face and topped off by an old straw hat. The scarecrow was a little creepy looking, but the two large black birds seated on its shoulders made Shiloh smile.

Shiloh turned toward Doc to point out what a poor job the scarecrow was doing and found him eyeing the birds intently. Suddenly the birds begin cawing and screaming loudly. Shiloh looked back and forth between the birds and Doc, wondering what was happening. Doc then mumbled, "What are you up to, Samuel?"

Suddenly, a familiar mechanical roar in the distance drew Shiloh's attention toward the front of the cart. He knew this noise, but couldn't place it. A second roar sounded from behind the cart and Shiloh again looked to Doc for an explanation, but Doc appeared just as confused and concerned.

The farther down the road they traveled, the louder the rumbling became. Shiloh felt that the reeds and cornstalks were enveloping them. "You might want to get a hold of the cats," Doc directed as wisps of smoke became visible just ahead of them.

Shiloh's True Nature

Confused as to why, Shiloh grabbed Cheepie and Lovie and placed them on the seat between himself and Doc. Doc then began maneuvering a second set of reins that Shiloh hadn't noticed previously.

The loud rumbling came closer and closer, accompanied by a swishing sound. Doc turned to Shiloh and shouted, "I'm sorry! I thought coming this way would be safer!"

Shiloh yelled back, "Safe from what? What do you mean?"

A moment after the words left Shiloh's mouth, the source of the noise was revealed when a gigantic combine harvester slashed out of the cornfield and just missed slicing into the rear of the cart with its giant rotary blades. Shiloh's heart began to pound and he placed his hands on the cats to be sure they remained stationary. He looked back and found the combine's spinning blades approaching the rear of the cart. He gazed up at the cab of the harvester and, though the glare from the sun obscured his view, he could've sworn there was no one inside.

When Shiloh turned back toward the front of the cart, another combine flew out of the field ahead of them in the distance, turning directly into their path.

Shiloh yelled, "What's going on?"

"Just hang on!" Doc shouted as he pulled on the second set of reins.

Shiloh watched as the coverings on the horses' backs flew up into the air and right onto the windshield of the combine behind them. He might have smiled at this good fortune, but before he had time to think about it he was shocked by what the coverings originally hid. The horses pulling the cart had huge, brown wings.

Shiloh watched as the horses stretched out their append-ages and began flapping them rhythmically. The combine ahead of the cart drew dangerously close, but Doc tugged on the reins and the horses leapt off the ground, pulling the cart into the air behind them.

As they took flight, a tickling sensation in Shiloh's stom-ach made him feel sick. Doc was smiling and cried out, "Woo-hoo! Are you having fun yet?"

Shiloh looked at his grandfather as if he were crazy and stammered, "I think I'd like to go back home now."

Doc's smile faded slightly and he asked, "What? Go home?"

"Yes, home. I'd like to go home please," Shiloh uttered.

Doc tried not to laugh and returned, "I'm sorry, Shiloh. There are a lot of things I haven't told you about . . . but I promise I will. In the meantime, maybe you could try to enjoy it."

"Enjoy what?" Shiloh shot back.

"We're flying, Shiloh! We're flying!" Doc said, unable to control his smile.

Shiloh pushed aside his queasiness and began to question if these things were really happening. "I'm dreaming, aren't I?" he wondered aloud.

Doc laughed and shook his head.

Shiloh gazed off into the distance toward the setting sun and noticed the rolling hills. They caught the sun's rays in such a way as to give them a glorious, golden haze. The hill they were flying toward was a little wider and a little taller

Shiloh's True Nature

than the rest. Shiloh had a strange feeling he'd seen it before, but he knew that wasn't possible.

As they descended, the hill obstructed the sun's remaining rays, casting an immense shadow on everything at the base. Shiloh peered down into the darkness, but everything seemed blurry because of their height. However, as they descended farther, he began to notice rows of peculiar glowing lights, which he took for streetlights. Through the darkness Shiloh thought he saw rooftops mixed in amongst the massive amounts of trees, but it was hard to tell. As they passed overhead, he noticed what looked like a giant, floating ball. It resembled a huge, multicolored beach ball.

Shiloh felt the cart descend sharply, and they landed with a thud onto a stretch of dirt road. Doc slowed down the horses and Shiloh examined the unique streetlights as they passed. They looked like palm trees without any leaves, with glowing, egg-shaped tops that swirled with a fascinating light.

Doc noticed Shiloh's fixation with the lights and commented, "Those are trees that attract Torchbugs."

Shiloh frowned. "What are Torchbugs?"

"You know lightning bugs?" Doc asked.

Shiloh nodded affirmatively.

"Kind of like them. They swarm together at night on top of the trees to provide light."

Doc slowed the horses down to a walk as they approached a house. It was a two-story, white Victorian that reminded Shiloh very much of his farmhouse, with one exception; trees had been built into the home. Instead of the four sides of the house connecting in right angles, tall maple trees stood at each of the corners.

Doc pulled the cart to a stop next to the front porch and said, "Wait here while I put away Peggy and Isis."

Shiloh frowned and wondered, "Peggy and Isis?"

Doc smiled and pointed toward the front of the cart, "My horses."

Shiloh nodded, grabbed his duffel bag, and stepped out of the cart. As it pulled away, he turned toward the front porch, where two large black birds sat on the railing. He slowly approached and, though he couldn't see them very well, the birds looked familiar.

Shiloh stopped in his tracks when he heard a creaking noise from the porch. He scanned the dark area and saw a small, orange glow. He squinted and realized there was someone in a rocking chair smoking a pipe. He couldn't see the person's face, so he took a step back to wait for Doc.

A moment later, Doc walked by Shiloh and up onto the porch with Cheepie and Lovie following him.

"Why are you sitting in the dark, Crow?" Doc asked, as he turned a small dial on the bottom of a lamp next to the door.

The light wasn't very bright and pulsed intermittently. Suddenly, a swarm of glowing insects gravitated toward the lamp, fully lighting up the porch.

Shiloh was now able to see a Native American gentleman sitting in a unique rocking chair made entirely from bent tree branches. The man had long, black hair and dark, leathery skin, as if he had spent far too much time outdoors. The man leaned forward in his chair with a big, comforting smile that

Shiloh's True Nature

rivaled Doc's. Shiloh forced a little grin and looked into the man's eyes, finding one was brown and the other green. That brought the total number of human beings Shiloh had met with different-colored eyes up to two.

Shiloh gazed down to see Lovie rubbing her chin against the man's ankle while Cheepie stood staring up at him. "Well, well, well . . . look who we have here." The man leaned down and petted both cats simultaneously.

Doc held open the front door while saying, "Crow, this is my grandson, Shiloh. Shiloh, this is one of my oldest and dearest friends, Screaming Crow."

Shiloh gave Crow a small wave of his hand. Crow winked and nodded, then rose from his chair and walked into the house. Shiloh followed Doc and the cats into the foyer and laid his duffel bag at the foot of the staircase.

Shiloh was amazed at how Doc's house was laid out so similarly to his own home. The kitchen area to the left seemed identical, right down to the wooden table and chairs. The only differences were that it had an open doorway and the floor was wooden, not tiled. The living room off to the right also matched his home, with the exception of an odd-looking door in the far corner next to the fireplace.

Doc walked into the kitchen and started heating up some leftover stew for them to eat. Shiloh was starving, which he demonstrated by stuffing himself with bowl after bowl. Barely a word was spoken throughout the meal, though Shiloh did catch Crow looking in his direction several times as if he had something to say.

When Shiloh finally had his fill, he pushed the bowl away

and slid back in his chair.

Doc smiled at him. "Had enough?"

Shiloh nodded.

"I heard you had a rough trip over?" Crow questioned, looking in Shiloh's direction.

Shiloh frowned, wondering how Crow could know that when neither he nor Doc had mentioned it.

"Shiloh. That's a unique name. Do you know what it means?" Crow asked, smiling broadly.

Shiloh shook his head.

Crow slid his chair back from the table and pulled out a brown briar pipe. "It means 'gift'," he noted, as he lit the pipe.

Shiloh had no idea that's what his name meant. He knew of a town not too far from his home by the same name, but nothing beyond that.

Crow exhaled the sweet-smelling smoke, then smiled at Shiloh and asked, "So, are you a gift?"

Shiloh squinted at Crow, confused by the question and unsure how to answer.

Doc rose from the table and announced, "You look tired. Let me show you to your room."

Shiloh stood up without looking back and followed Doc into the hallway and up the stairs. He found the upstairs, like the downstairs, was comparable to his home. The bathroom was at the top of the stairs and a bedroom stood at each end of the hall.

Doc led Shiloh to the dimly lit bedroom on the left where the cats had already made themselves at home. Lovie was at the foot of the bed and Cheepie was in a chair by the win-

Shiloh's True Nature

dow. Though everything was laid out just like his home, Shiloh was still uncomfortable in his new surroundings. He had a million questions and was just about ready to repeat his earlier request to be taken home when Doc spoke up.

"I want to apologize," Doc began.

"For what?" Shiloh asked.

Doc smiled and shook his head, "I hardly know where to begin. Let's see, there's my eccentric friend downstairs."

Shiloh chuckled slightly.

"He may seem a little odd, but I've never had a more loyal friend," Doc explained as he moved around the room, turning dials on the bottom of what appeared to be pieces of rounded, molded glass embedded into the walls.

As the room slowly began to grow brighter with each turned dial, Doc continued, "And, of course, there are the many happenings related to our journey here."

Shiloh realized that, like the device on the porch, these things in the walls were lamps. Only these lamps were closed to the interior of the house, designed to light the room yet keep the light-emitting insects out.

Finishing with the last dial, Doc turned to Shiloh. "Explaining everything to you will take some time. So I'll make a deal with you. If you give me one day, I will show you some amazing things that most people never get to see or experience in their entire lifetime."

"Like flying horses?" Shiloh proposed, squinting through the room's now complete illumination.

Doc smiled. "Yes, like flying horses. If after that you still want to go home, I will take you."

Shiloh was intrigued by Doc's offer, wondering what these amazing things could possibly be and thinking how foolish it would be to miss out on such an opportunity.

Doc stood waiting by the door for an answer as Shiloh examined a pinecone-shaped hive inside one of the lamps, still thinking about Doc's offer.

"All you have to do is turn the dial to adjust the light level," Doc noted.

Shiloh smiled at him, asking, "Just one day?"

Doc replied, "Just one day, and I'll answer any questions you have."

"Like why everyone calls you Doc?" Shiloh suggested with raised eyebrows.

Doc smiled. "Well, if you're around long enough, maybe I'll get to show you."

As Doc turned to exit the room, he added, "Get some rest, and let me know if you need anything."

Shiloh looked around the room, examining its contents. The large four-post bed was centered against the back wall underneath a small window. Against the wall by the door sat a big, wooden dresser with an oversized, shiny mirror attached to it. Two rocking chairs, like the ones on the porch, sat at the foot of the bed by a fireplace.

The room contained no electrical devices of any kind— no radio, no television, not even a clock. This seemed very peculiar to Shiloh, and he wondered if the house even had electricity. He then searched the room for electrical outlets and switches, finding nothing.

Contemplating how someone could exist without electricity, Shiloh took a seat on the edge of the bed with the palms of his hands flat by his sides. He then noticed a curiously comfortable sensation, as if the bed had molded itself to him. His hands felt as if they had been inserted into form-fitting, fur-lined gloves.

Shiloh turned his body toward the center of the bed and began examining its earth-toned covering. It was like no bed covering he had ever seen. The colorful patterns on the blanket were moving, flowing from one shape to another. The only stationary symbol appeared to be a giant, sideways figure eight located directly in the center.

Shiloh's attention was drawn away from the bed when he saw Cheepie climb up on a nightstand and stretch upward on his hind legs to examine one of the wall lamps. He seemed fascinated by the moving light and began pawing at the glass. Smiling at Cheepie, Shiloh turned away to find Lovie just as captivated by her new surroundings. She felt it necessary to walk on and sniff just about every object in the room.

A set of long, thin, white drapes caught Shiloh's eye. They were moving ever so slightly, as if a breeze had blown through them. Shiloh walked over and pushed the drapes apart to discover a large window behind them, open just a crack.

Shiloh looked out the window, finding a small white-tiled balcony with flowerpots around the ledge of its railing and an odd, gray statue sitting in the center of the platform. Shiloh pushed up the window to take a better look, and a cool breeze washed over him.

As he gazed out into the darkness, he reflected on the bizarre turn his summer vacation had taken. All he wanted was to spend some time with his friends, do a little swimming, and maybe go on some rides and play a few games when the carnival came to town. Instead, he found himself in a house in a dark forest, in the middle of nowhere, with no electricity, and a statue of some unknown creature towering over him.

Shiloh could have sworn the statue was staring at him. The incredibly detailed craftsmanship made it seem lifelike. Well, as lifelike as something with the body of a large dog, the hooves of a horse, the scales of a fish, and the face of a dragon could seem. The statue's expression perplexed Shiloh. He couldn't tell if it was growling fiercely or smiling with an openmouthed, toothy grin.

An irresistible urge to touch the figure came over Shiloh, so he leaned a little farther out of the window to reach for it. However, he quickly withdrew his arm when he discovered the statue really was staring at him. Shock overcame him as he watched the creature come to life.

It stretched its legs, rolled its neck, and looked down at Shiloh cowering at the window's edge. The creature smiled and winked at him. Shiloh gave a frightened smile and watched as the creature burst into flames and jumped off the balcony. Shiloh stared as the burning creature blazed a glowing trail into the darkness.

Stupefied, Shiloh closed the window, pulled the drapes, and walked over to the bed. He lifted the blanket and went to bed without removing any of his clothing or his shoes. He pulled the covers over his head, thinking the sooner he went to sleep, the sooner he could see what Doc had to show him and go back home.

July 22nd

Shiloh stumbled out of bed with his new favorite blanket wrapped around him and walked downstairs. He entered the sunlit kitchen to find his grandfather and Crow seated at the table having breakfast.

He pulled out a chair and sat down as he yawned, "Good morning."

"Ah, there's the gift," Crow joked with a smile.

"Good morning, Mr. Screaming Crow," Shiloh smiled, shoving a piece of wheat toast in his mouth.

Crow laughed at Shiloh's politeness. "You can call me Crow."

Shiloh smiled and looked around the table searching for whatever food might help him shake off the morning rust. There were a multitude of choices ranging from breads and pastries to fruits and nuts. He couldn't make any complicated decisions this early in the day, so he grabbed a bowl and started pouring some pillowed-wheat from a glass canister.

Doc handed Shiloh a jug of milk and asked, "How did you

Shiloh's True Nature

sleep?"

Shiloh shrugged as he lifted his first spoonful of cereal.

Doc poured a cup of green tea and pushed it at him, saying, "We're going into town shortly."

Shiloh paused between bites to inquire, "To Pike Creek?"

Doc shook his head no and Shiloh frowned in confusion.

"To Fair Hill," Doc added, as he watched Shiloh take another bite.

"Fair Hill? Where's Fair Hill?" Shiloh asked with a mouthful of cereal.

Crow let out a little laugh and grinned, "You're in it."

Still confused, Shiloh remarked, "I thought you lived in Pike Creek."

Doc grinned slyly and asked, "Do you remember yesterday when you asked why we went through Old New Castle?"

Shiloh nodded, so Doc continued, "We went that way because you can't get here by any road, and I needed a more discreet route to fly you in."

"I've been over here before and didn't have to fly in," Shiloh noted.

"Whenever you came to see me previously we met in Pike Creek, which is nearby, but I actually live in Fair Hill," Doc answered.

Shiloh put down his spoon, sat back in his chair, and began asking questions in rapid succession. "What do you mean you can't get here by road? Flying horses aren't supposed to exist, are they? And how come you don't have any electricity? Don't you have a telephone? What is Fair Hill?"

Crow laughed hard, "All very good questions."

Doc leaned forward toward Shiloh. "Fair Hill is a special place where special people live."

Frowning, Shiloh picked up his spoon to resume eating. "What do you mean, 'special'?"

"The people who live in Fair Hill have come here from all over the world to be with others like themselves," Doc revealed.

Shiloh continued frowning. "Okay. What do you mean, 'like themselves'?"

Doc paused for a moment before answering. "All the people of Fair Hill have unique talents and abilities."

Shiloh wondered what sort of talents or abilities might bring people together. "Can they sing or dance or something?"

Crow roared with laughter. "I sure can't."

Doc slid his chair away from the table. "Perhaps it would be easiest to just let you see for yourself. Finish eating and we'll head into town."

Shiloh quickly shoveled in a few more bites of his cereal and, with a full mouth, said, "Let's go."

Despite being sandwiched between Doc and Crow on the ride, Shiloh tried to appreciate the warm, sunny morning. He looked around at the lush environment waiting to see something remarkable, but all he saw was an overabundance of trees. He wondered why the place was called Fair Hill when it was clearly in a valley surrounded by hills.

Shiloh's study of the environment was interrupted when a voice out of nowhere called, "Good morning."

On the right side of the cart, a smiling man moving in an

Shiloh's True Nature

odd fashion came up next to Crow. He was rocking back and forth, but Shiloh couldn't tell how he was keeping up with the cart.

"Morning," Crow greeted the man, while Doc nodded.

The man then surged ahead of the cart and Shiloh saw he was riding on a giant, white bird. The creature had long, thin legs, an S-shaped neck, and large wings protruding from its egg-shaped body. At first, Shiloh wondered how the bird was able to support itself given its seemingly disproportionate dimensions. However, he noticed, with each step it took, its broad wings extended outward from the body to keep everything in balance.

"What is that?" Shiloh questioned, as he watched the speedy, pallid bird run into the distance.

Doc pointed. "That, Shiloh, is a Prodigian Ostrich. They are the largest birds in the world."

"Prodigian Ostrich? If they're the largest birds in the world, how come I've never heard of them before?" Shiloh inquired.

"Because they can only be found in Fair Hill." Doc smiled.

The farther along they went, the wider the road became and more people were moving around. Many were walking, some were traveling on ostrich-back, and a few people were riding on the backs of gigantic bugs. The massive insects had shiny, green-and-brown, oval-shaped bodies with six legs and a pair of antenna. Shiloh stared at the bizarre creatures until Crow leaned toward him and chuckled. "Cyclopean Beetles . . . in case you were wondering."

The townspeople seemed normal enough, going about

their business—all very friendly, saying hello to Doc and Crow as the cart passed. However, Shiloh noticed something different about them that he just couldn't place. He thought maybe it was their friendliness. The people of Salem weren't unsociable, but the people of Fair Hill seemed overly hospitable by comparison.

Shiloh's focus turned to the rear of the cart when he heard a fluttering noise. When he turned around, two large black birds were walking toward him on the bed covering.

"Ah, there are two birds back here," he stammered, leaning away from the bed as the birds drew closer.

Crow turned briefly to glance at the birds. "They're with me."

"Are they your pets?" Shiloh inquired with a scowl of curiosity.

Crow answered, "I don't think of them as pets. That would signify ownership and you can't really own an animal. They are my friends."

"So these are the same ones that were on the porch last night?" Shiloh inquired.

"Yup," Crow confirmed.

Shiloh squinted at the birds. "You know, I think I've seen these same birds several times in the past few days. Not just here, but at home too, and on the way here yesterday."

Crow smiled at Shiloh. "You might have. They get around."

Shiloh saw Doc and Crow look at each other and smile. He then asked, "Is that why you're called Screaming Crow? Because you have these birds?"

Crow leaned over to Shiloh and whispered, "It is. But I'll

Shiloh's True Nature

let you in on a little secret. They are actually ravens."

Shiloh grinned. "What's the difference?"

Crow laughed. "The difference is that all ravens are crows, but not all crows are ravens."

Shiloh was puzzled by Crow's assertion and looked at them again. Without turning, Crow asked, "You see that shiny tint to their feathers?"

"Yes," Shiloh replied.

"If you see that shine when the sun hits them, they're ravens. They are the largest of all crows."

In town, more than just people and creatures caught Shiloh's attention. The unique designs of the buildings fascinated him as well. Plenty of trees still flourished, but in town they were fully integrated into the surroundings. As with Doc's house, many buildings had trees as their corners. Other more massive trees had stores built right into the base of their trunks. Shiloh found it particularly amusing to see some trees growing out of the tops of buildings. He grinned at them, thinking they resembled humongous, leafy, green wigs.

The one thing that captivated Shiloh above all else was a giant, levitating object in the center of town. From a distance, he thought it was a rainbow-colored hot-air balloon. However, as they moved closer, he realized there was no basket for anyone to ride in. The object was made up of colored panels that resembled huge, curved flower petals with gaps in between them. Shiloh then recognized it as the object he saw when they flew over last night.

Staring up at the balloon, Shiloh was astounded when a

levitating man floated out from behind it and opened one of the petals like a door. A moment later, another man walked up on stilts carrying a toolbox and assisted the levitating man.

On the ground beneath the balloon, a tall, thin man with scraggly, blond hair was talking to a heavy-set, dark-haired woman who was shuffling through some papers and occasionally pointing upward. Doc slowed the cart down as it approached them and called out, "How's it coming along, Regina?"

Breaking off her conversation, the well-dressed woman turned toward the cart. She looked very officious in her business suit and clipboard as she stepped forward. Squinting through the bright sunshine, she answered, "Oh, can't tell for sure yet, Doc. But we had an unexpected breakthrough last night. We're thinking it might be back up within an hour or so."

"Then I have no doubt it will be," Doc said with a nod.

Doc's words drew a smile from Regina's round face and a return nod from the tall, blond man.

Just past the balloon, Doc brought the cart to a stop in front of a large brick building. Shiloh thought it resembled a bizarre, old-west saloon because of the many ostriches and beetles tied up out front. A sign on the building read DEER PARK. Wooden decks wrapped around both of the building's levels. Thick hedges hugged the railing all the way around the lower deck. Trees stood at each corner with one gigantic tree growing out of the top.

Doc led the way up onto the deck where Shiloh took in

the surroundings. Patrons sat eating and conversing at the many tables filling the deck. The empty tables were meticulously set with shiny, metal silverware, plates, and cups sparkling against the white, linen dining cloths. Ornate, dragon-shaped carafes were lined up around centerpieces filled with exotic wildflowers.

As they turned a corner and continued down the side-deck, a question popped into Shiloh's head. "Why is it called 'Deer Park'?" Neither Doc nor Crow answered; they just kept walking until they reached the rear of the building.

The rear deck expanded outward from the building, overlooking a large, grassy area where many deer were frolicking and foraging. Shiloh smiled in amazement as some of the deer fearlessly approached the deck, where people tossed them apples and other whole fruits.

Doc and Crow took seats at a table, but Shiloh stood staring out at the beauty of the park. Beyond the lush field was the area's largest hill. Shiloh didn't know the difference between a mountain and a hill, but the mound of earth before him sure looked massive with its innumerable trees. Despite the bright sunshine, the tree density created pockets of total darkness on the hill.

"There's a lot more to the town than just a hill, Shiloh," Doc said smiling.

Shiloh returned the smile and inquired, "Like what?"

"Well, why don't you take a walk around to see if you can figure out what's so special about the town and the people who live here. Come back around one o'clock or so and we'll have some lunch."

Shiloh was already amazed by the balloon, the park, and the hill, among other things, but said, "Okay. How will I know when it's one o'clock? I don't have a watch."

Doc grinned. "If all goes well, I don't think you'll need a watch."

Shiloh was confused by Doc's assertion, but turned to leave anyway. Before he could take a step, Doc added, "By the way, if you want to have some fun, find the Arcadia. Oh, and stay away from Acacia street."

Shiloh nodded up and down. "Arcadia, good. Acacia, bad."

"That's correct," Doc chuckled.

"Okay. Got it," Shiloh confirmed.

Shiloh left Deer Park and began exploring the town. The road they arrived on, which wasn't so much a road as it was a dirt path, was clearly the main thoroughfare for the town's residents. People paraded up and down the road, going in and out of the little shops and stores nestled in between trees and other interesting plant life. Shiloh found it amazing how everything seemed to fit perfectly within the surrounding environment.

His jaw dropped when he came across the biggest oak tree he had ever seen. He remembered reading a plaque once at the base of a huge oak tree in Salem that estimated the tree's age at over four hundred years. The tree before him was at least twice the size of Salem's, and its base alone covered an area the size of a small house. The massive tree stretched so high it's top couldn't be seen from the base.

His focus on the mighty oak was broken when a middle-aged gentleman with gray hair and a snow-white goatee

Shiloh's True Nature

rushed by with a wheelbarrow full of fruits and vegetables. Curious, Shiloh followed him around the oak until the man brought the pushcart to a stop in front of a produce store that was built into the base of the giant tree.

The man reached under his denim overalls to the pocket of his short-sleeve, plaid shirt and pulled out a handkerchief to wipe his brow. A middle-aged woman wearing a plaid dress and a denim apron exited the store and the couple began placing the produce in the appropriate bins. As he watched them work together to empty the wheelbarrow, Shiloh noticed their matching attire and smiled.

At the far end of the bins, a frizzy-haired old woman wearing a long, pink- and white-checkered dress, a large straw hat, and matching shoulder bag, kept pacing back and forth examining the produce. She seemed unsure about what she wanted and lost her grip on each piece she chose to inspect. He wondered if she was indecisive or just clumsy.

Reaching for an apple from a pyramid-shaped stack, the old woman sent the entire pile crashing to the ground. Shiloh smiled, retrieving the pieces that rolled closest to him. He returned the apples to their bin where the old woman was trying to rebuild the stack she'd demolished.

"Thank you very much, young man," the old woman said, taking the fruit from him. She squinted at him with a crooked little smile and looked directly into his eyes. She hesitated for a moment, a quizzical look on her face, but then looked away to resume remaking the bin. Shiloh wondered why she gave him such a strange look, but chose not to ask, fearing he might spend his entire afternoon rescuing fallen produce.

Shiloh continued with his exploration until he came across an amusing sign for a store called Jeremiah's. The wooden sign had a carving of a bullfrog wearing reading glasses and seated in front of a fire place with an open book. He smiled at the absurdity of a literate, farsighted frog. The store itself looked like a huge tree house with large stone stairs leading up from the road.

As he stood admiring the store's architecture, a thin young woman in a white sundress approached. Her waist-length, brown hair blew in the breeze as she moved along with a spring in her step. She passed right by him on her way up the stone steps, but hesitated when she reached the door and looked back.

Lighting around the door was dim, but Shiloh noticed there was something different about the girl's eyes. She smiled at him before opening the door. As she entered the store, Shiloh was stunned as the girl's hair changed from brown to blond before his eyes. He thought it had to be an optical illusion and raced up the stairs after her.

Once in the store, Shiloh found a counter directly ahead where a young man was stacking books. He gazed around and saw some patrons seated at small wooden tables, but none were the young lady with the color changing hair. A tall thin woman with long, straight, dark-brown hair moved quickly from aisle to aisle placing books on the shelves.

The store's many tall bookcases, shelves, and cabinets obstructed his view in all directions, so Shiloh began walking around, peering down each aisle for the girl. Unfortunately, the young woman was nowhere in sight. He shrugged,

Shiloh's True Nature

wondering how she could have disappeared so quickly, and turned toward the door to leave.

Before he could exit, the tall woman with the long, brown hair appeared out of nowhere, blocking his path. The woman's beautiful face moved closer to Shiloh's as she placed her hand under his chin and stared directly into his eyes. Shiloh returned her gaze, but immediately focused on her eyeglasses. The oval spectacles pointed out toward her shoulders, resembling two perfect water droplets turned on their sides. Behind the glasses were two different-colored eyes: one blue and one brown.

"What is your name, young man?" the woman questioned.

Shiloh was a little surprised by her in-your-face greeting, but replied, "Shiloh."

She smiled at him. "Hello, Shiloh. My name is Saige. Come with me."

She grabbed him by the wrist and led him down an aisle of books. She paused in the middle of the aisle, raising her hand toward one of the shelves. Shiloh watched as a small book floated off the shelf and flew right into her hand. He was speechless as Saige thrust the book into his hands. He briefly looked at the book's title, *True Nature*, before realizing Saige had left him behind.

"All new arrivals in Fair Hill should have a copy," Saige announced. Shiloh tried to catch up to her, still gazing at the colorful jungle scene on the cover.

When they reached the counter, Saige took the book from Shiloh and placed it into a small paper bag.

"Sorry, but I don't have any money," Shiloh admitted,

shrugging his shoulders.

With an odd smile, she handed him the bag and proclaimed, "Welcome to Fair Hill."

"Thank you," Shiloh replied, puzzled by her generosity.

He walked toward the door, but then stopped to ask, "Can you tell me how to get to the Arcadia?"

Saige smiled like she were about to laugh and called out, "Bryce!"

A tall young man with short, brown hair who looked to be about sixteen, the one who was stacking books when Shiloh entered the store, came out of a door behind the counter. Saige extended her hand toward the young man. "This is my son, Bryce. Bryce, this is Shiloh."

Shiloh gave the young man a small wave of his hand and Bryce nodded in return.

Saige continued, "Shiloh is new in town and is looking for the Arcadia. Perhaps you could show him?"

"Definitely," Bryce grinned, seeming eager to help.

Saige then added, "Please don't linger, though, because I need you back here."

Bryce's expression briefly turned serious. "Of course. I'll be back shortly."

He then jumped over the counter with a smile and led Shiloh out of the store. Shiloh stopped for a moment, stuffing his new book into his back pocket. As they began walking, Bryce directed them down a side street to the right and Shiloh asked, "So what is this Arcadia anyway? My grandfather said to go by there if I wanted to have some fun, but he didn't say what it was exactly."

Shiloh's True Nature

Bryce laughed, "Arcadia is where all the kids go to play games."

Intrigued, Shiloh asked, "What kind of games?"

"There are all kinds of games. Some you can play by yourself; some you play with others. The coolest part is you can win tokens and trade them in for prizes," Bryce explained.

"So what's your favorite game?" Shiloh inquired.

"It's called 'Atmosphere'," Bryce answered with a smile, as they made another right-hand turn.

"Atmosphere? What's that?" Shiloh inquired.

Bryce's face lit up at the opportunity to talk about it. "It's really a simple game. There is a big, ten-foot, circular table that is divided in half. There are ten pockets: five on each half. Each player begins with five spheres, and the object of the game is for one person to get all of their spheres into the five slots on their opponent's side of the board before time runs out. You just aim and roll your spheres across the table."

"That's it? It doesn't sound very exciting," Shiloh noted, expecting something more.

"Well, there's a little more to it than that. You'll just have to see for yourself," Bryce added.

"Okay. So how about we play a game then?" Shiloh suggested.

Bryce hesitated. "I don't know if I should. Sometimes the game can take a while."

Shiloh frowned at him, so Bryce smiled as he turned right again and said, "Well, I guess I could play one quick game."

Shiloh scowled in confusion at all the right-hand turns they had made, but kept quiet to wait and see where they ended up. At the next intersection, Bryce turned right again and Shiloh stopped. "What's going on?" Shiloh demanded.

Bryce stopped and turned around. "What do you mean?"

"I mean, we've turned right four times, which means we've walked in a complete circle. So where is this Arcadia?" Shiloh asked in perplexed tone.

Bryce pointed across the way. "It's right there."

Shiloh looked in the direction Bryce was pointing and saw a building resembling a giant tiki hut with bamboo walls, a thatched roof, and an emerald-green sign that read ARCA-DIA. "What? How? I don't understand," Shiloh stammered.

A huge smile came to Bryce's face as he joked, "Welcome to Fair Hill."

As they entered, Bryce led the way and Shiloh looked around at all the happy children running around laughing and playing games. The farther they went inside, the older the children became and the more complex the games looked. Bryce stopped when they reached the back.

"So where is Atmosphere?" Shiloh asked.

"Right here," Bryce said pointing to a waist-high, round, black board in front of them.

Shiloh frowned, thinking the game would be boring. However, Bryce walked to one end of the table to press a button and all of Shiloh's assumptions about the game disappeared.

A wave of white light rolled from one side of the table to the other and the table went from black nothingness to what looked like a grassy meadow. Shiloh gently lowered his hand to the tabletop and touched what felt like real grass.

Shiloh's True Nature

He then heard what sounded like water running and looked toward the middle of the table to find a tiny blue river flowing, evenly separating the two sides of the table. A suction-cup sound returned his attention to the green field in front of him, where five pockets had suddenly appeared.

Shiloh was still examining the playing field when Bryce asked, "Would you like to be the Earth or the Moon?"

"Earth, I guess," Shiloh stammered, unsure how to answer the question.

Bryce pressed another button and a basket popped up in front of Shiloh, spilling five little round, Earth-like spheres on the table in front of him. Down at Bryce's end, five little Moon-shaped spheres appeared on the table as well.

"You ready?" Bryce asked.

"Wait a minute. What do I do?" Shiloh inquired.

Bryce smiled. "You just roll your spheres to get them in the pockets on my side of the board before I can get all of mine on your side. But one player has to get them all in before sundown or it's a draw and we move to the next level. Understand?"

"I guess," Shiloh lied.

Sundown wasn't for hours. *Could the game really go on that long*? Shiloh wondered.

"You ready?" Bryce questioned.

"I guess," Shiloh lied again.

Bryce pressed another button and the grassy board began to brighten further, like an invisible sun was rising on it. Shiloh stared at the board, fascinated by the seemingly solar illumination, until a short, loud beep caught his attention.

Shiloh looked down to find Bryce had rolled a Moon-sphere into a pocket on his side of the board. He quickly grabbed one of the Earth-spheres before him and rolled it across the table.

Shiloh watched his sphere roll past a pocket on Bryce's side of the table. He thought it was going to fall to the floor, but the sphere came to an abrupt stop, like it had hit an unseen wall. Once it stopped, it then vanished, only to reappear at Shiloh's end of the table. Shiloh was again in awe at the magnificence of the game, but one short, loud beep after another sent him scrambling for his spheres.

As the table reached a peak of brightness, Shiloh began just rolling his spheres down the other end of the table and hoping for the best. However, his just-keep-throwing strategy brought him no success. A fourth loud beep and a look down at four filled pockets in front of him signaled to Shiloh that he was about to lose the game. He needed a new strategy fast.

Shiloh decided, since he couldn't drop a sphere into a pocket on the other side, perhaps he should try to keep Bryce from sinking his last sphere. The last empty pocket on Shiloh's side of the table was the one closest to him. This worked perfectly with his new strategy, because each time Bryce rolled one of his Moon-spheres, Shiloh waited and rolled one of his Earth-spheres to knock it off course.

As the illumination on the table faded, Bryce continued frantically rolling, trying to seal his victory. Shiloh persisted with his defensive approach and even managed to a put a sphere into a pocket on Bryce's side by sheer luck.

Shiloh's True Nature

Suddenly, a long, loud beep sounded and the table went dark. Shiloh looked around in confusion, wondering what happened. "Did it break or something?" he asked, gazing toward Bryce at the other end of the table.

"No. The round is over. Now, we move on to a second day." Bryce smiled as the table came to life again.

The table looked the same to Shiloh, with the grassy meadow, the little river separating the sides, and the pockets all reappearing. However, as the spheres popped back onto the table, several lumps grew up out of the field, creating little hills and valleys.

Shiloh smiled as the table began to brighten for the second round. He continued his strategy of defense right from the start and even put a couple spheres into their pockets before the round ended in a stalemate again. The third round concluded the same way, despite the addition of little trees, rocks, and other environmental obstacles appearing around the playing field.

By the fourth round the landscape on the table became more lifelike than ever. There was wind and rain for brief periods. A fleeting hailstorm dropped tiny pieces of ice onto the table, which in turn altered the direction of any sphere rolling nearby. Snow fell on some of the hilltops, slowing the momentum of any sphere trying to pass. None of the elements affected Shiloh's play though, because his sole intent was to keep the game going.

Between the fourth and fifth rounds, Shiloh's sense of elation was matched only by Bryce's look of frustration. Shiloh couldn't believe he had avoided losing, while Bryce appeared stunned by his denied victory. Shiloh noticed a crowd of kids gathering around to watch the game. They stared at him and the board, whispering to one another like they were witnessing something of genuine importance.

At the start of the fifth round, all the elements of the playing field remained the same as they were in the previous round. However, the board began tilting randomly in different directions, leaning left and right, rising forward and back, making the conditions more difficult than ever. Shiloh tried to concentrate on his defensive strategy, but he found it very difficult.

Bryce seemed to find the environment less irritating, which he demonstrated by quickly pocketing four of his spheres despite Shiloh's best efforts to stop him. As was the case in the first round, Shiloh found the pocket closest to him was the last empty one on his side. So he tried to focus on defending it, but he found the growing crowd around the table distracting.

In between defending Bryce's rolls, Shiloh kept looking up at the murmuring kids crowding around the table. There was something unusual about the kids and Shiloh was unable to keep from staring at them. Eventually he figured out what it was; everyone had two different-colored eyes, one brown and one blue. When Shiloh returned his full focus to the game, a loud buzzer went off and the remarkable playing field returned to a dull black board.

Disappointed in himself, Shiloh looked down the other end of the table with a grimace. Bryce exhaled a sigh of relief and smiled at Shiloh.

Shiloh's True Nature

As the crowd began to disperse, Bryce made his way around the table to Shiloh and held out his hand. "Good game."

Shiloh shook Bryce's hand. "Yeah. It's a pretty cool game."

"I hope we can play again sometime," Bryce added.

"Sounds good," Shiloh agreed.

"Well, I've got to get back to the store. I'll see you around," Bryce remarked, moving away.

Shiloh waved good-bye and turned back toward the blank Atmosphere board. The kids who had watched the game had scattered, except for three who looked to be about Shiloh's age. They were still standing nearby and arguing. Shiloh tried to listen to what they were saying, but they suddenly went silent and faced him.

A boy, about Shiloh's size—with shoulder-length, sandy-blond hair—smiled and said, "That was an incredible game."

Shiloh looked away, frowning down at the blank board. "I lost."

The boy laughed. "Yeah, but no one ever beats Bryce. Usually, no one ever comes close."

Shiloh felt a little better knowing he did better than most.

"I'm Bud," the boy announced. He nodded toward a tall, stout girl. "This is Brinda." A girl with beautiful, cocoa-brown skin brushed the straight, black hair out of her face to reveal a bright smile. Shiloh gave a little wave of his hand. Bud then pointed to a short, sallow-skinned boy with short, black hair. "And that's Kaz."

The boy gave Bud a backhanded slap to the arm. "I told you to announce me as Kazuhiro whenever we meet someone for the first time." He then stepped forward and gave a little bow. "Kazuhiro Watanabe."

Shiloh was slightly taken aback by Kaz's formality, but smiled nonetheless. "My name's Shiloh."

Bud pushed Kaz out of his way and said, "Hey, Shiloh, we need a fourth player for 'Waterfowl'. You wanna play?"

Shiloh frowned. "What's Waterfowl?"

"Come on. We'll show you," Bud responded with a wave, walking toward a nearby table.

At first glance, the table appeared to be nothing more than a large rectangular box. Bud pushed a button on the side and, just like the Atmosphere board, the box transformed before Shiloh's eyes. A small, egg-shaped lake filled the center, while a sandy shoreline with trees filled in around it. Four small birds appeared at equal distances apart on the shore in front of the kids. A swan sat in front of Brinda, a duck in front of Kaz, a goose in front of Bud, and the tiny bird before Shiloh was a Great Blue Heron.

"So what do we do?" Shiloh inquired.

"You push your bird down to the other end as fast as you can. Whoever gets their bird across the finish line first wins," Brinda explained, pulling out a plastic water pistol from a compartment in front of her.

Shiloh looked down and reached into an opening where he found his own pistol. As he began to examine the toy gun, a bell rang, catching him off guard. He turned to find the others rapidly squeezing their triggers and aiming the streams of water from their nozzles at the birds' backs. He followed his new friends' actions, but he didn't have much success. In

Shiloh's True Nature

fact, none of the boys seemed to be doing very well. Brinda, on the other hand, had managed to push her bird over half-way to the finish line.

"What am I doing wrong?" Shiloh asked.

Bud, who was right next to him, softly said, "Nothing. Just keep going."

Shiloh kept at it and was able to catch up to the other boys, but he couldn't put a dent in Brinda's lead.

After a noisy series of beeps, Brinda roared with laughter, having pushed her bird across the finish line. Shiloh looked to the other boys, who rolled their eyes. A rapid succession of clanging noises came from the other end of the table where Brinda stood, and she reached down to retrieve a handful of shiny, little coins.

"Well, just a few more wins and I'll have enough for my hat," Brinda gleefully announced.

Bud looked at Shiloh and mumbled, "Yeah, because she cheats."

Brinda frowned. "I do not cheat."

Kaz chimed in, "And I suppose the water pressure from your gun just happened to be more powerful than the rest of ours."

"I can't help it if you jerks don't know how to play the game," Brinda snorted.

Shiloh was confused as to what they were arguing about. He didn't see how Brinda could have cheated and was about to say so when he was startled by a thunderous, vibrating chime. He looked around, trying to determine where the chime had come from, but he didn't think there was a game capable of making such a noise.

When everyone began cheering, Shiloh looked to Bud and asked, "What was that noise?"

Brinda and Kaz giggled at Shiloh's question, while Bud smiled and answered, "That's the Stone Balloon." Shiloh looked confused, so Bud added, "It's the town clock. It's been broken, but apparently it's fixed now. The single chime means it's one o'clock."

Shiloh grinned, realizing what Doc meant by 'if all goes well'. He thought of the Deer Park and how to find his way back there. Recalling his confusing path to the Arcadia, Shiloh turned to his new friends and asked, "Can you tell me how to get to the Deer Park? I'm supposed to meet someone, but I'm not sure how to get back."

Brinda and Kaz laughed again.

Feeling a little foolish, Shiloh turned to Bud. "What's so funny?"

Bud smiled and remarked, "I'll show you. I'm meeting my parents at the Deer Park too." He turned to the others, "Are you guys staying here?"

Brinda said, "Yeah. I want to try to win some more tokens so I can get that hat."

"What is it with you and that stupid hat?" Kaz asked.

Brinda sneered. "It's not just some stupid hat. It's a water-proof, rainbow-colored, stovepipe hat."

Backing away to follow Bud, Shiloh called out, "It was nice to meet you."

Kaz waved good-bye, while Brinda smiled brightly, "Nice to meet you too."

Shiloh's True Nature

Once outside the Arcadia, Bud asked, "So who are you meeting at the Deer Park?"

"My grandfather," Shiloh said.

"Who's your grandfather?" Bud inquired.

Shiloh hesitated, but then said, "Well, I guess everybody around here knows him as Doc."

Bud seemed stunned to hear this. "Really? Wow, I've known Doc my whole life. I didn't even know he had a family."

Grimacing slightly, Shiloh grumbled, "Well, then you probably know him better than I do."

Bud detected Shiloh's resentful tone and continued leading the way in silence.

All of a sudden, Shiloh realized the surroundings had changed. Dense tree growth had given way to tall, wild grasses and brush. There were no people, shops, or crazy critters running around. "Bud, I'm sure you know how to get to the Deer Park, but I came from there earlier and I didn't pass any of this stuff on the way. What's going on?" Shiloh questioned.

Bud chuckled slightly and didn't answer right away. Shiloh huffed, "And why do I keep getting laughs when I ask questions?"

"I'm sorry, Shiloh. You're new here, so I guess you don't know," Bud replied.

Shiloh grumbled, "Know what?"

"That all the roads lead back to the center of town," Bud noted.

Shiloh laughed, "All of them?"

"Well, all of them except that one." Bud pointed down a path at a fork in the road they were approaching.

Shiloh looked toward the path at a barely visible sign in between a number of odd-looking trees with thorny protrusions on the branches. The sign read ACACIA STREET.

"How is that possible?" Shiloh inquired.

Bud replied, "I don't know. It just is."

As they reached the intersection, Shiloh noticed a peculiar sight. Acacia Street wasn't just another dirt path, but an actual street. It had remnants of a paved road hidden beneath some brush and wild growth. Even stranger was how the pavement looked new, but it had weeds and grass shoots growing out of numerous cracks. It was almost as if the plant life had forced its way through the paving to cover it.

In the distance, beyond the brush and weeds on Acacia, a young man with short, brassy-colored hair was walking toward the intersection. "Who is that?" Shiloh asked.

Without even looking, Bud replied, "That's Junior."

"Who is he?" Shiloh wondered aloud.

"No one, really. He and his family live on Acacia," Bud noted.

Shiloh paused for a moment, then added, "That seems like a pretty messed-up road to live on. I mean, compared to the rest of town."

"His family is the reason the road is messed up," Bud explained.

Shiloh turned toward Bud, a look of confusion on his face. Seeing he needed to clarify, Bud continued, "Junior's family doesn't really get along with the rest of the community."

Shiloh's True Nature

"What's that have to do with the road?" Shiloh asked.

Bud sighed. "They keep trying to extend their road out to a nearby town, but they're not supposed to do that. It used to be that every time they would clear out and pave a section, it would disappear overnight. The grasses and brush would just cover it, like it was just swallowed up. But for some reason, lately it doesn't disappear completely. And that's why it looks all messed up."

Shiloh wasn't sure how to respond, so he just said, "Wow."

As they walked away from the intersection, Shiloh continued looking back at Acacia. He noticed that Junior wasn't alone, but accompanied by what appeared to be several large greenish-gray dogs that walked strangely. They were tilted forward and hopped along, like their heads were too big for their bodies.

Once Acacia was behind them, Shiloh began to focus on the road ahead. He was still unsure of their whereabouts until he noticed the familiar giant levitating object in the distance. "What is that thing?" Shiloh asked pointing.

Bud smiled. "That's the Stone Balloon. It's the clock that made the chime you heard earlier."

"It doesn't look like any clock I've ever seen," Shiloh noted skeptically.

Bud thought about Shiloh's comment for a moment and then said, "Now that I think about it, you're right."

Shiloh frowned. "Right about what?"

Bud continued, "The Stone Balloon. You're right. It's not really a clock, but more like an acoustic sundial."

Shiloh laughed. "An acoustic sundial?"

Bud laughed too, saying, "Yeah. I'm not sure how the thing works, exactly, but I do know the balloon is made of thirteen different-colored Sun Crystals that vibrate and chime to indicate the time."

"That's a pretty elaborate sundial," Shiloh said, focusing on the Stone Balloon.

"Yes, it is," Bud agreed.

Shiloh frowned. "Wait a minute. You said it chimes on the hour, right?"

"Yeah," Bud confirmed.

"Well, I've been here since last night and I didn't hear it until today," Shiloh announced.

Bud nodded. "That's because it hasn't worked in a while. My dad has been leading the repair team, but they haven't had much luck until last night."

As they moved farther into town, the scenery became more familiar to Shiloh. He again saw people moving around, going from shop to shop. When he noticed the young lady he had seen earlier at the bookstore, walking along carrying some packages, Shiloh pointed and asked, "Who is that girl in the white dress?"

Bud caught a quick glimpse of her as she turned off the main road. "I think that's Bryce's cousin, Harmony."

"Do you know her?" Shiloh asked, craning his neck to see where she went.

"Not really. She hasn't been in town very long," Bud replied.

A moment later, the Deer Park came into view and Shiloh felt a slight sense of relief. While they hadn't really been

Shiloh's True Nature

walking all that long, Shiloh was starting to wonder if they were ever going to arrive. He gazed at the building and the unique critters out front, then he noticed the tall, thin man Doc had nodded to earlier. The man's scraggly, blond hair swayed back and forth as he limped along, apparently headed to the Deer Park also.

"Hey, Dad!" Bud called out.

The man gave a wave and a smile, walking up the Deer Park's front steps.

"That's your father?" Shiloh inquired.

"Yeah. He's been working non-stop to get the Stone Balloon fixed," Bud said proudly.

"Cool. I saw him by the balloon earlier when we rode into town," Shiloh added.

Making their way up the stairs and past the many people having lunch, Shiloh spoke, "Bud, I want to thank you for helping me get back here. It was nice to meet you."

Bud smiled. "No problem. Hey, we're going swimming at my house tomorrow. You should come."

Shiloh had wanted to go swimming all summer, but he hesitated nonetheless. "I'd like to, but I'm not sure if I'll still be here tomorrow."

Bud gave him a puzzled look. "Why? I thought you just got here."

Shiloh didn't answer as they rounded the corner onto the rear deck. Bud's father was limping just a few steps ahead of them. Shiloh saw Doc standing a little farther ahead, by some stairs that led down to the large grassy area where the deer were playing. He was talking to a short, plump woman with rosy cheeks and strawberry-blond hair. "There you two are," the woman called out.

Shiloh frowned slightly, wondering to whom the woman was speaking.

Doc extended his arm in Shiloh's direction. "Ah, perfect timing. Luther, Martina, I'd like you to meet my grandson, Shiloh. Shiloh, I'd like you to meet my dear friends Luther and Martina Miller."

Shiloh smiled and waved his hand. "Hello."

Luther nodded, and Martina stepped forward with a glowing smile and placed her hands on the sides of Shiloh's face. "Hello, Shiloh. It's wonderful to finally meet you. Your grandfather has been telling us about you for years," she beamed.

Shiloh squinted toward Doc with a slight smirk on his face. Doc avoided his gaze, just moving his eyes around, looking at nothing in particular.

Martina shifted her focus toward Bud. "I'm assuming by your arrival partner that you've already met our son, Bud."

"Yes, ma'am, I have." Shiloh smiled.

Martina glanced over her shoulder and continued, "And the rude, still-seated young man is our son, Jace."

The men chuckled slightly as Martina pointed to the table behind her. Looking past Martina, Shiloh saw a young man with closely-cropped, blond hair eating. Jace momentarily choked with laughter from his mother's scolding before wiping his peach-fuzz-covered chin and giving Shiloh a wave.

Shiloh looked around at the smiling faces of the Miller family, and realized all of them had one blue eye and one

Shiloh's True Nature

brown eye. Doc stepped forward and directed Shiloh toward a table next to the deck railing, saying, "Well, it's time for some lunch."

"It was nice to meet you, Shiloh. I'm sure we'll being seeing you again real soon," Martina said, pushing Bud toward the table where Jace was seated. Shiloh gave Bud a little wave and took a seat at his grandfather's table.

Before Doc could take a seat, Luther grabbed his arm and in a low voice said, "I didn't want to say anything in front of Regina earlier. You know how she likes everything neat and orderly, but truthfully, we have no idea how or why it's working."

Doc nodded and gave a little grunt. Luther paused and looked around for a moment before adding, "I mean . . . we did repair all the external damage Sam caused taking *it* out. But that doesn't explain why the internal mechanisms all just kind of kicked on by themselves last night."

Doc stroked his chin in thought as Luther asked, "What do you think it means?"

Out of the corner of his eye, Doc saw Shiloh listening to the conversation. He smiled and patted Luther on the back. "I'm sure you'll figure it out."

A hand appeared on Luther's shoulder, pulling him around. It was Martina. "Come eat some lunch."

Luther turned toward her and grimaced as he adjusted his stance. "Okay, okay."

Luther started to limp away, but then turned back, grinning, "Oh, Doc, I've got to show you this new knot I came up with. Come by and I'll show it to you."

Martina countered, "Yes, Doc. Come by. That way he can show you that toe of his too. He's been limping around for days now."

Luther frowned. "There's nothing wrong with my toe. It's fine."

Martina rolled her eyes. Doc looked down at Luther's foot and then turned toward Martina with a wink. "I'm sure he's fine."

Doc took a seat across from Shiloh and pointed down at the table. "So, are you hungry?"

Shiloh looked around the table with its numerous, shiny trays and bowls filled with things to eat, but decided he needed to quench his thirst first. He grabbed a shiny, metal cup sitting next to the empty plate and then reached for the gold carafe closest to him. Doc wagged his finger and advised, "Not the gold one."

Shiloh frowned and Doc explained, "The color of the dragon corresponds to its contents. Gold is honey-wine. The rest are water, juices, and teas."

As he poured himself some juice from a crimson carafe, Doc asked, "So what did you learn around town?"

Shiloh pulled the book from his back pocket and laid it on the table. "The lady at Jeremiah's is very generous. She gave me this book. Can you believe that?"

Doc smiled. "It's a wonderful book. You'll find most people in Fair Hill are very generous. And everyone finds ways to repay one another. It's how we live."

He wasn't sure what Doc meant, but before he could inquire, Doc asked, "What else?"

Shiloh's True Nature

"Oh, that balloon-looking thing is actually a clock. Or kind of a clock," Shiloh noted.

Doc nodded. "Pretty cool, huh?"

Shiloh nodded in agreement as he grabbed a sandwich from a nearby plate.

"Anything else?" Doc asked, as Shiloh took a bite.

His mouth still full, Shiloh questioned, "Yeah, how can all the roads lead back to the center of town?"

Doc chuckled. "All the roads?"

"Bud told me that Acacia road doesn't," Shiloh answered. He paused for a moment, waiting for an explanation from Doc. When none came, he shrugged his shoulders. "So?"

Doc looked at Shiloh, trying to find the right words. "It would take a lot of explaining, but if it helps you, just pretend it's magic."

Shiloh stopped eating. "Magic? Is it?"

Doc laughed. "No, Shiloh. Everything new can seem magical until you've learned about it. Then it becomes just as real as everything else you already know, doesn't it?"

Shiloh shrugged. "I guess so."

"Think about it like this. I'm sure you've noticed there are no automobiles in Fair Hill. Well, imagine you've lived in Fair Hill your whole life and you left the town for the first time and came across a car. You'd be amazed. It would seem magical. But it's not magic. It's just new," Doc said, hoping the explanation would suffice.

Shiloh continued eating, occasionally looking up at Doc, who sat watching him. "So, what else did you notice?" Doc asked with a wide-eyed grin.

Shiloh thought for a moment before responding, "Nothing really. I mean I saw some weird things." Shiloh paused, then quipped, "Oh, how come everyone here has two different-colored eyes? You're the only person I'd ever seen like that, until I came here."

"Now that's the question I've been waiting for," Doc said with a chuckle before continuing. "Do you remember earlier when I told you the people here are special?"

"Yes," Shiloh replied.

"Well, all the people in this town are what we call 'Movers.'" Doc could see a question about to escape Shiloh's mouth, so he continued, "... and no, they don't help anyone relocate to new homes. Each person here has an extraordinary ability and can do things regular folks might think is magic. As for having two different-colored eyes, it's how we know someone is a Mover."

"Like a birthmark or something?" Shiloh asked.

"Yes, very much like that," Doc agreed.

Shiloh glanced around at all the people having lunch, wondering about them and what they could do. His gaze went from one side of the deck to the other until he found himself looking at the chair next to his, which was empty except for a couple of long black feathers.

"Tell me about these extraordinary abilities. Like what are they? For instance, what's Crow's ability?" Shiloh inquired as he continued munching on various items from the table.

Doc waved his finger out at the field where the deer were frolicking. "Crow has a unique connection to animals. You should ask him about it. I'm sure he'd be able to explain it

Shiloh's True Nature

much better than I could."

Finishing the last of his food, Shiloh looked down at his reflection in the shiny metal plate. A feeling of exclusion washed over him as he looked to Doc. "My eyes are the same color."

Doc smiled at him. "Yes, they are."

Shiloh was about to continue but was interrupted by a loud thump and a cracking noise from down below off the deck. Luther and some others from nearby tables ran down the stairs leading to the field. Doc stood up and looked over the railing. "Everything all right?"

"You want to come have a look, Doc?" Luther asked.

Turning to Shiloh, Doc instructed, "Stay here please."

As Doc walked down the stairs, Shiloh peered over the railing. There were a few deer standing close by the deck, while Doc and the others were right below where Shiloh was seated. Shiloh craned his neck to and fro, but with the high hedges underneath the railing and people standing around, he couldn't see much.

A moment later, a deer jumped to its feet and Shiloh heard Doc utter, "There we go."

The people on the deck applauded as the deer walked off and Doc gave everyone a wave as he returned up the stairs to his seat.

"What happened?" Shiloh asked.

"I guess a couple of the bucks were playing a little too rough. That one must have hit his head and gotten knocked out for a moment. He seems fine now, though," Doc answered.

Shiloh watched the young buck as he rejoined the others. He then turned back to Doc, who smiled. "So what did you do?" Shiloh asked.

Doc shook his head. "Oh, nothing much. Listen, I have some errands to run. So we should probably get going."

Shiloh squinted, confused as to what just happened, but shrugged and agreed, "Okay."

Shiloh went along with Doc for the ride, but it was all a blur. He was lost in his thoughts about everything he had experienced in Fair Hill so far. He wondered how all this could be. The questions mounted in his brain about people with two different-colored eyes, flying horses, levitating clocks, and roads all leading to one place. It was all very exciting, like a wonderful dream. He was filled with questions, but wasn't sure what to ask or even where to begin.

They returned to the house late that afternoon, and as Doc put the horses away, Shiloh stood outside of the stall admiring a unique, colorful carving of a pair of giant wings on the doors. When Doc finished in the stall, he closed the doors and began fiddling with some odd-looking pieces of thin, tangled rope. He watched Doc fumble around trying to untwist the rope and asked, "What are you doing?"

"Trying to lock up the stall," Doc answered.

Shiloh chuckled slightly. "How is that rope going to keep anyone out?"

Doc finally untangled the rope, exhaling a sigh of relief. "First, it's mostly about keeping the horses in, not keeping anyone out. Second, this is no ordinary rope. It was created to be as strong as any lock you may have seen. It will keep out anyone who doesn't know how to untie it," Doc noted as he began tying the rope.

Shiloh watched Doc tie what appeared to be a simple square knot. However, as soon as Doc let go, the rope began to move on its own, turning into the most elaborate knot Shiloh had ever seen. He turned to Doc with raised eyebrows, looking for an explanation. Doc smiled, extending his arm toward the house. "You ready for something to eat?"

Doc made them dinner and Shiloh ate without saying a word. He was consumed by thoughts about the new wonderland in which he found himself. Doc occasionally looked his way and smiled, but Shiloh avoided eye contact by focusing on his food.

It was only after they had finished eating and moved out onto the rear porch overlooking the backyard that Doc broke the silence. "You've been awfully quiet," he mused, noting the obvious.

Shiloh gave a tight-lipped smile, unsure how to describe the trouble he was having believing all the things he had experienced since his arrival. Doc waited for an answer with raised eyebrows, until Shiloh blurted out, "This is all so crazy."

Doc gave him a wide-eyed, toothy grin and remarked, "Yes, well, we're all a little mad here." Doc laughed, but saw his joke didn't amuse Shiloh. "Have you ever been to China, Shiloh?"

Shiloh frowned, puzzled by the question. "No."

"But you believe it exists, don't you?" Doc asked.

Shiloh nodded. "Of course."

"Well, then you should have no problem believing winged horses exist, because there's two right in there," Doc pointed over at the stall.

Shiloh just smiled, unable to argue. He then thought for a moment before asking, "So, do all Movers live here?"

Doc shook his head. "No. Some live here, but not all."

"But only Movers live in the town?" Shiloh concluded.

"That's correct," Doc confirmed.

Shiloh frowned. "Why?"

"Well, Shiloh, we try to stay together to avoid regular folks discovering our gifts. We learned long ago how disastrous it could be to reveal ourselves to regular people," Doc explained.

"What do you mean?" Shiloh inquired.

"People are afraid of what they don't understand, Shiloh. In the past, Movers were put on trial, burned, and drowned because people were afraid of them. They thought Movers were evil or using magic," Doc revealed.

Shiloh was shocked to hear this. "Really?"

Doc nodded. "Yes. It even happened right across the river in your town."

With a look of disbelief, Shiloh questioned, "In Salem?"

Doc nodded affirmatively.

Shiloh let his grandfather's words sink in before continuing, "So Movers avoid contact with regular people?"

Doc shook his head. "No, not completely. But most of us try to keep our distance."

"Most?" Shiloh inquired.

Doc sighed. "Well, some Movers have different ideas and

Shiloh's True Nature

opinions about our relations with the outside world."

"Like how?"

A somewhat pained look fell over Doc's face as he explained, "Some—not many mind you, but some—think our gifts make us better than regular people and that we should do as we please and use our gifts how, when, and where we please."

Shiloh stared at his grandfather for a moment and then pointed out, "You never told me what your gift is."

Doc smiled at Shiloh and pointed off the porch. "Why don't you have a look around my yard a little bit? Maybe you'll find something interesting."

Realizing Doc wasn't going to reveal his gift to him, he stepped off the porch and started looking around the backyard. The first thing that struck him was how the yard was not simply a squared-off piece of land. The boundaries of dense trees and vegetation made it more of a jagged, V-shaped niche.

Walking along the edge of the yard, he noticed something peculiar about the far corner. The color of the vegetation in that spot seemed slightly different from the flanking plants. Approaching the spot to investigate, Shiloh realized he was the victim of an optical illusion. There was no difference in the coloring of the plant life. It only appeared that way at a distance because there was an opening to a path that led into a darker, denser section of the woods.

On his return trip around the yard, Shiloh found there was more foliage than just dense trees and brush to the yard. Numerous types of exotic wildflowers grew all around.

One particular plant that fascinated Shiloh had red, yellow, and blue cone-shaped flowers that attracted butterflies. He smiled as he watched the insects dance around in the air, hopping from flower to flower.

The butterflies suddenly stopped moving, taking positions near the tops of the flowers. Thinking this was odd, he looked closely at them to see what had changed. There was no visible change in the insects, but he did hear a noise coming from the thick leaves at the plant's base, like something was moving. So, he took a step back and bent down.

Suddenly, a cat jumped up and out from under the leaves, swatting at the flowers. The butterflies took flight together in the direction of the house and the cat gave chase. Shiloh recognized the tiger-striped pursuer as his cat, Cheepie. He watched as the butterflies flew up and down just out of Cheepie's reach, until they finally reached the house and flew upward toward the roof. Refusing to give up, Cheepie clawed his way up some lattice running up and around the tree at the corner of the house near the kitchen window.

Shiloh heard Doc laughing from the porch. "He was chasing them all morning before you got up," Doc hollered. Shiloh grinned before returning to his inspection of the yard.

Several ornate wood sculptures with unusual carved symbols captured Shiloh's attention. One piece particularly amused him because it resembled a fedora. Upon closer inspection, the carvings weren't the only unique feature of the pieces. The wood had been smoothed or weathered, like it had begun eroding before it was used for the sculptures. As Shiloh ran his hand across the surface of one piece, Doc

Shiloh's True Nature

called down to him, "It's driftwood. Luther made them."

In the center of the yard, Shiloh found Lovie stretched out atop a raised rectangular platform made of gray marble. She was sprawled over a chiseled, circular image of what appeared to be a sundial. She flicked her tail from one side of the dial's vertical, brassy fin to the other. The dial was carved into eight sections with unfamiliar symbols at the center of each.

The fin sat on a line between the two symbols ζ and , and was pointed directly at the setting sun. However, to Shiloh's surprise, the fin cast an improper shadow. Shiloh looked around and found everything in the yard, including him, was casting a long shadow toward the house, but not the fin. Its shadow was directed away from the house, straight toward the sun.

Shiloh shook his head and walked toward the house, rubbing his brow. As he walked up the porch steps, Doc stretched out his arm with a book in his hand. He recognized it as his gift from Saige. Doc said, "Why don't you head on up to your room. Maybe read it over a little."

Shiloh took the book from Doc and gazed at the title, *True Nature*. It then suddenly sprung open to the first page. He looked at the pages and found a picture on each. On the left was a picture of a caged lion with a caption, 'this is not a lion.' On the opposite page was a picture of a lion running in the wild with the caption, 'this is a lion.' Doc then smirked and added, "Get some rest. If you still want to go home in the morning, I'll take you."

July 23rd

Shiloh woke before dawn in a half-seated position, a crick in his neck and his new book in his lap. He pushed the book away, rolling onto his side to go back to sleep, but some faint, rustling noises and a whistling sound caused him to open his eyes. He saw his cats over by the window, staring intently out into the darkness. Closing his eyes, he wondered what had them so mesmerized, but had no desire to wake up.

The whistling continued, growing louder until it sounded like it was directly outside the window. The melody, while soothing and sweet, kept him from falling back to sleep. It seemed to be calling to him, and he couldn't help but pull himself out of bed to investigate. He stumbled over to the window and squinted down into the darkness, but found nothing. The only thing he could make out in the predawn light was the gray platform in the center of the yard.

He was ready to turn away when a sudden bright light appeared at the rear of the yard. It bounced up and down between the trees and bushes. The whistling grew as the flut-

Shiloh's True Nature

tering, white object moved closer to the house. Shiloh tried to determine what it was, but every time he caught a glimpse it would skip out of view.

The object left a glowing trail in its wake, and the thought of a ghost crossed Shiloh's mind. He had already seen so many fantastic things in Fair Hill that the possibility of a ghost didn't seem out of the question. However, all of Shiloh's speculation was put to rest when the object passed beneath the window.

The unidentified object was no longer just a thing, but an unidentified girl with long, blond hair in a bright, flowing white dress. She whistled her tune, swinging a small basket in one hand as she skipped close to the house and around some of Doc's wooden sculptures before drifting toward the rear of the yard again.

Shiloh watched with a feeling of contentment as she bounced to and fro, occasionally disappearing behind the yard's many obstacles. As the whistling faded again, Shiloh lost sight of the girl. He squinted hard into the distance, wondering where she had gone. He contemplated investigating, but was still very tired and decided to go back to bed.

A couple of hours later, Shiloh woke again and saw the cats by the window basking in the sunlight. He immediately went to the window and was greeted by the warmth of the sun on his face. He gazed down into the backyard for signs of his early morning visitor, but found only the usual things present. The only whistling came from the local songbirds, which wasn't nearly as appealing as the tune he heard earlier. Wondering if he had dreamt the whole thing, Shiloh tried to recall the tune and what he had seen before dawn, but it was all a blur.

Hoping something to eat might clear his head, Shiloh left the bedroom and went downstairs to the kitchen. He walked in, finding Doc seated at the table reading a book, and a number of breakfast items spread around the table. Shiloh didn't speak; he just poured himself some cereal and began eating while staring out into space. Doc watched him with a raised eyebrow for a moment before saying, "Good morning."

Shiloh didn't answer; he just grunted. Doc snorted with laughter. "For a farm boy, you're not much of a morning person."

Shiloh ignored Doc's observation and continued shoveling spoonful after spoonful of frosted pillows of wheat into his mouth. Doc could see he wasn't going to have any conversation from Shiloh, so he returned to his book. Shiloh then blurted out, "Did you see anyone in the backyard this morning?"

His grandson's abrupt alertness puzzled Doc, but he answered, "No."

Shiloh grunted. "Hmm. Never mind then."

Shiloh finished off a second bowl of cereal, some toast, and was working on devouring a pear when a knock came to the front door. "Come in," Doc called.

Shiloh heard the screen door squeak as Doc said, "Good morning, Bud."

"Hey, Doc," Bud replied, brushing his messy, blond hair from his face to behind his ear.

"What can we do for you this morning?" Doc asked with

Shiloh's True Nature

a smile.

"Oh, nothing really, I just wanted to see if Shiloh was still here and wanted to go swimming."

Shiloh's eyes widened and he looked to Doc. "May I?"

Doc smiled, tilting back in his chair slightly. "I don't see why not. It's supposed to be very hot today."

Shiloh slid his chair away from the table to stand up. Doc, with a big grin on his face, added, "That is, unless you still want to go home."

Smirking at Doc, Shiloh stood and said to Bud, "Wait here."

Shiloh ran upstairs and began looking around the bedroom for his duffel bag. He found it on one of the chairs by the fireplace, but Cheepie was laying on it. Shiloh tried to shoo him away, but the feline wouldn't budge. He started to pull the bag out from underneath the cat, but Cheepie dug his claws into the bag, unwilling to part with his pillow.

Shiloh eventually won the game of tug-of-war and began rummaging through the bag for his swim trunks. Once he found them, he quickly put them on and ran back to the kitchen.

"I'm ready," Shiloh announced, grabbing an apple from a bowl on the table.

"Cool," Bud smiled. He then turned to Doc and said, "Have a good afternoon, Doc."

"You too, Bud," Doc replied.

Bud started out of the kitchen and Shiloh nodded to Doc as he took a bite from the apple. Doc smiled. "Have fun."

Shiloh followed Bud out of the house and into the late-morning sun. Bud led them in a direction Shiloh hadn't been before, so he was eager to take in the surroundings. At first, there didn't appear to be much of anything but forest on both sides of the dirt road. However, as they walked on, Shiloh began to notice little cottages and bungalows nestled in between the trees off the road. The homes were integrated with the surrounding plant life, just like the stores in town, with trees growing out of the rooftops or used as their corners.

One house in particular caught Shiloh's eye. Not so much because of its uniqueness, but more because of its familiarity. It was close to the road and looked like a house one might see in Salem. The simple, two-story, white house had a wraparound porch with pink shutters. The only unique thing Shiloh noticed about it was an octagonal, stained-glass window with a depiction of a pink rose above the gabled archway over the front door.

As they passed by the house, Shiloh thought about his home and how he hadn't wanted to come to Fair Hill at first. He smiled to himself, thinking how glad he did. He reflected on all the amazing things he had seen since he arrived, and realized that no traveling carnival could be as exciting. Now he was going swimming with some new friends, and couldn't be happier about his father making him come to Fair Hill.

Still smiling, Shiloh spoke, "Thanks for inviting me to come along today."

"Well, I know you just got here, and Doc is like a part of our family, which pretty much makes you family. So, you're welcome," Bud replied, returning the smile.

Shiloh's True Nature

Shiloh then asked, "So, has your family always lived in Fair Hill?"

"Yeah, I think so. I mean, we've lived here my whole life," Bud responded.

Shiloh was ready to ask another question, but before he could, Bud asked, "You live across the river, right?"

"Yeah, I live in Salem," Shiloh replied.

"Wow, Salem," Bud sounded intrigued.

Shiloh grinned, wondering why anyone would ever think of his sleepy, little farm town as fascinating. "We used to have some relatives who lived there, I think," Bud added.

"Oh? Where do they live now? I mean, do you have relatives who don't live here?"

Bud nodded in return. "Yeah, we have some relatives outside of Fair Hill. We don't see them much though."

"Are they . . . ah . . . you know, special people too?" Shiloh asked, unable to remember what they called themselves.

"Movers, you mean? No. Well, some, but not most of them . . ." Bud fumbled with his words before explaining, ". . . You see, if a family has anyone special, it's usually just one person." Shiloh scratched his forehead as Bud continued. "I guess what I'm trying to say is, it's extremely rare for there to be a whole family of Movers like mine."

"Oh, okay," Shiloh replied, thinking he understood.

Bud smiled, snapping his fingers. "Kaz and Brinda."

Shiloh frowned slightly. "What about Kaz and Linda?"

Bud laughed and Shiloh retorted, "What?"

"Brinda, not Linda," Bud replied, chuckling.

"So, what about them?" Shiloh asked with a smirk.

Bud informed, "They are good examples of most Movers, and most of the people in Fair Hill."

"How so?" Shiloh inquired.

"Brinda was sent here to live with Mina and Maximo. They are these huge twins who talk funny. I once heard they're from some hidden island in the Mediterranean Sea," Bud answered.

Shiloh thought for a moment, "What do you mean she was sent here?"

A solemn look washed across Bud's face. "Not too long ago, her parents kind of freaked out when they found out about her gift and didn't know what to do about it. So she ended up here."

Shiloh wasn't quite sure what to say, only mumbled, "Hmmm."

Bud added, "It's cool though. I think she's happier living here."

As they continued along, Bud related, "Kaz lives with his godmother, Regina, but he's not actually related to her. I think you might have met her. She's the town magistrate."

"What's a magistrate?" Shiloh asked.

Bud laughed. "I don't really know, but she oversees all of the town's affairs. If there's a problem of some kind, people usually go to her and she sees that it's taken care of. Anyway, Kaz came here to live with her."

"Same deal as with Brinda?" Shiloh asked.

Bud chuckled. "No. Kaz needed help learning to control his gift and came here to get it."

Shiloh nodded in understanding.

Shiloh's True Nature

A moment later, the road curved and sloped down slightly as they came to a stop just above a beautiful open area. The area, like most of Fair Hill, was surrounded by a forest of hickory, oak, and pine trees. A number of little streams rolled out of the forest, all flowing into a long, thin lake.

Shiloh gazed down at the lake, seeing how it stretched into the distance and bent out of view. Bud motioned with his arm. "It connects to the river way over there."

When Bud began walking again, he pointed down by the edge of the lake. "There's my house."

Shiloh saw a green bungalow with a wrap-around porch snuggled in amongst some trees and said, "Cool."

As he looked around the house and the surrounding forest, Shiloh noticed a few unusual trees. One particular tree with red, yellow, and orange leaves caught his eye. He thought it was a little early for the leaves to be changing color and continued staring at it, trying to figure out what type of tree it was. A gust of wind then blew through the trees and the multicolored leaves appeared to catch fire.

Shiloh turned to Bud, a look of panic on his face, but Bud just smiled. "Relax, it's a Fire Tree. When the wind blows hard enough, the stirring leaves make it look like the tree is on fire."

Shaking his head, Shiloh sighed in relief as the breeze died down and the leaves returned to normal. His focus shifted to a few fir trees scattered around the edge of the lake. The trees appeared to be decorated for Christmas, but since that was over five months away, Shiloh assumed the decorations must have been left up from last year.

As they came closer to the water, someone emerged from behind the trunk of a giant pine tree near the edge of the lake. It was Kaz. Bud gave him a wave, but Shiloh was focused on the tree behind him. It had a massive trunk with thick, spaced branches creating a spiral staircase leading all the way to the top. At the peak, there was a large, manmade platform sitting just under the tip.

Shiloh pointed toward the tree. "What is that?"

Bud joked, "That's Kaz."

Shiloh laughed and said, "No. I mean up on that tree."

"Oh, that's the tower," Bud replied. "We mostly use it to look at the stars. There are so many trees around that it's hard to see much of the sky from the ground."

"Cool," Shiloh said, grinning.

"Hey, guys," Kaz called out as Bud and Shiloh reached the edge of the lake.

Shiloh gave a little wave and Bud echoed, "Hey, Kaz."

Kaz gave a sly smile, "Any chance of getting into the shed today?"

Bud shook his head. "No chance. My mom is home."

Kaz had a disappointed look, prompting Shiloh to ask, "The shed?"

Bud pointed over toward his house, where Shiloh noticed a small green shed off to the side. "That's where my dad keeps all his tools and toys and stuff," Bud noted.

Shiloh found it amusing that the shed looked like a miniature version of the bungalow. He noticed the doors were held closed by a piece of rope and asked, "Is that one of those special knots?"

Shiloh's True Nature

Bud smiled. "Yeah, it's special all right."

Shiloh nodded. "I saw my grandfather using one on his stall doors yesterday. It was weird the way it worked."

"My dad makes them. He's real good with puzzles and devices, but he likes to work with string and rope mostly," Bud added.

Bud then turned to Kaz. "So where's Brinda?"

Kaz started to answer, but before he could speak a splash of water drenched the three boys. Shiloh was stunned and looked toward the lake, but no one was there. Confused as to what had happened, he turned to Bud and Kaz, but they seemed just as dazed. Then a girl's voice said, "You jerks went swimming without me. How rude."

The boys turned around to find Brinda standing behind them with a big grin on her face.

"Nice one," Bud chuckled.

Kaz scowled. "Oh, you're going to get it, Brin."

"You're getting in the water anyway, Kaz," Brinda joked, sticking out her tongue.

As she began walking toward the lake, Brinda smiled at Shiloh. "Hello, Shiloh. It's nice to see you again."

Shiloh was still a little puzzled and stammered, "H-hello."

Brinda waded into the lake, with Bud and Kaz right behind her. Shiloh hesitated for a moment, but then followed. He walked in slowly to let his body acclimate to the cool, refreshing water. When he was about waist-deep, Shiloh looked down at his reflection in the crystal-clear lake and smiled. He then closed his eyes, took a deep breath, and let his feet slide out from under him. He stretched out his arms, letting the surrounding water cool his entire body.

Shiloh surfaced, wiping the water from his eyes as Kaz said, "We should play a game or something."

Brinda splashed Kaz in the face and smiled. "How about a race?"

"No. Nothing that gives you the opportunity to cheat," Kaz sneered.

Brinda made a funny face and said, "Fine."

The kids thought for a moment, and then Bud asked, "So what should we play then?"

Shiloh kept quiet, because he didn't care what they played, as long as it involved being in the water. "How about Marco Polo?" Kaz suggested.

"Fine, but you're it," Brinda answered with a demanding tone.

"Fine," Kaz responded, making a funny face back at Brinda before turning away and moving toward the lake's edge.

Brinda, Bud, and Shiloh waded a little farther out into the lake and Brinda yelled, "And no cheating, Kaz!"

"You're the cheater, Brinda," he shot back.

The three separated from each other a little and Bud yelled, "We're ready!"

"Okay. Marco?" Kaz called out.

None of the three kids answered, so he called out again, "Marco?"

Shiloh looked back toward the edge of the lake before answering, but no one was there. Bud and Brinda yelled, "Polo!"

Shiloh looked all around, but he didn't see Kaz anywhere.

Shiloh's True Nature

He noticed some bubbles and ripples on the water in the distance and thought Kaz must have gone under. To his surprise, he again heard Kaz call out, "Marco!"

Brinda and Bud again yelled, "Polo!" but Shiloh was still trying to figure out where the voice came from and didn't answer.

Kaz went silent and Shiloh continued watching the ripples in the water, waiting for him to pop-up from underneath. The ripples moved toward Bud's position across the way from Shiloh. He watched the bubbles, thinking it was unbelievable how long Kaz could hold his breath.

When the ripples were nearly touching him, Bud's entire body rose up out of the water and hovered in the air above the surface. Shiloh's mouth hung open in awe and he quickly turned toward Brinda to see her reaction. She had a gigantic smile on her face and cupped her hand over her mouth to keep from laughing out loud.

Though nothing surfaced from underneath the water, Shiloh looked around as he again heard Kaz's voice call out, "Marco."

Shiloh looked toward Brinda, who nodded rapidly to him. The two of them called out together, "Polo."

The ripples in the water moved in their direction, so Shiloh remained still. Brinda swam off noisily and the ripples followed her. When she stopped, Brinda turned back toward Shiloh's position, raising her hands out of the water slightly. Suddenly a large wall of water burst from her location, spreading out in all directions. Shiloh's eyes nearly popped out of his head, watching the rushing water fly at him, but he submerged just in time to avoid being hit.

Shiloh resurfaced, swimming to a new location, but he ran into something. He looked around, but couldn't see what was blocking his path. He stretched out his arm and his hand touched something he could not see. It was almost like he had run into an invisible wall. Suddenly, the unseen barrier appeared before Shiloh's eyes. It was Kaz, who grabbed him, crying out, "Gotcha."

Once the shock of learning of his new friends' abilities wore off, Shiloh began to enjoy himself. He realized they were just ordinary kids who could do extraordinary things, and he found it exciting and challenging to keep up. If there was one thing working on a farm with his father had taught him, it was how to keep up.

The kids swam and played hard until morning turned into afternoon. When they needed a break, they took to floating around on the gigantic lily pads lining the edges of the lake. Shiloh was curious about his friends' abilities and took the opportunity to ask about them. "So what else can you do, Bud?" Shiloh inquired, as his lily pad slowly rotated.

Bud was reclined with his eyes closed and his face pointed up toward the sun. "Well, it's all air-related stuff. I'm still learning how to do different things. You've already seen the coolest thing I've learned to do so far: float in the air for a short while."

"What about you, Brinda? Is everything you do water related?" Shiloh asked.

"Oh, no. I can manipulate all kinds of liquids. Water is just the easiest to work with. It has something to do with

Shiloh's True Nature

its weight or something. I'm still learning, too," Brinda confessed. She paused for a moment, and continued, "Let me give you an example." She placed her hand on the water and a small wave washed away from her toward Kaz, who was resting his eyes. Kaz's lily pad upended and he fell backward into the water.

Brinda roared with laughter and then said, "If this were a thicker, heavier liquid, I would have to be closer to do that."

Shiloh chuckled, but realized Kaz had not surfaced. "Is he all right?"

Bud opened his eyes and looked around. Suddenly, Brinda was upended from her lily pad, falling face-first into the water. "He's fine," Bud laughed, closing his eyes.

Brinda surfaced, and Kaz materialized next to her and yelled, "Stop doing that!"

Brinda again roared with laughter, while Bud and Shiloh snickered. Kaz shook his head, smiled, and swam back to his lily pad.

Still giggling, Brinda said, "And as you can see, Jerk-o here is an invisible man."

Climbing back on to his lily pad, Kaz differed, "I do not become invisible. I have a camouflage-like reflex that I am learning how to manipulate."

Bud snorted as Brinda mimicked, "A camouflage-like reflex."

Shiloh then said, "I'm not sure I understand the difference, Kaz."

"Well, Shiloh, it's kind of like how a chameleon changes its skin color to blend into the background," Kaz tried to clarify.

"Sound good, Shiloh?" Brinda laughed, mocking Kaz's explanation.

"I don't know, dude. You looked pretty invisible to me," Shiloh chuckled.

Bud and Brinda both burst into laughter again.

Kaz smirked, trying to hold in his laughter. "Shut up."

Shiloh leaned back and closed his eyes. A moment later, a splash of water hit him in the face. Shiloh thought it was Brinda being funny, but when he opened his eyes he was surprised to find a giant frog had leapt onto a lily pad next to him. The frog had slimy, dark-green skin with black stripes running down its back and enormous, bulging, maroon-and-gold eyes that swirled in opposite directions.

The huge frog stared at Shiloh, and he expressed his concern. "This thing isn't dangerous is it?"

Brinda laughed as Bud answered, "No, it's just a Mondo Frog."

Kaz added, "Don't stare at it too long, though, or it might put you to sleep."

Brinda saw the worried look on Shiloh's face and argued, "That's a myth, Kaz."

Kaz seemed irritated by Brinda's contradiction. "It's not a myth. Staring at them for a long time has a hypnotic effect."

Brinda snorted. "Whatever, Kaz."

Brinda placed the palm of her hand on the water and Shiloh's lily pad quickly floated over next to hers. "I'll protect you from the dangerous Mr. Sleepy Frog, Shiloh."

"You know, that's the first frog I've seen all summer," Bud noted, gazing toward the frog out of the corner of his eye.

Shiloh's True Nature

"I'll have to mention that to Regina, because the water must be getting cleaner if the frogs are returning," Kaz said, running his hand through the water.

Brinda sighed. "This is the nicest the water has been all summer."

Shiloh was curious and inquired, "What was wrong with the lake before now?"

Kaz quickly answered, "Some sort of pollution made its way into the lake recently. No one knows where it came from."

"The town has been testing the water to see what could be done to make it cleaner, but they haven't had much success," Bud added.

"Well, whatever it was is gone. Whatever they did seems to be working, because the water has been just beautiful the last couple days," Brinda said, happily pushing off of Shiloh's lily pad and spinning away from the lake's edge with her arms raised in the air.

"I wonder when the Moon Whales will return to the lake," Bud pondered.

Kaz let out a little chuckle. Bud raised his hands, questioning, "What?"

Shiloh turned to Brinda, who had drifted back next to him. "What's a Moon Whale?" Brinda rolled her eyes, shaking her head and smiling.

Kaz pointed toward Brinda. "Now there's your myth."

Bud raised his voice a little. "It's not a myth. I've seen them. They sleep in the lake during the day and head out to the river at night."

Bud looked around at the others, who just bit their tongues. "If you don't believe me, when they return, just walk along the river some night. You can see their tusks glowing in the dark as they swim out," Bud pled.

Shiloh looked at Bud with a confused smile. "So they're whales who have a glowing horn sticking out of their heads or something?"

Kaz and Brinda snorted as Bud answered, "Exactly!"

"If you don't believe me, we'll look for them tonight," Bud offered.

"I'll pass! I remember last summer's exciting Moon Whale hunt. We snuck out two nights in a row and stared at the lake for hours," Brinda huffed. "And what did we see? Nothing!"

"Yeah, I don't want to do that again," Kaz said, with a grimace.

Bud grumbled, waved his hand at the others in disgust, and returned to a reclined position.

As they floated around, Shiloh realized how remarkably quiet it was in Fair Hill. All he could hear was water flowing. Shiloh's farm was far from boisterous, but there was always some kind of background noise, whether it was his father's farm equipment or cars in the distance. Fair Hill, on the other hand, was completely noise-free, except for the sounds of nature.

The tranquility was then interrupted by a voice calling out in the distance. "Bud! Get up here!"

Bud sprang up from his lily pad. "That's my mom. I better see what she wants. I'll be right back."

While Bud waded out of the lake, Shiloh, Brinda, and Kaz

Shiloh's True Nature

continued quietly floating around. Shiloh began to think about all of the cool things his new friends could do. He felt a little awkward knowing they had such amazing abilities and he didn't. He wasn't envious or ashamed, but felt like an outsider.

Shiloh's self-reflection ended when an odd, buzzing sound echoed through the trees. He frowned, listening intently as the noise grew louder and closer. He then realized it was a motorized noise of some kind. "What is that?" he asked, looking toward Kaz and Brinda to see if they were familiar with it.

Kaz just shrugged his shoulders, but Brinda scowled and said, "I'll bet it's him."

Confused by Brinda's comment, Shiloh repeated, "Him?"

Before Brinda could reply, Shiloh saw a black watercraft speed into view in the distance, spewing a trail of white smoke in its wake. "What is that?" Shiloh questioned, raising his voice to be heard.

Kaz groaned. "It's Junior!"

Shiloh squinted, "What's he riding?"

"It's a water bike," Brinda hollered.

As the craft drew near, Shiloh saw what appeared to be a cross between a small boat and a motorcycle gliding across the water's surface toward them. The water bike came closer and closer, and didn't appear to be slowing down. The kids turned to one another with looks of apprehension, and then simultaneously scrambled to move out of the way.

Junior sped the craft directly toward the lake's edge, only to make a U-turn at the last second, sending a wave crashing into the backs of Kaz, Brinda, and Shiloh, who were still moving away. Shiloh looked back to see the brassy-haired boy complete his U-turn and slow the water bike down to a crawl. Junior glanced over his shoulder at the kids and laughed before speeding away.

"What was that?" Bud called out, rushing down to the lake's edge.

"Junior," Kaz replied, wading toward the edge of the lake.

Brinda fumed, "I should've knocked that jerk over."

Bud shook his head in exasperation. "You know what, forget about him and come have some lunch."

Kaz, Brinda, and Shiloh climbed out of the lake and followed Bud into the bungalow, where Bud's mother, Martina, had prepared them a midday meal. Shiloh, while having a wonderful time, was relieved to have a respite from the sun. The kids stuffed themselves for over an hour with every delectable treat Martina provided, replenishing their energy for an afternoon of recreation.

The meal ended with the kids resting in rocking chairs on the front porch while eating icy fruit pops. Shiloh happily nibbled on a raspberry pop and gazed out at the lake, anxious to return to the water. As he scanned the area, Shiloh noticed a girl with long, brown hair by the lake. The girl walked back and forth between one of the decorated fir trees and the lake, where she was tossing something into the water.

"Who is that?" Shiloh asked.

The kids briefly stopped consuming their fruit pops to have a look. Bud smiled with a squint. "It looks like Bryce's cousin Harmony again."

Shiloh's True Nature

"Oh." Shiloh nodded before returning to his fruit pop.

Brinda looked back and forth between Bud and Shiloh, asking, "What do you mean 'again'?"

Bud started to answer, but Shiloh cut him off. "I saw a girl at the bookstore yesterday and I could have sworn her hair changed colors right in front of me. When I saw her again later, Bud was with me, so I asked him who she was." He paused, and then pointed toward the lake. "It was her."

Brinda gave a nod of understanding. "I think the hair thing is part of her ability, but I don't know for sure."

"Hasn't anyone asked her?" Shiloh inquired.

Bud smiled again, "Well, it's like I said, she just arrived not too long ago."

Clearing his throat, Kaz commented, "I met her when she first got here, but she didn't have much to say. Now that I think about it, I don't think she even spoke."

Brinda shook her head. "I know what you mean. She seems kind of weird. She just stares with those big spooky eyes."

Shiloh finished his fruit pop and continued watching the girl move between the tree and the lake. He wondered what she was tossing into the water. "What is she doing?"

Kaz looked down to the girl. "It appears she's feeding the fish," he observed.

"What is she getting from the trees to feed the fish?" Shiloh asked.

Brinda giggled. "Fish food."

"Fish food grows on trees?" Shiloh questioned.

"No, Shiloh, it's a Present Tree," Bud pointed out.

"What's a Present Tree?" There was so much to learn about Fair Hill.

Bud stood up, giving Shiloh a little wave to follow. Kaz and Brinda trailed after them as Bud walked to the closest Present Tree by the edge of the lake. Shiloh smiled when he saw the tips of each of the tree's branches had little ornate boxes with tiny, golden bows on them. Bud pointed to one of the presents and explained, "If you need something, you open the box, and the tree will give it to you."

Brinda grinned and quipped, "I'd really like another one of those fruit pops."

She reached for one of the boxes, but Kaz pushed her hand away, saying, "It's not supposed to be used like that."

Brinda made a funny face and stuck her tongue out at him. Kaz raised his hand and pointed to a bandage wrapped around his middle finger. "On my way here this morning, I cut my finger and it wouldn't stop bleeding. I clearly needed a bandage. So, when I got here, I opened a box and a bandage was there."

"Why don't you give it a try?" Bud suggested with a smile.

Shiloh eyed the tree and its little boxes, trying to think of something he wanted. He gazed around at his friends and Brinda was smiling at him, while silently mouthing 'fruit pop'. Shiloh grinned. "Those fruit pops were really good."

Kaz huffed, and Shiloh reached for the closest box. When he opened the box, Shiloh peered inside to find nothing but his own reflection in the bottom of the box.

"There's nothing in here," Shiloh said, looking quizzically at his friends.

Shiloh's True Nature

Brinda frowned, Bud shrugged his shoulders, and Kaz just shook his head. Shiloh tried the next closest box, but with the same result.

"You have to concentrate on what you want," Bud said.

Kaz again huffed. "I told you guys; it's not supposed to be used for trivial things like that."

"You take the fun out of everything, Kaz," Brinda scoffed.

The kids began drifting toward the lake while they continued to debate the issue, but Shiloh hesitated. He stared into the little present box, wondering why it didn't work for him. When he turned to follow his friends, he was startled as a girl appeared from behind the tree and reached for one of the boxes. It was the girl he saw from the porch; only her hair was no longer brown, but a light golden blond.

Slightly tongue-tied, Shiloh stammered, "H-hello."

She smiled at him while opening the box. "Perhaps there is nothing you really need."

Shiloh tilted his head and looked into her eyes, pondering what she meant. He marveled at the size of her eyes, but didn't find them spooky at all. He thought they were amazingly beautiful. One was amber, the other hazel, and both had flecks of auburn and blue. He then watched as she walked over to the lake and began sprinkling flakes of fish food across the surface of the water. He smiled to himself as he watched her, but was again startled as Brinda called out, "C'mon, Shiloh."

Shiloh looked toward the lake and found his friends drifting around on the lily pads again. He turned back toward the girl to say good-bye, but found she had begun walking away into the forest with her blond hair diffusing into brown. Shiloh was puzzled by her abrupt departure, but decided not to dwell on it and returned to the lake with the others.

The kids spent the rest of afternoon swimming, playing, and enjoying the lake. They lost all track of time until Bud spun toward the house on his lily pad and noticed his father arriving home.

"What's he doing home already?" Bud questioned.

Shiloh looked at Bud and asked, "Why? What time is it?"

Suddenly, the Stone Balloon began chiming in the distance. After hearing several chimes, Brinda said, "I can't believe it's five already."

Kaz grunted his displeasure at the time as well.

As the kids began to leave the lake, Shiloh observed, "You know, I didn't hear that Stone-Balloon thing all afternoon until just now."

Brinda and Kaz laughed heartily and gave a wave goodbye as they headed off. Shiloh looked at Bud with his hands raised. "What are they laughing at?"

"You never hear it, unless you want to hear it," Bud answered.

Shiloh gave him a look of confusion. Bud started toward the house, opening his mouth to explain, but Shiloh waved him off, saying, "Never mind."

When they reached the porch, Shiloh stopped Bud and said, "I should probably get going too. Thanks again for inviting me over today."

Bud smiled and started to say something, but stopped when the front door swung open. Luther poked his head out

Shiloh's True Nature

of the door. "You two get in here and eat."

Shiloh tried to explain he was leaving. "But my grandfather . . ."

Luther cut him off, "He knows exactly where you are, and I told him I'd feed you. So get in here before Jace eats everything."

Shiloh looked to Bud, who extended his arm to the front to door as if to say, 'after you.'

After another wonderful meal with Bud and his family, Shiloh headed home content. He thought this day was exactly how he wanted to spend his vacation, swimming and laughing with friends, and being well fed was a nice bonus.

As Shiloh walked, he found out there was a price to be paid for his day of fun in the sun. His skin was sunburned. It was taut, dry, and every movement felt uncomfortable.

As he approached his grandfather's house, Shiloh heard talking inside. When he came close enough to hear a deep, gruff voice, he knew Crow was over for a visit. He stopped at the porch steps to listen and rub his knees, which were burning from the walk.

"Oh, I've been meaning to tell you, Doc. I've been getting reports of a drastic improvement in the environment, but they say there's still something strange going on with the water," Crow's voice carried through the house's open windows.

Intrigued, Shiloh waited for Crow to continue. "They've been keeping an eye on Samuel, like we talked about. They believe he's up to something, building something. Oh, and he went over to Salem again."

Hearing about Salem further piqued Shiloh's interest, and questions began to swirl in his head. Who was reporting to Crow? Who was Samuel? And why was he going over to Salem?

Shiloh wanted to learn more, but his sunburn was annoying him. He thought if he could take a seat in one of the rocking chairs on the porch, he could continue listening. However, when he put his foot on the bottom porch step, it creaked loudly. Shiloh cringed and froze in place until Crow resumed talking.

"Molly was telling me that Henrietta has been having a lot of trouble with her hands lately. Some others mentioned her constantly dropping things as well. So you may want to look in on her," Crow said.

"I'll be making my rounds the day after tomorrow, and I'll swing by and have a look," Doc replied.

Crow chuckled, adding, "You may want to think of a good excuse for the visit. You know how independent Henrietta is."

"I'll figure something out," Doc laughed.

Crow then asked, "So where's that grandson of yours? I haven't seen him all day."

"He went to the lake with Bud this morning. I bumped into Luther, who said he'd make sure he was fed. I expect he should be home any time now."

Shiloh couldn't stand anymore. He was now feeling the sunburn pain on his skin from his head to his feet. When he entered the front door, he was greeted with a roar of laughter from Crow, who was seated in the living room with Doc.

Shiloh's True Nature

"So much for wanting to go home, huh?" Crow laughed.

"How was your day?" Doc asked with a smile.

Shiloh tried to return the smile. "It was great, except now I'm burnt."

Doc saw how much pain Shiloh was in, so he rose from his chair and tore off a pointy branch from a plant sitting on the window sill. Doc handed the branch to Shiloh and said, "Bend it in half lengthwise and rub the gel that comes out on your skin. It will stop the burning."

Shiloh took the branch and slowly climbed up the stairs to his room. He took a seat on the edge of the bed and did as instructed, snapping the branch and rubbing the gooey, green gel all over his arms and legs. As he finished covering himself, Doc entered the room and said, "It takes a little while for the gel to sink in . . . why don't you lie back?"

Shiloh leaned back, resting on the pillow, while Doc spun the ceiling fan. The cool breeze made Shiloh feel a little better. Doc took a seat at the foot of the bed and asked, "So you had a good time today?"

Shiloh nodded, smiling.

Doc winked and pointed. "See, I knew you'd like it here."

Shiloh moved slightly, wincing in pain. Doc grabbed Shiloh's big toe and shook it. "I'll bet if you close your eyes, the pain will go away and you'll fall right to sleep."

Shiloh wanted to question Doc's optimism, but he didn't have the strength. He was starting to feel sleepy and could barely keep his eyes open. So he smiled at Doc, closed his eyes, and a moment later he was asleep.

July 24th

Shiloh found himself standing in a dark cornfield with no idea how he arrived there. As he gazed around at the giant, deformed cornstalks, flapping and fluttering noises came from all directions. He scanned the dark skies above for the moon or a familiar star to direct him, but there was nothing he recognized.

When a loud groan echoed out of the darkness, Shiloh became frightened and started to run. He had no idea where he was going, but it felt safer to be moving than stationary. He ran and ran, but the cornfield seemed never ending. It was only when he heard a gentle, seductive whistling that he began to slow down.

Without thought, Shiloh stopped looking for a way out of the field and began searching for the source of the sweet, soft melody. The whistling seemed to be coming from all around him. It was so relaxing he no longer had the urge to run. He felt like he needed to lie down and close his eyes. So he did.

Suddenly, he opened his eyes and sat up in bed, realizing

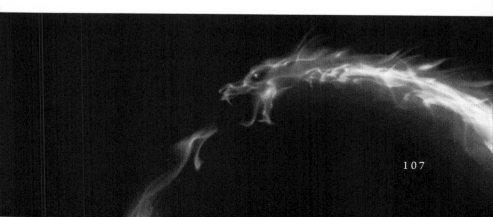

Shiloh's True Nature

he had been dreaming. He looked toward the window and found the cats side by side, staring outside, just like the previous morning. He fell back on his pillow, thinking he would return to sleep, but a part of the dream kept him from doing so. He could hear the whistling from the dream ever so faintly in his head. He tossed and turned as the whistling grew louder and louder. Eventually, he came to the understanding that it wasn't in his head, but right outside his window.

Remembering the previous morning, Shiloh quickly jumped up and looked outside. Though first light had yet to hit, he could clearly see the girl with long, blond hair skipping around the backyard again. Just like the previous morning, she whistled her tune and carried a basket as she skipped, only the basket she carried this morning seemed much larger.

Shiloh was much better rested and thinking more clearly this morning as he watched her skip around. He wondered what she was doing bouncing around his grandfather's yard so early, and was determined to find out. He thought about calling down to her, but she abruptly moved off toward the rear of the yard. He quickly pulled on his shoes and raced through the house and out the back door to follow.

Shiloh ran down the back porch steps, finding the girl nowhere in sight. He continued toward the rear corner of the yard until he reached the path. Hesitant to enter the dark trail, but too intrigued to turn back, Shiloh walked into the opening and began moving along quietly, listening for any signs of the girl.

The path was dark, but Shiloh's eyes slowly adjusted, allowing him to take in the surroundings. There was a sweet smell to the morning air as he passed through the glistening, lush vegetation. His pace was dictated by the morning dew, which had made the ground very slick. He nearly slipped several times before coming to a four-way junction.

At the open intersection, the passageways to the left and right appeared dark and overgrown. The pathway directly ahead seemed the least hazardous choice, so he continued forward. This section of path had some oddly-shaped flowering plants lining both sides of it. The plants' circular flowers gave off a crescent-shaped sliver of glowing light, making it much easier to maneuver through the area.

When the trail came to an end, it opened up into a clearing overlooking a small valley. Shiloh saw the girl nearby, unfolding a blanket, so he quietly ducked behind a tree, hoping to see a glimpse of her face. She placed the blanket by the embankment, then knelt down and opened the picnic basket. Shiloh watched as she pulled a steaming teapot, some cups and saucers, and a plate of biscuits from the basket.

Shiloh looked past the girl and across the valley's misty treetops at the unobstructed view of the horizon, which grew brighter with the pending sunrise. It was a beautiful, peaceful sight, and he drank it all in, until he was startled by a voice saying, "I thought you might like to have some tea and biscuits and watch the sunrise."

Shiloh again ducked behind the tree, but felt foolish for hiding when he had clearly been discovered. So he stepped out from behind the tree to find Harmony smiling at him. He walked to the blanket where she was seated and said, "Good

Shiloh's True Nature

morning."

"Your name is Shiloh, right?" she asked, brushing her long, blond hair over her shoulder.

Shiloh nodded. "Yes, it is."

She started pouring some tea into the cups and smiled, "Good morning, Shiloh. We haven't been formally introduced. My name is Harmony."

Shiloh took a seat on the blanket next to Harmony, and she handed him a cup of tea. "Thank you," he said, placing his hand under the saucer.

Harmony held up a plate covered with round, golden pieces of fluffy bread with pieces of fruit baked into them. "Biscuit?"

Shiloh shook his head as he took a sip of tea. "If you don't mind my asking, why have you been skipping around my grandfather's backyard the past couple mornings?" Shiloh questioned.

"It's the easiest way to get here. I sometimes find the roads in Fair Hill a little confusing," Harmony explained.

Shiloh grinned, understanding that confusion all too well. "So why here?"

Harmony replied, "To watch the sunrise, of course."

Shiloh frowned, wondering to himself why anyone would wake up so early to watch the sunrise if it wasn't required of them. He'd had to wake up before sunrise all summer long to help his father on the farm and dreaded it.

Harmony saw Shiloh's frown. "You see, I used to live by the ocean, and every morning I watched the sunrise over the water. When I first arrived here, with all the trees and hills,

110

it seemed unlikely I would find a suitable place to watch. So one morning, when I was feeling homesick, I began walking and thinking how much I missed the sunrise. As I walked past your grandfather's house, I felt drawn to his backyard, then to the path, and I ended up here."

Shiloh nodded. "I see. I've been up before dawn quite a few times, but I don't think I ever actually just sat and watched the sun come up."

"That's too bad." He tilted his head, wondering what she meant. She continued, "It's a remarkable thing, the birth of a new day. It's a simple pleasure that no one seems to appreciate."

Excitement for the pending sunrise filled him and he felt as if there were nowhere else he would rather be. It was only when she grasped his wrist and pointed into the distance that his attention shifted.

A tiny amber dot broke the horizon. Shiloh watched it grow from a flickering speck, to a bright half-circle, to a glorious, radiant sphere. He then turned to Harmony to see the sun glowing off of her face. The beauty of her eyes was fully revealed by the sun's glow. The auburn and blue fleck patterns throughout the irises made her amber and hazel eyes sparkle and shimmer like kaleidoscopes.

Harmony felt Shiloh's gaze and blushed slightly. "So, you're new here, right?" she asked, brushing the hair out of her face to behind her ear.

Shiloh smiled. "Yes, but I'm only staying another week or so."

"Why?" Harmony asked, her blush replaced with a look

Shiloh's True Nature

of curiosity.

Shiloh looked away without answering, feeling a little like an outsider again.

"Shiloh?" she pressed, awaiting an answer.

He sighed and turned toward her, opening his eyes very wide while slowly moving his head from side to side.

She smiled at him, unsure of what he was doing. "What?"

He grimaced slightly while pointing to his eyes. "My eyes. They're the same color. I'm not . . . ah . . . you know, a Mover."

"Oh, how old are you?" Harmony asked, seeming to change the subject.

Shiloh frowned. "Twelve, but my birthday is in a few days."

Harmony smiled again, and advised, "Then I wouldn't worry about that."

Her comment confused Shiloh. "What do you mean? You wouldn't worry about what?"

Harmony didn't answer as she focused toward some rustling noises in the trees in the valley below them. Shiloh followed her gaze and saw nothing.

"So what do you mean? You wouldn't worry about that?" Shiloh asked again.

Harmony divulged, "You have to hit the age of ascension for your eyes to change."

"Age of ascension?" Shiloh whispered back.

Smiling, Harmony whispered, "Shhh. I think they're coming."

Shiloh frowned nervously. "Who's coming?"

Suddenly, the heads of two creatures poked through the brush just below the embankment. Shiloh recoiled at the sight of them, but exhaled a sigh of relief as Harmony leaned forward and hugged each of them with an excited giggle. Harmony then reached for the picnic basket, while Shiloh examined the animals. One had the body of a zebra, but the neck and head of a giraffe. The other was a bird of some sort. At first Shiloh though it was an ostrich, but with its pointed beak and rainbow-colored wattle, it reminded him of a giant turkey.

"What are these things?" Shiloh asked, watching Harmony feed the zebra-giraffe creature a raw carrot and the bird a dark-blue plum.

"They're not things. They are my friends," Harmony said.

Shiloh shrugged his shoulders. "Sorry. They startled me."

"That's okay," Harmony replied with a smile.

She pointed to the creature closest to Shiloh, the zebra-giraffe mix. "This is an okapi." She then fed the giant bird another plum, saying, "And this is a cassowary."

"I've never seen anything like them before," Shiloh admitted, looking back and forth between the two creatures.

"Not many people have," Harmony replied, tossing Shiloh a couple of carrots and plums.

Shiloh picked up a carrot, but hesitated. "Go ahead. He won't bite you," Harmony promised with a little giggle.

Shiloh rose to his knees, extending his arm with the carrot in hand. The okapi leaned forward and took the bright-orange vegetable from him. Marveling at its uniqueness, he reached up and petted the okapi's head as it crunched away on the carrot.

Shiloh lost track of time while he ate some biscuits and

Shiloh's True Nature

listened to Harmony explain where the okapi and cassowaries came from, along with various other details about them.

It wasn't until they began walking back through the path to his grandfather's that Shiloh was able to change the subject. "I've noticed that your hair changes colors. Except for today, each time I've seen you it was dark and then it turned light all of a sudden," Shiloh noted.

Harmony responded, "Yeah, it just started doing that recently."

"Really? Do you know why? I mean, is it part of your ability?" Shiloh curiously inquired.

"I don't know. I guess it must be, right?" Harmony giggled.

"I guess so. You would know better than I," Shiloh added, shrugging his shoulders.

As they walked along the path, Shiloh realized the oddly-shaped plants with the circular flowers were no longer glowing. "These flowers were lit up before. I wonder what happened to them," he wondered, examining them as they passed.

"They're Moon flowers. They bloom and glow at night, but only when the moon is visible. The amount of light they give off corresponds to the moon's cycles," Harmony explained.

"What do you mean 'the moon's cycles'?" Shiloh asked.

Harmony elaborated with a smile. "When the moon is full, the whole flower lights up. If it's half full, the flower is half lit. They mimic whatever the moon looks like."

Shiloh found the plants' correlation to the moon fascinating, and gave them one last look before they reached the intersection.

When they exited the path and stepped into his grandfather's backyard, Shiloh saw Lovie and Cheepie lying on the gray platform in the center of the yard. He smiled to himself as he watched them contently flicking their tails as they soaked in the early morning sunshine.

As they reached the rear porch, Harmony turned to Shiloh, saying, "Well, I'm off. I have to get to the bookstore soon or my aunt will wonder where I am."

"Well, thanks for an interesting and educational morning. I enjoyed it," Shiloh confessed with a smile.

Harmony returned his smile. "I did too. I hope we can share another sunrise soon."

Shiloh watched Harmony walk around the corner of the house and out of sight. He sighed contently, and then started up the stairs to the porch with a smile on his face. When he reached the top step, he realized Crow's birds were perched on the railing watching him. The ravens continued staring at him as he approached the door, so he stopped and blurted, "What?" The birds flinched when Shiloh spoke to them, and then turned to face the yard.

Shiloh chuckled to himself as he entered the kitchen, where Crow and Doc were seated at the table. "Good morning," he said, greeting them with a smile.

"Well, you seem to be feeling much better this morning," Doc noted, looking Shiloh over.

"I feel fine," he replied. Shiloh thought for a moment, and added, "I guess it was the rest. I mean, I must've been really exhausted. I can't remember ever falling asleep so quickly

Shiloh's True Nature

before."

Crow snorted and let out a little laugh. Doc scowled at Crow, and then turned to Shiloh. "So where have you been?"

Shiloh smiled widely. "I had the most interesting morning."

"Really? What happened?" Doc asked, intrigued.

"Do you remember yesterday morning when I asked you about anyone being in the backyard?" Shiloh asked.

Doc nodded. "Yes."

"Well, the girl I saw was out there again today, so I followed her."

Doc's eyes widened. "Really?"

"I followed her into the path at the back of your yard and through the woods to the hillside. It was the niece of that nice lady at the bookstore, Harmony."

Doc nodded. "Hmmm. So then what happened?"

"We sat and watched the sunrise. I had the most amazing feeling being there," Shiloh responded.

Crow laughed. "I'll bet you did."

"Be quiet, Crow. What kind of feeling, Shiloh?" Doc asked.

"I don't really know how to describe it. I had never actually watched the sunrise. Harmony talked about it and made me excited to be seeing it for the first time. I never felt that way before," Shiloh explained.

Crow chuckled and Doc frowned at him again.

"What is he laughing about?" Shiloh asked.

"Just ignore him," Doc said, smiling at Shiloh.

Shiloh looked around the table at the plates and bowls of

food. Doc saw him and pointed at the table. "Would you like anything?"

"No, thank you. I already ate," Shiloh replied, looking around the table. He then added, "I do have a question for you though. What is the age of ascension?"

Doc didn't answer right away, and Shiloh turned to find a startled look on his face. Shiloh then looked to Crow, who wore a giant grin.

"How do you know about the age of ascension?" Doc asked with a squint.

Shiloh shrugged his shoulders. "I don't really. It was something Harmony said, but she didn't explain."

Doc cleared his throat and said, "Well, Shiloh, the age of ascension is the age when a person becomes a Mover."

"I don't understand. How does one 'become' a Mover? I thought you were born that way?" Shiloh asked.

Before Doc could formulate an answer, Crow said, "Oh no, Shiloh. After the twelfth year of life, the soul is ready to see the world for what it is, and ready to be seen for what it is."

Shiloh frowned in confusion at Crow's response. Doc raised his hand and said, "What Crow is trying to say is, it's at age thirteen that a Mover's true nature emerges."

Shiloh reflected for a moment, thinking about the *True Nature* book Saige gave him, and then suddenly his eyes widened as he blurted out, "You mean when someone turns thirteen, that's when they find out if they're a Mover?"

"Yes, exactly," Doc replied.

"So I might be?" Shiloh asked anxiously.

Shiloh's True Nature

"You might. If it's meant to be," Doc added with a smile.

Shiloh thought for another moment, and then rattled off a series of questions. "How does it happen? Do you just wake up that way? Does it hurt?"

Doc and Crow both saw Shiloh's growing anxiousness. Crow slid forward in his chair with a big smile on his face, "It just happens."

Shiloh frowned at Crow. "What does that mean, 'it just happens'?"

Crow laughed and Doc shook his head. "Again, I think what my friend is trying to say is, there is no one way it occurs. It's different for everyone," Doc answered.

Shiloh stared intently at Doc. "How did it happen for you?"

Doc sat back in his chair and smiled. "There was nothing to it. I just woke up one morning and my eyes had changed colors. I didn't know anything had happened."

Shiloh turned to Crow for a response, but the usually jovial Crow didn't give one. He stood up from his chair and declared, "You'll have to excuse me, I have some things to tend to."

Crow turned and exited through the back door. Shiloh watched the screen door close and wondered why Crow had departed so abruptly. He looked to Doc for an answer, but Doc just shrugged his shoulders and began clearing off the table.

Shiloh sat watching Doc clean up, still wondering about what might happen when he reached thirteen. "You know, if you're genuinely interested, there's something you can do to look for some answers," Doc offered. Shiloh looked at him inquiringly and Doc continued, "It's probably a good idea for you to stay out of the sun today anyway, after getting burnt the way you did yesterday."

"What can I do?" Shiloh asked.

Doc finished placing some dishes in the sink and said, "Come with me."

He led Shiloh to the living room, moving to the odd-looking door in the far corner by the fireplace. Shiloh hadn't noticed it before, but there was a complex knot—no doubt one of Luther's creations—holding the door closed. Doc fumbled around with the many string pieces for a moment before finally removing them and opening the door.

Doc opened the door and extended his arm, inviting Shiloh to enter. "This is my study," Doc said, as Shiloh gazed into the room. He was astounded by what he saw. The study was a perfectly rounded room, which extended up two stories to a high, flat ceiling that had a painting of a dragon encircling it. Other than a couple of rocking chairs with matching side tables, the room seemed very out of place with the rest of the house.

Curved, wooden bookcases encircled the room, sitting perfectly flat against the round, white wall. The floor was made of grayish-white marble with gold streaks through it. A circular, sea-blue rug covered the center of the floor. The edge of the thick rug had a depiction of a bluish-green dragon swallowing its own tail, identical to the painting on the ceiling above.

Hanging from the center of the ceiling was a magnificent

Shiloh's True Nature

chandelier with dozens of lit candles, making the room as bright as the outdoors on a sunny day. Directly below the chandelier, in the center of the rug, was the centerpiece of the room: an ornate, wooden pedestal, carved with a fire motif and covered in symbols Shiloh had never seen before.

Doc smiled at Shiloh, and then looked around the room. "I've been collecting these books for most of my life. They should contain the answers to any questions you have about Movers. You may have a look around, if you'd like."

Shiloh was still stationary, but managed to nod his head. He began to slowly circle the room, looking at the countless number of books on the shelves, but he mostly focused on the pictures, drawings, and paintings hanging on the walls in the gaps between the bookcases.

Shiloh soon realized all of the images were of the same subject: a dragon. One painting he found particularly amusing was a depiction of the earth as a cube with a sea dragon going over one of the edges. Another curious image was an old, meticulously hand-drawn map of the Earth with a sea dragon's body stretched throughout all the oceans of the world.

The most fascinating picture of all to Shiloh was an old, faded painting that depicted a dragon in a circle, swallowing its own tail, with a multicolored flame in the center. Doc noticed Shiloh lingering by the painting. "That's the Prime Mover's symbol," he conveyed.

Without taking his eyes off it, Shiloh asked, "What's the Prime Mover?"

Doc paused for a moment, then remarked, "The Prime

Mover was a special Mover who lived long ago and saved the world from total destruction."

Hearing this finally pulled Shiloh's attention away from the painting. "Total destruction?"

Doc nodded.

Shiloh turned back to the painting. "So what happened to this Prime Mover?"

"Well, it's said that once the Prime Mover saved the world, he disappeared. But before he vanished, he left behind a symbol: that symbol," Doc replied.

"So what does the symbol mean?" Shiloh questioned.

Doc shook his head side to side. "Honestly, I don't know. One belief is that it's a symbol of reincarnation. That the Prime Mover was trying to tell the world he would return if needed."

Shiloh then turned back to Doc, inquiring, "And did he? Return, that is?"

Doc smiled at Shiloh's question. "Yes. In fact, it's believed the Prime Mover reappeared six more times after."

"Six times?" Shiloh questioned in disbelief.

Doc nodded his head in confirmation.

"That's hard to believe," Shiloh countered with a scowl.

Doc grimaced. "Sadly, you're not alone in your skepticism."

"What do you mean?" Shiloh asked.

"Well, it's been quite a while since the 7th Prime Mover, and some wonder if another will ever manifest. In fact, it's been so long since the last Prime Mover, some people have begun to question whether any of the Prime Movers ever ex-

Shiloh's True Nature

isted," Doc answered, sounding disappointed.

Shiloh turned his attention to the pedestal in the center of the room. An old, large, leather-bound book with gold clasps sat atop the pedestal. "What is that?" Shiloh wondered why it was out when all the other books in the room were neatly organized on the shelves.

Doc smiled. "I believe that book once belonged to the last Prime Mover."

"Really? What's in it?" Shiloh asked, reaching for the book.

"No!" Doc shouted before Shiloh could touch the book.

Shiloh flinched and took a step back, a little unnerved by the aggressive response. It was the first time he could ever remember hearing his grandfather raise his voice. Sighing, Doc smiled and apologized, "Sorry, Shiloh. The contents of that book are for the eyes of the Prime Mover only."

"I don't understand. What's so special about it?" Shiloh asked.

"I don't know exactly, because I've never opened it. It is my understanding, whatever knowledge is contained in that book, only the Prime Mover will need, and only the Prime Mover will understand it," Doc explained.

Eyes wide, Shiloh scratched his head, shrugging at Doc's explanation.

"Feel free to look at any book in here you like. Heck, look at all of them. Just not that one," Doc implored, pointing to the pedestal.

Shiloh didn't answer, just shrugged his shoulders again. However, this was not enough of an answer for Doc. "Okay?"

Shiloh drew his arms up to his chest, the palms of his hands facing outward. "Okay, okay. I won't look at that book."

A slow smile crept across Doc's face and he turned to leave. "Okay then."

Doc shut the door behind him, and Shiloh shook his head as he heard Doc's footsteps fading away. Shiloh turned and looked at the many filled bookcases, wondering where to begin. He saw countless unfamiliar authors' names inscribed down the books' spines. Aristotle, Emerson, Locke, Rand, Wittgenstein . . . *Who were these people? What did they have to say?* Shiloh wondered.

As he looked through the shelves, Shiloh came across a book with an oddly shaped spine and slid it off of the shelf. When he retrieved it, he was amused to find the book was in the shape of a turtle. There was little on the cover except for a depiction of a smiling turtle fitting the book's shape and one word: "Russell." So Shiloh started flipping through the pages.

Shiloh never thought of himself as much of a student, but he found himself utterly fascinated by everything he pulled off the shelves. He read and read, continuously exploring one dusty, old book after another. It seemed for every answer a book provided, it raised at least one question he wanted answered. If one book mentioned something briefly, there was another book somewhere in the room completely devoted to the subject.

After a while, Shiloh found himself sitting on the floor in the center of the carpet, surrounded by open books. He leaned back against the pedestal and smiled to himself, won-

Shiloh's True Nature

dering what his mother would say if she saw him. She always had to nudge him to do his homework, and here he was studying all on his own. Knowing his mother, she probably would have told him a person can only read one book at a time and to straighten up the mess.

Shiloh decided he better start returning some of the books to their places on the shelves. He closed the nearest books he was finished with and stood up to return them. When he stood, he bumped the pedestal and it began to teeter. He stood frozen, eyes wide as he watched the Prime Mover's book slide off the edge, headed for the floor.

Shiloh dropped the volumes in his arms and lunged forward to catch the falling book. He caught the book one-handed in midair by the spine, but it was so heavy he could barely hold it. He quickly grabbed the other end of the spine with his free hand and lifted it upward. As he turned the book over to take a better grip and return it to the pedestal, it popped open in his hands.

Shiloh looked at the open book, dumbfounded by what he saw. It was his reflection staring back at him from inside the pages. Smiling in confusion, he flipped through the pages, wondering if the book was supposed to be some kind of joke. All the pages were shiny, framed mirrors, which explained why the book was so heavy. However, there were no words, nor explanations of any kind. This puzzled Shiloh deeply.

Staring at his own reflection, Shiloh waited for the book to do something or show him something, but it did not. It was only when he heard footsteps approaching that he returned the book to the pedestal. Shiloh knelt down to retrieve the books he had dropped as the door to the study opened.

"You've got to be getting hungry by now. How about you forget about this stuff for a while and we take a ride to get something to eat?" Doc asked with a smile.

Shiloh avoided eye contact with his grandfather, feeling guilty about having looked at the Prime Mover's book. "Yeah. Sure. That sounds good," Shiloh responded, continuing to pick the books up off the floor.

Doc squinted and tilted his head. "Everything all right?"

Shiloh gave a half smile, "Yeah, yeah. I just have to figure out where these books go."

"Oh, you can just leave them on the floor. They have a way of finding their proper places on the shelves," Doc replied.

Shiloh held the stack of books and frowned at Doc, wondering what he meant. Doc stuck out his hand and lowered it, indicating Shiloh should set the books down. So he set the stack of books back on the floor and followed Doc out of the study.

Shiloh's stomach growled the entire ride into town. When they stopped at the Deer Park, Doc tied Peggy and Isis to a post and announced, "I need to go speak to someone for a moment. You can get us a table or have a look around for a few minutes if you want."

"Okay," Shiloh answered, starting up the stairs to the deck.

Shiloh took a seat at an open table at the top of the stairs and began watching the people walking by in the street below. He poured himself some juice from one of the carafes and was starting to take a drink when he saw Harmony carrying some books through the crowd in the distance. He

Shiloh's True Nature

waved to her, but she wasn't looking his way. He considered calling to her, but felt a little self-conscious about doing so. Instead, he rose from the table and walked after her.

Shiloh followed and never lost sight of her, but with all the foot traffic he couldn't seem to close the gap between them. He followed until he saw her enter Jeremiah's, and he did the same a moment later. However, when he entered the bookstore, she had vanished again. There were a few patrons seated around the store reading, but Harmony was nowhere in sight.

After looking up and down the aisles with no luck, Shiloh decided he had better head back to the Deer Park. Turning to leave, a hand appeared on his shoulder and he turned to find Saige smiling at him. "Can I help you with anything, Shiloh?" she asked.

Shiloh scratched his head, trying to think of something to say, because he certainly wasn't going to admit he was only there trying to chase down her niece. "I just wanted to thank you again for the book," he said, trying to cover his embarrassment.

Saige smiled widely, pushing him down a nearby aisle. "I'm so glad you liked the book. There are many other fascinating and informative works you should see," she said, walking and pointing to various books.

Shiloh followed along after Saige, but wasn't really listening as she rambled on. Most of the works she pointed out were ones he had already examined in his grandfather's study. One particular book did catch his eye though. It had a beautifully colored picture of the Prime Mover's symbol on the cover. The dragon was a vibrant bluish green with a reddish-yellow underbelly, and the luminous, center flame looked alive in a rainbow of color. The book's gold inscribed title read, *The Eternal Flame*.

Saige was still walking and talking two aisles down from Shiloh when she discovered she had left him behind. She turned around and walked back to where he stood. Shiloh pointed to the book he was admiring. "I saw this symbol at my grandfather's. He said it was the Prime Mover's symbol. But what is this Eternal Flame thing?"

Saige didn't answer right away; she just smiled at him for a moment. Shiloh noticed Bryce at the other end of the aisle, smiling as he placed some books on the shelves. He gazed back and forth between the two, wondering what they were grinning about. "What?"

Saige took Shiloh by the hand and led him past Bryce to a table with some chairs at the end of the aisle. Once they were seated, Saige took a deep breath and began to tell him a story.

"Shiloh, long ago there were a group of Movers who called themselves the Society. The Society believed they were put here to rule the world, and made it their goal to do so. They decided the best way to achieve this goal was to use their powers of influence and intellect to deceive the non-Movers of the world and seduce them with new and supposedly bet-ter ways of doing things. By doing that, the Society would ensure that the non-Movers would always be dependent on the Society to lead them. Unfortunately, the non-Movers were all too eager to conform and never questioned the new path the Society laid out before them."

Shiloh's True Nature

Shiloh saw that Bryce had moved a little closer to listen, so he turned to Saige, frowning. "What does that have to do with the flame?"

Saige smiled. "I'm getting to that. The Society soon found there was another element of the world that wasn't so co-operative: Nature. You see, the planet is a self-correcting system, and the new technologies the Society provided to the non-Movers began to adversely affect the world around them. Over time, the Earth grew colder and colder, rendering the Society's new and better methods old and unsafe. The Society's plan had backfired, because the Earth became frozen, inhospitable, and on the verge of uninhabitable."

"So then what happened?" Shiloh inquired, fully engrossed in the story.

Saige continued, "A young Mover was born to parents who were not part of the Society. On the day he reached the age of ascension, he transformed into a dragon that was so big it could reach the sun. The dragon roared and stretched to the heavens, where it tore off a little piece of the sun and brought it back to the Earth. That piece thawed and healed the Earth, eventually returning everything to normal. That piece of the sun is the Eternal Flame."

Shiloh smiled at Saige and looked to Bryce, who had stopped to listen to his mother's tale. Shiloh turned back to Saige, "Wow. That's an amazing story."

Saige waved her index finger at Shiloh. "It's more than just a story."

Shiloh squinted. "What do you mean?"

Saige moved closer to Shiloh and, in a hushed voice,

shared, "The Flame is real and in this town. It's been here for a long, long time."

The skeptic in Shiloh had him pondering all the impossibilities of Saige's story. "The Flame is real?" Shiloh asked, making sure he had heard her correctly.

"Yes," she immediately answered.

Shiloh tilted his head sideways. "And it's in this town?"

Saige nodded. "Yes, but while it used to belong to all of us, it has been taken by a selfish man for his own selfish purposes."

"Who would do such a thing?" Shiloh questioned, scowling in confusion.

Saige opened her mouth to answer, but then paused. "Perhaps that's a question you should ask your grandfather."

Cocking his head to the side, Shiloh responded, "Okay, but I have one question for you. If the Flame is real and belongs to everyone, why doesn't someone just take it back?"

Saige didn't immediately answer, so Shiloh looked toward Bryce, who was nodding as if he agreed and wanted an answer to the question as well. Saige sighed, "I think that's also a question best answered by your grandfather."

Hearing Saige mention his grandfather a second time reminded Shiloh he was supposed to be at the Deer Park having something to eat. Standing from his chair, Shiloh said, "Well, thank you for the story. I have to be getting back. My grandfather is waiting for me."

Saige stood as well, saying, "Anytime, Shiloh. See you soon."

Shiloh smiled and walked away, nodding to Bryce as he

Shiloh's True Nature

passed to exit the store.

Shiloh was very hungry and made his way back to the Deer Park quickly. Upon his arrival, he found Doc seated at a table on the front deck talking with a middle-aged gentleman who sported a bright, white goatee. Shiloh recognized him as the man who was pushing the wheelbarrow full of fruit and vegetables the other day by the produce store in the oak tree.

When Shiloh walked up on the deck, Doc spotted him. "There you are. I was beginning to wonder where you'd gone."

The man, who wore the same denim overalls and short-sleeve, plaid shirt he'd had on the other day, rose from his chair, and Doc said, "Shiloh, this is Jasper Jackson."

"Mr. Jackson," Shiloh nodded with a smile.

"Hello, young man. You can have my seat," Jasper said, tapping the back of the chair.

"No, sir. I can take one of the others," Shiloh offered.

Jasper waved Shiloh to the chair. "I was just leaving. It's all yours."

Shiloh reluctantly sat in the newly vacant chair and watched as Jasper patted Doc on the shoulder and asked, "So you'll be by to have a look then, Doc?"

Doc nodded with a smile. "You're on the top of my list."

Jasper returned the nod and stepped off the deck, blending into the crowd as he walked away.

"So what kept you?" Doc asked, as Shiloh looked around the table, trying to decide what he wanted to eat.

"I'm sorry. I was at Jeremiah's talking to Saige. She wanted to tell me a story," Shiloh explained, smiling as he began filling up a plate with a little of everything available.

Doc laughed, "Yeah, she'll do that. Saige loves to tell stories." Doc paused for a moment before asking, "So which one did she share with you?"

"The story of the Eternal Flame," Shiloh replied, biting into a strawberry muffin.

Doc scowled slightly, but then a smile crept across his face. "She loves those stories."

"Stories? Plural?" Shiloh asked, continuing to eat.

"Yes, plural. There are so many stories about the Flame's origin that it's hard to distinguish which, if any, is true," Doc added.

Shiloh swallowed what was in his mouth and said, "Saige told me the Flame is real, and was stolen by someone from the town. Is that true?"

Doc hesitated for a moment and admitted, "Yes. It's true."

Shiloh opened his mouth to ask another question, but Doc quickly held up his hand. "Wait."

He looked to Doc for an explanation, but found him staring intently down the road. Shiloh followed Doc's gaze and found the sea of townspeople parting as a man in black shorts and an orange shirt approached.

The man looked familiar to Shiloh, but he was unsure where he had seen him before. As he drew closer, Shiloh noticed the man's short, wavy hair had a strange, brassy tint. The man's eye color was an even more peculiar sight. One eye was a very dark brown, and the other was a burnt-orange color Shiloh had never seen before.

Shiloh's True Nature

A sly smile came to the man's lips when Doc caught his eye. He then walked up to the edge of the deck and nodded. "Williams."

Doc nodded in return. "Haines."

The man then turned to Shiloh with a squint and extended his hand through the deck railing. "Samuel Haines."

Shiloh was still chewing, but wiped the muffin crumbs from his hands to shake Haines'. Before Shiloh had a chance to speak, Haines said, "I've seen you before, young man. But for the life of me I can't remember where."

Shiloh was going to concur, but Doc interjected. "This is my grandson, Shiloh."

The sly smile returned to Haines face, "Ah, yes, Joseph and Mary's son." He tilted his head, looking Shiloh over for a moment before asking, "Tell me, young man. Is Fair Hill to be your new home?"

The question confused Shiloh and he wanted to ask Haines for the meaning, but was again preempted by Doc. "No, he's just visiting. He'll be going back to the farm in a few days."

Haines snickered slightly. "Really? Will he now?"

Shiloh was again confused by Haines' comment and looked to Doc, but he appeared just as baffled by the remarks. Haines stood smiling at them both for a moment, until a voice called out from the crowd, "Dad!"

Haines gazed over his shoulder to the street and chuckled, "Well, I was looking for my son and it seems he's found me. Have a good afternoon, gentlemen."

Haines turned and the crowd again gave him a wide berth

as he walked back into the street. The young man with short, brassy-colored hair who Shiloh had seen accompanied by the greenish-gray dogs the other day—the one who rode the water bike and the kids referred to as 'Junior'—walked out of the crowd toward Haines. The resemblance between the two was uncanny; Junior was simply a younger version of his father.

Shiloh watched as Haines threw his arm around Junior's shoulder and they walked off into the crowd. He then turned to Doc. "He's the man that was at our farm the other day. He's the one you were telling me about on the way to Fair Hill, isn't he? The man who owns the 'pollution' factory?"

Doc nodded in confirmation. "Yes, he is."

Shiloh continued, "I guess he's not a very nice man."

Doc sighed and said, "Well, normally I'd suggest that you try not to judge someone before you truly get to know them. However, in this case, your perception happens to be accurate. He's not a very nice man. But I'm still hoping he'll come around."

Shiloh pondered Doc's comment for a moment, and then asked, "What do you mean, you 'hope he'll come around'?"

Doc smiled. "I mean, I believe there is good in everyone, Shiloh. That everyone innately knows right from wrong. If we selfishly lie to ourselves, if we try to make ourselves believe that doing the wrong thing isn't really wrong at all, a voice deep down inside lets us know. So, I keep hoping the voice deep down inside will one day reach him."

Shiloh again thought for a moment, considering Doc's assertion. "How would you know if the voice reached him?"

Shiloh's True Nature

Shiloh asked.

"I don't know. An act of kindness or a gesture of good-will," Doc suggested.

"Like what kind of gesture?" Shiloh questioned.

Doc tilted his head, confiding, "Well, he could start by returning the Flame."

Shiloh's eyes widened as he asked, "What Flame? The Eternal Flame?"

Doc nodded. "Yes. He's the one who took it."

July 25th

Shiloh yawned and shook his head, trying to keep himself awake while Doc drove them through the muggy morning air. As they approached the Stone Balloon, he gazed up and saw how the morning sun's rays made the colorful stones twinkle. He noticed each of the crystals had a faint symbol carved into them. It was a symbol that was becoming all too familiar to him: a flame encircled by a dragon.

Once they passed the Balloon, Shiloh began to wonder where they were headed. Doc hadn't shared their destination before they left. He had just mumbled something about house calls, and Shiloh didn't bother to ask what that meant. He just figured he would know when they arrived.

The farther they traveled, the less familiar things looked to Shiloh. It was like they had left the town entirely. However, when Shiloh saw a fork in the road and a barely visible street sign that read Acacia, he sort of knew their location.

The sign caused Shiloh to reflect on what he had learned the previous day. *Why would Haines take the Eternal Flame?*

Shiloh's True Nature

he wondered. He didn't know the purpose of the Flame or why it mattered that it was taken, so he turned to Doc and said, "I don't understand the Eternal Flame."

"What do you mean?" Doc asked, looking at Shiloh out of the corner of his eye.

"Saige told me that story, and you said there are many others about where it came from. And that man Haines took it, but I'm not sure I understand what that means or what it really does."

"That may be hard for me to explain, Shiloh," Doc said with a slight grimace. Doc could tell Shiloh was unsatisfied with the response, so he asked, "Do you know what would happen if our planet moved much closer to or much farther from the sun?"

"What?" Shiloh asked, mystified by Doc's question.

Doc repeated himself in a serious tone. "Just tell me what you think would happen if our planet moved closer to or farther from the sun?"

"I think it would be bad," Shiloh replied, shaking his head in confusion.

Doc gave a small chuckle. "It would be very bad. If it moved too far away, everything would cool down and eventually freeze. Plants wouldn't grow, so there would be no food for us or any creature to eat. We'd all freeze or starve to death. If it moved much closer, the planet would get hotter and be scorched. And again, the plants, animals, and people would all die. So, my point is, everything in this world is dependent upon the sun being where and how it is. It is this balance that makes life possible and preserves it."

"I understand, but I still don't see what that has to do with the Flame," Shiloh injected.

Doc raised his hand. "Just bear with me. Now try to imagine for a minute that the Eternal Flame is the sun . . ."

Shiloh interrupted. "Saige said the Flame is a piece of the sun."

Doc closed his eyes and sighed before continuing. ". . . I'm sure she did, but just listen. Imagine the Eternal Flame is the sun, and the place it's supposed to be is in Fair Hill . . ."

Shiloh interrupted Doc again. "I thought it was still in Fair Hill, but that . . ."

"It is, but try to imagine it's supposed to be in one specific place, the center of town in Fair Hill," Doc said, pointing up in the air.

Shiloh looked up, shocked to discover they were passing the Stone Balloon again. He suddenly felt disoriented and began babbling, "How? It? We?"

He looked to Doc, who was still pointing upward. "If the Flame isn't where it belongs, everything is out of balance."

Shiloh closed his eyes, trying to comprehend how they had returned to the center of town. He knew they had passed the Stone Balloon once already, and they couldn't have gone in a circle.

A moment later Shiloh opened his eyes and was ready to start asking questions, but he was again startled when the Stone Balloon was nowhere in sight. They had returned to where they were prior to the start of their conversation, just past Acacia.

Shiloh looked to Doc and demanded, "What just hap-

Shiloh's True Nature

pened? And please don't tell me how hard it is to explain. Just tell me."

"Okay. I wanted to show you where the Eternal Flame is supposed to be, inside the Stone Balloon, and suddenly, there we were," Doc explained.

"What?!" Shiloh screeched in disbelief.

"You know how you said you discovered all roads lead to the center of town?"

"Yeah," Shiloh answered.

Doc scratched his forehead and elaborated, "Well, that's not completely accurate. Yes, if you just keep walking, you'll end up back at the center of town, eventually. However, if you want or need to be somewhere and you focus your thoughts, you'll turn a corner or go around a bend and be there."

"So you're telling me all I have to do is think about where I want to go and I'll be there?" Shiloh stated.

"Not exactly. First of all, you have to be a Mover. Second, you have to be moving and close your eyes and concentrate on where in town you want or need to be," Doc answered.

Shiloh shook his head and mumbled, "This is unbelievable."

Doc chuckled. "I'm actually surprised it worked. Since the Flame was stolen, nothing seems to work properly."

Shiloh again mumbled, "Unbelievable."

Doc's nodded. "I know, but you get used to it."

"How is all this possible?" Shiloh asked.

Doc shook his head again. "I have no idea, but it is. It's the Flame. It's this town. There's something about this place, Shiloh. It's . . ."

"Magic?" Shiloh questioned.

Doc smiled. "I was going to say, it's Fair Hill."

Doc returned his focus to the road ahead and began steering the cart around a bend. The thick weeds and overgrown brush cluttering the landscape gave way to open fields. The fields contained perfectly spaced rows of fruit trees as far as the eye could see. A small white farmhouse with a maroon barn beside it sat in the center of the fields.

When they pulled into the dirt driveway in front of the farmhouse, Shiloh turned to Doc. "So, what are we doing here?"

Doc smiled. "Making a house call."

Shiloh wanted to inquire further, but before he could, the front porch door swung open and a man with a familiar, white goatee walked out, waving and hollering, "Hey, Doc!"

Doc gave the man a wave. Shiloh recognized Jasper Jackson, who was dressed in his usual attire. Jasper approached the cart with his hand extended and proceeded to vigorously shake both Doc and Shiloh's hands. "Thanks for coming, Doc. I can't tell you how much I appreciate it," Jasper said as he led them toward the side of the house.

"You don't have to thank me, Jasper. I'm always happy to help out whenever I can. You know that," Doc answered as they walked through a gate into a fenced-in clearing in front of the barn.

As Jasper opened a door on the barn, Doc said, "So tell me again what the problem is."

Stepping inside, Jasper explained, "It's Ol' Lucky, Doc. He hasn't left the barn in days, much less been able to pull the

Shiloh's True Nature

cart up to the stand."

Doc grunted as they walked along. "Hmmm. Has he been walking around at all?"

"No, not much," Jasper replied. "I've been using a wheelbarrow to cart the fruit up to the store myself. I'm afraid if Lucky is down much longer, I'll be needing Doc's services myself," he continued, laughing and patting Shiloh on the shoulder.

Shiloh wasn't sure who Lucky was, or to what services Jasper was referring, until they stopped at the opening of a stall. Inside was an old, flea-bitten, gray horse lying on his side.

"Well, let's have a look," Doc said, stepping into the stall with the horse.

Shiloh remembered the other day when the buck at the Deer park was injured, and wondered if Doc was a veterinarian.

Doc knelt down next to the old horse and slowly ran his hand from the hoof up one of the front legs. When he reached the shoulder, Doc said, "Nope." He moved to the other leg, and when he reached the elbow, the horse began to neigh and tried to pull the leg away. "That's the one. Easy, boy. Easy, Lucky," Doc whispered, trying to soothe the creature.

Shiloh watched intently while Doc ran his hand up and down the horse's leg several times. Doc then pulled away and stood up. "That should do it."

Do what? Shiloh thought to himself.

Suddenly, Lucky sprang to his feet and walked out of the stall. Jasper cheered. "Thank you, Doc. I'm sure Lucky would thank you too . . . if he could."

Shiloh wasn't quite sure what had happened, but Doc had somehow healed the horse.

The men followed the horse as it walked out of the barn and into the clearing. As he watched Lucky begin grazing, Shiloh noticed the woman from the produce store approaching. She again wore a plaid dress and denim apron. When she reached the gate, she stopped and noted, "Lucky seems to be feeling better. That's the first time I've seen him eat in days."

Doc led Shiloh over to where the woman stood. "Jasmine, I'd like you to meet my grandson, Shiloh. Shiloh, this is Jasmine Jackson."

"Hello, young man. It's wonderful to meet you," Jasmine replied with a wide grin.

Shiloh couldn't help but return her smile as he said, "Hello."

Jasmine turned her attention back to Doc. "We can't thank you enough for helping us out with Lucky. Is there anything we can do for you?"

Doc held up his hand. "Oh, no. I'm fine. I'm just happy to help out."

"You sure, Doc? I got to tell you, our early season pears are particularly sweet," Jasper added, still watching Lucky graze.

Doc laughed at Jasper's enticement. "I'll tell you what, you can bring some by the house when Lucky feels up to it. Okay?"

"Will do," Jasper promised.

As they pulled away from the Jacksons, Shiloh couldn't help but wonder what he had witnessed in the barn. "What

Shiloh's True Nature

did you do?" Shiloh asked.

Doc looked at Shiloh, raising his eyebrows in question, "What do you mean?"

"What I mean is the horse. When you first touched his leg, he was clearly in pain. Then, you touched him again and he got up and started walking around. So what did you do to fix him?" Shiloh asked.

Doc gave that familiar grimace and said, "Well . . ."

Shiloh rolled his eyes, groaning. "Ugh. Just tell me."

Doc burst into laughter. "Okay, okay. I am able to heal the sick and injured with my touch. That is my gift."

Shiloh's eyes widened. "So that's why everyone calls you 'Doc'?"

"Yup," Doc confirmed.

Shiloh stared at his grandfather, thinking how amazing it was that he had such a gift. Doc felt Shiloh's stare and asked, "What?"

Shiloh didn't answer at first, but then he asked, "Can I call you 'Doc' too?"

Doc let out a laugh. "You can if you like."

Doc returned his focus to the road ahead. "I'm very fortunate to have such a special gift. All Movers have unique gifts, but mine is extremely rare. So rare, in fact, it was once thought I might be the Prime Mover."

Shiloh perked up and asked, "Really? How do you know you're not the Prime Mover?"

Doc chuckled. "Well, I'm sure I'd know by now. You see, the Prime Mover emits radiance, has a powerful life force." Doc saw Shiloh frown and continued, "The Prime Mover has a connection to all living things, Shiloh. I can heal on a small scale—like one person or animal—but the Prime Mover would be able to do much more than that, and without even trying or thinking about it."

Shiloh had enough trouble understanding how Doc could heal a horse, much less how the Prime Mover could do much more. He just scratched his head and grinned, pretending to comprehend.

"I'm not sure I'm doing a great job explaining all of this. If the Prime Mover ever comes back I'll ask him . . . or her," Doc said with a laugh.

"Her? The Prime Mover can be a girl?" Shiloh asked.

"Of course. A person's gender has no bearing on their abilities, Shiloh," Doc answered.

"I know that, but I assumed that since the first Prime Mover was a male, that he would always be . . . if he returned," Shiloh added.

Doc nodded. "Ah, now I see the confusion. When you think of the Prime Mover, you see a single person being reborn over and over throughout time?"

Shiloh nodded in agreement.

Doc continued, "See, when I think of the Prime Mover, I think of different individual Movers throughout time that emerged with power beyond all of their contemporaries, and the wisdom to use that power properly and for a purpose."

"And is that right? What I mean is, is what *you* think how they actually are?" Shiloh asked.

Doc let out a laugh. "Now I'm confused. I don't know, Shiloh. But again, if a Prime Mover shows up, I'll be sure to ask

Shiloh's True Nature

for you."

"There's our next stop." Doc pointed before pulling the cart into a semicircular driveway in front of a little white cottage.

The exterior of the dwelling could barely be seen due to countless berry bushes surrounding it. As they exited the cart and started up the front steps, Shiloh took note of how stained the porch was from the berries lying all over it. "We'll have to get her a broom," Doc chuckled, knocking on the door.

A frizzy-haired, old woman wearing a heavily stained, yellow apron opened the door. Shiloh thought he recognized her, but his focus drifted when a sweet smell wafted from the doorway.

"My, Henrietta, that is one heavenly scent. Are you making your delicious preserves?" Doc asked, slowly inhaling.

A crooked smile crept across the old woman's face as she shook her head. "You know I am, you old fool. You can probably smell it all the way to your house."

Doc snorted, and then pointed his thumb toward Shiloh. "This is my grandson, Shiloh."

She squinted at him and nodded. "Ah, yes. I've seen him before."

Shiloh raised his hand and gave her a little wave, trying to remember where she might have seen him. He looked her over and noticed underneath the yellow apron was a long, pink- and white-checkered dress. He then recognized her as the woman who kept dropping things at the fruit stand.

"So what can I do for you, Doc?" Henrietta inquired.

Doc cleared his throat, "Well, Henrietta, Crow mentioned Molly might be in need of some attention."

Henrietta frowned. "Attention? For what?"

"I don't know, dear. It's just something Crow brought up, so I thought I'd stop by to check on her," Doc answered, giving Shiloh a wink out of the corner of his eye.

"I have no idea what he's talking about, but you might as well come in," Henrietta grumbled, pushing open the screen door.

Doc and Shiloh stepped into the house, as Henrietta mumbled to herself, "I just saw her five minutes ago and there was nothing wrong with her. That Crow. What does he know?"

Shiloh grinned as he gazed around at the dozen or so cats lounging around. He then flinched as Henrietta called out, "Molly!" He waited for someone to walk in from another room, but no one did. Henrietta paused in the center of the living room as several of the cats advanced and began rubbing against her ankles. She looked around erratically and Shiloh frowned, wondering what she was doing.

Henrietta then said, "Ah, there she is," and stepped over the felines at her feet to a table underneath a nearby window. A huge calico cat was stealthily nestled between two overgrown ferns on the table. Henrietta reached for the cat, but had trouble lifting the feline because she was only using one hand.

Eventually, Henrietta managed to lift Molly by sliding her off of the table and holding the cat against her chest. She then carried Molly to Doc, supporting the feline with just

Shiloh's True Nature

one arm. Doc took Molly from Henrietta, sat down on the couch, and began examining the cat somewhat haphazardly.

"She looks just fine to me," Doc said.

Henrietta raised her hands and huffed. Shiloh noticed Henrietta's right hand was clenched oddly.

While continuing his supposed examination of Molly, Doc asked, "How's your arthritis, Henrietta?"

Henrietta slid her right hand to her side. "Just fine. It's not bothering me too much."

"That's good. And I think you're right, there doesn't seem to be anything wrong with Molly," he noted, setting the cat down on the floor in front of him.

"See, I told you. That Crow. He doesn't know what he's talking about," Henrietta insisted, agitated.

Doc stood and extended his hand. "I'm sorry to have interrupted you, Henrietta."

Shiloh watched as Henrietta extended her clenched fist, trying to open it to shake Doc's hand. Doc slid the open palm of his right hand under her fist. He then placed his left hand on top, pressing down upon her fist to push the hand open between his two palms. Henrietta closed her eyes for a moment. When Doc released his grip, Henrietta retracted her hand, easily opening and closing it a couple times.

"Well, I guess we'll be off," Doc said with a smile.

"Fine. On your way then," Henrietta said, extending her fully open right hand toward the door.

"I'll stop back to check on Molly in a week or so, just in case," Doc added on his way out.

Henrietta smiled at him. "Thank you, Doc."

Shiloh gave Henrietta a 'good-bye' smile and climbed up into the cart.

"I'll send you over some preserves when I'm finished, Doc," Henrietta hollered.

"Sounds good," Doc replied with a wave as he began to maneuver the cart out of the driveway.

As soon as the little white cottage was out of sight, Shiloh asked, "We didn't go there for the cat, did we?"

Doc let out a long laugh. "No, we didn't."

Shiloh thought for a moment before asking, "How come you never told me about your gift before?"

Doc shrugged. "What difference would it have made? Besides, I couldn't have you running around telling people your grandfather can heal with his touch. They would think you were crazy."

Shiloh grimaced, nodding in understanding.

"Well, you kind of knew anyway," Doc added.

Shiloh frowned. "What do you mean?"

Doc smiled and asked, "Don't you remember the time you broke your leg? On your birthday?"

Shiloh thought for a moment about his recent birthdays, and then suddenly flashed back to his eighth. It was a hot summer day, and every friend he had was at the farm for the party his mother threw him. He had a mountain of presents, including a shiny, new bicycle. It was also the last birthday party Doc attended, but the presents he gave were priceless. That was the day Doc gave him Cheepie and Lovie.

He remembered running around playing tag with his friends and jumping from a pile of hay bales to avoid being touched. When he landed, his knee twisted awkwardly and he felt a snap accompanied by a sharp pain in his thigh. Tears filled his eyes as he realized he had broken his leg. His parents were distraught. As they prepared to take him to the hospital, Doc knelt at Shiloh's side to comfort him. Doc then touched Shiloh's leg and the pain was gone. Shiloh stood up, wiped the tears from his face, and returned to playing with his friends like nothing had happened.

"I remember," Shiloh said, a smile creeping across his face. He looked at Doc, the smile lingering.

"What?" Doc asked with a curious grin.

Still beaming, Shiloh said, "I never thanked you."

Doc was a little confused about what Shiloh was talking about and asked, "For what?"

"For fixing my leg that day," Shiloh answered.

"Well, I . . . you're my grandson . . . you're welcome." Doc stammered due to his usual discomfort with praise.

After a couple more house calls, the morning turned into afternoon and Doc drove the cart to Deer Park so they could have something to eat. They took a long lunch before continuing on to more and more houses. Shiloh marveled at Doc's ability, watching him fix anything and everything, from people's stomachaches to their sick pet turtles. He felt a true sense of admiration for his grandfather when he realized what Doc meant to the people of Fair Hill.

When Doc announced they were about to make their final stop, Shiloh became curious about the unfamiliar forest area they were passing through. The trees were thinning on his side of the cart, and Shiloh noticed a body of water. He wasn't sure what it was at first, but as the trees grew sparser, he could see a familiar, green bungalow in the distance. He then realized the water was the lake and they were approaching Bud's house from the far side.

"So where are we headed?" Shiloh asked.

Doc replied, "Luther—your friend Bud's father—has a broken toe, but he's been ignoring it. I don't know whether it's because he doesn't want to admit it or doesn't want to make a fuss. In any case, it needs to be fixed."

Shiloh nodded, so Doc smiled and said, "And I could use your assistance."

"What can I do?" Shiloh questioned, unsure of how he could be helpful.

Doc grinned widely. "Distract him. Get him to talk to you about his knots so he won't be focused on why we're there. I'll figure out the rest."

Shiloh chuckled. "Okay. I'll do my best."

Doc parked the cart out front of the bungalow and walked up the porch steps with Shiloh following. He knocked on the front door and Martina immediately answered.

"Hi, Doc," she greeted him with a smile and her usual hug. She then turned her attention to Shiloh. "Hey there, Shiloh. It's wonderful to see you again."

"Nice to see you too, Mrs. Miller," Shiloh replied.

"Well, I guess we're having two more for dinner," Martina said, spreading her arms to welcome them.

Doc waved his hand. "Oh, no. That's not why we're here."

"Come on now, I insist," Martina said, grabbing Doc by the wrist and leading him in the house.

Shiloh's True Nature

As Doc and Shiloh entered, they found Luther seated at the dining room table surrounded by boxes of rope, string, and thread. When he noticed their presence, Luther dropped the knot he was fiddling with and stood up. "Hello, Doc . . . Shiloh. What brings you by?"

Doc said, "Well, Luther, we were just passing by on our way home and Shiloh . . . um . . . ah."

Hearing Doc fumble his words, Shiloh took the opportunity to jump in, saying, "I've been curious about your knots, Mr. Miller. I've come across a few since I've been in town and I was wondering about them. For instance, how can you make such sophisticated locking mechanisms out of such simple materials like string?"

Hearing Shiloh's words, Doc tried to suppress the smirk that appeared on his face. He gave Shiloh a sly wink and turned to Luther, who stood staring at Shiloh with a joyous grin. It was like he had been waiting his entire life for someone to ask him that very question. "Well, have a seat, Shiloh. I'll show you this new knot I've been working on."

Doc and Shiloh took seats opposite one another at the large rectangular table as Luther untied the knot in his hands. Luther held up the string. "You see, Shiloh, ever since I was young, I've been fascinated with puzzles, riddles, and knots. Especially knots. I used to spend days playing with them."

Shiloh watched as Luther began twisting the thin, white string around in unbelievable ways with his hands as he spoke. "When I became a Mover, something happened. I would hear a riddle and just know the answer. I would see a puzzle and knew how all the pieces fit together. I could just touch a knot and know how to untie it," Luther said, placing an incredibly intricate, figure-eight-shaped knot in front of Shiloh.

Shiloh picked up the knot, admiring the multiple loops on each end of the figure eight as he tried to locate the ends of the string. He turned it over and over looking for the ends, but he couldn't find them. Shiloh looked to Doc, who shrugged his shoulders. He turned to Luther, who smiled, saying, "To untie this particular knot, the loops have to be pulled in just the right way or it will tighten, making it even harder to come off."

Shiloh tugged on the loops a few times unsuccessfully and was amazed when the knot tightened before his eyes. Luther watched as Shiloh tried and again failed to untie the knot. "You get three chances to pull the loops in the correct sequence. Otherwise the knot will completely tighten and you'll have to wait 24 hours before trying again."

Shiloh became slightly irritated and decided to examine the knot further before trying again. He looked over the thin piece of string, wondering how it would make anything secure. He thought if he pulled hard enough, he could break the seemingly delicate string with his hands. He then grabbed the string from both ends and pulled as hard as he could. With his right hand, he pulled one side of the loops toward his body, and with his left, he pushed the other set away.

Suddenly, the string tightened and sprang out of Shiloh's hands, flying across the table, hitting Doc in the chest and falling to the floor. Luther laughed. "See what I mean?"

Winking at Shiloh, Doc said, "I'll get it."

Shiloh's True Nature

Doc slipped under the table and Shiloh leaned back in his chair, tilting his head to peek underneath. The knot had landed right next to Luther's feet, and Shiloh smiled as Doc squinted at them, trying to figure out which of Luther's toes was broken. To distract Luther, Shiloh asked, "So, do you prefer to work with string?"

Luther frowned. "Oh no, I like to work with . . ." He paused, a glazed look falling over his eyes for a moment, like he was in a trance.

Doc then popped up and tossed the knot onto the table in front of Luther. "There's the little bugger."

Shiloh looked to Doc and they exchanged smiles. Luther shook his head, blinked his eyes, and asked, "What was I saying?"

"I had asked if you preferred working with string," Shiloh replied.

"Ah, right. Actually, I like working with anything I can use to make knots, Shiloh," Luther answered.

Luther rambled on continuously about 'the glory of knots' for what seemed like an hour. When Martina placed a magnificent meal on the table, he still managed to keep talking in between bites. When the meal was finished, Doc and Shiloh could take no more and headed for the door. They thanked Martina for her hospitality and were nearly out the door when Luther hollered, "Doc, let me know if you need any knots!"

Rolling his eyes, Shiloh whispered, "I'm never helping you again."

Doc snorted and pursed his lips, suppressing his laughter

as he led Shiloh out the door.

As they headed home, Shiloh reflected upon all the people and creatures Doc had healed that day. This reflection led to many questions. However, there was one thing Shiloh really wanted an answer to, so he blurted, "Can you save people from death?"

Doc's eyes widened at the sudden query, and he stared at Shiloh for a moment before responding, "Sometimes."

Shiloh frowned slightly. "What do you mean, 'sometimes'?"

Sighing, Doc rubbed his chin before answering. "Well, it all depends, Shiloh. If their life force has gone, I can't help."

"Life force?" Shiloh questioned.

"All living things have energy and emit radiance. If that energy—that radiance—is gone, they're gone," Doc explained.

"I'm not sure I understand," Shiloh said, staring out in front of the cart.

"Think of it like this. You know how at your parent's house you have those round, glass light bulbs you can turn on and off by a switch?" Doc asked.

Shiloh chuckled. "Yeah."

Doc smiled. "Well, I don't know if you've ever looked inside a light bulb, but there's a filament. It's a tiny little thread of metal that looks like a spring. That little filament is what gives off the light. If that spring—that filament—is broken, you can flick the switch on and off all day and all night, but nothing will happen."

"So if a person's filament is broken . . ." Shiloh began.

"Then I can't help," Doc finished with a solemn look.

Shiloh's True Nature

As they continued on, Shiloh noticed an odd sight in the distance. A woman approached, riding on the back of a cyclopean beetle and wildly waving her arms in the air. Shiloh chuckled, thinking the woman had lost control of her ride. As she came closer, Shiloh realized it was Regina, the town magistrate. She continued frantically waving her arms, though she was clearly in sight, and Doc said, "Gee, do you think she's trying to get our attention?"

Shiloh giggled and smiled as she reached them.

"Doc, please come quickly," Regina begged, a worried look on her face.

The smiles left Shiloh and Doc's faces after hearing her serious tone. Regina turned around, and they followed her until she came to a stop in front of a white house with pink shutters. Shiloh looked up above the gabled archway over the front door and saw an octagonal window with a pink rose on it. He realized this was the house he had passed on the way to Bud's the other day.

Doc exited the cart and said to Shiloh, "Stay here."

Nodding, Shiloh watched as Doc and Regina entered the house.

Shiloh stood at the foot of the steps for a moment, then began pacing back and forth, examining the house and the surroundings. He noticed a rather large rock jutting out of some brush off to the side of the house. The greenish-gray rock, with its rough, sharp edges, was partially hidden from the road by wild grass and tall weeds.

Shiloh walked the perimeter of the rock until he discovered someone was sitting on its flat top. He thought it was a woman, but he wasn't sure because the person's head was tilted down, a long, ashen mane covering the face.

"Hello?" he called, trying to draw the person's attention. The head tilted upward toward Shiloh and his heart began to race. "Harmony?" Shiloh asked, shocked at her gloomy appearance and trying to confirm her identity.

"Hello, Shiloh," she answered, forcing a little smile.

"What's going on? My grandfather and I were on our way home and that magistrate lady, Regina, stopped us and brought us here."

Harmony seemed a little distant, but managed to say, "Its Bryce. He's hurt."

Shiloh frowned. "What happened?"

Harmony shook her head, saying, "I don't know. He was still out when I went to bed last night. He didn't come to breakfast this morning. And he never came to the store today."

Shiloh thought for a moment, "So how do you know he's hurt?"

Giving Shiloh another little smile, Harmony said, "When we got home with Regina, my Aunt Saige went upstairs to look for him. A moment later she screamed down the stairs, begging Regina to find Doc."

Shiloh gave a concerned sigh, but he remembered everything he had seen Doc do that day. "Whatever it is, I'm sure my grandfather can fix it."

He looked toward the house, and seeing the octagonal window slightly open gave Shiloh an idea. He patted Harmony on the shoulder and said, "I'll be right back."

Shiloh's True Nature

She stared in curiosity as he stood and walked over toward the front door.

Shiloh pulled himself up the porch railing and began quietly climbing up the gabled archway. When he reached the peak, Shiloh peered into the opening of the stained-glass window. He could see the upstairs hallway and the top of the staircase, but no one was there. He listened carefully, hearing nothing until Doc and Saige exited a room at the far end of the hall. When he saw them, he immediately ducked down to avoid detection.

Though he only caught a brief glimpse of her, Shiloh could tell that Saige had been crying. Her eyes were puffy and he could hear her sniffling. "Is he going to be all right, Doc?" Saige asked, clearing her throat.

Shiloh heard Doc give a loud sigh. "Well, his injuries are pretty severe. I've done all I can do for now. I'm hoping it'll be enough." There was silence before Doc added, "Saige, he has a very odd combination of burns, cuts, and bruises. Do you have any idea how this happened?"

"I don't. He hasn't been able to talk. He was fine yesterday. I found him this way," Saige answered, breaking into tears.

Shiloh poked his head above the window sill to see Doc comforting Saige at the end of the hall. He ducked down again, thinking he better climb down off the archway, but before he could, he was taken off guard by a gasping, raspy voice calling out, "Mawwwth."

Shiloh's eyes widened and he looked back in the window to see the noise had spooked Doc and Saige as well.

As the pair moved back into the room, Shiloh climbed

down off the archway. He walked back to Harmony, who looked up at him for some reassurance. Shiloh gave her a little smile and said, "I heard my grandfather say his injuries were odd, but I'm sure he'll be fine."

Harmony smiled at him for a moment, but her eyes were drawn over his shoulder as the porch screen door opened. Doc walked out the front door with Saige and Regina close behind him. Shiloh gave Harmony a little wave before walking to the front of the house and climbing into the cart.

"Thank you for coming so quickly, Doc," Saige said, giving him a little hug.

"Don't worry. I'll be back a little later to check on him," Doc replied, rubbing Saige's shoulder.

Saige reentered the house and Doc's attention turned to Regina. "Keep me apprised of any changes in his condition," Doc advised in a serious tone.

"Okay. I'll stay here until you return, and will let you know if anything changes," Regina added with a nod.

"All right, I'll be back in awhile," Doc said, stepping off the porch and into the cart.

Doc was silent on the ride home, and Shiloh could sense his tension, so he kept quiet as well. When they arrived at the house, Shiloh was stunned to see the entire porch was covered with baskets of fruit, crates of vegetables, and boxes of various other items. "What is all this stuff?" he asked, gazing around at the filled porch.

Doc didn't answer, but knelt down at the foot of the porch steps to pick up a note that was stuffed into a box of glass jars. As Doc began reading the note, Shiloh took a peek at it, but

Shiloh's True Nature

he found the writing illegible except for the signature, which read 'Henrietta Holt'. When he finished with the note, Doc reached into the box and held up a jar of what appeared to be raspberry preserves. He waved the note at Shiloh. "A thank you gift from Henrietta."

Shiloh smiled and said, "Well, at least it's not a box of cats."

Doc let out a little laugh as he started up the steps. Shiloh followed him, carefully making his way around the baskets and boxes to the front door. When they entered the house, they found Crow reclining at the kitchen table with his feet up next to a basket of pears.

"I was arriving just as Jasper was wheeling over some fruit, so I helped him unload the wheelbarrow," Crow announced, taking a big bite from a pear.

Doc and Shiloh watched Crow chew for a moment. Crow then made a pleasurable grunting noise and said, "The Jacksons always have the sweetest pears. Doesn't it seem odd only a week ago their orchard was struggling and now it's thriving?"

Crow smiled, looking directly at Shiloh. Shiloh was confused, wondering if Crow wanted an answer to his question. Shiloh turned to Doc, who, with a raised eyebrow, said, "If you say so, Crow."

Without taking his eyes off of Crow, Doc pointed toward Shiloh and said, "Shiloh, maybe you could continue your research about Movers while I have a chat with my friend here."

Crow continued smiling at him, so Shiloh shrugged his shoulders. "Okay."

Shiloh walked out of the kitchen, passing through the living room to reach the study. He heard the two men start talking, and hesitated in the doorway to eavesdrop on the conversation. He felt a little guilty about trying to listen in, but his curiosity overrode his shame.

Doc and Crow kept their voices down, so Shiloh struggled to discern what they were saying. He overheard Doc mention something about Bryce's injuries, but none of Crow's responses were audible. The conversation then turned to something that made Doc angry.

"I cannot believe he's even considering it," Doc said with agitation in his voice.

Crow mumbled something Shiloh couldn't hear, to which Doc responded, "I better go talk to that fool before he makes a decision he'll regret."

Shiloh wondered what had Doc so riled up. Who was the 'fool'? What was the 'decision' they would regret? "Tomorrow! I'll go tomorrow!" Doc insisted. Shiloh then closed the study door, not wanting to be discovered listening.

July 26th

The late-morning sun shone down upon Shiloh and his friends as they ate a late breakfast on the back deck of the Deer Park. Shiloh was a little uncomfortable, partly because Doc had left him behind after mumbling something about running some errands, but mostly because no one had spoken a word since they sat down at the table.

Luther, Martina, Crow, and Regina were one table over, and relatively quiet as well. The people at the surrounding tables murmured softly to one another, but occasionally Shiloh could overhear them say one word: Bryce. It was the news of Bryce's condition that had the whole town subdued.

Kaz quietly broke the silence. "Does anyone actually know what happened to Bryce?"

The kids looked around at one another for a moment. Jace then leaned over the table and said, "I overheard my dad saying he was attacked." Bud nodded in agreement.

"Attacked? By whom?" Kaz asked.

Bud sighed. "No one knows. I think that's why everyone

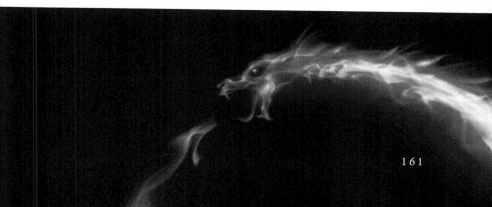

Shiloh's True Nature

is freaked out."

Brinda shook her head.

"What?" Bud asked with a frown.

"Regina was at our house early this morning. She told Mina and Maximo she thought Bryce had been burned somehow," Brinda answered.

"Burned?" Kaz questioned, his eyes widening.

"That's what she said," Brinda responded. "And she was at Saige's until late last night."

"Did she actually see him?" Bud asked.

Brinda shook her head again. "I don't know, but I think so."

"My grandfather saw him," Shiloh interjected.

The kids turned toward him, quizzical looks on their faces. Shiloh pointed to Bud and Jace and said, "We went there after we left your house yesterday." They leaned toward him, wide eyed, and he added, "Regina flagged us down on our way home and we followed her there. He went inside to help and I stayed outside and talked to Harmony."

"So what happened? What did Harmony say?" Bud asked.

Shiloh answered, "Harmony didn't really know anything. She only said she thought Bryce was hurt. I don't think anyone knows exactly what happened to him, because Saige said he hasn't been able to talk."

Brinda gave him a curious look. "You spoke to Saige?"

"Not exactly." Shiloh grimaced.

"What do you mean, 'not exactly'?" Kaz asked.

Rubbing his forehead, Shiloh tilted his head down, and said, "I sort of climbed up on the archway over the front door.

162

D.W. Raleigh

I looked in, but mostly just listened through the window."

The boys all smiled and snickered, while Brinda frowned.

"Did you hear anything else, Peeping Tom?" Brinda asked with an indignant tone.

Shiloh blushed and cleared his throat before answering, "My grandfather said Bryce's injuries were odd. He had cuts, bruises, and burns."

The kids looked around at one another, wondering what really happened, when Jace spoke up, "I don't think we're going to know anything until Bryce can talk."

Bud frowned. "He must have been hurt pretty bad if he hasn't said a word."

Everyone nodded in agreement.

Shiloh thought back to the previous day. "You know, he did say something."

"Who? Bryce?" Kaz asked.

"Yeah. It was weird. I was getting ready to climb down from the archway and he moaned something," Shiloh said.

"What? What did he say?" Brinda asked.

Shiloh squinted, frowning. "It was something like 'Marf' or 'Mawf', I think."

The kids all scowled, except for Kaz, who had a worrisome look on his face. "You don't think it was . . . the Mothman? Do you?"

Brinda sneered and rolled her eyes.

"What's the Mothman?" Shiloh inquired.

"I never should have told you that," Bud said, shaking his head at Kaz.

Shiloh looked at Bud with a questioning shrug.

Shiloh's True Nature

Bud leaned toward Shiloh and whispered, "One time, right after it was taken, I overheard my dad saying something about a Mothman guarding the Eternal Flame. At least, I thought that's what he said."

Brinda scoffed and said, "Yeah, right. Maybe Bryce was trying to steal the Flame and was attacked by a Mothman."

Kaz sneered. "Maybe that is what happened, Brinda. You don't know."

"I know there's no such thing as a Mothman, and that you're stupid. There's nothing else I need to know," Brinda answered.

Kaz took offense and said, "No, you're stupid. You make up your mind about something and start name-calling anyone who disagrees with you without even listening to their point of view."

Brinda pointed to herself. "I'm stupid? This coming from . . ."

Jace frowned at the pair and Bud interjected in a low voice, "Guys, you're getting kind of loud."

Jace rose from his chair and walked away as Bud tried to mediate the disagreement. Shiloh wasn't really listening. He ignored his friends' argument, his thoughts turning to the memory of his conversation with Saige at the bookstore two days prior. He remembered Bryce being nearby and nodding vigorously in agreement when he asked Saige why someone didn't simply take the Flame back. He hoped his question hadn't influenced Bryce's behavior.

"You don't think that's what really happened do you? Bryce getting hurt, trying to steal the Flame?" Shiloh asked, a note of apprehension in his voice.

Brinda broke off her argument with the others and shook her head, frowning. "I seriously doubt it."

Shiloh looked at Kaz, who answered, "I don't know, but it's possible."

He turned to Bud, who shrugged his shoulders.

Shiloh thought for a moment before asking, "Does anyone know what Haines did with the Flame?"

Bud quietly answered, "No one knows for certain. He must have it somewhere on his property."

"Then it must be well hidden, because the Flame needs to be outside," Kaz added.

Shiloh squinted and asked, "Why is that?"

Kaz pointed up toward the sky. "Because it needs to have contact with the sunlight."

Brinda grunted in displeasure at Kaz's answer.

"What?" Kaz asked, wondering what she was objecting to this time.

Brinda shook her head again. "As usual, you've got it half right. It has to be outdoors because it can't be contained. It needs unlimited oxygen to burn freely."

"If it has nothing to do with the sun, why is the Stone Balloon made of Sun Crystals? And if it can't be contained, why then is it placed inside the Stone Balloon, huh?" Kaz questioned.

Brinda bit her lip and tapped the side of her fist on the table as she answered, "The sun crystals are for the clock purposes. And if you ever bothered to look, you'd see the Balloon isn't completely enclosed."

Shiloh's True Nature

Bud smiled at Shiloh, trying not to laugh at the tension between Kaz and Brinda. Attempting to draw their attention, Shiloh asked, "Has anyone ever been to Haines' place?"

Kaz and Brinda ceased fighting long enough to shake their heads.

Shiloh then looked to Bud, who replied, "I know where the house is. I've seen it from a distance, but never up close." His eyes narrowed and Bud asked, "Why do you ask?"

Shiloh shrugged. "I don't know. I guess I was just wondering about Bryce, and if he really did get hurt trying to retrieve the Flame. If it has to be outside, for whatever reason, maybe he thought he could just go get it. I mean, can't you just go down Acacia Street to get there?"

Bud scowled. "You can get there down Acacia, but it would be difficult with all the overgrowth. And you would definitely be seen."

Brinda added, "No one in their right mind went near Haines' home before the Flame went missing, much less since he stole it."

Shiloh scratched his head, saying, "Well, if the only way is Acacia, and it's too obvious a route, Bryce wouldn't have gone over there. Right?"

Kaz nodded in agreement, while Brinda and Bud gave an uncertain frown. "Well, Acacia isn't the only way over there," Bud noted, motioning over his shoulder at the field behind him.

Shiloh looked toward the park where the deer were frolicking and asked, "What do you mean?"

Bud answered, "Old Pottle Path runs along the hill. It

166

leads over to the far side of Fair Hill, where Haines' house is."

Kaz looked stunned to hear this. "I thought the path was washed out years ago, and that's why no one uses it anymore."

Brinda looked at Shiloh with a big grin. "It never ceases to amaze me how he believes everything he hears."

Astounded he was being contradicted again, Kaz cried out, "What?"

Brinda turned to Kaz, patting his shoulder. "Kaz, honey, that's just what the adults say to keep us from going over there and up into the Crosskut Caves."

Kaz threw his hands in the air in frustration.

"Crosskut Caves? What's that?" Shiloh inquired.

Smiling, Bud pointed toward the hill. "There are dozens of caves in the hill. You can see some of them from here. They look like real dark spots. We've been told to stay out of them because they're dangerous."

Scanning the hill, Shiloh noticed a number of places seemed to be in total darkness, despite the bright sunshine. "I just thought those were dense patches of trees."

"Nope. Caves," Bud confirmed.

Kaz sat wondering what else there was he didn't know about and mumbled, "I can't believe this."

Brinda patted him again. "Don't worry about it, Kaz. We've all been told wild stories about things in Fair Hill." She then stared up at the hill for a moment and added, "I know Mina and Maximo have been up there a couple of times. They talked about the caves being shortcuts through the hill."

Kaz sneered, halfheartedly asking, "Now who believes everything they hear?"

Shiloh's True Nature

Brinda chuckled and shook her head, a curious grin on her face. She began tapping her fingers on the table, her focus on the hill. "You know, I'd really like to see those caves for myself."

Shiloh turned toward the hill again, wondering how Bryce was injured. Did he creep along the path or sneak through those caves only to be discovered and attacked by someone or something?

Bud noticed Shiloh's intense stare. "What are you looking at Shiloh?"

The question broke Shiloh's concentration and he shook his head. "Nothing. I was just wondering if someone could get over there and have a look around without being noticed."

A cocky smile fell over Brinda's lips as she answered, "I bet we could." She looked around at the boys with a wide grin. "I've often wondered what was around the other side of the hill. What it looks like and all."

Unnerved by Brinda's comments, Kaz lashed out, "Are you crazy? Let's say you can avoid any problems with the supposedly washed-out path or the potentially dangerous caves and actually get within viewing distance of Haines' house. Have you forgotten what just happened to Bryce? What if there really is some Mothman or something over there?"

Bud saw Brinda was about to lay into Kaz, so before she could, he leaned into the table and quietly said, "I shouldn't be telling you all this, but, ever since the Flame was stolen, people have been watching Haines closely. I overheard Regina talking to my dad, Crow, and Doc about Haines' building something over there. It's some sort of mechanical structure or something next to his house." He paused for a moment to look around before continuing. "You know if Haines is doing something like that, or anything else he shouldn't be, he isn't going to allow people to just stroll up and take a look. He will have some sort of security in place. Or worse yet, what if there really is a Mothman guarding the place?"

Brinda tilted her head. "Oh, no. Not you too. Will you guys stop with the Mothman nonsense? There's probably no such thing. Even if there were, we could just make our way over there carefully and have a look around without actually going on the property."

Kaz shook his head. "You are crazy."

Frowning slightly, Bud motioned out to the field again. "It would have to be at night though, otherwise we could be seen."

"Now you want to go at night. This is not good," Kaz added.

Brinda chuckled. "Oh, quit complaining and think of it as an adventure. We haven't snuck out to do anything since last summer's thrilling Moon Whale hunt. It's about time we did something exciting."

She looked around, waiting for one of them to say something, but when no answer came, she blurted out, "So when do you guys want to do this?"

Bud knew Brinda's enthusiasm wasn't going to be contained and said, "I'll have to be quiet, but I can get out pretty much any night."

They turned to Kaz, who said, "I don't know. Whenever.

Shiloh's True Nature

Regina goes to bed early so she can get up at the crack of dawn . . . so it shouldn't be a problem."

They all looked to Shiloh, but he was silent. Brinda smiled at him with raised eyebrows as Bud asked, "Can you get out without Doc knowing?"

Shiloh looked a bit shocked by the question. "Me? Oh, no. I can't go."

"Why not? This was your idea." Brinda smiled at him.

Shiloh's eyes widened at Brinda's assertion. "What? No it wasn't! I was just thinking about whether Bryce tried to get over there, and whether or not it was dangerous. I can't go over there, and I don't think you should either."

Seeing the frown on Brinda's face, Shiloh explained, "Look, I'd kind of like to know what's over there too, but I can't do what all of you can do."

"What do you mean?" Bud asked, tilting his head.

"What I mean is, you can blow yourself up and float home on a brisk wind. Brinda can just step into any one of the dozen streams of water and ride it away. Kaz can just blend into the background and walk home without anyone noticing. I can't do any of those things," Shiloh replied, feeling inadequate.

Brinda smiled at Shiloh. "C'mon, it'll be fun. I'm sure you'll be safe. We're just going to have a look."

Shiloh looked to Bud, who was grinning also. "It wouldn't be any fun if it was completely safe. If anything weird happens and I have to float home, I'll carry you."

Shiloh smiled at the friendly persuasion, but said, "I don't know, guys. I don't think I should."

"Finally, we have a friend who actually thinks," Kaz said, pointing at Shiloh.

Brinda sneered. "Shut up, Kaz."

Kaz sneered back, "No, you shut up."

As the kids argued amongst themselves, Shiloh tuned them out again when he noticed Doc walk around the corner of the deck. Crow immediately stood up from the nearby table and walked over to him. Shiloh watched the two men talking, and he could tell that Doc was slightly agitated. When their conversation ended, they looked in Shiloh's direction before starting toward him. Shiloh pretended not to have noticed them talking and returned to the conversation at the table.

"Guys, I'm sorry, but I'm with Kaz on this one. It's not such a good idea," Shiloh announced.

Bud and Brinda frowned, but before they could respond, Doc and Crow reached the table.

"Good morning, everyone." Doc smiled, looking around the table.

Everyone returned Doc's smile and gave him a wave. Doc looked at Shiloh and said, "Shiloh, I need to head out of town for a bit, and Crow was hoping you might assist him with some things this afternoon."

Seeing an opportunity to avoid further talk of a trip to Haines' property, Shiloh stood up and smiled at Doc and Crow. "I'd be happy to help out."

"That's great," Doc beamed.

Crow smiled slightly and nodded at Shiloh. Shiloh turned to his friends and said, "I guess I'll see you guys later."

Shiloh's True Nature

Shiloh followed Doc and Crow as they marched around the deck to the front of the Deer Park. When they reached the street, Doc immediately jumped into his cart. "I should be back by suppertime."

"Okay. Where are you going?" Shiloh asked, curious about Doc's destination.

Upon hearing the question, a frustrated look swept across Doc's face. Shiloh recognized the look as the same one Doc had when he argued with Shiloh's father. Doc then stammered, "I . . . ah . . . I've gotta go look into something."

Shiloh smiled at Doc and said, "See you when you get back then."

Doc smiled back and nodded before pulling the reins and heading off.

Shiloh watched Doc ride away and turned to Crow. "So where are we heading?"

"Follow me." Crow pointed over his shoulder with an extended thumb.

Shiloh walked along behind Crow in silence as they passed Doc's house, then Harmony's house, and finally Bud's house. It was only when they reached the forest at the base of the hill by the lake that Crow stopped. Shiloh stared out into the forest, amazed at how little sunlight made it through the dense treetops to the ground. He turned to Crow to mention this, but found him kneeling, examining the ground, intently scanning the surroundings.

Shiloh watched with a frown, wondering what Crow was doing. "So, what are we looking for?" he finally blurted out.

Crow didn't explain. He simply pointed off in the distance

and said, "This way."

Shiloh wondered how he was supposed to assist if he had no idea what they were doing. He tried to engage Crow in conversation, saying, "My grandfather told me you have a connection to animals. Is that right?" However, Crow was more focused on the environment than Shiloh's inquiry and just grunted, "Uh-huh."

Shiloh wanted to ask another question, but before he could Crow was on the move again.

Crow moved swiftly over the terrain and Shiloh did his best to keep up. It was only when Crow began to slow down that Shiloh was able to fully observe the surroundings. When he noticed a dark spot up the hill, he thought back to the conversation at the Deer Park about the caves. "Is that a cave over there?" He pointed, hoping Crow might share some information.

Crow looked up the hill in the direction of the dark spot, so Shiloh knew he heard him, but he gave no answer.

When Crow came to a stop again, he knelt down to examine some broken branches at the base of a hickory tree. Shiloh caught his breath, his frustration spilling out. "Since you haven't liked any of my other questions, maybe you could tell me why you didn't want to discuss your age of ascension the other day."

Crow looked up at Shiloh with a frown of his own, but it faded into a little smile. "It's a sore subject for me, Shiloh. You wouldn't understand," Crow said, looking over the branches.

"One thing is for sure. I'll never understand if you won't give me a chance to," Shiloh said, eyebrows raised.

Shiloh's True Nature

Crow squinted. "The ways of my people have been corrupted over time, Shiloh. They have forsaken the customs of their ancestors. For me, there is no clearer example of that than when I reached the age of ascension. It was then I developed a unique connection to nature. In the distant past, having such a connection would have been looked upon as a tremendous gift. It should have been celebrated, but instead it made me an outcast."

Crow stood up and began walking again. Shiloh followed, asking, "What do you mean by 'connection to nature'?"

"I can communicate with animals," Crow revealed.

Shiloh chuckled. "So what? You can talk to cats and dogs and birds?"

Crow let out a little laugh. "Not exactly. It's more like seeing and exchanging thoughts with them."

"Wow. That's pretty cool," Shiloh responded. He thought for a moment before saying, "There's one thing I don't understand though. Why would your ability make you an outcast?"

The frown returned to Crow's face. "In the past, my people thought a connection to nature was one of the most important things in life. Today, however, they are like most people: concerned with making money and buying things. They have decided to consume nature instead of communing with it. They no longer care about the power and miracles of life, and that's unfortunate. I'm an outcast because my gift reminds them of how they turned their backs on their ancestors."

The irritation in Crow's voice was evident, but Shiloh couldn't keep himself from asking, "What are the power and miracles of life?"

Crow kept walking, only smiling at Shiloh without answering.

Shiloh shrugged his shoulders. "Can you give an example or something?"

Crow chuckled. "You know, I can. And it's an example you above all others will be able to appreciate."

Shiloh frowned slightly, but was intrigued by Crow's assertion.

"A few years back, I was traveling down south one summer and came across a sign in front of an old run-down house that read 'Get your picture taken with a Tiger–$10.' At the time, I was on a muddy road in a marshy area and thought it must be a joke or something. As I passed the beat-up, old shack, I could see an enclosure; a rusty cage by a thicket at the rear of the property. The cage appeared empty, but something drew me to it; a feeling of hunger. As I got closer, my chest grew heavy and I struggled for air. When I reached the chained and locked gate of the enclosure, all I found was what appeared to be an old, dirty, rolled-up striped carpet lying in the back shaded corner. I turned to leave, but looked over my shoulder a last time to see two eyes staring at me. I was shocked when I realized the dirty carpet wasn't a floor covering at all, but a large cat of some kind covered in dirt and mud, and the poor thing was so thin I could see just about every bone in its body. I then realized it was a tiger. A tiger that was being starved, kept weak so it wouldn't escape and could be used for taking pictures."

Shiloh gasped, "That's awful."

Shiloh's True Nature

Crow scowled and said, "It is disgraceful. It's despicable. It's a crime against nature. I was so angry. I didn't know what to do. I wanted to scream. I wanted to find the person who had done this and find out what gave them the right to possess such a creature, much less abuse it as they had."

"So what did you do?" Shiloh asked.

"I was enraged and began kicking at the gate. The chain and lock were relatively new, but the cage itself was old and rusty. I just kept kicking at the gate until it broke off at the hinges. I threw the gate out of the way and knelt down with my arms apart. The tiger came to me. He could barely walk. It was so sad, Shiloh. Not only was the tiger being starved, but the lack of proper nutrition and hot, humid, southern air caused him to develop breathing problems. I knew immediately I had to get the creature away from there or he wouldn't last long. So, I picked him up and carried him out of the cage. Just as I did, the owner of the house, the savage who had nearly starved the tiger to death, came out of the house and began firing a shotgun at us. Fortunately, that dense thicket was nearby and I quickly ducked into it with the tiger in my arms. That fool just kept firing, but we managed to escape."

Shiloh was so focused on Crow's tale he nearly walked into a tree, but caught himself at the last moment. "Then what happened?"

"I carried the tiger through the thicket to get us as far away from the house as possible. We continued on through the swamp, and when I could no longer carry the tiger, I found us a place to rest. The next day, the tiger seemed to be doing a little better and could walk on his own, so I began to lead us north. However, at one point the tiger wanted to turn west, deeper into the swamp. I tried to get him to follow me, but he wouldn't. I tried to communicate with him and read his thoughts, but all I could get from him was a feeling of being trapped. So, I followed him for a bit to see if his feelings would subside and let me change our direction. He led me to an embankment where I discovered the cause of his feelings. When I looked down, I found an old swamp panther caught in a hunter's spring-loaded, steel trap. She was probably chasing something through the area and stepped on it by accident. So I climbed down and freed her from the trap. Luckily, the trap was old and not very sharp, so the teeth didn't bite into her flesh. However, the force of the trap snapping shut had broken her leg. So, I lifted her up onto the embankment and tied a splint around her leg with a piece of my shirt. Despite her leg and age, she was in much better shape than the tiger. So I decided to leave her behind. But when I started to lead the tiger away, she limped along after us . . ."

Shiloh interrupted, "Crow, this is an amazing story, but I'm not sure how it is an example of the power and miracles of life?"

Crow smiled. "I'm getting to that. You see, I decided to bring them home to Fair Hill. I thought if I brought them here, I might be able to restore their health. I was wrong. The journey was difficult for them and, not long after we returned, their health began to fail. The panther developed an irreversible infection in her leg that spread throughout her body. And the tiger was too far gone. It was a tragedy. Their bodies were breaking down even though their spirits were

Shiloh's True Nature

strong."

Crow saw that Shiloh was about to say something and raised his hand to stop him. "I tried to make them as comfortable as possible and waited for the inevitable. Then, one morning I was walking on the hillside and found a couple of kittens crying underneath some brush. Their eyes were still closed, and they couldn't have been more than a few days old. I looked around for their mother, but it seemed she had disappeared. I tried to care for them, but they refused to eat. Unlike the big cats, they had no will to live, no spirit. So I knew what I had to do. Later that night, I brought the cats together, big and small, and performed an ancient ceremony of my people; the Ethereal Transference rite. As both sets of cats lay dying, I performed the rite. While burning the sacred wood, I chanted and danced about crying out to the heavens to take the decaying bodies and broken spirits and leave the new life and hungry souls behind. I would know it worked if the kittens would eat, so I offered them milk. At first they would not take it, but the tiger and panther both cried out at the same time in one last gasp, and suddenly, the kittens began to drink the milk. I fed them all night long and when the morning came they opened their eyes for the first time and spoke to me in my mind, thanking me. That's the power of life, Shiloh."

Shiloh walked, shaking his head in amazement, and asked, "You're telling me, the spirits or souls or whatever of the tiger and the panther left their dying bodies and moved into the kittens?"

Crow nodded.

Shiloh continued to shake his head. "That's incredible. So what happened to the cats? Are they still around?"

A big grin washed over Crow's face as he said, "They're still around, but I haven't seen them much in the past few years."

Shiloh frowned. "Why? After all that, I thought they would have been with you forever."

Crow continued grinning as he said, "Well, a friend of mine—the best friend I've ever had in fact—he needed an extraordinary birthday present, but he just couldn't find anything that seemed right. He wanted something that would be cherished and enjoyed every day. So I told him the only gift I could think of that would be that way was the gift of friendship. He agreed. So I suggested the cats. He accepted them and passed them on."

Shiloh smiled. "Wow, that's an amazing birthday present. Does the person who got the cats know how special they are?"

Crow smiled back at Shiloh. "He does now."

Shiloh stopped in his tracks and his eyes widened. "Are you saying what I think you're saying?"

Crow turned and nodded with a grin.

Shiloh stammered, "You mean, my cats were your cats? The kittens? The big cats?"

Crow smiled widely. "That's right."

Crow began walking again and Shiloh followed, asking, "Are the cats different somehow? I mean, are they different than other cats?"

Crow answered, "Not really. But the spirits of the big cats

Shiloh's True Nature

can transform the felines in ways."

Shiloh thought for a moment and asked, "Transform? In what ways?"

Crow chuckled. "If it happens, you'll know."

Shiloh wasn't sure what Crow meant and wanted to inquire further, but he noticed Crow had stopped moving and was looking around intently. "What is it, Crow? What are we looking for?" he asked in a low voice.

Crow shook his head and whispered, "I'm not sure yet. We'll know when we find it."

"It's an animal of some kind, isn't it?" Shiloh asked.

Crow nodded, walking forward slowly.

Shiloh kept his voice down and asked, "Does your ability work with all animals?"

Crow shook his head. "Not fully. I am able to communicate best with animals that behave as individuals. My gift doesn't work as well with pack animals. I have no problems communicating with birds and cats, but dogs for the most part I can't reach. Though, I can usually reach the lead dog—the alpha dog."

"That is so cool. I wish I could do that," Shiloh remarked.

"Maybe you will," Crow responded.

"What do you mean?" Shiloh inquired.

Crow answered, "My gift isn't completely exclusive. There have been other Movers who had a touch of it."

"Really?" Shiloh asked.

"Yes. A few people have developed connections to a single animal or even a specific species, but none has the connection the way I do. Not too long ago, there was a boy here who

I thought had the same type of ability, but sadly he wasn't able to develop it beyond a certain point," Crow noted.

Crow stopped ahead of a small clearing and looked around. Shiloh scanned the area, but didn't see anything. Crow startled him by pulling him behind a large tree. Crow placed his index finger to his lips and whispered, "I believe we've found what we've been searching for."

Shiloh frowned, unsure of what Crow was referring to, and then peered around the tree. Suddenly, a deer rushed into the clearing and began charging violently around the area. It jumped back and forth, kicking its hind legs in the air, shaking its head wildly.

As Shiloh watched the deer, Crow said, "Some animals in this area have been behaving very strangely. I'm hoping we can find out why."

"What are we going to do?" Shiloh asked nervously.

Crow said, "In order for me to communicate with an animal for the first time, I have to be in physical contact with it, touch it."

"What? Are you crazy? You can't get near that buck. It could gore you with its antlers," Shiloh responded.

Crow smiled at him. "I have to try to help it, Shiloh. Everything will be fine. Just stay here."

As Crow slowly stepped out from behind the tree, Shiloh called after him, "Wait. Don't go out there."

Ignoring Shiloh's plea, Crow walked very slowly into the clearing. The frenzied buck noticed Crow's presence and stamped its feet, making a loud screeching sound. "Easy, boy, easy," Crow soothed, trying to calm the deer as he crept to-

Shiloh's True Nature

ward it.

The buck thrashed its head from side to side at first, but then stopped and allowed Crow near enough to touch it. Crow slid his hand across the animal's back, petting it very slowly. He did this several times, until bringing his hand to a rest on the back of the deer's neck.

The buck seemed to have completely calmed down, and Crow motioned for Shiloh to join him. Shiloh wasn't completely certain it was safe, but he stepped out from behind the tree and joined Crow at its side. Crow closed his eyes to focus. "His mind is racing. His thoughts a jumble. I need to reach deeper to find out what happened, why he's acting this way."

Shiloh watched as Crow shook his head erratically, squinting and scowling, his eyes closed. Suddenly, the buck broke away from them. It ran straight away, crashing with a crunch into the tree they were hiding behind just moments ago.

Crow ran after the creature and Shiloh followed, wondering what happened. The buck lay motionless at the foot of the tree, and Shiloh's thought back to the deer knocked unconscious the other day at the Deer Park. Crow knelt down, felt the buck's neck, and shook his head. He moved his hands to the deer's face, lowering the eyelids with his fingers. "Sleep the eternal sleep, my friend."

Shiloh was stunned and asked, "What just happened?"

Crow shook his head as he stood up. "I'm not sure. I think the deer was trying to tell me something about water. The only clear thought I read was of it drinking from a stream."

"There must be a dozen streams around here. What do

you think it means?" Shiloh asked.

Crow didn't answer right away. He closed eyes his and listened to the surroundings for a moment. "Let's find the closest stream and go from there," Crow suggested.

Crow led Shiloh across the clearing to where the deer had emerged, and they began searching the forest for the nearest stream. As they walked along, Shiloh started to feel queasy. He wasn't sure if something he ate wasn't sitting right, or whether his stomach was upset from witnessing the deer's erratic behavior. However, one thing he was sure of was something didn't feel right.

It was then Shiloh heard the sound of moving water nearby. Crow heard it as well, and led them to a small brook that wound its way down the hillside. Crow bent down to look at the flowing water, which Shiloh thought looked a little odd. It had a peculiar shine to it, like it was oilier than it should be. Crow cupped his hands together, scooped up some water, and took a long whiff of it.

"There's something wrong with the water, isn't there?" Shiloh asked.

Crow nodded. "It smells very peculiar."

Shiloh frowned. "How could the stream get polluted? There aren't any factories or plants in Fair Hill are there?"

Sighing, Crow stood and answered, "I'm not certain how it got this way, but I have an idea."

Shiloh scowled and asked, "It's that man, isn't it? The one who owns the factory across the river? The one who stole the Flame? Haines?"

Crow frowned, nodded slightly, and quickly changed the

Shiloh's True Nature

subject. "We need to bury the deer."

Shiloh nodded. "Okay."

Crow led Shiloh out of the woods in silence. They walked to Crow's home, where they retrieved a couple of shovels, and immediately began the trek back. As they made the hike back up the hillside, one thing occupied Shiloh's thoughts: Haines. Shiloh wondered why so many unpleasant things seemed to bear his mark: Acacia street, the suicidal deer, the polluted stream, Bryce's injuries. Why was Haines in such discord with the community? Everyone there seemed so unique and wonderfully pleasant, except him.

All those thoughts relating to Haines led Shiloh to an even more burning question; why did Haines steal the Eternal Flame? So he blurted out, "What do you know about the Eternal Flame?"

Crow smiled at the sudden break in the silence, and asked, "What do I know?"

"Yeah. I mean, my grandfather told me Haines stole the Flame from the center of town, and that it's not supposed to be moved from there, but he never really said what it is. I've read about it a little bit, but the books never gave a clear answer. In fact, the only person who seems to have an answer at all is that lady from the bookstore, Saige. She told me a story about the Prime Mover turning into a dragon or something and tearing off a piece of the sun. I guess I just don't know what to believe."

Crow squinted for a moment, and then said, "Well, Shiloh, if you're looking for a definitive answer, I'm afraid I'm probably going to disappoint you along with the rest."

Shiloh huffed in displeasure.

Crow smirked and responded, "Did you ever stop to think that maybe those books, Saige, and Doc told you what they did because they don't really know either?"

Shiloh tilted his head in confusion.

"You see, the foundation of all knowledge is the realization that you don't understand something. If you want to know about something, you investigate and ask questions until you accumulate enough facts to make your own conclusion. Maybe Doc told you the Flame isn't supposed to be moved because that's the only fact he is sure of. And I imagine the books you read did the same thing: stated a few facts without ever saying what the Flame is," Crow said.

"And Saige? What about her story?" Shiloh asked.

Crow smiled widely. "Well, without being disrespectful to anyone else's beliefs, I can tell you I do not believe the Eternal Flame is a piece of the sun. There are a lot of fanciful stories about the Eternal Flame, Shiloh. The story Saige told you stems from the fact that we are all pieces of a sun."

"We are?" Shiloh asked.

"That's right. Every molecule in your body, my body, and everything around us once came from the dust of exploding stars, but that's not my point," Crow answered. He thought for a moment and then raised his hand, saying, "What you need to keep in mind with all the stories you may have heard or read, including Saige's, is that there are always pieces of truth in them."

Shiloh smiled. "Okay. If the Flame isn't a piece of the sun, what do you think it is?"

Shiloh's True Nature

Crow returned Shiloh's smile. "I believe the Eternal Flame is an example of the power of life. More specifically, I believe it is the last living piece of the Prime Mover."

"What do you mean, 'last living piece'?" Shiloh asked scowling.

"The Prime Mover has an immense radiance, a powerful life force, Shiloh. When the last Prime Mover left this world, he left a little piece of himself behind. I believe the Eternal Flame is the last remnant of the Prime Mover's radiance: the last living piece of himself."

Scratching his head, Shiloh asked, "How could that be possible? I mean, no one is made of fire. Are they?"

Crow chuckled and explained, "No. No one is made of fire. However, when Movers pass away, we have a ceremony called a Funus. For the Funus, the body of the deceased is placed inside something called a Revenant, which is sort of a combination of a coffin and a small boat. The exterior of the Revenant is filled with the branches of a special type of wood. The Revenant is then lit on fire and pushed into the water. The sacred wood burns extremely hot and fast to consume the body and Revenant before extinguishing. After that, the celebration begins."

Shiloh's eyes widened. "Celebration?"

Crow nodded and smiled. "Yes, Shiloh. We celebrate the life of the deceased. We don't look at their passing as a bad thing, but as a completion of their journey through this world. We are happy for them and the opportunity we had to share this life with them."

Shiloh wasn't sure what to make of what Crow told him.

He had always seen death and funerals as sad things. He then realized his original question hadn't been answered and asked, "So what does this have to do with the Eternal Flame and the Prime Mover?"

"Well, everything is done the same way when a Prime Mover passes on. There is a Funus, a Revenant, and the sacred wood, but once the fire is lit, it never goes out."

"What? That's hard to believe. What happens when the fire touches the water?" Shiloh asked in disbelief.

"The fire consumes the body, the Revenant, and most of the wood. Afterward there's a piece of the sacred wood found floating on the water still burning with a flame, and it won't go out. That is why it's called the Eternal Flame," Crow explained.

"What you believe sure is different from what Saige believes," Shiloh noted.

Crow chuckled. "Yes, it is."

Shiloh squinted at Crow with a little smile. "So how do I know what you believe about the Flame is correct?"

Crow let out a big laugh and said, "You don't. It's the conclusion I have come to after investigating and accumulating facts. I have no way of knowing for certain. It's been a long time since the last Prime Mover was with us, so I suppose I'll never know the absolute truth."

When they returned to the clearing to bury the deer, Shiloh helped Crow dig while pondering all he had learned. He tried to think of what facts he could attribute to the Eternal Flame, but he couldn't think of many. He had never seen it. He had no definitive answer as to where it came from, or

Shiloh's True Nature

what it was. All he really knew was that it existed and that it was stolen.

Shiloh didn't like having so little information, so, as he continued to dig, he asked, "How is it possible that the flame can't be extinguished? I mean, have you tried to put it out?"

As he shoveled, Crow chuckled. "No. I have not tried to put it out. Although I did see it in the pouring rain once. The water just bounced right off of it. It was the most amazing thing I've ever seen. And I have seen a lot of amazing things."

"So you'd say it's a fact that the Eternal Flame can't be extinguished?" Shiloh asked.

"As far as I know, it can't be. Although, I did read in a book once that there were a couple ways it could be put out," Crow said.

"Yeah?"

"If the Prime Mover comes back, he or she can extinguish it," Crow answered.

Shiloh found that interesting and asked, "Really? How would they put out the flame?"

"I don't know, but I'm sure the Prime Mover will." Crow chuckled.

"And the second way?" Shiloh asked.

Crow scowled slightly. "That one I didn't really understand. It just said 'by the blood of the innocent.'"

Shiloh frowned and asked, "Blood of the innocent? What does that mean?"

Crow shook his head. "I don't know. I suppose it could mean many things. Usually when Movers refer to 'the innocent', it means those who have not yet reached the age of ascension."

Once Crow and Shiloh finished digging the grave for the deer, they placed the poor creature into the ground and went on their way. Neither spoke as they slowly made their way down the hillside. When they emerged from the woods by the lake, Shiloh's stomach growled and he asked, "Do you think my grandfather is back yet?"

"I hope so. I'm hungry," Crow answered, patting his stomach with a grin.

Shiloh laughed and asked, "Where'd he go anyway?"

Crow looked at Shiloh, saying, "I'm not going to lie to you, Shiloh."

Crow seemed to have stopped mid-sentence. Shiloh turned toward him to find out what was wrong and asked, "What?"

Crow smiled and looked at Shiloh out of the corner of his eye as they walked along, but said nothing.

"You're not going to tell me, are you?" Shiloh asked, realizing Doc must have told Crow to keep his destination private.

Crow chuckled. "Like I said, I'm not going to lie to you."

Shiloh laughed and kept walking.

A little farther down the road, Shiloh noticed they were approaching Saige's home, and he began to wonder about Bryce. He hoped Bryce's health was improving and he was able to speak. Mostly, Shiloh hoped he was in no way responsible for inciting the actions that led to Bryce's predicament.

As they passed the house, Shiloh slowed his pace to have a long look around. He hoped someone would see them passing and emerge to give them an update on Bryce's condition.

Shiloh's True Nature

When no one seemed to be around, Shiloh craned his neck to see if perhaps Harmony was seated outside on the big rock again, but the wild grass and brush blocked his view.

Crow realized Shiloh had fallen a bit behind and looked over his shoulder to locate him. Shiloh caught Crow's glance and picked up his pace to rejoin him.

Crow smiled at Shiloh and said, "You have a birthday coming up, don't you?"

"Yeah," Shiloh confirmed halfheartedly as he continued looking backward toward the house.

Crow squinted at Shiloh and asked, "What's wrong? You look like something is bothering you."

Shiloh shook his head, frowning. "I don't know what you mean."

Crow gave Shiloh a sly smile. "It's the same look you had earlier at the Deer Park when you were talking with your friends."

Shiloh pursed his lips and shook his head, but said nothing.

"So what were you and your friends talking about?" Crow inquired.

Shiloh answered, "Nothing much."

Crow chuckled and noted, "The lips need not move to say nothing, my friend."

Shiloh chuckled while quickly trying to think of an answer to give Crow. He certainly didn't want to mention Bryce or Haines or a Mothman, so he tried to deflect the question. "I don't remember making any face. When was that?"

"Right before Doc arrived, that loud girl, Brinda, was all

excited about something," Crow answered.

Shaking his head, Shiloh replied, "I'm not sure, but I think we were talking about their abilities, and how I don't have one."

Crow stared at Shiloh with a grin.

Shiloh felt the stare and asked, "What?"

"Does that bother you?" Crow asked.

"Ah . . . well . . . a little . . . I guess," Shiloh stammered, realizing it did bother him. He wanted to be able to do something amazing. He wanted to sneak out with his friends to go on an adventure. Mostly, he just wanted to feel like he belonged in Fair Hill.

"It's your thirteenth birthday, isn't it?" Crow asked.

Shiloh nodded.

"Well, like I told you before, the thirteenth birthday is when a boy becomes a man. It's when men and women become Movers. So we'll just have to wait and see," Crow said with a smile.

"What if I'm not a Mover? What if I'm just an ordinary person?" Shiloh questioned.

"You'll be who you are, whether it be Man or Mover. And remember this, Shiloh: who you are isn't measured by powers or abilities, it's about what's in your heart and what's in your head. In any case, I think you'll have a good birthday," Crow said with a wink.

Shiloh gave Crow a little smile and noticed they were approaching Doc's house.

As they came closer, Shiloh looked to the porch and found Doc sitting in one of the rocking chairs. Doc gave them a

Shiloh's True Nature

little wave of his hand and Shiloh smiled, picking up his pace.

As he stepped up on to the porch, Shiloh said, "You're back."

"Yes. I had some things to do across the river," Doc noted.

This drew Shiloh's interest, and he asked, "Were you in Salem?"

Doc nodded.

"Did you go by the farm?" Shiloh noticed Doc's hesitation and gave him a questioning shrug.

"Yes, I did," Doc finally responded.

"So how are my parents?"

Doc hesitated again before saying, "I don't know. No one was home when I stopped by."

Shiloh was concerned. "Not home! In the middle of the day? That doesn't make any sense . . ."

Doc raised his hand. "Shiloh, I wasn't there very long. I may have just missed them. They may have gotten home right after I left." Doc paused for a moment before laughing, "For all I know, they may have been out buying you birthday presents."

Shiloh doubted the likelihood of Doc's explanation, but gave an 'I guess so' shrug anyway. It just seemed very odd to him that no one would be there at all. In fact, he couldn't ever remember a time during growing season when some-one wasn't tending to the field.

Doc smiled at Shiloh and said, "Why don't you head on in and get cleaned up for dinner? I'll join you shortly."

Shiloh sighed. "Okay."

Shiloh purposely removed his shoes as he walked through

the front door, because he had no intention of missing Doc and Crow's conversation. He went to the staircase and made sure to stomp his feet on the way up, but immediately stopped at the top and crept back down. When he reached the bottom, Shiloh tiptoed to the side of the open window between the porch door and the kitchen and began listening.

He heard Crow say, "It has to be something Haines is doing. I don't know what else it could be."

"And the deer?" Doc asked.

"Shiloh and I gave him a proper burial," Crow responded.

There was a pause in the conversation for a moment and Shiloh wondered what was happening. He looked toward the doorway, watching for a shadow, but none came. He then knelt down and peered out the window.

"Any word on Bryce?" Crow asked, causing Shiloh to pull away from the window.

"I stopped by there on my way back," Doc answered.

"And?" Crow asked.

Doc sighed. "It's not looking good. I've done all I can. I guess time will tell."

Crow grunted at the unwelcome news.

After another brief pause, Crow asked, "So what did you find out across the river? Is it true? Is he going through with it?"

Doc huffed. "I don't know what's going on. I wanted to get some answers, but as I mentioned, that didn't work out."

Crow grunted again. "You want me to have my birds keep an eye out?"

"Nah, that's not necessary," Doc replied.

Shiloh's True Nature

A final pause went by and Doc said, "Well, I better get inside and feed my grandson. Are you staying for dinner?"

"Of course I am," Crow replied with a chuckle.

Both men laughed and Shiloh quickly snuck up the staircase.

July 27th

Shiloh woke in a pool of sweat and immediately sat up in bed. He threw off his blanket and rushed downstairs into the kitchen. "Have you reached my parents yet?" he asked, seeing Doc seated at the table.

Doc looked up from his book. "Good morning. And, no, I have not. But I haven't tried to contact them, either."

Doc watched as Shiloh took a seat at the table with a scowl on his face. "Are you feeling all right?" he asked, concerned with Shiloh's troubled look.

Shiloh nodded, saying, "I'm fine. I just had a bad dream."

Doc gave an understanding nod.

A moment later, Shiloh blurted out, "It's not like them to just take off. There's all kinds of work that has to be done on the farm. They never just go out."

Doc raised his hand. "I think you're overreacting. I'm sure everything is fine."

Doc watched as Shiloh wiped the sweat from his brow and again asked, "Are you sure you're all right?"

Shiloh's True Nature

"I'm worried that something bad has happened," Shiloh said.

Doc set his book down and slid his chair closer to the table. "What do you mean 'bad'?"

Shiloh sighed. "The night before you brought me to Fair Hill, something chased me through the cornfield: something big."

Doc squinted at Shiloh, stroking his chin. "Tell me about it. What do you think it was?"

Shiloh shook his head. "I don't know. There were two of them."

"Two?" Doc asked with a frown.

Shiloh continued, "Yes. I was walking along in the dark and there was a flapping noise, like something was flying around me. When the noise stopped, a loud thumping sound replaced it. The thumping followed me as I walked, like it was stalking me. I started running, but fell. Whatever it was came up behind me. I thought it was going to attack me."

"So what happened?" Doc asked, intrigued by the story.

"I decided to get to my feet and run to the house. When I looked up, something else was blocking the direction I needed to run. It was lower to the ground with reflective eyes and it made a growling sound. It jumped over me and went after whatever was behind me," Shiloh recounted.

Hearing the latter part of Shiloh's story brought a little smile to Doc's face. Seeing this Shiloh hollered, "I'm not making it up!"

Doc's smile faded, his eyes widened, and he raised his hands as he sat back in his chair. "I believe you, Shiloh."

Shiloh shook his head and frowned. "My father didn't believe me either."

Doc smiled and in a calm voice said, "I believe you. And I understand your concern after being chased, but I'm sure there's a logical explanation involving either foxes or deer or countless other animals. Whatever the case may be, I don't think there's any reason for you to be concerned about your parents' well-being."

Shiloh hung his head and tapped his fingers on the table, staring down at nothing in particular.

"Honestly, Shiloh, you should stop worrying about this, eat something, and head over to the lake for a swim," Doc suggested.

Doc watched Shiloh continue to tap his fingers on the table and said, "You know, a week from now you'll be wishing you were here having fun, instead of being put to work every morning by your father."

Grinning, Shiloh grabbed a bowl and poured himself some cereal.

After he ate, Shiloh made his way out into the midmorning sun and walked over to the lake. When he arrived, he found his friends huddled in front of the small green shed off to the side of Bud's house. Jace was in the center, closest to the door, doing something Shiloh couldn't see.

As he approached, Shiloh stepped on a stick lying on the ground, cracking it. Jace, Bud, Kaz, and Brinda simultaneously flinched and turned toward him with wide eyes. They all exhaled a sigh of relief at seeing him, which led Shiloh to ask, "What are you guys doing?"

Shiloh's True Nature

"We're trying to untie the new knot my dad used to lock up the shed," Bud replied.

"What do you mean 'we'?" Jace chuckled.

Shiloh watched as Jace played with the loops in the rope and asked, "Can't you just cut it? I mean, it's rope, right?"

Jace shook his head. "No can do. Cutting it off would take forever, because it's a special type of rope. And, if we did cut it off, our parents would know we were in the shed, and we're trying to avoid that."

"Well, aren't they going to think it's odd if they look out the window and see us all standing around?" Shiloh asked with a chuckle.

Bud answered, "They went into town and shouldn't be back for a while."

Examining the knot more closely, Shiloh recognized the design and realized the difficulty of the task. It appeared to be the same knot Luther had shown him the other day. "You're never getting that thing off," Shiloh declared, remembering the incredibly complicated knot.

"That's exactly what I said," Kaz noted to Shiloh.

"Oh ye of little faith. Watch this." Jace snickered as he tugged at one of the knot loops with a smile.

Shiloh watched closely, waiting for the knot to untie or fall away, but it didn't. The knot made a tightening sound and Bud said, "Nice going. That's strike two. Once more, and it's over."

"I don't know what the problem is. Dad always uses the same three or four patterns," Jace answered apologetically.

Shiloh watched as Jace began again. "What's so interesting in the shed anyway?"

"Give me another minute and I'll show you," Jace said, tugging on the loops in a specific sequence.

Shiloh watched as the rope fell limp and Jace pulled it off the adjacent door handles. Bud, Brinda, and Kaz all had big smiles on their faces as Jace opened the doors and said, "I told you I'd get us in."

As Jace walked into the shed, Shiloh scanned the interior, noting the various benches and open cabinets holding all sorts of odd tools and equipment. A strange dark and feathery object hanging from a hook on the back wall of the shed caught his eye. He tried to identify it, but it only reminded him of a gigantic, gray feather duster. Shiloh soon found out this was the very thing the shed had been breached for, because Jace grabbed it off the hook.

As Jace exited the shed, Shiloh realized he was carrying not one, but two of the big feathery things. The kids followed Jace, and Shiloh turned to Bud, asking, "What are those?"

Bud answered, "They're wings." Shiloh looked confused, so Bud added, ". . . for flying."

Shiloh frowned. "For flying what?"

Brinda and Kaz laughed at Shiloh's question, but Jace glanced over his shoulder with a smile and said, "People."

Shiloh was shocked to hear this and looked to Bud, who nodded at him with a big grin.

They proceeded to the giant pine tree by the lake, where Jace began to climb the spiral staircase of branches. Bud, Brinda, and Kaz waded into the lake, while Shiloh stared up at the platform sitting just under the tip of the massive tree.

Shiloh's True Nature

Jace circled in and out of view as he ascended, and Shiloh began to wonder exactly what he planned to do upon reaching the top.

A thin wave of cool water slapped into him from behind, breaking Shiloh's upward stare. He turned toward the lake to find Brinda smiling at him. "Are you getting in the water or what?" she asked with a laugh.

Smiling, Shiloh shook his head at Brinda's sassiness. He then waded into the lake to join his friends, who were floating around on the giant lily pads off to one side.

"So what's this all about? Why were those things locked up?" Shiloh was still curious about the wings.

"My parents don't like us using the wings when they're not here. Well, my dad doesn't mind too much. My mom doesn't like us using them at all. She makes Dad lock them up," Bud explained.

"I understand, but what are they for?" Shiloh asked.

"Just watch," Bud said, pointing upward.

Shiloh looked to the platform and saw Jace at the top. His eyes widened as Jace slipped the wings on to his arms and jumped off the edge of the platform. Shiloh's jaw dropped and he quickly looked to the others. They cheered as Jace stretched out his arms and slowly descended into a graceful glide just above the lake's surface.

Once he realized Jace was in no danger, Shiloh's tension eased and a smile came over his face. He continued watching until Jace landed with a light splash. Turning to Bud, he said, "That's amazing. You can really fly with those, huh?"

Bud smiled and said, "You can, but you have to do it just

right." Shiloh frowned in confusion and Bud explained, "If you start off in a glide and flap your arms every once in a while, in just the right way, you can coast for miles. If you're just jumping from the platform, you don't need to do that."

Jace emerged from the water on the side of the lake. He grabbed a small stake with a flag on it out of a nearby bucket and placed it in the ground parallel to where he landed. Watching Jace, Shiloh inquired, "What are the wings made of? How do they work?"

Brinda answered, "The wings are made of a bunch of different types of waxes. What look like feathers are actually thin strands of wax. And they float." Smiling at Shiloh, she added, "Mina and Maximo made them."

As Jace walked back toward the tower, the kids began to taunt him.

"Is that the best you can do?" Brinda hollered with a laugh.

"Yeah. Hurry up, Jace! I've seen turtles move faster than you!" Kaz yelled. Jace shook his head, smiling at the taunts.

Shiloh leaned toward Bud and asked, "Was that not very far?"

Bud chuckled. "Actually, that's probably farther than any of us will make it. Jace is the best glider, except for my dad."

"Your dad?" Shiloh questioned, thinking it odd Luther would participate in such an activity.

Bud smiled, saying, "Yeah. The wings are his."

As soon as Jace reached the edge of the lake by the giant pine, Brinda quickly jumped out of the water and grabbed the wings from him. She ran up to the platform as fast as she could, and stepped to the edge, where she slid the wings over

Shiloh's True Nature

her arms, yelling, "Now this is how you do it!"

Shiloh watched Brinda jump, but something didn't seem right. Her arms and body shuddered, unlike Jace, whose body had seemed stiff as a board on his descent.

The boys all chuckled at Brinda's glide, which seemed more like a fall. Shiloh winced as she sped toward the water, waiting for her to crash into the lake. However, just before she hit, an enormous plume of water rose up from the lake and caught her, cushioning her fall and gently lowering her into the water.

When Brinda surfaced, Jace yelled out, "So that's how ya do it, huh?"

The boys burst into laughter and Brinda yelled, "Shut up!" after which she smacked them all with a wave of water.

Shiloh watched as Kaz and Bud took their turns and marked the distances of their glides. After his turn, Bud tried to give the wings to Shiloh, but Shiloh looked up at the tall tree while shaking his head, "No way."

Bud tried to think of something encouraging to say, but before he could, Jace pulled the wings from him and re-marked, "You heard the man. It's my turn again."

Shiloh floated around on his lily pad soaking up the sun as he watched the others jump and glide in turn. The kids made it sound like an exciting carnival ride and encouraged Shiloh to give it a try, but when Bud asked after his second glide, Shiloh again declined.

As each of his friends took another turn, Shiloh enjoyed their glides vicariously with no intention of participating; that is, until Jace, who had been silent on the matter to this point, explained how to glide properly. "It's actually very simple. You just need to keep your body stiff and stretch out your arms as wide as you can. When you first jump, you'll feel the urge to bring your arms in closer to your body, but don't. That's what happened to Brinda on her first jump. You'll know you're doing it right if you feel a tickling sensation in your stomach. It feels like you're being pulled along."

Shiloh smiled at Jace's advice and looked up to watch Bud take his turn. As Bud jumped and began his glide, Brinda said, "If you want to try, I promise I'll catch you if things don't go right."

Shiloh turned to Brinda, who gave him a silly, surprised look as she conjured a small plume of water next to her lily pad like the one that caught her on her disastrous first glide.

After Bud marked his longest glide of the day, Shiloh reluctantly made his way out of the water to the edge of the lake. Bud met him there and asked, "Are you going to try it?"

Shiloh sighed. "I must be crazy, but I guess so."

Bud smiled and said, "Cool. You're gonna love it. Just throw your arms wide open and keep the rest of your body tight."

"Thanks," Shiloh responded, taking the wings.

Shiloh slowly approached the tree, looking up toward the platform and beginning to have second thoughts. He nearly gave in to his fear of heights, but his mother's words of wisdom 'to focus elsewhere' echoed through his head. He began to climb the staircase of branches, focusing directly on the trunk. He didn't look up. He didn't look down. He just climbed until he reached the top.

Shiloh's True Nature

Reaching the platform, Shiloh found a magnificent view in all directions. The forest-covered hills, and the river in the distance, gave him a new appreciation for the beauty of his surroundings. He then looked down to the lake at his friends lounging around on their lily pads. "You can do it, Shiloh!" Bud hollered up to him.

As he prepared to make his jump, Shiloh examined the wings and saw the giant feathers were indeed made up of waxy broom hairs. The underside of the wings had three hoops through which his arms would fit. One slid up to the pit of the arm, another around the elbow, and a final one on the wrist. There were also handle-like grips to hold onto at the tips.

As he pulled the wings onto each arm and stepped to the edge, Shiloh's nervousness returned. He took a deep breath and gazed around again at the beautiful surroundings. Once calm, Shiloh closed his eyes and ran off the edge of the platform to the cheers of his friends below. Though he threw his arms open, the force of air immediately caused the wings to shudder, compelling him to pull in his arms. His jump turned into a virtual nosedive.

Jace cried out, "Stretch out your arms!"

Shiloh forced his arms straight out to his sides with all his might. As he rapidly descended toward the water, the pressure on his arms subsided and was replaced by a slight tickling sensation in his abdomen. He narrowly missed the water by twisting his arms, which sent him upward. However, he had overcompensated, and his body was now moving vertically. He rotated his arms downward, trying to move his body parallel with the lake, but he again went too far and began moving headfirst toward the water.

The process continued, with Shiloh veering up and down in a battle to keep from crashing into the water. His friends laughed and cheered at his awkward glide, until his momentum finally slowed on a downward turn. He briefly slid across the surface of the water until submerging into the lake. The wings' buoyancy pulled Shiloh back to the surface, where he found his friends cheering and racing toward him.

As he stepped out of the lake, Jace teased, "That was the ugliest glide I've ever seen."

Bud sneered at Jace and said, "I don't remember your first glide being very graceful."

"It may have been an ugly glide, but it looks like a new record to me," Kaz noted, pointing to the side of the lake.

Shiloh looked just beyond the lake's edge and found his landing spot was well beyond any of his friends' marks, including Jace, who'd had the longest glide of the day. Jace pointed to a shiny blue and brown marker with a knot tied around it. "Oh, no. Dad's not going to like that."

Shiloh looked to Bud, who stood with his mouth hanging open. "What?" Shiloh inquired, pulling the wings from his arms.

Bud nodded toward the marker, "That mark is my dad's."

As Shiloh examined the ornate marker from a distance, Jace pulled a blue-green, metal marker from the bucket, pushing it into the ground a couple of steps beyond his father's mark. Jace then knelt and bent the top of the thin metal marker into the shape of an 'S'.

Shiloh's True Nature

Everyone was hushed in awe. Shiloh couldn't understand why, and again blurted out, "What?"

Jace pointed to his father's marker and said, "That's the farthest anyone had ever gone..." He then turned, pointing to the new marker he just placed, "... until now."

Frowning, Shiloh looked at the gap between the new and ornate markers. What did Jace mean? Shiloh thought his clumsy, awkward glide couldn't be the farthest anyone flew before.

The kids stood in silence admiring the distance of Shiloh's glide, when suddenly a woman's voice yelled out, "What is going on here?"

They looked toward the house simultaneously to find Bud's parents at the lake's edge by the house. Martina looked particularly angry. Luther tried calming her. "Go ahead inside, dear. I'll handle this."

Luther marched toward them with a menacing gait as Martina stomped up the porch steps, slamming the door as she entered the house. The kids hung their heads in anticipation of the reprimand, but it never came. When he reached them, Luther shook his finger at them with a slight smirk on his face. "Is she still watching?"

Jace looked over his father's shoulder toward the house. "Yeah, she's looking out the window."

"Well, keep your heads down then... otherwise we'll all be in trouble," Luther chuckled.

The kids did their best not to smile as Luther asked, "So, did you have fun?"

They all nodded, but Jace grimaced and said, "But there's

some bad news."

Luther frowned and asked, "What? No one got hurt did they?"

Bud looked at his father out of the corner of his eye trying not to smile. "No one got hurt, but . . ."

"But what?" Luther questioned.

Jace pointed to Shiloh's blue-green marker and Luther gasped. "Who did this?"

"Shiloh," Jace informed his father.

Shiloh looked to Luther, worry on his face, wondering what he was going to say. He was surprised when Luther smiled at him and said, "Well done, young man. Truly remarkable."

Bud added, "And that was his first try."

Tilting his head, Luther folded his arms and surveyed the distance between his marker and Shiloh's. Jace interrupted his father's examination, saying, "We thought you would be in town for a while."

Luther turned to the kids with a somber look and mumbled, "Yes, well, we would have been . . . unforeseen events."

Bud frowned. "What?"

Luther sighed and began to answer, but then Martina yelled in the distance, "Luther."

Luther looked back toward the house to find Martina marching toward them. He quickly turned back toward the kids and whispered, "Who got the knot off?"

Bud, Kaz, and Brinda simultaneously pointed in Jace's direction. Jace let out a long sigh and Luther said, "Sorry, son. You've got to take one for the team."

Shiloh's True Nature

Luther looked to Shiloh, giving him a wink as he pulled the wings away from him. He then hollered, "And don't any of you ever get into my shed without permission again, or you'll be punished!"

Luther turned to Jace and whispered, "Sorry, Jace." He then grabbed Jace's earlobe and began pulling him toward the house as he announced, "I've found the culprit, dear."

Martina yelled, "Jace! How many times have we told you not to use those wings without our permission?"

When Luther reached Martina with Jace in tow, she grabbed Jace's other earlobe, pulling him away from his father. The kids watched as she continued yelling at him the entire way into the house.

When the porch door slammed shut, the kids looked at one another with sighs of relief. Grateful to have escaped Martina's scolding, they started into the lake. However, before they could re-enter it, the porch door swung open again and Martina hollered, "You four! Get in here and eat! Now!"

The kids hurried into the house, where Martina had quickly thrown together some lunch for them. The meal came with a price; they had to endure a stern lecture from her about the wings and their dangers while they ate. They finished as fast as they could to escape the house and return to the lake.

When they returned outdoors, the kids swam around for a while, but it was a bit of a letdown after the excitement of playing with the wings. They eventually retreated to the gigantic lily pads, where they floated around watching the Mondo Frogs.

As they relaxed, Shiloh tilting his head back to soak in some sun, Bud asked, "Has anyone heard anything about Bryce?"

Brinda responded, "Mina and Maximo were talking about him when I came down to breakfast this morning, but they stopped before I could hear anything."

"Regina said he isn't doing well. She didn't give any details," Kaz noted.

Things went silent for a moment and Shiloh opened his eyes slightly to find his friends all looking in his direction. "What?" he asked.

"If anyone would know Bryce's condition, Doc would," Bud said, raising his eyebrows.

Shiloh frowned a little, saying, "I heard him telling Crow yesterday that he had done all he could. He said things didn't look so good."

As Bud, Kaz, and Brinda gave a collective, somber sigh, Shiloh added, "But if anyone can help him, my grandfather can."

Thinking of Bryce reminded Shiloh of the previous morning's conversation, so he asked, "Did you guys sneak over to Haines' place to look around last night?"

Brinda sneered. "We planned to, but most of us weren't able to get out."

Kaz immediately went on the defense. "I told you Regina usually goes to bed early because she gets up early. For some reason she was up late last night. I can't help that."

Brinda rolled her eyes at Kaz and then looked at Bud. "My folks were up late, too," he answered with a shrug. "I want to

Shiloh's True Nature

go with you, Brinda, but if I can't get out, I can't."

Brinda huffed, "Well then, maybe we can try again to-night. Okay?"

Kaz raised his hands. "Okay."

After Bud did the same, Brinda turned to Shiloh with a smile and asked, "So? Have you changed your mind about coming along?"

Smiling slightly, Shiloh shook his head. "I seriously doubt I could get out undetected." He wasn't sure whether he could or couldn't sneak out, but he wasn't comfortable with the whole idea, and figured it was easier to make an excuse than to argue with Brinda.

As the afternoon slipped into evening, Shiloh left his friends at the lake and began the walk back to Doc's house. He was hungry and marched along at a brisk pace, but as he approached Saige's house, he slowed down, wondering about Bryce's condition. He recalled what Doc had said to Crow about Bryce's recovery and felt a little sad. *If the man who heals people with his touch said he had done all he could do and things didn't look so good, that doesn't sound promising,* Shiloh thought.

Slowly passing, Shiloh stared up at the house, feeling sadness wash over him. He shook his head, focusing on the road ahead, and told himself Bryce could still pull through. It was then Shiloh heard a sniffling noise coming from the area around the large, jagged rock by the house. He walked around the greenish-gray boulder and, like the other day, found a woman seated there. Also like the other day, he could not readily identify the person. There was again an ashen mane, but this time it was an almost silver color.

Harmony swept the hair from her face and turned to Shiloh with swollen, puffy eyes. "Bryce is gone," she announced, a look of despair in her eyes.

Shiloh felt like he had been punched in the stomach. Needing to sit, he flopped down with a thud next to Harmony. "I'm so sorry, Harmony," Shiloh said, pausing to watch the tears drip from Harmony's cheeks. "I wish I had never said anything in the bookstore the other day."

Harmony looked to Shiloh with a sniffle and asked, "What do you mean?"

Shiloh sighed and rubbed his forehead. "Your aunt told me that story about the Eternal Flame and how it was stolen. When she finished, I asked why someone didn't just go take it back. Bryce was there and seemed to agree. The next day he turned up injured." Harmony appeared as though she were going to say something, but before she could, Shiloh continued, "I don't know if that's how Bryce got hurt or if what I said had anything to do with it, but if I played any part, I'm sorry."

Harmony looked into Shiloh's eyes with a teary smile for a moment and then suddenly threw her arms around him. When she released him from the hug, Harmony said, "It wasn't your fault, Shiloh."

Shiloh felt slightly relieved that she didn't think so. He was unsure what to do or say, so he put his arm around her and she placed her head on his shoulder.

"They're planning to have a Funus for Bryce tonight. Will you be there?" Harmony asked with a sniffle.

Shiloh's True Nature

Shiloh remembered Crow telling him a Funus was a Movers' funeral rite and he replied, "Of course I will."

Shiloh and Harmony sat in silence, leaning on one another for comfort, until a woman's voice called out, "Harmony?"

"I'll be right there, Aunt Saige," she replied.

Shiloh walked Harmony to the door and gave her a hug good-bye before continuing down the road to Doc's place.

He couldn't stop thinking about the desolate look in Harmony's eyes. It was as if a lingering sadness walked beside him. Like Harmony, he could hardly believe it possible that Bryce was gone forever. *How could that be*, he wondered.

The more Shiloh thought about it, the angrier he became. He grew even more agitated by the fact that the only unpleasant memories he had of Fair Hill seemed to all stem from one person: Haines. Shiloh thought if it wasn't for him, none of this would have happened.

When he reached Doc's, he found Doc and Crow sitting in the rocking chairs on the front porch. He assumed from the somber looks on their faces they knew of Bryce's passing. Crow cleared his throat, stammering a bit. "Ah . . . Doc has just informed me. I don't know if you heard."

Shiloh answered, "I heard."

Crow nodded and hung his head, avoiding Shiloh's gaze.

Shiloh turned to Doc and asked, "So what happens now?"

Scratching his neck with a grim look, Doc said, "Well, after dinner, we're going to help Saige put together a Revenant for Bryce. Then later tonight we'll have a Funus."

Shiloh huffed and raised his voice, "Put together a Revenant? Have a Funus? That's not what I meant! Did Bryce get hurt trying to get back the Flame from Haines?"

Doc looked to Crow and then back to Shiloh with some hesitation. He then nodded. "We think so."

Shiloh's eyes widened with anger as he exclaimed, "You think so? Then why isn't anything being done about it?"

Doc sighed and answered, "I understand your agitation, Shiloh. Most of us believe Haines was involved somehow, but we have no real evidence. No one saw anything, so no one knows exactly what happened. There's not much that can be done for now."

Doc's answer did not calm Shiloh. "How can Haines get away with stealing the Flame? What gives him the right to take what isn't his?" Throwing his hands in the air, his questions poured out, "What is he doing with it? Why does he need it? I don't understand all of this."

Crow leaned forward and, in a low, calming voice, said, "Shiloh, no one is happy about the Flame's theft. Haines and his family have believed for years that they are the living descendants of the last Prime Mover. Believing so, they have always felt they had the right to do whatever they wanted with the Flame. Until recently, that meant nothing, because the Flame was left undisturbed in the center of town where it's supposed to be. But when Sam became the head of his family, he had ideas of his own."

Narrowing his eyes, Shiloh thought for a moment before asking, "What do you mean 'ideas of his own'?"

"Haines isn't like the rest of us, Shiloh," Doc answered. "He doesn't seem to care about the true nature of things. His only concern is how to use and exploit them, regardless of the consequences."

"I'm not sure I understand," Shiloh said, rubbing his forehead.

Doc sighed again and asked, "Do you remember our previous conversation about the Flame and where it's supposed to be?"

After Shiloh nodded, Doc continued. "By removing the Flame from its proper place, Haines has also taken away the protection it provided to the world."

Shiloh frowned. "Protection to the world?"

"Shiloh, the Flame is more precious than you know. It shields the entire world from much harm. Not the least of which is the presence of man," Doc answered.

Shiloh started to inquire what that meant, but Doc raised his hand, cutting him off. "People sometimes do things that damage the environment. The Flame balances those things out. So, like in the case of Haines, the Flame neutralizes poisoning of the land, water, and air in and outside of Fair Hill. By taking the Flame, Haines has compounded the problem, because if the Flame isn't in the Balloon, it adds to the environmental problems instead of repairing them. And it pains me to say this, but the world would be better off with the Flame extinguished than in the hands of that man."

Shiloh stared back and forth between Doc and Crow, genuinely disturbed by the scope of the problem. "Why would anyone do such an awful thing?"

The grim look returned to Doc's face as he answered, "I don't know, Shiloh. It could be that Haines doesn't believe in the power of the Flame, or he just doesn't care. It seems all he really cares about is the Flame's immense energy and how he can use it, regardless of what it does to the environment."

Shiloh grimaced and said, "That seems like all the more reason to take it back from him."

Doc nodded in agreement. "Most of the people in the town would agree with you, Shiloh. However, they're afraid."

"Afraid of what?" Shiloh asked.

"Of Haines," Crow said in disgust.

Shiloh looked to Doc, who said, "Haines is a very powerful Mover, Shiloh. Most of the people just try to stay out of his way."

Shiloh tilted his head, pondering everything he had just learned, and Doc added, "So, as you can see, while we're all upset about Bryce's passing, the problem here is much deeper than the passing of one young man."

July 28th

Just before midnight, Shiloh walked down the stairs into his grandfather's foyer. Doc emerged from the kitchen and asked, "Ready?"

Shiloh nodded and followed Doc out the front door. Stepping off the porch, Doc said, "Wait here while I get Peggy and Isis."

Shiloh nodded again, looking to the sky as Doc walked away.

It was a cloudless night and the heavens were dotted with countless twinkling stars. Shiloh took a deep breath and noticed the air had cooled down significantly from the day's heat. He thought if it were any other night, it would be wonderful to be outside, but not tonight.

A peculiar, swishing sound broke through the din of the singing insects, reminding Shiloh of something running through sand. He tried to imagine what sort of bug would make such a noise, but, before he could think of one, the source of the noise revealed itself as Crow rode out of the

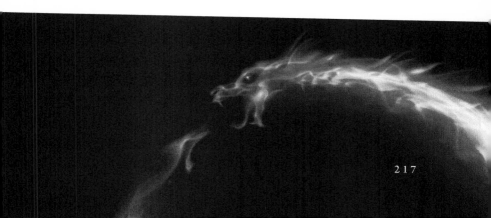

Shiloh's True Nature

darkness on a Prodigian Ostrich.

Shiloh gave a puzzled frown as Crow dismounted from the giant bird. Crow nodded to him and Shiloh asked, "Why didn't you just walk over?"

Crow looked away, fumbling with the reins of the ostrich, avoiding eye contact. "I want to travel alone tonight."

Shiloh was again puzzled, unsure what Crow meant by travel.

Wondering what was keeping Doc, Shiloh started toward the side of the house. He stopped when he saw a cart approaching from down the road. He was confused as to how Doc could have been coming from that direction. As the cart drew near, Shiloh saw it wasn't Doc, but Bud and his family.

Luther brought the cart to a stop in front of the house and Shiloh gave a little wave. Bud, Jace, and Martina all nodded, and Luther said, "Hello, Shiloh."

Shiloh tried to smile as he replied, "Hello, Mr. Miller."

"Where's your grandfather?" Luther asked with a subdued smile.

Before Shiloh could respond, Doc appeared from the side of the house, bringing the cart to a stop by the front porch. "Sorry for the delay. I had a little trouble getting the knot off the door," Doc said, rolling his eyes and smiling in Luther's direction.

Shiloh climbed into the cart and Doc snapped the reins to encourage them to move toward the center of town. As they gathered speed, Shiloh watched Crow race by on his ostrich. He still wasn't sure why Crow was riding the big bird when they needed to be airborne to reach their destination.

The answer came when the enormous bird jumped in the air, spread its long wings, and suddenly took flight.

Stunned to see the bird flying, Shiloh turned to Doc, ready to ask how this could be. However, before the question escaped his mouth, the horses also took flight, pulling the cart into the air behind them. Shiloh clung to his seat with his eyes closed as the familiar, tickling sensation he associated with flight rippled through his stomach.

Once they rose above the trees and leveled off, the feeling in Shiloh's abdomen dissipated and he opened his eyes to admire the view. He turned to face the rear of the cart, where Bud and his family flew along behind them. Looking down, he smiled when he saw a number of townsfolk popping out of the treetops in carts and on ostriches and beetles.

As they flew through the cool night air, Shiloh took a deep breath and looked up at the beautiful sky again. The waxing moon and twinkling stars almost made him forget why he was in flight. He felt almost guilty about enjoying the ride— if it weren't for a tragedy, he wouldn't even be in the air.

Doc watched Shiloh sigh and noted, "You're very quiet tonight."

Shiloh shrugged, saying nothing.

Doc smiled and said, "Just a few hours ago you were yelling at me, and now you're silent."

"The other day Crow told me about the Funus ceremony."

Doc waited for a moment and then asked, "Yeah. And?"

"I never thought I'd be attending one, ya know?" Shiloh said.

Doc nodded, "I know."

Shiloh's True Nature

Shiloh heard the midnight chime of the Stone Balloon in the distance, and the weight of the cart shifted forward. He gazed off to the side of the cart, toward a cornfield below, wondering if it was where he and Doc had taken to the skies to avoid the combines. As they descended, Shiloh saw some lights from Salem shimmering off the river's surface. He squinted at the far southern shoreline, trying to find his farm, but all he could see were the lights from Haines' immense factory.

As they drew closer to the river, Shiloh wondered where they were going. He scanned the area and noticed a small dark spot just offshore. It was a tiny island, hidden and inaccessible from land due to the reed-covered riverbank.

Doc set the cart down in a center clearing on the dark islet and steered it around, stopping it on the riverbank near some reeds. Following Doc's lead, those landing after them positioned their carts, big birds, or gigantic bugs along the edge of the islet, creating a semi-oval procession.

Doc walked to the rear of the cart, reaching into the bed and retrieving two long, thick sticks with white, fuzzy tips. Shiloh smiled, because they reminded him of gigantic cotton swabs. Doc then withdrew something from his pocket and touched it to the white tips, causing them to burst into flame.

Doc handed Shiloh one of the lit sticks and then proceeded from cart to cart, lighting the torches of those arriving. As Doc made his way around, Shiloh watched as the other Movers landed. He recognized almost everyone: Bud and his family, Kaz and Regina, Crow, and some other familiar faces from town. When he came across an unfamiliar couple,

Shiloh studied them. The man and woman were unusually large, with dark, thick heads of hair. When Brinda joined the couple, he assumed they were her guardians, Mina and Maximo.

Once Shiloh had surveyed the procession, his focus turned to an open space in front of Doc's cart, where a downward-sloping dirt ramp led straight into the river. He started to think back to what Crow had told him about Funus ceremonies, but he became distracted by the landing of one final cart. Instead of joining the outer oval, it swung around just past Doc's cart and came to a stop with its bed facing the dirt ramp.

The bed of the cart was covered with a bulging tarp. Shiloh stared at the covering, wondering what was hidden beneath. His gaze was eventually broken by Doc, who handed him a torch and said, "Hang on to this while I help them unload the Revenant."

Shiloh watched Doc detach the tarp from the side of the cart-bed and begin rolling it up and over to expose the contents underneath. The cart-bed contained an ornate, wooden vessel with beautiful carvings on it. Shiloh remembered Crow's description of half-boat/half-coffin and thought it was fitting.

As Doc, Crow, Luther, and Maximo lifted the Revenant off the cart, Shiloh peered at the vessel. He sensed something familiar about it, and watched as the men placed the Revenant at the mouth of the sloped dirt ramp. He let out a sad sigh, realizing the vessel contained the remains of Bryce.

When the men began stuffing the edges of the Revenant

Shiloh's True Nature

with straw, reeds, and some strange, wooden branches with hooked thorns, the cart moved toward the end of the procession. Wondering as to the whereabouts of Saige and Harmony, Shiloh gazed around the oval, but didn't see them anywhere. He craned his neck to and fro until he saw Harmony step out of the cart that had delivered the Revenant. Saige followed, and the two stood shoulder to shoulder in silence, staring at the Revenant.

Shiloh watched Saige and Harmony with a heavy heart. Saige's solemn look was matched only by Harmony's, which was fully evident from her silvery-gray hair, which she had pulled back out of her face into a ponytail. Shiloh wanted to go to her. He wanted to hold her hand, or put his arm around her, or do something to make her feel better, but he didn't. He doubted there was anything he could say or do to make her feel better about losing her cousin.

Shiloh's thoughts cleared as the men walked away from the Revenant and returned to their families. After handing torches to Saige and Harmony, Doc walked to the Revenant, clearing his throat before speaking.

"We are gathered here on Peas Isle for the Funus of one of our fellow Movers. You know that I'm not long-winded . . ." Doc paused, allowing a few people to chuckle. ". . . at least, I try not to be. You also know it's not our way to mourn one's passing. We are different. We celebrate their passing into the next life by reflecting on their achievements and showing gratitude for having been able to share this life with them."

Doc again paused for a moment, placing his hand on the tip of the Revenant. "However, in the case of this young man,

Bryce, I can only say that he was taken from us far too early. We will never know how much greatness he held inside of him." Doc's eyes welled and he placed the side of his hand to his mouth as he cleared his throat again. "Bryce... Bryce was fair and kind, helpful and grateful, and he always... always beat me at Atmosphere," he added, mustering a smile and eliciting a few chuckles.

Doc motioned to Saige, who came forward and tossed her torch onto the Revenant. Doc gave the Revenant a little push, and the vessel began to slide slowly into the water. Everyone followed Saige's lead, coming forward to toss their torches into the vessel, except for Shiloh. He wasn't sure if he was supposed to, since he was not a Mover.

Shiloh stood waiting as the others dispersed, until there was only one other torch still lit besides his own. It was in the hand of Harmony. She looked to Shiloh with an ever-so-slight smile and nodded her head toward the Revenant. He wasn't sure, but assumed she wanted him to come forward. He stepped toward the vessel, Harmony matching his pace. They met side by side in front of the Revenant, and simultaneously tossed their torches. Doc then said, "As we commit this Revenant and these remains to the waters, I can think of nothing in the world more true to say, Bryce will be missed."

The Revenant burned rapidly, the smoke carrying a strong, sweet odor through the air, making Shiloh sniffle. As the fire died, the vessel all but disappeared, Shiloh and Harmony parted. Shiloh returned to Doc's cart, thinking the ceremony was over. However, he found that everyone's attention lingered on what was left of the flames consuming

Shiloh's True Nature

the Revenant.

When the vessel finally disappeared, the islet went dark and Shiloh climbed into the cart. He waited for Doc to join him, but realized each person was still focused on the spot where the Revenant had burned away. Finally, after a collective sigh, Doc said, "I hope all of you will be joining me back at the Deer Park to celebrate Bryce."

Doc watched for a moment as everyone prepared to depart. He then stepped up into the cart and asked, "Ready?"

Shiloh nodded and, before he knew it, they were once again climbing into the night sky. As they ascended, Shiloh glanced back over his shoulder for a final look at the tiny island, the river, and Haines' factory in the distance. He had a lingering feeling of injustice surrounding Bryce's passing.

On the flight back to town, Shiloh was lost in his thoughts, prompting Doc to ask, "Is everything all right?"

Shiloh started to answer, but before the words left his mouth, he broke into a sneezing fit. When the sneezes finally subsided, Shiloh said, "I can still smell the stench of the fire. I can almost taste it. What was that odor it gave off?"

Doc smiled and said, "That scent came from the burning acacia wood."

"Was that those branches with the thorns?" Shiloh asked.

Doc nodded. "Yes, it's always been an important part of the Funus. It burns very hot and very fast. More importantly, the wood symbolizes purity, vitality, and the endurance of the soul."

Shiloh sniffed and asked, "That smelly wood means all that?"

Doc chuckled. "Well, no. But that's the meaning many have attached to it."

Upon their arrival back in town, Doc, Shiloh, and everyone from the Funus gathered at the Deer Park. Doc joined Saige at a center table on the rear deck with Luther, Martina, Crow, and some others. Shiloh stood listening as everyone around him sat discussing fond memories of Bryce. He was somewhat stunned by the upbeat mood, and didn't feel comfortable sitting at the table with the adults.

When Luther began to tell a story about how Bryce solved one of his puzzles, Shiloh knew it was time to escape. He looked around, trying to locate Harmony, but she was nowhere in sight. He spotted his friends a few tables away in a dark corner of the deck, so he walked over to join them.

The mood at the kids' table was much more subdued. Bud, Brinda, Jace, and Kaz weren't talking, but quietly eating some rainbow-colored puffballs. Shiloh took a seat, grabbed one of the sticky confections, and began to look it over.

"What is this?" he asked, rolling the light, colorful treat around in his hand.

Brinda smiled slightly and said, "It's a rice-puff. It was one of Bryce's favorites. Give it a squeeze."

Shiloh frowned at her, but then closed his hand around the puff. With a crunch, the ball disintegrated into a sticky dust.

The table went silent again, and Shiloh looked toward the center table, where he made eye contact with Doc. Doc smiled at him, but Shiloh only managed a little grin before turning his attention to the dark field off the deck. He was

Shiloh's True Nature

staring down into the darkness at nothing in particular, when the empty chair next to him moved.

Shiloh turned and watched Doc take the seat next to him. Doc smiled at everyone and grabbed a rice-puff. "You know, I can remember the very day Bryce arrived in Fair Hill. He was smiling from ear to ear as he sat here on the deck eating one of these things. When I introduced myself, he spit a mouthful of rainbow-colored crumbs all over me trying to say hello," Doc noted, letting out a little laugh.

Everyone chuckled, except for Shiloh. Looking at him, Doc said, "You should try one."

Shiloh shook his head with a frown. "No thanks."

Doc stared at Shiloh for a moment, but his gaze was broken when Bud said, "I didn't know you played Atmosphere, Doc."

Doc smiled. "Oh, yes. I really enjoy it, but I don't get to play as much as I used to."

He then paused for a moment before saying, "It was unbelievable how good Bryce was at that game. I don't think anyone ever beat him. I never saw anyone come close."

Brinda pointed to Shiloh and said, "Shiloh came close."

"Really?" Doc's eyes widened as he turned to Shiloh.

Kaz sat up and said, "Yeah. Took him into the fifth round."

Doc grinned and said, "That's amazing. Well, this I have to see."

Shiloh sat staring at the table, disengaged from the conversation. Doc tapped him on the shoulder and asked, "What do you say? Are you up for it?"

Shrugging his shoulders, Shiloh sighed and said, "I guess

so."

He followed Doc and his friends as they eagerly marched away from the Deer Park for the Arcadia. Shiloh's apathy was evident as he trailed behind, with more interest in the low-lying mist covering the road than their intended destination.

Along the way, the reminiscence continued. "You know, it seemed to me, once Bryce jumped ahead in Atmosphere, no one could catch up," Doc said.

Bud and Kaz nodded in agreement. Brinda begged to differ, saying, "Bryce jumped ahead of Shiloh, but it didn't bother him, because he nearly won."

Doc smiled and gazed around looking for Shiloh, but didn't see him. He frowned slightly as he looked back over his shoulder finding Shiloh lagging behind. When they made eye contact, Doc smiled again, but Shiloh quickly averted his gaze into the distance.

As they approached, Shiloh thought the Arcadia's normally lit-up appearance seemed a little dimmer than usual. Once inside, they headed straight for the Atmosphere table in the rear. When they reached the table, Bud walked to the far end and pressed the button to begin the game. "Would you like the first game, Doc?" he asked.

As the round, black table turned from nothingness to a grassy meadow in a flash of white light, Doc shook his head with a smile and said, "Thank you, Bud. But I think I'd like to see Shiloh play."

Shiloh's eyes widened at Doc's suggestion, but he decided not to argue and stepped up to the table. As the tiny, blue river flowed across the center of the table and the ten pock-

Shiloh's True Nature

ets appeared, Bud asked, "Do you want to roll the Earth or the Moon?"

"Moon," Shiloh answered, thinking the insipid, hollow spheres would match his mood.

The five little Moon-shaped spheres fell on the table in front of Shiloh and he reached down, taking one in each hand. Bud smiled at Shiloh. "You ready?"

"Just do it," Shiloh said with an irritated sigh.

The grassy board suddenly lit up and Shiloh waited for Bud to make his first roll. When Bud released one of his Earth-shaped spheres, Shiloh immediately and forcefully threw the two moon spheres he had been clutching.

Doc, Kaz, and Brinda stood in awe as Shiloh's spheres slammed into Bud's and ricocheted into two pockets on Bud's side of the table. Two loud beeps sounded as Bud's Earth sphere slowly rolled back to him, coming to a stop right where he had released it. With a stunned look on his face, Bud quickly grabbed the sphere and threw it again. Shiloh grabbed two more and hurled them across the table the very moment Bud released, duplicating the previous result.

Kaz made a noise like all the air had escaped from his body and Brinda cackled at Shiloh's play. Doc eyed Shiloh with a frown, waiting to see what happened next. Shiloh had no idea how he had done it. He only knew he didn't really want to play, only wanted the game to be over. Bud was dumbfounded and grabbed two of his spheres, hoping to catch up somehow.

As soon as Bud released his two spheres, Shiloh flung his final one and it bounced off of each of Bud's, rolling into the final open pocket on the far end of the table. The loud buzzer sounded, the board went black, and Brinda let out a roar of laughter.

"Aw man, Shiloh. That is unbelievable. I don't think Bryce himself could have beaten you tonight," Kaz said, shaking his head.

"I guess we'll never know. Will we?" Shiloh said with a look of sadness.

Brinda excitedly moved to the end of the table, pushing the still stunned Bud out of the way. "It's my turn!"

Her excitement, though, was not enough to keep Shiloh from duplicating his success. Every roll Shiloh made was perfect, and before Brinda knew it, his spheres were resting in the pockets on her side of the table. With a look of confusion on her face, Brinda threw her hands into the air. "How are you doing that?"

Shiloh shrugged nonchalantly and shook his head. He then looked to Kaz, wondering if he wanted to be beaten too. Kaz shook his head, backing away from the board, indicating he wanted no part of Shiloh's Atmosphere aggression.

"You know what?" Brinda smiled at everyone and said, "I want to play something where I can win some tokens. I want that stovepipe hat."

Kaz rolled his eyes and said, "Oh, again with the hat."

The kids started away from the table, Bud pausing to look at Shiloh. "You coming?"

Doc raised his hand and said, "He'll catch up with you in a few minutes."

Bud smiled at Doc and walked off to join Brinda and Kaz.

Shiloh's True Nature

"That was a pretty amazing display, Shiloh," Doc noted.

Shiloh frowned. "What's so amazing about it? It's just a stupid game."

Doc huffed and said, "That's where you're wrong. It's not just some stupid game. Look around."

Shiloh gazed around at all of the fascinating and unique games he'd seen previously, but wasn't sure what Doc meant.

Doc continued, "Every game in the place is designed for Movers to sharpen their abilities."

"If you say so." Shiloh shrugged.

Doc stepped to the far end of the table and said, "How about one more game?"

"Fine," Shiloh said, rolling his eyes.

Doc pressed the button and the table came to life. As the sunshine began to spread across the miniature landscape, Shiloh reached down and clutched two spheres. He looked to Doc, waiting for him to make a move. However, Doc seemed to be doing the same.

Shiloh shifted his focus from the table to Doc's face and found Doc staring back at him. Shiloh quickly looked down at the table with a frown. As the table moved past its peak of brightness, Shiloh wondered what Doc was doing. Why wasn't he rolling? He kept thinking. Suddenly, a long, loud beep echoed and the table went dark.

Shiloh raised his hands in the air and said, "Are we playing or what?"

"We're playing," Doc said with a grin.

Shiloh frowned again as daylight swept over the table for the second round. He looked over the newly emerged little hills and valleys in the table as he waited for Doc's roll, but it never came. Losing his patience, Shiloh threw one of his spheres across the table. At the moment of Shiloh's release, Doc tossed one of his Earth spheres, hitting the moon sphere and knocking it back down to Shiloh's side of the table. Shiloh tried to throw two of his spheres at the same time, but Doc threw two of his and successfully defended his side of the board.

With increasing agitation, Shiloh began to think of how to combat Doc's strategy. Smirking as an idea popped into his head, he threw one of his spheres. Doc responded in kind, but Shiloh immediately and forcefully threw another of his. Doc successfully defended the first of Shiloh's rolls, but the second managed to drop into one of the pockets with a beep.

A second beep then sounded and Shiloh looked around frowning. While Shiloh was aggressively rolling his second shot, Doc had lazily rolled one of his spheres down to Shiloh's end and into one of the pockets. Shiloh tried some more trickery, but the result was always the same. If he managed to sink a sphere, he left himself open for Doc to do the same.

The stalemate continued on through the round, and for two more after that. Shiloh's play became increasingly more aggressive and cunning as he began to incorporate the obstacles on the table into his approach. However, by the beginning of the fifth round, he was agitated by his lack of success.

Seeing Shiloh's irritation, Doc tried to engage him in conversation while they played. "The reason I said it was amazing that you were able to compete with Bryce is because he had a unique adaptability that was perfectly suited for the

Shiloh's True Nature

complex, environmental changes of the game. That's why no one ever came close to beating him. The fact that you were able to play him so well, and nearly win, is unbelievable," Doc noted, eyeing the table and defending against Shiloh's aggressive throws.

Shiloh sneered at Doc's comment and a loud beep sounded. He looked down at the table, realizing victory was within his grasp. Eight pockets had been filled, four on each side of the table.

"It's not unbelievable," Shiloh said, grabbing his final sphere. "Everyone plays the game wrong."

"Really? How so?" Doc chuckled.

Shiloh looked Doc in the eye, a tight grip on his sphere, and said, "You all play to win the game . . . instead of playing to keep your opponent from winning. So if your opponent is better, you're always going to lose."

As he finished speaking, Shiloh kept eye contact with Doc and quickly threw his sphere, hoping Doc would be distracted by his gaze. Doc never broke eye contact with Shiloh, but reacted by throwing his final sphere in defense. Doc's sphere hit Shiloh's, causing both of them to slowly roll onto Shiloh's side of the table.

As Shiloh watched the spheres, hoping they would stop, Doc said, "So what you're saying is, playing the game with aggression causes misjudgment and carelessness."

Doc's sphere then dropped into the final open pocket on Shiloh's side of the table. Shiloh bit his lip, sighing as the long, loud buzzer sounded and the board went blank. Rubbing his forehead, Shiloh stared down at the vacant table, contemplating his loss.

Doc cleared his throat as he came around to Shiloh's side of the table. "I suppose that lesson works in life, as well as in games. Fortunately, Atmosphere is just a game." Shiloh looked up at Doc and sighed again. Patting him on the shoulder, Doc said, "I'm going to head back to the Deer Park. You should try to have some fun with your friends."

Shiloh forced a little smile and nodded. "Okay."

Shiloh watched Doc walk away and then began looking for his friends. He found them at the Waterfowl table, tightly gripping plastic water pistols to push their fowl to victory. "I've got to win. I only need a few more tokens and that hat is mine," Brinda announced.

Kaz responded, "You're not going to win this time, cheater."

Brinda scoffed at Kaz's comment, while Bud laughed.

Shiloh stared down at the rectangular box, with its tiny lake, shoreline, and trees, to find the game remarkably close. He was stunned, considering Brinda's margin of victory the last time they played. When the birds reached the far end of the table, a noisy series of beeps echoed and Kaz threw his arms in the air. "In your face, Brinda!" Kaz howled.

Brinda rolled her eyes. "Yeah, yeah. You've beaten me once out of a hundred times."

"Who cares? I win! You lose!" Kaz roared with laughter.

A rapid succession of clanging noises rang out from the end of the table and Kaz strutted over to retrieve his pile of shiny little coins. "So what are you going to buy?" Bud asked with a smile.

Shiloh's True Nature

Kaz looked toward Brinda with a wide grin. "I don't know. But you can be absolutely, positively certain it won't be a stupid, rainbow-colored stovepipe hat."

Brinda gave a backhanded motion for Kaz to go away. Grinning widely, Kaz shook his winnings in Brinda's direction and then walked away with Bud.

Brinda turned to Shiloh, saying, "First, a Funus. Now I lose tokens to Kaz. This is a really crummy way to start my birthday celebration."

"Today is your birthday?"

Brinda sighed and responded, "No. Tomorrow, the twenty-ninth, is."

Shiloh nodded. She paused for a moment, smiling at Shiloh. "You'll be coming to the party tomorrow, won't you?" Brinda asked.

"Yeah, of course," Shiloh confirmed, forcing a smile.

"Great. It wouldn't be any fun if you weren't there," Brinda added with a sly grin.

Shiloh's brow furrowed and he started to question her meaning, but before he could, Bud and Kaz returned.

"So what did you get?" Brinda inquired.

Kaz crumpled the top of the bag he was carrying and said, "Just a bunch of little things I've been wanting but was never able to get before because I always play games with people who cheat."

Bud snorted and Brinda laughed, saying, "Let's go play something else before I punch him."

Bud, Brinda, and Kaz started to move off, but Shiloh stood still, staring toward the front of the Arcadia. Bud noticed Shiloh hadn't followed and looked back, "You coming, Shiloh?"

Shiloh didn't answer, his gaze fixated on something. The others followed his stare to determine the source of his distraction and found a young man with short, brassy-colored hair in the distance. It was Haines' son, Junior. He chatted boisterously with a couple of people as he entered the Arcadia.

Shiloh continued staring at Junior, until they made eye contact. Junior's smile faded into a frown before he looked away, walking out of view. Bud patted Shiloh on the back and said, "What do you say we go find something fun to play?"

Shiloh sneered slightly and asked, "Are you guys still planning to go over to Haines' place to have a look around?"

Brinda, Bud, and Kaz looked at one another for a moment. Brinda then said, "We were thinking about it. Why? Do you want to come along?"

Shiloh grinned at his friends. "I'm thinking about it. Let me know when you plan to go."

"Cool," Brinda said with a smile.

"C'mon, let's go play something," Bud suggested.

Shiloh shook his head. "You guys have fun. I think I'm going to head back to the Deer Park."

After saying good-bye, Shiloh started back to the Deer Park alone. Along the way, he began feeling tired and realized he had never been up so late before. Thanks to his father, he had always kept farmer's hours: early to bed and early to rise.

With every step he took, Shiloh became more inclined to return to Doc's to go to sleep. When he eventually reached

Shiloh's True Nature

the Deer Park, Shiloh continued past with no intention of stopping. However, he took notice of a young woman with long, brown hair sitting alone, reading by the faint light emanating from the Stone Balloon. He wasn't sure who it was at first, but then realized it was Harmony.

A smile came to his lips as he approached her. "I'm glad to see your hair is no longer gray."

Harmony flinched with wide eyes, startled by Shiloh's sudden appearance. When she realized who it was, she let out a relieved sigh and smiled. "Oh . . . hello, Shiloh."

Shiloh started to speak, but his eyes widened as he saw Harmony's hair transform from the dark brown to light blond right before his eyes. Harmony chuckled slightly and asked, "What?"

Shiloh pointed to her hair and mumbled, "Your hair did that thing it does."

Harmony placed her hand to her mouth, covering a little smile, and closed the book she was reading.

Shiloh cleared his throat and said, "So why are you out here reading?" He paused and tilted his head to see the title of the book in Harmony's lap. "*Hearts*? Is that what it's called?" he asked.

Harmony nodded and he asked, "Why are you reading *Hearts*, instead of 'celebrating' with everyone else?"

Harmony tilted her head down with a frown. "I don't feel much like celebrating."

Shiloh nodded. "Me neither."

"Besides, they're not really celebrating," Harmony said, shaking her head.

"They're not?" Shiloh asked.

"No. They just tell themselves that to avoid the fact that Bryce is gone and he's not coming back," Harmony said.

Shiloh nodded with a sad smile.

He noticed the area had begun to brighten, and he heard some ticking and clicking sounds coming from overhead. He looked up, searching for the source of the noise and saw a luminous pulse growing from the Stone Balloon. "You might want to cover your ears," Harmony said.

"What for?" Shiloh asked, looking at Harmony.

The pulsing light grew more intense and Harmony placed her hands over her ears. Shiloh did the same just a moment before the Stone Balloon gave off a thunderous, vibrating chime. When the chime started to dissipate, Shiloh withdrew his hands. However, he replaced them when he saw that Harmony still had hers in place. A second chime pulsed out, followed by a few more.

When it was clear the chimes had stopped, they dropped their hands and Shiloh said, "I guess this is not the place to be standing at the top of the hour, huh?"

Harmony frowned, looking up at the Stone Balloon.

"What's the matter?" Shiloh asked.

"I've never heard it chime so loudly before," Harmony noted, still staring upward.

Looking up, he said, "Hmmm. Well, we are right underneath of it." Shiloh stared at Harmony, trying to think of something to say. He blurted out, "You know, I've never stayed up all night like this before."

"I haven't either," Harmony responded. "If it takes a Fu-

Shiloh's True Nature

nus for me to be awake at this hour, I hope I'm never up this late again."

Shiloh nodded. "I agree." He paused before adding, "Perhaps we could do something life-affirming to put this night behind us."

Harmony squinted with a hint of a smile and asked, "What do you have in mind?"

"Maybe a simple pleasure, like seeing the birth of a new day, might do the trick."

Harmony blushed, realizing he remembered her words. She nodded at Shiloh and he raised his index finger, saying, "Wait here."

Harmony watched as Shiloh quickly ran over to the Deer Park and began taking things off one of the tables. He grabbed a tablecloth, a basket full of fruit, a loaf of bread, a carafe, and some glasses before returning to her. Smiling, Harmony stood as Shiloh approached, and they set off down the road.

When they reached their secluded, sunrise spot, the surroundings began to lighten as Shiloh laid out the tablecloth by the embankment. He stretched out his hand, inviting Harmony to take a seat. He joined her and watched as Harmony set her book down to wait for the event.

Shiloh was able to see the book better this time and he marveled at the radiant cover. It had a depiction of two sparkling hearts of pink and red, which intertwined and melded into one. "What is your book about?" Shiloh asked.

Harmony pushed the book aside and said, "It's probably nothing you'd be interested in."

"What makes you say that?" Shiloh inquired frowning.

Harmony sighed and with a little smile said, "It's about how each Mover has a complimentary counterpart. How their hearts become inextricably entwined once they have found one another."

Shiloh scowled and thought for a moment. Harmony blushed and explained, "It's about love. How it connects and transforms Movers in ways they never imagined."

"Ah, I see." Shiloh nodded with a smile.

The blush still evident on her face, Harmony began to fidget, moving the book out of sight and adjusting her position several times trying to get comfortable. When she finally came to a rest, Shiloh noticed a unique, bluish-green glow over her shoulder off in the distance. It wasn't in the direction from which the sun would be rising, but around the far side of the hill.

Shiloh pointed and asked, "What is that?"

Harmony looked over her shoulder and shook her head. "I've seen it before, but I have no idea what it is."

Shiloh continued staring toward the glow, wondering about its source, until Harmony tapped his leg and said, "It's starting."

As Shiloh looked toward the horizon, Harmony reached down and took his hand, folding her fingers in between his with a squeeze. Shiloh smiled and glanced down at their interlocked hands. He then panned up to Harmony's face, where he could see the rising sun's reflection sparkling in her teary eyes.

"It's beautiful, isn't it?" Harmony said, as her eyes welled.

Shiloh continued staring into Harmony's eyes, marveling

Shiloh's True Nature

at their exquisite shimmer and answered, "Yes. Very beautiful."

He then kissed the back of Harmony's hand before turning toward the sunrise.

After the sun's ascension above the horizon, and a short visit from the okapi and cassowary, Shiloh and Harmony were exhausted. Taking Harmony by the hand, Shiloh quietly led them back through the dimly lit path.

When they reached Harmony's house, Shiloh didn't want to let go of her hand. He wondered when he would see her next and asked, "Are you going to Brinda's birthday party?"

"I don't know Brinda very well, but I'm sure I'll end up there." Shiloh smiled and Harmony chuckled, adding, "It's a small town, you know."

Shiloh laughed. "Yes, it is."

Shiloh reluctantly let go of Harmony's hand and watched as she walked up the porch steps to the house. Harmony looked back with a little smile and waved good-bye before she entered the door. Once she was out of sight, Shiloh smiled up at the archway, thinking about how he had climbed it just a few days prior. When he remembered why he had climbed up, the smile drained from his face.

Two things continually ran through Shiloh's mind as he walked back to Doc's house; the first was how he had been awake for almost 24 hours straight and desperately needed sleep. The second was the reason he had been up so long. Being in Harmony's presence had eased his agitation about Bryce's death temporarily, but the walk coupled with his exhaustion brought the anger back.

When he arrived at Doc's, Shiloh found Doc and Crow seated in the rocking chairs on the porch. Shiloh stopped at the foot of the porch and stared up at them for a moment. No one spoke, so Shiloh started toward the door. Before he could go inside, Doc leaned forward in his chair and said, "You need to let it go, son."

Shiloh stopped, holding the door open, and asked, "Let what go?"

"The anger that's eating at you," Doc said, pointing toward Shiloh's torso. "It's bad for your radiance."

Shiloh scoffed. "I'll give it a try."

Shiloh started into the house, but paused in the doorway. "Hey, you know what? Maybe you could help me let go of the anger that's eating at me by telling me how the injustice isn't eating at you."

Doc and Crow looked to Shiloh with wide eyes, seemingly caught off guard by the comment. Shiloh waited for a moment, but when neither answered, he said, "No? Okay then. Good night. Or I guess I should say, good morning." With that said, Shiloh headed to bed.

July 29th

Shiloh slowly opened his eyes to let them adjust to the sunlit bedroom. He squinted, noticing a white, gold-trimmed envelope lying next to him on the bed. He yawned and picked up the envelope to see it was addressed: 'To: Shiloh–c/o Doc'. In the upper-right corner, someone had scribbled, 'It's tonight.'

Curious about the letter's contents, Shiloh tore it open. It was an invitation which read, "You are cordially invited to witness the escalation of Brinda on the anniversary of her Ascension. Her departure from the thirteenth into the fourteenth year of existence begins precisely at 7:47 P.M. on July 29th. Festivities will be held at Luther and Martina Miller's by the lake. An early arrival is highly recommended, so as not to miss escalation."

A droll smile came to his lips as the slumber wore off and he realized the letter was an invitation to Brinda's birthday party. He looked around the room, wondering what time it was, when suddenly the Stone Balloon chimed in the dis-

Shiloh's True Nature

tance. He sat up to wait for more chimes, but none came. Confused, he looked toward the window and found bright midday sunshine. He realized just how disoriented he was from staying up so late after the Funus. He had lost an entire day in a blur of eating and sleeping.

Determined to make the most of the day, Shiloh quickly dressed and went downstairs with the party invitation. He entered the kitchen to find something to eat and found a note lying on the table. 'Shiloh Van Winkle, I have some errands to run. I'll be back by five for dinner and to prepare for the party.'

Shiloh poured himself a bowl of pillowed wheat and began eating. As he chewed, he gazed back and forth between the invitation and Doc's note. He realized he needed to find Brinda a birthday gift, but didn't have a lot of time. He quickly finished his cereal, grabbed an apple, and ran out the door.

As soon as he exited the house, Shiloh ran into an oppressive wall of heat. The journey into town found him ducking into every store he came across just to avoid the stifling air. He even walked into stores where he had no chance of finding a present for Brinda simply to move out of the heat temporarily.

Going from store to store, Shiloh saw many interesting things, but nothing seemed appropriate. He eventually concluded he wasn't familiar enough with Brinda to know what she would like. When he passed the Arcadia, Shiloh smiled to himself, thinking he did know one thing she wanted. However, he just walked by, because he knew he didn't have nearly enough tokens to buy her a silly stovepipe hat.

When Shiloh approached the one place he had avoided all afternoon—Jeremiah's bookstore—he hesitated. Since the Funus, the thought of being in Saige's presence made him uncomfortable, and he didn't want to go inside. He had visited almost every other store in town, and Jeremiah's seemed like his last shot. He told himself Harmony might be there and she could help him find something for Brinda.

Shiloh's hesitation ended when the Stone Balloon gave off four loud clangs. He walked up the stairs and opened the door, scanning the store for Harmony. He saw Saige down one of the aisles and immediately moved out of her line of sight. Unfortunately, Harmony was nowhere to be found, so he turned to exit. However, he found himself face to face with Saige.

"Hello, Shiloh," Saige said with a smile.

Shiloh avoided eye contact, looking down and saying, "Hi."

Saige squinted and asked, "Is there something I can help you with?"

"Ah... I... ah... need to get something for a friend," Shiloh stammered.

Tilting her head, Saige said, "Okay. Well, what does your friend like?"

Shiloh scratched the side of his cheek. "I'm not really sure. I don't know her that well yet."

Saige grinned at Shiloh with a raised eyebrow and asked, "So you're shopping for a young lady, are you?"

Confused by Saige's look, Shiloh answered, "Ah, yeah."

"Hmmm. Well, let's see what we can find," Saige said, leading him down an aisle toward the back of the store.

Shiloh followed along until Saige stopped walking, extending her hand toward the top shelf of one of the cases. "There are many books in this section your friend might be interested in."

A book levitated from the shelf and flew into Saige's hand. She turned the book toward Shiloh to show him the title, *The Young Movers Guide to Complex Emotional Issues*. Shiloh winced and recoiled, waving his hands with revulsion.

Seeing his reaction, Saige said, "No. Okay," and returned the book, scanning the shelves for another title.

Looking past Saige, Shiloh became intrigued by a doorway at the end of the aisle opening into an area of the store he had not seen before. He walked past Saige to look in the doorway. The area contained a number of long, glass display cases filled with distinctive items. There were rings, necklaces, bookmarks, and many other interesting little items, but none of them seemed like an appropriate gift for him to give to Brinda.

Shiloh noticed a unique display in the back corner. Floating in midair was a hexagonal, glass display case with gold edging. Inside was a beautiful, levitating crystal tree, slowly rotating. Hanging from the tree's branches were colorful pairs of wristlets.

As he stood admiring the display's contents, Saige appeared over his shoulder and said, "They're friendship bracelets."

She stepped around Shiloh and opened the display doors, which stopped the crystal tree from rotating. Shiloh moved a bit closer, admiring the colorful patterns and intricate weaving of the bracelets. "These are really cool," he noted, his eyes moving from pair to pair. He then pointed to a multihued bracelet toward the top of the tree. "I like those."

Saige squinted and pursed her lips. "Hmm. I don't know if that's something you want to give someone." She paused for a moment, then asked, "Is this a special friend?"

Shiloh was fixated on the bracelet, not really listening, but answered, "Uh, sure."

She tilted her head with wide eyes and said, "Okay."

As Saige began to remove the pair from the display, Shiloh frowned. "I only need one."

"Friendship bracelets always come in pairs," she said with a smile.

Shiloh shrugged his shoulders. "Okay."

On their way back to the counter, Saige tried several times to make eye contact with Shiloh. He deliberately focused elsewhere whenever he felt her glance, causing her to ask, "Is something bothering you, Shiloh?"

He raised his eyebrows, shaking his head without looking in her direction. Saige frowned and continued staring, until they reached the counter, where she asked, "Are you sure there's nothing on your mind? You've seemed uncomfortable since you walked in here."

Not answering, Shiloh hung his head and sighed. After Saige wrapped the bracelets in a small box, she placed her index finger under his chin, and lifted Shiloh's head. "Shiloh, look at me."

Shiloh saw she had a sad little smile on her face as she

Shiloh's True Nature

said, "Harmony told me you felt bad about what you said in the store the other day, and there is something you need to know..." Saige paused for a moment to find the right words before continuing, "We all make our own choices in life. Others may influence us, but every decision is ultimately our own. Your question about why someone hadn't simply gone and taken back the flame is one that many people in this town have asked, including my son. Asking a simple question does not make you responsible for his actions or the outcome. So you need not feel responsible for Bryce."

Shiloh didn't know what to say; he just gave her a subdued smile.

Saige placed the little box into a bag and handed it to Shiloh. He patted his pockets and she gave him a funny look. "What are you doing?"

"I don't know. I guess I still haven't gotten used to not paying for things," Shiloh said, rubbing his forehead. She chuckled slightly at his comment and he waved the bag in his hand, saying, "Thank you."

Upon exiting the bookstore, Shiloh heard the Stone Balloon chiming again and knew he was running late. Needing to return to Doc's house for dinner, he quickened his pace through the late-afternoon heat. He walked along, occasionally wiping the sweat from his brow, until he came to the Deer Park, where he saw Bud.

"Hey, Shiloh," Bud said, stepping off the deck and into Shiloh's path.

"Hey, Bud." Shiloh hesitated before stopping.

Bud smiled. "You're coming to the party, right?"

"Yeah, but I've got to get home to eat and get ready," Shiloh answered, slowly sidestepping Bud to continue on his way.

"Oh, okay. Don't forget the start time is 7:47. You don't want to be late," Bud added, watching Shiloh walk backward away from him.

Shiloh continued backing away with a wave, saying, "I won't."

When he arrived at Doc's house, Shiloh walked up the porch steps, slowing to take in the heavenly smell wafting through the open porch door. He closed his eyes and thought of how, after a hard day of work on the farm, he loved the smell of his mother's cooking emanating from the house. This was the first time he had thought about home in a couple of days. He continued into the house, marching directly into the kitchen, where he found Doc cooking dinner.

"You're finally awake I see. Are you hungry?" Doc asked, seeing Shiloh enter.

Shiloh smiled and nodded, taking a seat at the kitchen table.

"So where have you been?" Doc asked, continuing to cook.

"I was just going to ask you the same thing," Shiloh answered.

Doc smiled without looking at Shiloh. "Oh, I had some things I needed to do and left early." He paused for a moment to stir a pot, then asked, "And you?"

Shiloh answered, "Oh, I had some things I needed to do and left late."

Shiloh's True Nature

With a slight grin, Doc looked at Shiloh out the corner of his eye. "Something on your mind, Shiloh?"

"Well, now that you mention it, there is. Have you heard from my parents yet?" Shiloh asked, eyebrows raised.

Doc's expression changed into a frown. "As a matter of fact, I have."

Shiloh perked up in his chair. "You have?"

Doc nodded. "Yes. Well, to be precise, I spoke to your father. That's where I went this morning."

Hearing this caused Shiloh to rattle off a series of questions. "How are they? Where were they the other day? How's the farm?"

"They're fine, Shiloh," Doc answered with a frown. "But there is something I want to talk to you about."

"What's that?" Shiloh's eyes narrowed.

Doc sighed, starting to answer, but abruptly stopped, looking toward the back porch.

Shiloh impatiently raised his hands. "So?"

The screen door to the back porch opened and Crow walked in. Shiloh smiled to himself, thinking it was funny how Crow always seemed to show up right when it was time to eat. Crow nodded to Shiloh as he entered, then turned to Doc with an odd look on his face.

Shiloh scowled and sat up in his chair, wondering what was on Crow's mind. Doc turned to Shiloh and said, "I need to have a word with my friend here. Perhaps you could go upstairs and get cleaned up for the party. I'll call you when dinner is ready."

Shiloh raised his hands in frustration. "But . . ."

Doc immediately cut him off. "Please, Shiloh. It's very important that I speak to Crow. We'll continue our conversation later."

Shiloh rolled his eyes, rose from his chair, and left the kitchen. He stomped up the staircase, stopping when he reached the top. Squatting down, he tried to overhear what was so important. He turned his head left and right, trying to listen to the conversation. He could barely make out Crow asking, "So you went over?"

"First thing this morning," Doc replied.

Shiloh waited intently for the conversation to continue, but he flinched when something rubbed against the back of his legs. He looked around to find not one, but both of his cats staring at him. They took turns rubbing against him and purring loudly. He attempted to quiet them by holding them down, but his touch only made them purr louder.

He was about to give up trying to listen when he heard Crow raise his voice. "I can't believe it. He's really going through with it?"

As Doc started to answer, Lovie and Cheepie began meowing and squirming in Shiloh's grasp. He let them go and they walked away into the bedroom, but he had missed Doc's response.

Shiloh stood up, deciding to abandon his eavesdropping efforts, but Crow raised his voice again. "Do you want me to send them over to Salem now?"

Doc replied, "It can wait until after dinner. That is, if you're staying for dinner."

Crow snorted with laughter.

Shiloh's True Nature

Shiloh wondered what they were talking about. Who was going through with what? And who was Crow sending to Salem? This was the second time he had overheard a cryptic exchange between Doc and Crow. Both times he heard too little information to make sense of the conversation, so he dismissed their exchange. Though annoyed with a lack of details, Shiloh was somewhat relieved to know Doc had at least spoken to his father. He assumed everything on the farm had to be fine or else Doc would have said so.

After dinner and a brief rest, Shiloh, Doc, and Crow were off into the sticky evening air to attend Brinda's party. On their way to the lake, Shiloh noticed Crow frequently scanning the surroundings. He kept looking up, like he was searching the treetops for something. Shiloh was just about to ask about this when Crow announced, "I don't see them anywhere, Doc. I'll find them, send them off, and meet you at the party."

"See you shortly, my friend," Doc said with a little wave, as Crow stepped off the road and into the woods.

Shiloh frowned, unsure of what or whom Crow was talking about, but he shrugged it off as just another of their odd exchanges. Crow's departure gave Shiloh the opportunity to resume his earlier conversation with Doc. "So what was it you wanted to talk to me about?"

Doc focused on the road ahead, but answered, "Oh, we were talking about my trip over to Salem. Right?"

"Yeah. You said there was something you wanted to tell me," Shiloh confirmed.

Doc nodded. "Okay. As I said, I spoke to your father and

it seems he is planning to . . ." Doc hesitated, looking over his shoulder with a raised eyebrow.

Scanning the area with wide eyes, Shiloh threw up his hands. "Planning to what?"

Doc raised his hand and waved. Turning, Shiloh found Regina and Kaz walking toward them. He rolled his eyes and grunted in aggravation. Doc chuckled. "It's nothing important. I'll tell you about it later."

When Regina and Kaz caught up to them, the four of them continued to the party. As they walked, Shiloh looked over the amusing, if not confusing, birthday invitation. "Why is the start time 7:47 P.M.? Wouldn't it make more sense to be at 8:00? Or 7:45?" he blurted out.

Regina and Kaz smiled, while Doc chuckled, answering, "The party always starts at the exact time of day the person was born."

Shiloh frowned. "Why is that? And what does it mean, 'so as not to miss escalation'?"

This time Regina and Kaz laughed. Doc squinted and stroked his chin for a moment, like he wasn't sure how to respond. Finally he answered, "The reason it starts at the time the person was born is because of escalation. As for escalation, you're just going to have to see that for yourself to understand."

Shiloh shook his head, still puzzled.

When they arrived at the lake, it looked like the party had already begun. There were people seated in chairs and standing around tables by the lakeside. Shiloh looked over the cheerful crowd searching for familiar faces. He smiled

Shiloh's True Nature

when he saw Brinda seated at a center table in front of a giant cake, surrounded by a pile of presents. He knew from the enormous smile on her face she loved being the center of attention.

He continued to inspect the crowd, until he felt a tap on his shoulder. He turned, and Kaz motioned to Bud and Jace, who were standing just beyond the tables by the giant pine tree. Kaz started walking away to join them, so Shiloh followed. They reached the base of the spiral staircase of branches, and Bud nodded, saying, "Hey guys."

Kaz nodded in return and Shiloh said, "Hey, Bud. Hey, Jace. What's going on?"

Jace wiped his brow and said, "I wish this escalation would start so we can have some cake and get into the water."

The boys chuckled, and then they heard a man with a thick accent call out, "Gather around everyone. It's just about time."

"Finally," Jace grumbled, pushing his way past the others to get to the tables.

"Come on. I want to get a good spot," Bud added, following Jace.

Shiloh frowned. "A good spot? For what?"

"Escalation," Kaz answered with a smile, starting to walk away.

"Guys, what is this escalation exactly?" Shiloh asked, trying to keep up.

Bud continued walking, but looked back over his shoulder smiling. "You're about to find out."

The boys came to a stop across from the center table,

while everyone else began lining up in a semicircle. Brinda, who was still seated in front of her cake and presents, smiled brightly as an unusually large couple with dark, thick hair moved by her sides. Shiloh remembered them from the Funus and recalled they were Brinda's guardians, Mina and Maximo.

While Maximo alternated between looking at the crowd and staring down at something in his enormous hand, Mina cleared her throat to catch everyone's attention. "Thank you all for coming to the escalation of our little Brinda," she said with a thick accent and proud grin.

Jace snorted and whispered, "Little?"

Bud and Shiloh snickered, while Kaz immediately but discreetly punched Jace in the arm. Jace winced as Mina continued, "And our thanks to Luther and Martina for letting us share their space for the gathering."

Maximo remained silent, focused solely on the object in the palm of his outstretched hand. Shiloh was curious as to what he was looking at, but he assumed it was a timepiece when Maximo announced, "It's time."

Brinda stood up and the crowd began to murmur and fidget. Shiloh looked around, trying to figure out what was going on, but his curiosity faded when he saw Harmony and Saige join the semicircle of onlookers across the way. He stared in Harmony's direction until he caught her eye and then mouthed 'hello'. Harmony smiled and raised her hand. Shiloh thought she was going to wave, but with wide eyes and a raised brow, she frantically pointed toward the center table.

Shiloh's True Nature

Shiloh shifted his focus and was flabbergasted to see a pulsing, white glow emanating from Brinda's body. He watched in awe as the pulses grew progressively more intense until a blinding flash burst forth from her body in all directions. A cheer of 'Happy Birthday' erupted from the onlookers, and everyone crowded around Brinda offering their congratulations.

The boys moved away from the crowd and over toward the giant pine tree again. Shiloh followed, still dazed by what he had witnessed. When they reached the tree, Shiloh blurted out, "Guys, what just happened?"

Bud and Jace laughed, but Kaz explained, "On our birthdays, once we have reached the age of ascension, at the precise moment of the anniversary of our birth, we display an involuntary burst of radiance from our bodies."

Shiloh shook his head, rubbing his hands over his face. and asked, "What?"

Bud answered, "Brinda was born at 7:47 P.M., so every year on her birthday at exactly 7:47 that bright light shoots from her body as a sign that she's a year older."

"That's it? And that's escalation?" Shiloh asked.

Bud nodded. "Pretty much. I mean, what Kaz said is technically more accurate, but generally, that's it."

"That's not it," Kaz huffed in dissatisfaction with Bud's simplified answer. "You forgot to mention how Movers' powers usually escalate or increase on their birthdays. Sometimes a little, sometimes a lot."

Bud nodded to Kaz. "Oh, yeah, and sometimes their powers change."

Kaz grinned in return, adding, "And sometimes they add new powers."

"That's really rare though," Bud countered.

Jace pushed his way past the others while growling, "Who cares? Let's get some cake, you idiots."

Shiloh burst into laughter and followed Jace to join the festivities.

After taking some cake, the boys watched as Brinda began ripping open her presents. She slowly tore into the mountain of gifts, reveling heartily in each of her birthday treasures.

As the sun began to fade, Brinda's slow pace and the lingering heat had pushed Jace's patience to the breaking point. "If she doesn't hurry up, I swear I'm going to scream."

Shiloh chuckled as Bud said, "Will you relax? She's almost done."

Luther approached the boys and said, "I could use some help setting up the attractors before it gets dark."

Bud immediately answered, "Take Jace. He's going to lose his mind soon if you don't give him something to do."

Punching Bud in the arm, Jace said, "Fine, I'll help." Bud winced, rubbing his arm.

"What's he going to help with?" Shiloh asked.

"They're going to put up Torchbug attractors along the edge of the lake so everyone can see. They help keep away the mosquitoes," Bud answered.

"Really?" Shiloh asked in a surprised tone.

"Yeah. The Torchbugs eat them."

Kaz was quiet as Brinda opened her gifts. He stared intently until she reached for a box covered in rainbow-colored

Shiloh's True Nature

wrapping paper. He tapped Bud and Shiloh with the backs of his hands and excitedly said, "Watch this."

Brinda enthusiastically tore off the rainbow-colored wrapping paper to reveal a white box with writing on it. She read the box and then looked at Kaz with a big smile. Brinda opened the box, letting out a squeal as she pulled out a rainbow-colored stovepipe hat. As she placed the hat on her head, Shiloh and Bud turned to Kaz and found him grinning from ear to ear.

Shiloh reached into his pocket and pulled out the little box containing Brinda's bracelets. He thought about walking over and giving them to her, but he felt awkward about doing so with so many eyes focused on her. He decided to wait for a less-intrusive moment and pushed the gift back into his pocket.

As Brinda continued opening presents, Luther and Jace placed the attractors around the edge of the lake, causing swarms of Torchbugs to gravitate out of the woods. The insects lit up the area well, particularly the far side of the lake at the base of the hill. It was there Shiloh saw Harmony by a Present Tree. She appeared to be feeding the fish, walking between the tree and the lake, tossing something into the water.

Like the Torchbugs to the attractors, Shiloh gravitated toward Harmony. He forgot about Brinda's present and walked over to the far side of the lake.

"You're not celebrating, again," he said with a smile as he approached her.

"I'm just not in the mood," Harmony answered, dusting

off her hands and taking a seat on an incline at the base of the hill.

Shiloh took a seat next to her. "Wow. That escalation thing really caught me by surprise. I seem to discover something new every day here."

"It's an extraordinary place," Harmony said, looking into his eyes.

Shiloh smiled and fidgeted a little, trying to become comfortable sitting on the incline. He heard a jingling noise, followed by a soft thud. He looked down to discover the little box containing Brinda's gift had fallen out of his pocket and was lying by his side on the incline. He retrieved the box and began pushing it back in his pocket when Harmony asked, "What is that?"

"Oh . . . it's . . . ah," Shiloh stammered as he noticed Brinda approaching in her new hat.

"There you are, Shiloh. I've been wondering where you were," Brinda greeted him.

Shiloh's eyebrows went up. "Ah, yeah. I've been here. I just didn't get the chance to say hello."

Brinda stood staring down at Shiloh with a great big smile. He returned the smile, saying, "Happy birthday."

"Thank you," Brinda said before turning toward Harmony. "Hello, Harmony," she said in a subdued tone.

Harmony forced a little smile and said, "Happy birthday, Brinda."

"Thank you. And thanks for the book from you and your aunt," Brinda sneered, a note of sarcasm in her voice.

Harmony squinted toward Brinda. "Well, we clearly

Shiloh's True Nature

couldn't have come up with a present as ostentatious as that hat."

Brinda seemed puzzled by the comment, but smiled and said, "I know. It's great, isn't it?"

Harmony smirked and bit her lip to keep from laughing. Shiloh reached into his pocket and pulled out the little box. "This is for you, Brinda."

As Brinda took the present from him, Shiloh continued, "I forgot it was in my pocket. By the time I remembered, you were already opening your other gifts, so I figured I'd wait."

Shiloh paused when he heard Brinda gasp as she opened the box. He gazed up to see a look of elation on her face. He frowned at her reaction and turned toward Harmony, but Brinda quickly pulled him to his feet and threw her arms around him. Shiloh stood motionless as Brinda released him and tied one of the bracelets around his wrist. She then placed the other on her own wrist and Shiloh again looked to Harmony, wondering if she knew why Brinda was so over-joyed by the bracelets. Harmony appeared upset at the sight of the bracelets, which confused him further.

"I love it," Brinda gushed, fiddling with the bracelet on her wrist. She then took Shiloh by the arm and started pull-ing him toward the lake, saying, "We should get back to the party."

As Brinda dragged him away, Shiloh looked back at Har-mony. "Are you coming?"

Harmony's expression had not improved as she answered, "No. You two go ahead."

Shiloh frowned and wanted to know what was wrong, but

Brinda forcefully pulled him away.

Brinda loosened her grip as they reached the tables and Shiloh looked back over his shoulder to discover Harmony had gone. He wanted to go look for her, but, before he knew it, Brinda was pushing him into the lake, along with Bud and Kaz. He didn't want to be rude or hurt Brinda's feelings on her birthday, so he abandoned his thoughts of finding Harmony and soon found himself floating around on a lily pad.

Marveling at the star-filled heavens, Shiloh said, "The sky is just incredible here. On my farm, it gets pretty dark, but I can't ever remember seeing so many twinkling stars. It's so clear it looks like some of them have different colors too."

"It can get pretty dark in Fair Hill, especially in places without torchlights," Bud noted.

Kaz cleared his throat and added, "You know, the stars don't really twinkle. It's an optical illusion created by the layers of our atmosphere."

"Really?" Shiloh asked.

"Yes. It's called refraction . . ." Kaz paused, a spray of water suddenly hitting him in the face.

As Kaz wiped the water from his face, Shiloh and Bud looked to Brinda, who had water dripping from the tip of her index finger and her thumb extended upward, making her hand look like a gun.

"No science-chat on my birthday, Kaz. Fun only. Got it?" Brinda demanded.

"Brinda!" Bud said with a puzzled look on his face.

"What?" she answered.

"Did that water just come through your finger?" Bud

Shiloh's True Nature

asked.

She examined her finger. "I think it did."

Unsure what that meant, Shiloh watched as Brinda dipped one hand into the lake and with the other shot water out of her index finger at Kaz again. Brinda roared, pelting Kaz with a steady spray of water. Bud shook his head and said, "That's amazing."

Kaz wiped the water out of his face and yelled, "Stop doing that!"

Shiloh squinted at Brinda. "I don't understand. What's so amazing?"

Bud continued looking in Brinda's direction and added, "She never used to be able to do that."

"Do what? I've seen her move water around a bunch of times," Shiloh noted.

Kaz finished wiping his face and said, "You saw her manipulate liquids externally, but now it seems she's able to absorb and pass them through her body."

"That's what we were talking about earlier, about escalation," Bud said.

Shiloh frowned. "You mean she couldn't do that before today?"

"That's right. The escalation added a new dimension to her ability," Bud answered.

Kaz saw Shiloh still frowning, so he continued, "Think of it like this, Shiloh . . . when a baby is born, it can't run, right? It has to get strong enough and then learn to crawl, then stand, then walk, then run. Movers' powers are just like that. When escalation hits, it's like going from crawling to standing, or standing to walking, or walking to running. So, in Brinda's case, it's like she just went from crawling to having the ability to stand."

Shiloh thought for a moment before saying, "So, she could crawl and now she can stand."

Kaz nodded. "Sort of. She'll have to fully develop this new dimension of her ability to find out exactly what she can do with it."

Brinda added, "Shiloh, when I reached the age of ascension, I could only manipulate a tiny amount of water. I could barely move a drop of water across a table, but I practiced and learned how to use my gift. Now I can push a wave of water down the lake."

Kaz sneered. "Yeah, and we're all looking forward to seeing what havoc she'll be able to wreak with this new facet."

Brinda turned to Kaz and blasted him again with the spray from her finger.

Laughing at Kaz's third blast of water to the face, Shiloh sat back on his lily pad and looked off into the trees at the base of the hill. He marveled at how dark it was just a few feet away from the lake's edge. "I'll bet you can't even see your hand in front of your face in there."

Bud nodded. "If you think that's bad, you should see how dark it gets behind the Deer Park. The tree cover there is twice as dense along Pottle Path. It's like total darkness. When there's no moonlight anyway."

Brinda cleared her throat. "Speaking of the path, when are we going to Haines' place to have a look around?"

The boys looked around at one another, but said nothing.

Shiloh's True Nature

Brinda sat up and said, "I think we should stop talking about it and just go."

Kaz frowned. "When?"

"Right now," Brinda answered with a sly smile.

Kaz shook his head. "Now? Are you crazy?"

Shiloh looked to Bud, who rolled his eyes and shrugged his shoulders. Suddenly Shiloh's lily pad glided across the water and came to a stop next to Brinda's. Brinda locked arms with him and said, "Quit being a bunch of scaredy-jerks and go over there with me and Shiloh."

Bud threw up his hands in defeat, and Kaz begrudgingly said, "Okay."

With a wide grin, Brinda said, "Cool. Let me go see who's still around before we go."

Brinda let go of Shiloh and was suddenly carried away by a wave of water. Shiloh watched and chuckled as she sped away toward the edge of the lake. "She's really enthusiastic tonight. Are you guys this energetic on your birthdays?"

Bud laughed. "Brinda is always rowdy. But with this being her birthday, and you giving her that bracelet, she's certainly fired up tonight."

Shiloh frowned and asked, "What do you mean? What about the bracelet?"

"Nothing," Bud replied. "I guess, we just didn't know you liked her."

"Sure I do. I mean, why wouldn't I? She's a lot of fun to hang out with," Shiloh replied.

Bud grinned. "I guess what I mean is, we didn't know you like-like her."

"I'm not sure what you mean," Shiloh admitted, narrowing his eyes. Kaz burst into laughter, and Shiloh looked to Bud. "What's so funny?"

Kaz stopped laughing long enough to ask, "You don't know what those bracelets are, do you?"

"Sure. They're friendship bracelets," Shiloh answered with a curious look.

Kaz pressed his lips together and snorted. Bud chuckled and explained, "They are, but each pair has a specific meaning. The bracelets are meant to be symbols of a strong bond between two people, and different bracelets have different meanings."

Even though there was minimal light, Bud and Kaz could tell Shiloh's face had turned red. Kaz snickered. "Guess what those bracelets mean, Lover-boy?" He then made a funny face, accompanied by some kissing noises, causing Bud to roar with laughter.

Shiloh huffed, "I don't like her that way. I like . . . never mind."

Bud smiled at Shiloh. "You like Harmony, don't you?"

Shiloh looked away, saying nothing. Kaz snorted again. "Brinda's going to kill you when she finds out."

Bud was still laughing as Shiloh shouted, "I didn't know! I didn't know what they meant! I just thought they looked cool."

Bud and Kaz continued howling at Shiloh's predicament until Brinda called them up to the lake's edge. When they reached her, Brinda chuckled and asked, "What are you guys laughing at? I could hear you all the way up here."

Shiloh's True Nature

Shiloh scowled at Kaz and Bud. Kaz smirked as Bud shook his head, saying, "Nothing."

Shiloh glanced around and saw the party had all but ended. The few people remaining appeared ready to leave. "We can go just as soon as . . ." Brinda stopped when she saw Mina and Maximo approaching.

Mina waved and Maximo lifted Brinda off the ground in a bear hug. Brinda giggled and Mina said, "We're going home. Are you coming?"

When Maximo released her, Brinda hugged Mina and said, "No, I think I want to stay for a little while longer, if that's okay."

"It's okay. But don't stay out too late." Maximo smiled.

Mina and Maximo turned to leave, but Brinda grabbed their arms and said, "Thank you for my party."

They paused, smiling affectionately at her, before continuing on their way.

When they were certain everyone had gone, the kids quickly and quietly headed for town. They started out on the dirt roads, but soon began taking shortcuts through the woods to avoid being seen. At one point, Shiloh was baffled as to their whereabouts and only reoriented when they emerged from the woods near the Stone Balloon. The Deer Park was just up the road and still teeming with activity, so they hesitated to make sure they weren't seen.

When the opportunity presented itself, they crossed the road and ducked into the woods at the base of the hill. It was very dark, and the density of the vegetation made traversing the area cumbersome. After nearly walking into a tree,

Shiloh said, "Guys, if this is the path, I think we should turn around before someone gets hurt."

"No kidding. I can't see a thing," Kaz agreed.

"Just hang on. We're almost there," Brinda insisted.

The trees and vegetation eventually thinned a bit and opened into a wide-enough trail to walk along. It was still pretty dark, but, with the overhead cleared away, the waxing half-moon provided enough light for them to see a little ways. Brinda took the lead, with Bud following, and Shiloh and Kaz bringing up the rear.

As they walked along, Shiloh noticed something lit up behind the trees in the distance. When he realized what it was, he said, "You weren't kidding, Bud. You really can see the Deer Park from here."

"Which means they could probably see us, if it weren't so dark out," Bud responded.

The Deer Park wasn't the only glowing object Shiloh saw. Up ahead, on the hillside, there was an extremely dark spot with a peculiar, copper glow next to it, like something was reflecting the moonlight. "What's that shiny, orange thing?" Shiloh inquired.

"What thing?" Brinda asked, looking around.

Shiloh walked up next to Bud and pointed over Brinda's shoulder. "Right there. In the hill, next to the really dark spot."

Bud squinted ahead. "Oh yeah. I see it. I don't know what it is."

"Wait a minute. Didn't you say the dark spots were entrances to the caves, Bud?" Shiloh asked.

Shiloh's True Nature

"Yeah. Why?" Bud questioned.

Shiloh answered, "Well, maybe it's some kind of a marker to the cave's entrance or something."

"If it is, shouldn't there be more markers for the other caves?" Kaz questioned from behind.

The others heard Kaz's query, but had no answers.

As they passed by the first dark spot in the hill, Shiloh looked upward. Just off the path was a makeshift staircase of long, white stones leading up to the area with the copper glow. Farther up the hill's steep incline was another dark spot with another glowing object nearby.

"Look," Shiloh said, pointing up the hill. "Kaz was right. There's another one."

Brinda and Kaz looked up, and Bud said, "Cool. We should check it out on the way back."

Brinda snorted. "Check out what? We've got no way to see. You can't go inside of those caves without a light source."

"Yeah. If we're going to hurt ourselves needlessly, let's do it out here in the very dark woods," Kaz added.

Farther down the path, the tree density grew and the overhead light diminished. Though none of them said so, the kids began to feel like the woods were closing in on them. When they began to hear peculiar noises coming from all around, Brinda halted their progress, asking, "What is that?"

Shiloh listened intently to the odd sounds. At first he thought it was footsteps, but the cadence was different than the sound of someone walking.

"Guys, I'm beginning to think this isn't such a good idea," Bud said, sounding a little uncomfortable.

"I agree. I think we should get out of here," Kaz said.

Suddenly, a dark figure stepped out from behind a tree just ahead of them. "Buddy-boy is right. It's probably not a good idea for you kiddies to be wandering around in the scary woods."

As the figure stepped into view, Shiloh immediately recognized the young man by the moon's illumination of his short, brassy-colored hair. It was Junior. He appeared a little ominous in the moonlight as he grinned. "What are you rejects doing roaming around this time of night anyway? Did you think it would be cool to sneak out or something?"

Brinda sneered. "What's it to you, Junior? These aren't your woods."

Junior laughed. "You should listen to your little friend and get out of here, while you still can."

"Is that supposed to be some kind of threat?" Brinda fumed.

Junior snorted. "I don't need to make threats. I think we all know what happened to the last idiot who wandered over this way."

Junior's words inflamed the kids. He was no doubt referring to Bryce, and they knew it. Shiloh scowled in anger and wanted to say something, but Bud spoke up first. "You're out of line, Junior."

Junior snorted again and retorted, "Oh, I'm out of line? Let me tell you what's out of line: having to make sure the stupid local kids aren't trespassing where they don't belong, or having to keep them from trying to steal things that don't belong to them."

Shiloh's True Nature

"You mean kind of like how your father stole the Flame?" Shiloh asked.

Shiloh's question struck a nerve. Junior made a growling sound, and the noises from the surrounding woods resumed. As the kids searched the surroundings for the source of the noises, Junior barked, "Don't even speak to me, Outsider. It's a disgrace that you're even in this town, and much worse that you're accepted like you belong."

While Junior spoke, Shiloh noticed dark shapes moving around in the woods behind him.

With a smug smile, Brinda shot back, "Shiloh hasn't reached the age of ascension yet. He has just as much right to be here as anyone else. As for his being an Outsider and accepted; you must be thinking about yourself, or maybe your father, because with the way you treat people, one is what you are and the other what you will never be."

Shiloh frowned, looking between Brinda and Junior, confused by the meaning of their exchange.

Junior stood silently, hissing and screeching sounds coming from the woods behind him. He then pointed toward the kids and thundered, "Leave! Now!"

Brinda snorted. "Or what?"

"Or this." Junior sneered.

From the woods behind him, the hissing, screeching, dark shapes emerged, slowly approaching Junior. Shiloh identified them as the creatures that had been with Junior the prior week. When he saw them previously, Shiloh thought they were some odd breed of canine, but in the moonlight they looked like hopping reptiles with glowing, red eyes.

The beasts lunged toward the kids, who instinctively turned and ran. They sprinted down the path to escape, but the creatures moved fast and were gaining on them. They ducked off the path into the woods, but visibility was poor. As they wove their way through the trees, Shiloh began to fall behind. He tried to pick up his pace, but in doing so, tripped and fell. When he stood back up, the others were nowhere in sight. He wanted to call out to them, but was concerned about giving away his whereabouts to his pursuers and kept quiet.

Unable to see, Shiloh maneuvered through the area until he discovered a small clearing. He could see better there and scanned the vicinity, trying to determine which way to go. Unfortunately, he found the area impassable. The steep incline of the hill and the density of the surrounding brush made his only option retreating back into the woods.

Shiloh turned to leave, but froze when he saw a pair of glowing, red eyes staring at him from the forest. He was cornered and again thought about calling out for help, but this time he was too frightened to speak.

A beast the size of a small bear slowly hopped into the clearing. It had no fur, but a leathery, scaly, greenish-gray skin with spines running down its back. A sulfuric stench filled the air as the creature sneered at Shiloh, its forked tongue dangling over large fangs. Shiloh flashed back to the night before he came to Fair Hill, wondering if one of these creatures had chased him through the cornfield.

As the beast drew closer to Shiloh, he tried to back away, but with the steep hillside directly behind him there was no-

Shiloh's True Nature

where to go. He began to panic as the beast let out a loud screech and lunged at him. Shiloh squatted and covered his head with his arms, waiting to be attacked.

The attack never came though, because a loud roar came out of nowhere and echoed through the clearing. Suddenly, a giant, gray blur leapt off the steep hillside above Shiloh toward the attacking beast and chased it into a dark corner. Shiloh hesitated for a moment and, realizing the path out of the area was clear, ran for his life.

July 30th

Shiloh yawned as he entered the misty, lush woods with barely enough predawn light to show him the way. He didn't care how tired he was, or how just hours prior he had nearly been attacked by some sinister beast. His only concern was making his way to Harmony's secret sunrise spot to explain he didn't know the significance of Brinda's birthday gift.

The morning fog hampered Shiloh's pace through the woods, but once he reached the four-way junction, the Moon flowers guided him the rest of the way. The flowers' circular petals were almost fully lit, and glowing much brighter than when he had first seen them. He followed them until the path opened into the small clearing overlooking the valley.

When he arrived, Shiloh was disappointed to find the clearing empty. He gazed around, beginning to worry that Harmony's absence was due to the bracelets. Though the sky began to lighten, a look to the distant horizon brought on the realization there would be no visible sunrise this morning. A heavy cloud cover blanketed the sky in all directions.

Shiloh's True Nature

Oddly enough, the thick, dark clouds comforted Shiloh. He hoped they were what kept Harmony away and not his poor choice of birthday present for Brinda.

Shiloh fought his way back through the lingering mist, but when he reached Doc's, he decided to continue on to Harmony's house. He marched on through the gloom until the dirt road brought him to the white house with pink shutters. He looked up at the pink rose on the window above the archway before walking up the steps and knocking. When no answer came, he knocked again, receiving the same result.

Stepping off the porch, Shiloh sighed and wondered where else Harmony might be this early in the morning. The only place that came to mind was the lake. He thought perhaps she might be there feeding the fish, so he continued down the road toward Bud's house.

As he approached his destination, Shiloh found his view obscured by a thick fog hovering over the open area. He moved closer to the misty lakeside for a better view, but soon found his trip as fruitless as his other stops. Harmony was not there.

Dejected, Shiloh slowly walked away. On the way back to Doc's, he came to understand the only way he was going to feel better was to talk to Harmony, which meant he had to keep looking. He headed for town with hopes of finding her there.

By late morning, Shiloh had walked all over town with no luck. He had checked every place he had ever seen Harmony, until there was just one place left to look: Jeremiah's. He had hoped to avoid having to explain himself to Harmony in front of Saige at the bookstore, but it seemed if he really wanted to see her, it was going to be there.

Shiloh quietly opened the door and stepped into the store, trying not to draw any attention. There was no one behind the counter, so Shiloh began to stealthily scan the aisles. When he found the aisles bare, he decided to leave before Saige appeared out of nowhere like she always seemed to do.

As he turned toward the door, Shiloh flinched when a hand appeared on his shoulder. It was Saige, of course. "Good morning, Shiloh. Is there something I can help you with?"

Shiloh stammered, "No . . . umm . . . yeah. Actually, I was looking for Harmony. Is she here?"

"I'm sorry, but no. She . . . ah . . . isn't feeling well today," Saige answered, looking away.

Shiloh frowned. "I went by your house earlier, but no one answered."

Saige continued avoiding eye contact, but said, "I suppose she was still in bed."

"What's wrong with her? Is there anything I can do?" Shiloh asked.

"No, no. I'm sure she'll be fine," Saige answered. "She just needs her rest."

Shiloh wasn't sure he believed Saige, and felt frustrated. He looked around at nothing in particular, wondering what to do next.

"Is there anything else I can help you with?" Saige inquired.

Agitated, Shiloh sighed. "No. Wait. Yes. Why didn't you tell me what those bracelets meant?"

Shiloh's True Nature

Saige's eyes widened and a little smile came across her lips. "Whatever do you mean, Shiloh?"

"All I wanted was a cool birthday present for my friend, not the complications those stupid bracelets caused. Now, Brinda's all googly-eyed. Harmony's mad at me. And I'm running all over town trying to fix things."

Saige pressed her lips together trying to hide her smile. Waving his hands with a huff, Shiloh walked out the door.

By the time he arrived back at Doc's, it was noon and he was growing hungry. He entered the house, heading directly to the kitchen, where Doc was sitting down for some lunch. "Ah, there you are. I missed you at breakfast. Where have you been?" Doc asked, pushing a plate of sandwiches across the table.

Shiloh grabbed one and mumbled, "Got out early. Had some things to do."

As Doc grabbed a sandwich, he said, "I didn't see you after the party last night either. You must've come in late."

Shiloh just grunted and continued devouring his sandwich. Before taking a bite of his sandwich, Doc smiled and asked, "So what were you doing out so late?"

Shiloh looked up and could tell Doc wasn't going to take grunting for an answer, so swallowed the food in his mouth and said, "I was in the lake with my friends for a while. We went for a walk. Then I came home."

Doc squinted. "A walk, huh? I hope you and your friends didn't walk anywhere foolish."

Shiloh grinned and answered, "With all the roads leading to the center of town, I wouldn't even know how to get to anywhere foolish."

Doc chuckled and took another bite.

Grabbing another sandwich, Shiloh asked, "That reminds me, we never finished our conversation yesterday. You said there was something you wanted to talk to me about?"

Doc's expression changed and he mumbled, "I can't remember. I don't think it was anything important."

Shiloh frowned like he didn't quite believe Doc. "Something about home? The farm?"

Doc's shrugged and hesitated for a moment before answering, "Whatever it was, I'm sure you'll find out in a couple of days or so."

Shocked by Doc's response, Shiloh asked, "A couple of days?"

"Yes. When I take you home for your birthday party."

He stopped eating when he heard this. He set down his sandwich and said, "Oh, yeah . . . I almost forgot."

Shiloh then realized his days in Fair Hill were numbered. He had only been there a little over a week, but it felt longer. He was starting to think of Fair Hill as home, but it wasn't. Soon, all the experiences and new people he met would be a memory. He would be back at work on the farm until school started.

Doc saw Shiloh's demeanor had changed. Feeling Doc's eyes upon him, he stammered, "Yeah, it'll be nice to get back home . . . to the farm."

Despite what he said, Doc could tell by Shiloh's glum expression something was wrong. "What are you thinking about there, Shiloh?"

Shiloh's True Nature

Shiloh sighed. "I was just wondering what's going to happen."

Doc frowned. "What do you mean?"

"Well, I mean, my birthday. What if I'm a Mover? What happens then? And what if I'm not?"

Doc smiled. "If you're a Mover, then you're a Mover. If you're not, then you're not. What happens after is you continue living your life, just like you always have. Being a Mover doesn't make you any more or less important, Shiloh."

Doc's words of wisdom didn't make Shiloh any less anxious about the future. "If I'm not a Mover, can I still see you?" he asked.

Doc chuckled. "Of course you can. You're my grandson."

Shiloh felt a little relieved to hear this. "That's great. You know I've never really been able to spend much time with you. I'm glad I'll be able to come over to see you again, and everyone else too."

A slightly pained look crept across Doc's face and Shiloh saw it. "What's the matter?" Shiloh asked.

Doc grimaced, trying to find the words he needed to reply. "Shiloh, I'm not sure how to tell you this, but if it turns out you aren't a Mover, you won't be able to come back here."

"What? Why?" Shiloh asked with a dumbfounded look. "You just said I could see you. Didn't you?"

"Yes, you can. But I'm sorry to say it won't be here," Doc answered.

Shiloh stared at Doc for a moment and then asked, "What do you mean? I don't understand."

Doc sighed. "Shiloh, no one who has reached the age of

ascension may enter Fair Hill unless they are a Mover."

"So you're saying that once I've turned 13, if I'm not a Mover, I can't ever come here?"

Doc nodded. "That's correct. It's one of the reasons I asked your father to let you come for a visit, because, as you pointed out, we haven't spent a lot of time getting to know one another over the years. I meant to have you over sooner, but it never seemed like the right time. With your birthday coming up, I knew this might be our last chance. I wanted you to see this place, even if it was just for a little while."

Shiloh sat rubbing his forehead, trying to absorb this unpleasant news. Doc continued, "I need to be honest with you, Shiloh. It's highly unlikely that you're a Mover." Shiloh looked up as Doc added, "You see, neither of your parents are Movers. Even if just one of them was, it would still be unlikely. In fact, in recent times, there have been fewer and fewer new Movers emerging into the world."

Doc paused when he saw the look of deep disappointment on Shiloh's face. "I'm sorry, Shiloh. I guess I should have told you this sooner."

Shiloh went over the past week in his mind. He thought back to when he first arrived in Fair Hill and how its unique environment made him feel like he was at a carnival. Well, now it really felt like one. It popped in to brighten up his life for a while, but it would soon be gone.

Doc was determined to make Shiloh feel better. He wasn't quite sure what to say, but he decided to try, hoping the right words would come out. "Listen, Shiloh. I've really enjoyed having you here the past week or so, and we've still got a few

Shiloh's True Nature

days left. Let's not dwell on this or worry about what may come. Let's enjoy the moment. Make now the most important time and have no regrets about it."

Hearing this, Shiloh jumped up from his chair and said, "I've gotta go."

Doc was surprised by Shiloh's reaction. "Go? Where are you going?"

"Ah ... I've got to go ... ah ... meet my friends," Shiloh stammered as he backed away from the table. "I told them I'd stop by. You know, gonna try to enjoy myself."

Doc chuckled. "All right. Be back for dinner."

"I will," Shiloh said, running out the door.

Shiloh ran out into the foggy, white haze that hovered over the town, and resumed his search for Harmony. His possible exile from Fair Hill gave him a newfound sense of urgency. He was going to find Harmony and explain about the bracelets while he still had the time. With a new determination, he set off down the road to try her home again.

When he approached the house with the pink shutters, Shiloh immediately ran up the steps and started banging on the door. He knocked and knocked, but when no answer came, he started climbing up the archway. When he reached the top, his plan to call to Harmony through the stained-glass window was derailed when he found the window closed. Unsure of what to do next, he began climbing down from the archway.

Out of the fog, he heard a girl's voice in the distance. "What are you doing, Shiloh?"

The voice didn't immediately register, and he squinted

through the fog to see who was approaching. As the person drew near, Shiloh realized it was Brinda and gave a disappointed sigh. When she reached him, Brinda gave him an odd look. "What are you doing?" she repeated.

Shiloh mumbled, "Looking for someone."

"Who?" Brinda asked.

Shiloh didn't answer and turned to look at the house again.

"I was worried after we lost you last night. Are you all right?" she asked, noticing Shiloh's uneasiness.

Shiloh gave her a pained smile. "I'm fine. I need to find Harmony. You haven't seen her, have you?"

Brinda frowned. "No. Why do you need to find her?"

Shiloh looked Brinda in the eye. "Brinda, you are really cool, but I didn't know what those bracelets meant," he explained with a sigh. Brinda's expression changed and her face went flush. He continued, "I'm sorry if you got the wrong idea. I just wanted to get you a cool present."

Clearly agitated, Brinda tore the friendship bracelet from her wrist and threw it at him. Shiloh dodged the bracelet and it landed on the porch behind him. Brinda stormed away and Shiloh shouted, "I'm really sorry, Brinda!"

He felt bad about hurting Brinda's feelings, but he also felt a sense of relief. He had clarified her misinterpretation of the bracelets. Now, he needed to fix things with Harmony.

Before moving on, Shiloh heard a noise and looked up at the stained-glass window over the archway. The window was illuminated with a glorious glow. He squinted and smiled as he realized it was the reflection of the sun beginning to break

Shiloh's True Nature

free of the clouds.

With the day's gloom beginning to lift, Shiloh started down the road to the lake again. When he rounded the curve and the road began to slope downward, Shiloh scanned the shoreline for Harmony. His eyes gravitated toward the few Present Trees on the far side of the lake, but there was still a slight fog obscuring his view. He kept walking closer, but paused when he heard voices. Shiloh looked toward the Miller residence, where he saw Bud and Kaz standing on the porch.

"Hey, Shiloh," Bud yelled, jumping off the porch and running toward him with Kaz following.

Shiloh nodded a greeting and Bud asked, "What happened to you last night?"

His voice rising with anger, Shiloh asked, "What happened to me? What happened to you? You guys vanished into the woods and I almost got eaten by one of those things!"

Kaz could see how upset Shiloh was and lowered his head.

"When we turned into the woods, we all got separated. The three of us got away and eventually met back here. We figured you got away and went home. We didn't mean to leave you behind," Bud responded, staring down at his feet.

Shiloh sighed, looking between Bud and Kaz. "You gotta look out for your friends, you know. Especially the ones with no abilities and no idea where they're going."

"Sorry," Kaz and Bud responded in unison.

The boys were silent for a moment, until Shiloh asked, "So what were those things, anyway?"

"Chupacabra," Kaz answered in a low voice.

"What's a Chew-pa-cob-rah?" Shiloh asked with a frown.

Bud cleared his throat and said, "They're predators that suck the blood of other animals in the wild. Junior keeps them as pets."

"More like weapons than pets. They're dangerous and unstable, but fortunately for us they're kind of slow and stupid," Kaz added.

"They didn't seem all that slow last night," Shiloh noted.

"Junior has been training them. He has some kind of connection to them. He can command them, control them, or something," Bud said.

"What do you mean control?" Shiloh asked.

"It's like he has some kind of telepathy with them," Kaz said.

"You mean, kind of like what Crow has?" Shiloh asked.

"Yeah. I think it's kind of like that," Bud confirmed.

Shiloh thought for a moment and wondered if it was Junior who Crow had tried to help develop his power.

"So what are you up to?" Bud asked.

With a small smile, Shiloh said, "I've been looking for Harmony to explain about the bracelets. Which reminds me, I saw Brinda a few minutes ago."

Bud nodded. "Yeah. She was here a little while ago. She wants to try to go back to Haines' place tonight. Running into Junior last night has her more determined than ever to find out what's going on over there. She thinks going through the caves will help avoid running into anyone . . . or anything."

Shiloh's eyebrows lifted as he asked, "You're going back?"

Kaz shook his head. "I don't want to, but there's no reasoning with Brinda once she's made up her mind."

Shiloh frowned. "Well, after last night's narrow escape, I'm not going. Honestly, I don't think you guys should either." He paused for a moment before adding, "And even if I was crazy enough to go, I don't think I'd be welcome."

Bud and Kaz frowned at one another. "What do you mean?" Bud asked.

Shiloh tilted his head and grimaced. "When I ran into Brinda earlier, I kind of explained about the bracelets. I said I didn't know what they meant, and that I just thought they'd be a cool gift, nothing more."

Kaz tried to subdue a smile. "And how did she take the news?"

Shiloh shook his head. "Not well. So even if I wanted to go, I doubt she'd want me there."

Remembering why he was there, Shiloh turned toward the lake and began scanning the base of the hill for Harmony. As was the case earlier, she was nowhere around. "Have you guy's seen Harmony? Maybe around the lake? Feeding the fish?"

Bud and Kaz both shook their heads. Shiloh sighed and said, "I have to go."

Shiloh returned to town, hoping to run into Harmony. He kept passing Jeremiah's over and over, thinking maybe he would see her coming or going with an armful of books. At one point, he took a seat nearby and considered going inside, but decided against it at the thought of another encounter with Saige.

As the afternoon wore on, Shiloh realized he wouldn't

be seeing Harmony there. He didn't want to give up, so, as a last-ditch effort, he walked around checking places where he rarely saw Harmony. Eventually, Shiloh realized how foolish his search had become and stopped to take a seat by the Stone Balloon.

He let out a despondent sigh as he sat watching the people come and go from the Deer Park. He felt a little sad that his time in Fair Hill was almost over. If Doc was correct, and he wasn't a Mover, he was truly going to miss it.

Shiloh was gazing back and forth, soaking in the surroundings, when he heard ticking and clicking sounds coming from overhead. He looked upward to see the luminous pulse the Stone Balloon gave off just before it chimed. He smiled to himself as he placed the tips of his index fingers in his ears and stood up. As the Stone Balloon sounded its thunderous, vibrating chime, he began walking back to Doc's for dinner.

When he arrived back at Doc's, Shiloh walked into the kitchen to find Doc and Crow had finished eating. Doc was clearing the table and glanced up with a smile as he entered. "I guess I'm late for dinner," Shiloh said. "Sorry."

Crow chuckled. "Nonsense. You're only late when there's no food left."

Doc snorted at Crow's wisdom and pulled a clean plate from the cabinet, placing it on the table. "Have a seat," Doc said, pointing to a vacant chair.

Shiloh pulled out the chair and looked around the table at the selections. He honestly didn't care what was there. He'd had nothing but a sandwich the entire day and was famished. Shiloh had just sat and reached for a nearby bowl of red po-

Shiloh's True Nature

tatoes when Crow and Doc began moving toward the back door.

"We'll be outside on the porch. Holler if you need anything," Doc said, following Crow out the door.

Shiloh nodded and began putting a little bit of everything on his plate.

As he ate, Shiloh could hear Doc and Crow talking through the screen door. Parts of their conversation were louder than others. He heard some curious tidbits, and a little hushed innuendo about Crow going somewhere, but he was far too hungry to care. The more he ate, and he ate a lot, the more tired he became. When he finished, Shiloh placed his dishes in the sink, walked up to his room and fell asleep.

A few hours later, a crash on the balcony woke Shiloh from his nap. It was dark outside, but he could see someone through the open window. It was Bud. He was lifting one of the flowerpots off the balcony floor and placing it on the ledge. Bleary-eyed, Shiloh moved off the bed and walked over to the window. "What are you doing?" he asked, squinting into the darkness.

Bud slid the pot back to its spot on the ledge and turned toward the window. "Come on. We've got to stop Brinda. She's heading to Haines' place by herself. We tried to talk her out of it, but she wouldn't listen," Bud whispered, a note of urgency in his voice.

Rubbing his eyes and yawning, Shiloh asked, "What time is it?"

"It's a little after ten," Bud answered.

Shiloh stretched, trying to wake up.

"Come on. Let's go," Bud urged.

"Bud, I'm not going over there. If she wants to, that's her choice," Shiloh responded, leaning on the window sill.

Bud huffed. "Come on. After last night . . ."

"Oh, you mean last night, when you left me behind?" Shiloh interrupted with a tilt of his head.

Bud sighed. "Look, I'm sorry about that, but I'm taking your advice."

Shiloh gave him a curious frown. "My advice?"

"Yeah. You got to look out for your friends. Right?"

With a subdued smile, Shiloh slipped back into the room and walked over to take a seat on the bed. Bud stuck his head inside the window and watched as Shiloh leaned down and began slipping his feet into his shoes. Shiloh rose from the bed and climbed through the window to join Bud on the balcony. Turning away from Shiloh, Bud motioned over his shoulder to his back. "Grab on."

Shiloh threw his arms around Bud, and a moment later they were levitating. Bud lowered them to the ground, where they landed with a thud. Bud rubbed his neck and said, "You're heavier than you look."

Shiloh chuckled and nodded to Kaz, who was there waiting for them. The boys headed off to find Brinda.

As they did the prior night, they took some shortcuts through the woods until they emerged by the Stone Balloon. There they snuck across the road, making sure no one from the Deer Park saw them. They then made their way through the dense woods until it opened up into Pottle Path.

As they started down the dark path, Kaz said, "I don't

Shiloh's True Nature

know what we're doing here. If she's already gone into one of the caves, there's no way we're going to find her. We don't know where they lead. We don't know how to get through."

"I was hoping we could catch her before she went in. She said she was going around eleven. It should be close to that now," Bud noted.

They continued along until Shiloh noticed the familiar, copper glow in the distance. He stared toward it until they reached the white stones just off the path. "Didn't you say those glowing things were probably markers for the caves, Shiloh?" Bud asked, coming to a stop at the base of the makeshift staircase.

"Yeah, and I'm guessing this is where she'll try to go in," Shiloh answered.

"If she hasn't already," Kaz added.

The boys climbed up the white stones and stopped when they reached the entrance to the cave. Bud and Kaz examined the dark opening, while Shiloh inspected a copper plaque embedded in the wall of rock next to it. Shiloh couldn't discern much until some overhead clouds passed, letting through the bright moonlight.

The illumination revealed a depiction of a tree. The picture was rounded to give the tree the illusion of depth. It also had a number of raised branches spreading in different directions. At different points along the branches there were little empty holes. The one exception had a tiny green pebble lodged in it.

As Shiloh examined the little green pebble, he noticed there was an open hole on another branch just above and

to the left of it. He frowned to himself and took a few steps
back from the plaque. Kaz watched Shiloh back up and expressed some frustration. "What are we doing here? Brinda's
not here. And there's no way I'm just strolling into this pitch-
black cavern. How would we even know which way to go?"

Shiloh looked up at the hill, and saw another dark spot
with a copper glow just above and to the left of their location.
Shiloh chuckled and stepped forward to the plaque again.

"What?" Kaz asked, watching Shiloh run his finger over
the plaque.

"Come here and look at this," Shiloh said.

When Bud and Kaz were peering over his shoulder, Shiloh tapped his finger on the plaque just below the green
stone. "You see this pebble. This is where we are," he said
before pausing and sliding his finger up and slightly to the
left. ". . . and if you take a step back, you'll see this empty hole
here is a cave just above us."

Kaz and Bud stepped back, frowning upward to grasp Shiloh's assertion. Shiloh slid his finger back and forth from the
green pebble along a lower branch. "If I'm right, the holes
on this bottom branch are the lowest cave entrances on this
side of the hill." He then slid his finger to the far right on the
plaque. "By the looks of things, there are three openings in
the direction we need to go."

Kaz huffed. "Okay, let's say you're right. How are we supposed to see in there?"

Bud and Shiloh looked at one another, realizing Kaz was
correct. They had nothing to light their way through the
caves.

Shiloh's True Nature

Suddenly, a voice from the darkness said, "I knew you jerks wouldn't let me down."

The boys frowned at one another until Brinda came into view below and began climbing up the white stones. When she reached them, Bud asked, "What are you doing, Brinda?"

Brinda didn't answer, but reached into her back pocket and pulled out four long, odd-looking sticks. She shoved a stick at each of the boys. "What is this?" Shiloh asked.

Again, Brinda didn't answer. While holding one end of the stick, she broke off a small piece from the other end and suddenly the whole stick began to give off an orange glow.

Shiloh did the same to his stick, and marveled at its luminescence. "It's a fire-stick," Brinda announced.

Shiloh smiled. "Cool."

"Let's go," Brinda said, climbing into the cave opening.

"Wait a minute. We're not going in there. We came here to stop you, not join you," Kaz protested.

Brinda smiled. "Oh, come on. We're already here. And if I heard correctly, Shiloh just figured out how to get around. So let's go."

With a distressed look on his face, Kaz looked to the other boys for support. Bud just shrugged, while Shiloh said, "Fine. But if I get left behind again, you better hope I get eaten. Otherwise, you're all in big trouble."

Shiloh and Bud followed Brinda into the cave, while Kaz stood hesitantly at the opening. "Will you get in here," Brinda barked.

Kaz sighed and climbed in, finding the others standing at an intersection just inside the entrance. Straight across from the entrance was an inclined path leading upward. Off to the left was a path sloping steeply downward. The last path, to the right, was level, and the direction they wanted to go.

"I'll go first. Stay close," Brinda announced as she turned to the right.

The boys followed Brinda into the dark cavern, a small radius of light showing them the way. The only sounds present were their footsteps and an occasional, odd, screeching noise.

As they progressed through the cave, the screeching noises became constant and Kaz nervously asked, "What is that?"

Shiloh shook his head and Bud said, "I don't know."

"Who cares? Look," Brinda said, pointing to an illuminated opening in the distance.

Brinda led them forward through the opening, where they discovered the light source. The cavern ceiling opened upward, revealing the night sky. Against the moonlit backdrop were hundreds of unidentified, flying creatures. The screeching noises had reached a peak, and the flying creatures seemed to be the source.

"What are they? Birds?" Shiloh asked, watching the winged creatures swoop all around.

Bud held up his fire-stick and shook his head. "I'm guessing bats."

"Bats?" Kaz asked, sounding terrified.

Bud frowned. "Yeah. Bats, Kaz. Why?"

Kaz began to panic. "We gotta get out of here! I hate bats!"

"Why do you hate bats?" Shiloh inquired.

Shiloh's True Nature

"Because my ability is no good around them," Kaz answered.

Brinda extended her arm toward another opening and said, "Okay. Just keep moving."

As they entered the next section of caves, Shiloh whispered, "Why is his ability no good around bats?"

Brinda didn't bother keeping her voice down as she answered. "Because bats are blind and find their way using sound. So even if Kaz turned invisible, the bats would still know he's there."

Kaz cleared his throat and said, "Bats are not blind. It's true that most bats have very poor visual acuity, but they can see. Mostly they rely on sounds to survey their environment. And I don't actually turn invisible . . ."

"Who cares?" Brinda interrupted. "Just keep moving."

Kaz shot back, "Why do you have to be so rude all the time? Not only do you get everything wrong, but you're rude on top of it."

"Shut up, Kaz," Brinda replied, chuckling.

Kaz was about to respond to Brinda, when Bud said, "Shhhhh."

"What is it?" Shiloh asked.

"Do you guys hear water?" Bud asked.

Everyone went quiet, and Brinda slowed their progress to look for the source. "Here we are," she announced, pointing to a small stream of water running across the floor of the cave.

Brinda followed the path of the tiny stream with her firestick to find it emptied out through a fissure in the exterior cave wall. Bud bent down to look out of the horizontal opening and said, "It's big enough to fit through, if you lie down. But the incline looks way too steep for anyone to climb down."

The kids stepped over the little stream and continued on uneventfully until they reached a large opening. Outside of the cave was a modest incline with some trees and brush. A building unlike any Shiloh had ever seen lay just beyond the sparse vegetation. It appeared as if it were built out of cylindrical, rectangular, and triangular metal modules. The pieces were joined to form a single dwelling. Even more peculiar was a large cubed edifice just behind it. The structure looked like an enormous wire box with a gigantic, metallic ball sitting inside of it.

"Is this where Haines lives?" Shiloh asked with a frown.

Bud nodded. "Yup."

"Who would build their home here? I mean, it's on a ridge. You have a steep drop-off on one side and an incline to get to it on the other. It's ridiculous. Seriously, who would build here?" Kaz asked.

"Someone who didn't want anyone else to know what they were doing, I guess," Brinda surmised.

Just out of sight, and close to the ridge between the two buildings, Shiloh noticed a familiar, green glow. It was the same light he had seen while watching the sunrise with Harmony, except it was significantly brighter there. "What is that?" Shiloh asked, pointing toward the glow.

Bud shook his head. "I don't know."

Neither Brinda nor Kaz had any idea either.

Shiloh's True Nature

"Do you think it might be the Flame?" Shiloh asked.

Bud looked at Shiloh and said, "I'm not sure. I've never actually seen it." Shiloh frowned at Bud. Bud shrugged and continued, "It was always inside the Stone Balloon."

Brinda huffed. "It must be the Flame. It's outside, really bright, like an energy source that can't be contained."

Kaz waved his fire-stick back and forth, saying, "No, no. The flame needs to be outside because it needs to have contact with sunlight."

"You are such a jerk. Why do you have to contradict everything I say?" Brinda growled.

Kaz barked back, "I'm not contradicting you. I'm correcting you."

Brinda raised her voice slightly. "You see. That right there. That's what I'm talking about."

As Brinda and Kaz tore into one another, Shiloh and Bud smiled at each other. Bud closed his eyes, shaking his head and quietly saying, "Here we go again."

Shiloh snorted. "What? You mean you don't want to get in on this?"

Bud chuckled. "No, thanks." Bud then turned to Kaz and Brinda, saying, "Guys, you wanna keep it down before someone hears us?"

Brinda realized Bud was right and gave Kaz a dismissive wave of her hand. Kaz recoiled at Brinda's gesture and in the process dropped his fire-stick out of the cave opening. He quickly stretched to retrieve the stick, but it slowly rolled away from him. He leaned out of the cave to reach it, but slipped and suddenly began tumbling down the hill. He rolled past the fire-stick and crashed to a stop at the base of some brush.

Seeing the crash Brinda called out, "Kaz!"

"Are you all right, Kaz?" Bud asked.

Kaz didn't immediately answer, but stood up, appearing uninjured by the fall. He bent down, picked up his fire-stick, and waved it toward his friends with a little smile. The kids in the cave did not return his smile, only stared with wide eyes. Kaz threw his arms up as he started walking up the incline. "What?"

Bud slowly extended his arm out of the cave, pointing a shaking finger in Kaz's direction. "What?" Kaz called out again.

Shiloh leaned out of the cave and yelled, "Run, Kaz!"

Kaz looked over his shoulder to find several of Junior's Chupacabra charging at him. "Whoa!" Kaz exclaimed, dropping his fire-stick and using his gift to suddenly vanish.

The kids breathed a sigh of relief at Kaz's disappearance, but the respite was short-lived. With their closest prey gone, the Chupacabra set their sights on the cave opening. Shiloh was the first to his feet and, in his haste, turned right. He ran around a corner and immediately realized he had gone the wrong way. The cave came to an abrupt end, with an opening to a vertical drop into the valley below.

Shiloh stopped at the edge of the opening and caught a brief glimpse of the source of the green glow. It was emanating from the center of a small patio. Before he was able to discern much, Bud and Brinda charged around the corner, crashing into him. Shiloh nearly fell out of the opening, but Bud pulled him to safety. There was no time for thanks as

Shiloh's True Nature

they turned to run back the other way.

Brinda led the way as they sped by the opening to Haines' home. As they passed, the Chupacabra reached the cave and entered to pursue. They continued running, and jumped the small stream where Brinda came to a stop. Bud and Shiloh ran past her, but then stopped as well. "What are you doing? Let's go," Bud hollered, panting for breath.

"You go ahead. I'm going to try to hold them off," Brinda said, panting as well.

"What? No!" Shiloh yelled, as he watched a small horizontal wall of water begin to rise from the stream.

Bud yelled, "Come on, Brinda!"

"No! Just go, you jerks!" Brinda barked.

Bud stood shaking his head in disbelief, and Shiloh pulled his arm to move him along. Bud reluctantly followed, and the pair continued on, with Shiloh taking the lead. They made their way back through the area with the open cavern ceiling and seemed to be home free when suddenly both of their fire-sticks extinguished. They were running blind until Shiloh saw a faint light ahead in the distance.

Shiloh sped toward the light, coming to an abrupt stop when he realized it was where they had originally entered the cave. Not realizing Shiloh had stopped, Bud ran into him, sending both boys tumbling down the sloping incline. The boys yelled and screamed, sliding farther and farther downward. Finally, they tumbled out of an unknown hole, landing side by side with two loud thumps.

July 31st

As the vibrating chime of the Stone Balloon struck midnight, Shiloh and Bud lay on the ground, chuckling from their unanticipated exit from the cave.

"That was kind of fun," Bud said, staring up at the night sky with a smile.

Shiloh grinned. "Yeah it was."

Bud sat up and rubbed his side. "I could have lived without that landing, though."

Shiloh looked back into the opening and said, "I hope Brinda is all right."

"I'm sure she's fine. She's able to do some amazing things with water. Besides, she told us to go," Bud added.

The boys caught their breath, stood, and began to examine the surroundings. "I wonder where we are," Bud said, gazing around at the dense vegetation.

Shiloh saw a small ridge above the hole they tumbled out of and pointed. "Maybe if we climb up there, we'll be able to tell."

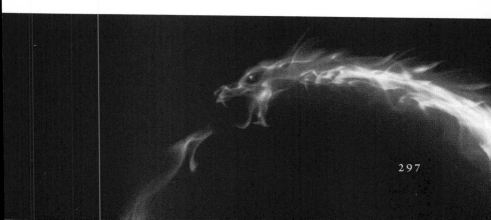

Shiloh's True Nature

They pulled themselves up onto the ridge and began to look around. The area seemed very familiar to Shiloh. When he saw glowing objects in the forest not far from them, Shiloh immediately knew where they were. The glowing objects were the Moon flowers, and they were standing in the clearing where he and Harmony watched the sunrise.

Shiloh pointed to the path. "This way."

Shiloh walked onto the path and Bud followed, asking, "What are these plants? I've never seen anything like them before."

Shiloh smiled to himself as he answered. "They're Moon flowers. Their brightness corresponds to the cycles of the moon."

"Really? That's cool." Bud continued examining the flowers as they walked.

They made their way back through the path, emerging at the rear of Doc's yard. Bud tapped Shiloh on the back and said, "Now that I know where I am, I gotta run before my parents realize I'm missing. I'll see you tomorrow."

"All right. See ya," Shiloh said, watching Bud trot away.

Shiloh slowly and quietly approached the rear of the house, trying not to be discovered by his grandfather. When he reached the back porch, he wondered how he could go back into the house undetected. He momentarily considered running after Bud to request a lift back up to his room. However, he saw the lattice on the corner of the house near the kitchen window and decided to climb it up around the corner to his balcony.

As soon as he began to climb, Shiloh heard some footsteps at the front of the house. He peered around the corner as a shadowy figure passed by. He assumed it was someone on their way to town, so he resumed his ascent toward the second floor.

A moment later, there was a knock at the front door, followed by two voices inside the house. He paused to find out who had arrived, and discovered the voices belonged to Doc and Crow. The two men entered the kitchen, and Shiloh's irresistible need to eavesdrop compelled him to take a couple of steps back down the lattice.

Leaning toward the window, he heard Crow say, "They said it just started to burn, Doc."

"Are they sure?" Doc asked, sounding shocked.

"They aren't close enough for me to get details yet, but it's what I'm getting from their thoughts. I just keep hearing 'it's starting to burn . . . it's burning,'" Crow answered.

"My god. I can't believe this is happening," Doc said.

The two men went silent for a moment and Shiloh waited, listening intently for any further information. Crow broke the silence, asking, "So what do you want to do?"

Doc didn't answer right away. After a couple of deep sighs, he said, "Let's just wait until the ravens get here to confirm what's happening."

"What about Shiloh?" Crow asked.

Shiloh's eyes widened when he heard his name.

"What about him?" Doc asked.

Crow responded, "Do you want to tell him?"

Doc immediately answered, "No! I'm not waking my grandson to tell him his farm—his home—is on fire until

Shiloh's True Nature

we are absolutely certain."

Shiloh was paralyzed with the shock from hearing Doc's words. He clung to the lattice, wondering what to do, but his only thought was he needed to go home to the farm. Loosening his grip, he dropped from the lattice to the flowerbed below.

Pacing along the side of the house, by the horses' stall, Shiloh tried to think of how he could get home fast. It occurred to him he could use Doc's flying horses, but when he approached the stall doors and pulled the handles, they wouldn't budge. He looked at Luther's knot and shook the doors in frustration. His gaze then drifted up to the unique carving on the wooden doors, and he smiled slightly before running off into the darkness.

Shiloh ran as fast as he could until he found himself approaching the lake. He slowed down and tried to be quiet as he passed by the Millers' house. It hardly seemed necessary, though, because he could hear Bud being scolded by his parents for sneaking out.

Walking past the house to the shed, Shiloh sighed when he discovered Luther had installed a new knot on the door handles. It appeared even more complicated than the one he had watched Jace remove. He knelt down in front of the doors, trying to remember what Jace had said about the patterns Luther used, and tried to mimic Jace's actions. It did not work. The knot didn't fall away, it tightened.

Shiloh sighed in frustration, wondering how he could enter the shed. It was then a twinkling light by the lake caught his eye. He stood up to investigate the visual oddity, and discovered it was one of the boxes on a Present-tree sparkling in the moonlight. He smiled to himself and said, "If you need something, you open the box, and the tree will give it to you."

He reached for the box, opened the lid, and looked inside. He couldn't see anything, so he reached in and pulled out the contents. It was a rock. Confused, Shiloh threw the rock to the ground. He then tried another box, but it also contained a rock. Groaning, Shiloh said, "I need something to help me get into the shed."

He grabbed another box, reached inside with his eyes closed, and slowly withdrew the contents: another rock. Shiloh shook his head and began walking back to the shed, holding the rock by his side. When he reached the doors, he held up the rock. "*How am I supposed to get into the shed with this?*" he thought.

Agitated, Shiloh lashed out, smashing the rock against the knot. It made a loud noise, but had no effect on the knot. He tossed the rock aside and slid to the ground with his back against the shed.

He closed his eyes for a moment, and when he reopened them, he saw a rectangular beam of light on the ground by the side of the shed. Curious as to the light's source, Shiloh stood up and stepped toward the illuminated spot on the ground. He frowned as the light disappeared, but then turned toward the shed and saw the nearly full moon's reflection off of the small side window. Smiling to himself, he picked up the rock and threw it at the window.

The glass shattered and Shiloh quickly reached inside. He knew he would have to hurry, because the Millers would

Shiloh's True Nature

come to investigate. The window was just large enough for him to pull out what he came for: the wings the kids used to glide over the lake.

After retrieving one wing and setting it by the shed, he leaned in for the second. As he tried to pull the second wing through, he hit a snag. His friendship bracelet caught on a shard of glass still wedged into the window frame. He tried to pull himself free, but was stuck.

Voices and movement from inside the house increased Shiloh's sense of urgency, so he forcefully ripped his hand away from the window. He freed himself, wincing in pain. He looked to the broken window, where blood dripped from the sill and the bracelet hung over a glass shard still wedged into the pane. He glanced at his hand, finding a deep cut across his palm.

Shiloh clenched his cut hand into a fist, grabbed the wings with the other, and ran toward the giant pine by the lake. The height of the pine with its spiraling branches seemed a little more menacing in the dark. That familiar tickling sensation rippled through Shiloh's stomach, but he did his best to focus and started up the spiral staircase.

As he ascended, Shiloh heard a commotion by the house. It was Luther, Jace, and Bud exiting to investigate. He kept climbing, but peered through the darkness at the three men moving toward the shed. When Luther discovered the broken window, he removed the knot from the door and entered the shed. He exited almost immediately and announced, "My wings are gone."

Shiloh heard Luther just as he reached the top of the

platform, quickly preparing to jump. He slid his arms into the three hoops on the underside of the wings and took a tight grasp of the handles at the tips. He took one last look back toward the house to see Jace watching Luther search all around the shed.

Bud meanwhile had moved toward the lake. Shiloh looked down to see his friend approaching and gave him a little wave. He then quickly turned away when Luther and Jace started toward the lake.

"Shiloh?" Bud called out.

He ignored Bud's call, took a deep breath, and jumped from the platform.

"Hey you!" Luther yelled after him.

Tense from the circumstances, Shiloh initially struggled with his dive, but just before reaching the water, he threw his arms open and soared upward. Luther yelled, "Get back here!"

Shiloh left the Millers behind, gliding his way down the lake and occasionally flapping his arms to keep up his momentum. The twists and turns of the lake made navigation hazardous. He was continually forced to make last-second course corrections to avoid hitting the trees along the lakeside. He contemplated increasing his elevation, but his fear of heights made him nervous.

When a close call with a protruding tree branch forced Shiloh to a lower altitude, he made an interesting discovery. There were several mysterious, glowing, white objects in the lake below. He had no idea what the objects were, but they appeared to be navigating through the center of the lake to-

Shiloh's True Nature

ward the river, so he followed.

When the river drew near, the glowing objects began to move erratically. Shiloh flew a little lower to investigate and heard splashing noises. Then, suddenly, a large grayish-white whale with a long, glowing tusk burst through the surface of the water. As it submerged with a splash, a huge smile came over Shiloh's face and he began laughing aloud. "I found your Moon Whales, Bud," Shiloh yelled.

When they reached the river, the Moon Whales dispersed, and Shiloh focused on his destination ahead. He increased his altitude for the flight across the river, and the cool night air made his eyes tear. His arms began to tire and his injured hand felt numb, but, seeing the glowing flames on the far shore, he ignored his fatigue and glided onward.

The closer Shiloh drew to the Salem shoreline, the more he detected smoke in the air. He could see the flames through the thick foliage along the river's edge, so he ascended slightly to pass over the trees. This brought the burning farmhouse into full view. His stomach churned at the sight, and he immediately became concerned with his parents' whereabouts.

As he closed in on the raging fire, Shiloh observed something flying lazy circles through the smoke. It looked like a large bird of some kind, but as he came closer he realized it was unlike any bird he had ever seen. Determined to have a better glimpse, he followed the creature's flight path from above while slowly descending.

Trailing along after the creature, he became mesmerized by the sight. Its large, furry-looking, brown wings had burntorange stripes across them, and it fluttered through the haze of smoke. The creature reminded Shiloh of a butterfly, but he'd never seen a butterfly at night, much less one so huge. He wondered what would look like a butterfly but be flying around at night. It then hit him; a moth would be flying at night. However, the creature was far too large to be a moth.

Shiloh refocused, descending toward the ground, but the lower altitude made breathing difficult. The heat and smoke filled his throat, and he couldn't help letting out a loud cough. The noise drew the flying creature's focus from the fire, and it began swooping around erratically to investigate the noise.

The creature halted in midair and Shiloh caught a glimpse of its underside. What he saw was not the body of an insect, but of a man. Shiloh gasped at the sight of the creature. It was not a moth, nor a man, but some hideous combination that his friends had called the Mothman.

Shiloh's immediate instinct was to flee, but the Mothman caught sight of his descent and flew toward him. Shiloh panicked and flapped the wings to escape. The creature gave chase and Shiloh flew around the house, trying to think of how to escape.

In his pursuit, the Mothman moved much more swiftly than when he was simply circling the house, so Shiloh knew he had to move away fast. He flew directly toward the house, remembering that moths were attracted to light. He hoped the flames would draw the Mothman's attention and give him the opportunity to flee.

Shiloh sped toward the roof where the flames were brightest, and at the last second twisted his arms, causing the wings to shoot him off in the other direction. When he looked back

Shiloh's True Nature

to see if his ploy had worked, he found the Mothman still in pursuit.

Without hesitation Shiloh ascended to make another pass at the fire. As he rose through the air, he inhaled a peculiar aroma. Not only did he smell smoke from the burning house, but he detected the odor of burning candles. He found that odd, but didn't have time to think about it and set course for the flaming roof.

Shiloh made his second pass, coming even closer to the roof. However, this time, when he twisted his arms to pull away, he was unable to control his direction and found himself hurtling through the air toward the back of the house. He flew head-on into the giant stack of hay bales near the back porch. The crash knocked the wind out of him, but he was thankful to hit the hay bales and not the ground.

Catching his breath, Shiloh held up his arms to discover why he lost control. The wings which had been so useful to him were virtually destroyed. Pulling their remains from his arms, Shiloh saw the waxy broom hairs had melted from the heat of the flames, hence the odor of burning candles.

Surrounded by fallen hay bales, Shiloh pulled himself up and looked around. His heart sank when he looked through the floating ash and gray smoke to find his home being consumed by the fire. His thoughts immediately turned to his parents. *Where are they? Are they still in the house?* He wondered.

Realizing there was no time to waste, Shiloh started for the back porch. His first step caused a sharp pain to shoot through his ankle, and he realized he had done more damage to himself in the crash than he thought. He grabbed his leg, wincing in pain, but the heat of the nearby flames compelled him to move on.

Shiloh limped toward the back porch, calling out, "Mom? Dad?" When no response came, he began hobbling up the porch steps. Flames were visible through the back door, but he kept moving toward it anyway.

The back door exploded outward, ejecting glass shards from the window panes. The force of the explosion knocked Shiloh backward off the porch, cutting his arms and face in numerous places. He pulled himself up from the ground to find the intensity of the fire had grown.

There was no way he could enter from the rear, so he started limping his way around to the front of the house. On his way, he noticed a number of spot fires had broken out in the cornfield, so he picked up his pace.

Wincing with every step he took, Shiloh reached the front of the house, where he discovered his father's pickup truck in flames, the engine running. A thick, dark smoke filled the cab of the truck, and Shiloh worried that someone might be inside. He went to open the passenger door, but as soon as he touched the handle, a searing-hot pain shot into his hand, causing him to recoil.

Grasping his burnt hand, Shiloh backed away from the flames licking out from under the truck and fell into a seated position. He stared, wondering how he could enter. It was then he noticed a fist-sized rock lying on the ground in front of him and recalled how a rock had come in handy earlier. He grabbed the rock and started to rise. Before he could stand

Shiloh's True Nature

up, a long, thin hand grabbed him by the shoulder, pulling him away.

Looking over his shoulder, Shiloh discovered the Mothman pulling him. He struggled to break free, but, with one hand cut, the other burned, his arms exhausted from the flight, and his ankle throbbing, he was incapable of escaping the Mothman's grasp.

When he was released near the dirt lane, Shiloh attempted to stand, but the Mothman pushed him back down. He tried a second time, but the Mothman bent down and stared at him forebodingly. By the light of the fire, the Mothman's eyes were mesmerizing. One eye was brown, the other a rusty-orange color split in half diagonally by a jagged maroon streak.

Shiloh forced himself to look over the Mothman's shoulder, where he gazed at the underside of the creature's wings. They looked like chalky, dark-brown feathers, but there was an asymmetry, like one had a small section missing.

His heart pounding, Shiloh waited for an attack, but the Mothman just stared. When he could no longer tolerate the penetrating gaze, Shiloh tried to roll away to stand. He was again thwarted as the Mothman grabbed him by the shirt and leaned in, coming face to face with him. Shiloh shut his eyes tight, certain he had provoked an assault, but again there was no attack.

When Shiloh opened his eyes, he found the Mothman looking to the sky. Suddenly, a huge swarm of black birds descended upon them. The Mothman briefly hesitated, but then jumped into the air, taking flight to escape. The birds gave chase and Shiloh finally stood, breathing a sigh of relief.

His respite was short-lived though, as he began choking from the nearby heat and smoke. The fire in the field was closing in on him, and Shiloh knew he needed to escape, but he felt very dizzy. He tried to remain upright, but fell to his knees and began crawling down the lane. He wheezed and coughed as he crawled, until collapsing to the ground on his stomach.

It was then Doc's cart landed in the lane with a thud. Doc brought the cart to a halt just in time to keep the horses from trampling Shiloh. Crow exited the cart and ran along the edge of the burning cornfield, looking toward the house. Doc retrieved Shiloh from the ground and placed him into the rear of the cart.

Crow ran back toward the cart and Doc yelled, "We've got to get out of here! The whole place is going up!"

Crow jumped into the cart and yelled, "Go! Go! That truck is going to explode any second!"

Doc snapped the reins and the horses began running. A moment later, they were headed into the sky over the river. A violent explosion caused Doc and Crow to look back toward the farm, a sea of fire engulfing the entire area.

August 1ˢᵗ

Heavy rain and an occasional clap of thunder in the distance woke Shiloh from a deep, sound sleep. He opened his eyes, feeling very groggy. Cheepie and Lovie were stretched out by his sides, purring and staring at him. He smiled at them as he slowly sat up, trying to remember how he had arrived in his bed at Doc's.

Shiloh gazed toward the mirror on the dresser and saw his reflection. It revealed only his usual features, and his need of a haircut. Raising his left hand to brush the hair from his eyes, he found a bandage tied around it. He frowned and reached for the bandage, but the sound of footsteps climbing the stairs stopped him.

Doc appeared in the doorway and smiled at Shiloh. "How are you feeling?"

Shiloh didn't answer; he just shrugged his shoulders. Doc walked over to the balcony window, pushing open the curtains and staring out into the gloomy downpour. "I've never seen it rain this hard, for this long."

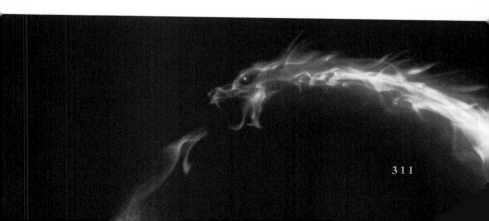

Shiloh's True Nature

Shiloh frowned, looking toward the foggy window. "How long has it been raining?"

"About forty hours," Doc said, turning from the window with an odd little smile.

Shiloh's eyes widened. "What? How long was I asleep?"

Doc gave no answer but his funny little smile remained. Shiloh grimaced and said, "I couldn't have been asleep for forty hours."

Doc nodded and Shiloh questioned, "How is that possible?"

Doc held up his hand, wiggling his fingers. "It's another facet of my little gift."

Shiloh gazed down at his bandaged hand again, and Doc said, "Try not to use that hand too much, and don't stretch open the palm. It's not fully healed, and you don't want to tear it open."

Shiloh looked up from his hand. "What happened? How did I get here?"

"You don't remember?" Doc asked with raised eyebrows.

Shiloh squinted, rubbing his forehead and stammering, "I . . . don't know . . . I'm still half-asleep."

"It's okay. It'll come back to you. Maybe I can help you fill in the blanks," Doc said, pausing to take a seat at the foot of the bed. "The night before last, Luther came running over here, said you took his wings and went gliding down the lake. As soon as he told me, I knew where you were heading. Crow and I jumped in the cart and flew after you. When we got to the farm, you were passed out in the lane."

As Doc spoke, Shiloh's expression changed from confusion to concern. He then gasped, "The truck. Did you look in the truck?"

Doc frowned and shook his head. "There wasn't time, Shiloh."

"What do you mean there wasn't time?" Shiloh asked with a look of despair.

"The fire was out of control and we had to get you away from there. We barely made it into the air before the truck exploded," Doc explained.

Tears began welling in Shiloh's eyes as he uttered, "So the farm was destroyed."

Feeling his grandson's heartache, Doc slid closer and patted Shiloh on the back. Shiloh sniffed. "What about Mom and Dad? Are they . . . gone?"

Doc shook his head. "I don't know."

Shiloh put his hand over his eyes and rubbed his temples as tears streamed down his face. Doc tried to comfort him. "Shiloh, we don't know that anything has happened to them. They may not have even been there. Maybe they were trying to fight the fire and went to get help. There's no evidence they aren't alive and well."

Sniffling, Shiloh moved his hand from his tearstained face. "Have you tried to reach them?"

Doc frowned slightly, rising from the bed and walking to the window again. "No. I've been taking care of you. I will, though, as soon as this infernal rain stops."

Shiloh thought for a moment, and then said, "I don't understand. How could this have happened? How could the farm have burned so quickly?"

Shiloh's True Nature

"That's what I was going to talk to you about the other day," Doc answered, pausing to stroke his chin.

Shiloh wiped his nose and looked to Doc, who continued, "The last time I was there, the farm didn't look so good. The crops had begun to wither. I suppose it was only a matter of time before the land went barren, with Haines' factory next door and all."

Rubbing his forehead, a sad look on his face, Shiloh said, "So my home has been destroyed. No one knows where my parents are, or if they are even alive."

"Shiloh, you have no reason to . . ." Doc stopped when he heard the front door open.

Eyes narrowed, Doc looked toward the hallway as the sound of pouring rain echoed up the stairs. A gruff voice called out, "Williams!"

Doc's look of compassion changed to one of irritation. He marched toward the hallway, pausing to say, "I'll be back in a moment."

As Doc left the room and started down the stairs, Shiloh climbed out of bed and went to the doorway to listen.

When Doc reached the bottom of the stairs, he found someone in a long, hooded raincoat dripping rainwater all over his foyer. Doc took a seat on the stairs. "What do you want, Haines?"

Throwing off his hood and shaking off some excess rainwater, Haines answered, "I'd like to have a little chat with you about your grandson."

"Come to wish him a speedy recovery, have you?" Doc questioned.

Haines tilted his head and frowned. "What? No. It seems he and a couple of the local kids have a bit of a fascination with my property."

"Is that right?" Doc questioned.

"Yes. A few nights ago they came strolling along Pottle Path, but were intercepted by my son. He drove them off, so I saw no need to mention it. However, the night before last they did it again . . . apparently using the Crosskut caves." Haines paused to gauge Doc's reaction. When no response came, Haines continued, "Now, I'm a patient man, Williams, but these intrusions need to stop. The path, the caves, my property . . . these are all potentially dangerous places. Someone could get hurt. There's already been one unnecessary death, we wouldn't want anymore."

"You mean Bryce?" Doc inquired.

"Precisely. One never knows what could happen," Haines stated firmly.

Doc stared at Haines for a moment and said, "Yes, that Moth you have guarding the Eternal Flame can be quite a handful." Doc paused briefly before asking, "Have him running any errands for you lately?"

Haines scowled and shot back, "I have no idea what you're talking about, Williams."

Glowering at Haines, Doc asked, "Really? So, you didn't know he's abandoned his post to frequent my son's home lately? Or that he just happened to be there when my son's farm burned to the ground two nights ago? And I suppose you didn't know he's tried to attack my grandson twice? Once, unsuccessfully, a couple of weeks ago . . . and again the

Shiloh's True Nature

other night as his home burned."

"Again, I have no knowledge of what you are talking about, Williams," Haines huffed. "In fact, you sound like you've taken leave of your senses."

Doc quickly stood and stepped forward. "Don't patronize me, Haines. You're a thief and a liar."

Haines gasped. "How dare you?"

"How dare I? How dare you! It still amazes me that after stealing the Flame you have the nerve to show your face in this town," Doc declared in an indignant tone.

Haines' face turned beet-red and he yelled, "That Flame belongs to me and my family! You and the pathetic rabble in this town . . . with your stories and your beliefs. You have no thoughts of the future, or what's going on around you."

Doc sat back down, folded his hands, and shook his head. "That's where you're wrong, Haines. When the Prime Mover returns, we'll see who is pathetic and what the future holds. In the meantime, get out of my house."

Haines scowled and shook his head, pulling on his hood and turning to exit. He stopped at the door, looking back at Doc. "I'm going to let you in on a little secret, Williams. There is no Prime Mover. There never has been and never will be. It's just a fictitious designation that has been used throughout the centuries by Movers who took charge in their time. They used the title to lead our people into the future."

Doc tried to contain a smile as he asked, "And what of the Flame? Is that fictitious too?"

Haines smiled slyly. "A creation of one of my ancestors. A source of immense power that had no real use, until this mechanized age in which we now find ourselves."

Doc shook his head. "Lies don't become the truth, Haines, no matter how much you want them to."

Giving Doc a sneer, Haines walked out the door.

When he heard the front door slam, Shiloh jumped back in bed. Doc climbed the stairs and entered the room, asking, "So, where were we?"

Shiloh shook his head. "I don't know." As Doc took a seat in one of the chairs at the foot of the bed, Shiloh asked, "So what happens now?"

Doc frowned. "What do you mean?"

"I mean, tomorrow. What will happen tomorrow?" Shiloh responded.

Doc stroked his chin and said, "Well, I'm supposed to take you home. I guess we'll head across the river and see if we can locate your parents."

Shiloh sighed. "And if we can't?"

Doc tilted his head and said, "Then we'll just have to come back here until we find them."

"And what if I'm not a Mover? I won't be able to stay here, will I?" Shiloh inquired.

Doc smiled. "Well, if Haines can break one of our most sacred rules without consequence, I don't suppose your being here is going to be the end of the world."

Shiloh returned Doc's smile.

The room fell silent and Doc frowned, looking toward the window. He rose from his chair and walked to the balcony, wiping off the foggy window. "What do you know . . . the rain stopped."

Shiloh's True Nature

Shiloh looked toward the window, watching as Doc pressed his nose up to the glass. "One of my flower planters is broken." His eyebrows then jumped and he turned to Shiloh to ask, "What happened to my Kirin?"

Shiloh frowned. "Your what?"

Doc pointed, tapping on the glass. "My Kirin. The statue that was out there."

Shiloh recalled his first night there, but hesitated to tell Doc about his experience for fear of sounding foolish. However, he remembered this was Fair Hill, which meant very little was unbelievable, so he blurted out, "My first night here I saw what I thought was a statue of a dog out there. At least it had the body of a dog. It came to life, burst into flames, and ran off into the woods."

Doc's eyes flew wide open. "It did what? That's impossible." He smiled with disbelief.

Shiloh shrugged. "That's what I saw."

Doc's shook his head, mouth hanging open. He looked like he wanted to say something, but just kept rotating his view between Shiloh and the balcony. Another knock at the front door then wiped the dumbfounded look from Doc's face. He turned from the window and walked toward the hallway, saying, "It sounds like we have more company." He paused before exiting the room, adding, "But at least they knocked this time."

Shiloh heard Doc trot down the stairs and open the front door. He listened carefully, trying to find out who had arrived, but there were no voices. The front door closed and he heard several sets of footsteps climbing the stairs. He frowned, wondering who it could be, but began smiling when Bud, Brinda, and Kaz filed into the room.

As they entered, Shiloh noticed his friends' drenched appearance and smiled. "Don't you have umbrellas in Fair Hill?"

Bud and Brinda grinned, while Kaz answered, "What's an umbrella?"

Shiloh chuckled, happy to see his friends.

Bud took a seat in a chair at the foot of the bed and asked, "How are you?"

"I'm fine . . . except for this," Shiloh answered, holding up his bandaged hand.

"What happened to your hand?" Brinda asked.

Shiloh sighed. "If I remember correctly, I cut it on a piece of glass when I . . . ah . . . borrowed the wings."

Kaz snorted. "Borrowed?"

The kids chuckled and Shiloh looked to Bud. "I guess your dad is pretty mad at me."

Bud shook his head. "No. He was at first, but Doc explained everything to him. So he's fine now." Bud paused for a moment, smiling and saying, "It was really cool watching you glide away down the lake."

Shiloh returned the smile. "What was cool was flying along and seeing Moon Whales swimming in the lake. I followed them all the way out to the river."

"Whoa," Kaz exclaimed.

Bud looked to Brinda and said, "Told you."

Brinda squinted at Shiloh and he said, "I saw them. They're real."

Shiloh's True Nature

Brinda looked at Bud and grunted, "Hmmm."

The kids went silent for a moment, looking around at one another. Brinda then gave Shiloh a sympathetic look. "We're sorry to hear about your home."

Shiloh cleared his throat, trying not to choke up, and said, "Thanks."

"So what exactly happened that night? There was a fire or something?" Kaz asked, frowning.

Brinda gave Kaz a backhanded slap and he yelped.

Shiloh smiled. "It's all right, Brinda. I flew across the river because my house was on fire. I wanted to find my parents, but I didn't have much of a chance."

Bud scooted to the edge of his chair. "Why not?"

Shiloh hesitated and then said, "Because of the Mothman."

"What?" Bud, Brinda, and Kaz exclaimed in unison.

Shiloh continued, "When I got to the farm, I saw something flying around the fire. When I got a closer look at it, I saw it was a man with wings: a Mothman."

Looking captivated, Kaz asked, "No way ... then what happened?"

Shiloh closed his eyes and thought for a moment before answering, "He chased me and I crashed. I tried to get a look around, but he grabbed me and pulled me away. If Crow's birds hadn't chased him off, who knows what he would have done."

"That's unbelievable," Bud said, shaking his head.

Brinda frowned. "What was he doing there?"

"I don't know, but I don't think it's the first time he's been over there," Shiloh answered.

"What do you mean?" Kaz asked.

Shiloh looked at each of his friends and said, "The night before I came to Fair Hill something chased me through the cornfields on my farm. I wasn't sure what it was, but now I'm thinking it was the Mothman."

A frustrated look washed over Brinda's face. "But why was he there? I mean, why would he have come to your farm to chase you? And why would he have been there again the other night? It doesn't make sense."

Shiloh threw up his hands. "I don't know. Maybe it has something to do with Haines' factory next door."

Surprised by Shiloh's suggestion, Bud, Brinda and Kaz again exclaimed, "What?"

Shiloh answered, "There's this great big factory next to the farm. Haines owns it. Maybe the Mothman was at the factory for some reason."

The three kids shook their heads, dumbfounded to hear this information.

"Sometimes I forget there's a world beyond Fair Hill," Kaz said.

Brinda nodded. "Really."

"What I can't believe is how much Haines interacts with the outside world. I mean, the whole point of this place is for Movers to avoid regular folks discovering our gifts. But he just comes and goes. Does whatever he wants," Bud noted with agitation.

The kids went quiet again, but Shiloh spoke up, "Haines was just here, you know."

Shiloh's True Nature

Brinda smiled. "We know. We saw him when we arrived. We hid and waited until he left. That's how we got soaked."

"So what did he have to say?" Kaz inquired.

"He was complaining about our last visit." Shiloh smiled.

The kids laughed for a moment, and then Bud asked, "What did Doc say to him?"

Shiloh's smile grew larger as he answered, "Let's just say, I've never heard my grandfather really angry . . . until today."

The kids chuckled hearing this.

Shiloh looked back and forth between Kaz and Brinda. "That reminds me. How did the two of you escape the other night?"

Brinda motioned toward Kaz. "Jerk-o over here just went invisible and ended up walking home because those dog-things came after us."

Kaz interrupted, mumbling in a low voice, "Chupacabra."

"I, however, wasn't as lucky," Brinda sneered, raising her left arm to reveal a bandage covering her wrist.

Shiloh's eyes widened. "What happened?"

Brinda smiled and said, "I had those dogs blocked by a nice wall of water. One of the best I've ever made. There was no way they were getting through. I decided to go through that horizontal opening in the cave, where the stream flowed through. But as I shimmied through to get away, I lost my focus for a split second and one of those dog-things managed to get through the wall of water and bit me. I pulled away and rode the stream down the side of the hill."

Shiloh smiled at Brinda's account of her escape and asked, "Why don't you get Doc to fix it for you?"

"He did. But apparently they aren't ordinary dogs," Brinda explained.

Kaz rolled his eyes and mumbled, "Chupacabra."

Brinda quickly turned toward Kaz, raising her voice, "Whatever they are, the bloodsuckers have very sharp teeth and secrete some sort of poison when they bite."

Shiloh recoiled slightly and asked, "Are you going to be all right?"

Brinda ran her index finger over the bandage and said, "Doc says I'll be all right, but it'll take a few days to fully heal. I bet it leaves a cool looking scar."

Shiloh shook his head, chuckling as he sat back on the bed and looked toward the balcony.

Bud then asked, "So what happens now?"

Shiloh frowned. "What do you mean?"

"I mean, with you. Are you staying in Fair Hill?" Bud inquired.

Shiloh's frown turned into a sad little smile. "I'm not exactly sure what's going to happen. Tomorrow is my birthday, and Doc said he'd take me across the river to see if we can find my parents. If we can't find them, I'll be coming back here, I guess."

Compassionate looks swept across the kids' faces. Shiloh scratched his forehead and choked up a bit as he continued, "We don't even know if they were in the house, my parents. If we find them, who knows where we'll live with the house and the farm gone."

"We're so sorry, Shiloh," Brinda said with a sympathetic look.

Shiloh's True Nature

Shiloh sat thinking for a moment before saying, "You know, my house, the farm, Bryce, the Flame. All of it has one thing in common: Haines."

The kids all nodded in agreement.

Shiloh continued, "Regardless of what happens tomorrow, whether I'm leaving Fair Hill for good or not, I'd really like to get back at him."

Bud and Brinda smiled, but Kaz looked confused and asked, "What do you mean?"

"I mean, I'd like to return the Flame to its rightful place," Shiloh answered.

Kaz's eyes widened and he tilted his head, pondering Shiloh's words.

"What do you think?" Shiloh questioned, looking around to gauge their reactions.

A wide smile came to Brinda's lips. "You know I'm in."

"Me too," Bud replied without hesitation.

The others looked to Kaz, who sighed. "Okay. But I am not going in those caves again."

Shiloh nodded, smiling at his friends.

"So how are we going to do it? I mean, how do we get over there undetected?" Kaz asked.

"The path to the caves again, I guess. That's the closest we can get without being seen," Bud answered.

Kaz huffed. "Do you think that's wise? You know Haines will have both the path and cave by his house watched or guarded in some way."

Bud threw his hands in the air. "Well, we certainly can't go down Acacia Street."

"Fine," Kaz sighed, "but I'm not going in the caves with those bats again. I'm sorry, I just can't."

Brinda smiled at Shiloh, rolling her eyes.

"All right, so we've established that Kaz isn't going into the caves. So how are we going to do this then? We can't take the path all the way there," Bud noted.

Shiloh left the bed, pacing back and forth trying to formulate a plan. Suddenly he stopped and pointed at Kaz. "Maybe we can use that to our advantage, Kaz not taking the caves."

Bud seemed a little puzzled by Shiloh's suggestion. "What do you mean?"

"What I mean is, if Haines is going to be on the lookout, maybe the best way to do this is by misdirection," Shiloh answered.

"Misdirection?" Kaz said, looking confused.

Shiloh opened his mouth to answer, but paused when he heard footsteps coming up the stairs. As the footsteps grew louder, he quickly jumped back into bed and said, "I have an idea. Just come and get me tonight after all of you get out."

Doc popped his head in the door and smiled. "Visiting hours are over."

After his friends left, Doc led Shiloh to the kitchen and fixed him something to eat. Shiloh stuffed himself and then returned to his room to wait for dark. When the gray sky faded into black, Shiloh dressed and took a seat in one of the chairs at the foot of the bed. He picked up his copy of *True Nature*, skimming through the pages to pass the time.

As night set in, Shiloh kept gazing toward the balcony window in anticipation of his friends' arrival. When Bud fi-

Shiloh's True Nature

nally landed on the balcony, Shiloh exhaled a sigh of relief before jumping up and climbing out the window. Bud immediately lowered him to the ground and, without a word, the kids headed to the path.

They made their way through the lingering mist, taking the usual shortcuts through the woods until emerging by the Stone Balloon. The decks of the nearby Deer Park were empty due to the drizzle, so they simply crossed the road into the dense woods, where they trudged through the damp vegetation until reaching Pottle Path.

"So what's this plan of yours, Shiloh?" Brinda asked, as they moved into the open trail.

Shiloh smiled and said, "I told you. Misdirection."

Kaz huffed. "I'm not going into those caves."

Shiloh saw the copper glow of an entrance plaque in the distance. "I know, Kaz . . . you're not. You're going to camouflage yourself and move along the path until you get to that steep cave opening where the water pours out. You know, the one with the horizontal opening."

Kaz frowned. "And then what?"

"Just wait there for Brinda," Shiloh answered.

"What are we supposed to do then?" Brinda questioned.

As they came to a stop by the white stones leading up to the cave opening, Shiloh answered, "Wait about ten minutes for me and Bud to get over to Haines' place. Then, I want you to run around and make as much noise as possible."

"What? Are you crazy?" Kaz exclaimed.

Bud let out a little chuckle and Brinda said, "Cool."

Kaz was still confused, and watched as the others began

climbing up the white stones to reach the cave entrance. "So I just walk along the path to that opening?"

Shiloh answered, "Yeah. Wait for Brinda there."

"And use your camouflage," Bud added.

"Unless you want to come through the caves with us," Brinda snorted, looking back at Kaz.

Kaz frowned and used his gift to disappear.

At the cave entrance, Brinda reached into her back pocket and pulled out some fire-sticks. She handed one to Bud and another to Shiloh. They each snapped off an end piece to light them and then stepped into the cave.

Just inside the opening, Brinda turned down the path at the right of the intersection and led them into the dark cavern. The boys followed her along and soon began hearing faint screeching noises in the distance. As the screeching grew louder, Shiloh knew they were moving closer to the horizontal opening. He gazed forward, noticing an illuminated opening in the distance, but it immediately dimmed.

"What's that light?" Shiloh asked, pointing forward as the opening lit up again.

"I don't know," Brinda said when the opening began to dim again.

They continued forward through the opening into the cavern with the open ceiling. Looking to the sky, they discovered the cloud cover had begun to splinter. The passing clouds intermittently obstructed the full moon's reflection, causing the cavern to momentarily dim and then relight as they elapsed.

As they entered the next section, the sound of flowing wa-

Shiloh's True Nature

ter could be heard echoing throughout the cave. When they reached the foot of the tiny stream emptying out through the horizontal opening in the cave wall, Brinda bent down and looked through the gap. "So you want us to create a diversion, Shiloh?"

"Yes, please. Give us about ten minutes to make it the rest of the way," Shiloh answered. "Oh, and try not to get bitten this time."

Snorting, Brinda slid through the opening.

Shiloh and Bud continued on through the cave until they reached the opening overlooking Haines' geometrically shaped home. Bud looked down at the house and said, "Even with Brinda and Kaz causing a commotion, it's going to take time to get down there and find the Flame."

"It might take less time than you think," Shiloh replied, motioning for Bud to follow him.

Shiloh led Bud around the corner to the farthest opening, with the vertical drop-off. Pointing out of the opening, Shiloh said, "Before you guys nearly knocked me out of here last time, I saw that."

Bud looked in the direction Shiloh was pointing to see a bluish-green glow emanating from the center of a small square patio. The four corners were occupied by large statues, facing inward toward a flickering, blue-green flame dancing in the moonlight.

"I wonder what those four scary-looking things are?" Bud asked.

"They look kind of like Kirins."

"What's a Kirin?"

Shiloh smiled and replied, "I don't really know. My grandfather had one."

Glistening in the moonlight, just beyond the patio, was Haines' metal monstrosity. The giant wire box with its interior, metallic sphere couldn't have looked more out of place amongst the lush vegetation.

"What do you think that's for?" Shiloh asked, pointing to the massive cube.

Bud shook his head. "Who knows with Haines?"

As they stared down upon Haines' compound, Shiloh had a funny feeling. He felt like they were being watched. He scanned the area, but found nothing out of the ordinary. However, he then noticed two familiar black birds seated on a piece of rock protruding from the outer cave wall. The birds seemed to be staring in the same direction as he and Bud.

Suddenly, one of the birds turned in Shiloh's direction and softly cawed. Realizing whose birds they were and what they were doing there, Shiloh blurted out, "Oh, no. We have to hurry."

Bud frowned and asked, "Why? What's going on?"

"Forget it. Can you get us over there to the edge of the embankment by the patio?" Shiloh asked.

Bud nodded and levitated off the ground slightly. "Grab on." Shiloh climbed onto Bud's back, and a moment later they were levitating out of the opening.

"They'd never expect anyone to be coming from this direction. Just stay below the sightline of the patio until Brinda and Kaz start making a racket," Shiloh whispered.

Bud nodded and maneuvered to the edge of the patio,

Shiloh's True Nature

where the ridge dropped off into the valley.

When they reached the ridge, Shiloh gasped and whispered, "Look."

Bud glanced up toward the patio and saw the Mothman walk from the shadows toward the Flame. He knelt down in front of the flickering, blue-green glow with a euphoric look on his face. He reached out for the Flame, but quickly recoiled with a look of pain. He clenched his hand for a moment, but as soon as the pained look faded he reached for it again, duplicating the result.

Bud whispered, "What's he doing?"

"I don't know. I guess he's attracted to the Flame," Shiloh whispered back.

Just as Shiloh answered, they unexpectedly dropped a little below the ridge. As they slowly rose back up, Shiloh asked, "What was that?"

"Sorry, but you're getting heavy," Bud replied. "How long has it been?"

Shiloh sighed. "More than ten minutes. What's taking them so long?"

"Who knows with those two? They're probably arguing about how long it's been. They better hurry, though, because I'm not going to be able to hold us up much longer," Bud noted.

"Just try to hang on for another minute."

Shiloh clung to Bud's back, watching the Mothman and listening for a commotion from Kaz and Brinda. More time passed with still no sound of distraction, and he was about to suggest they return to the cave. However, a light breeze washed over them and Shiloh caught a familiar, sweet odor. His eyes began to tear and he let out a sneeze. The Mothman rose from his crouched position and Bud flinched, quickly sinking below the ridge.

Shiloh rubbed his nose trying to purge the aroma of burning acacia from his nostrils. He held back another sneeze as Bud said, "I think we're going to have to return to the cave. I can't hold you anymore."

Shiloh nodded. "Okay. At least we tried."

Bud slowly rotated in midair back toward the cave opening, when a sudden ruckus broke out in the forest. He heard the uproar in the distance and looked back over his shoulder to see the Mothman leaving the Flame to investigate. Bud quickly reversed course and landed on the edge of the patio with a thump. Dismounting by one of the statues, Shiloh watched Bud stumble forward, rubbing his lower back.

"You all right?" Shiloh asked.

"I'll be fine. But there's one problem," Bud answered.

"What?" Shiloh asked with a frown.

"How are we going to take that?" Bud pointed to the Flame, which stood almost as tall as him.

Looking toward the Flame, Shiloh grimaced and wondered how they would transport it.

A loud scream echoed through the woods, startling them. Bud stepped to the edge of the patio and looked into the distance. He wanted to investigate, but he didn't want to leave Shiloh behind. Seeing Bud's hesitancy, Shiloh nodded toward the forest. "Go ahead. I'll stay and see if I can figure out how to move this thing. Just don't forget me this time."

Shiloh's True Nature

With a quick nod, Bud levitated off the patio toward the Haines' home and the woods beyond.

Still standing at the patio's edge, Shiloh returned his attention to the Flame. Its amazingly vibrant colors mesmerized him. For the most part, it was a beautiful blue-green flame, but flickering yellow and red streaks danced around the edges. The flame gave off no smoke and seemed unaffected by the light breeze.

As Shiloh took a step toward the Flame, it appeared to contract. He thought it was an optical illusion, but, by the time he reached it, the Flame appeared to be no larger than the palm of his hand. He knelt down and found the base of the flame attached to a thin piece of the acacia wood. The thorny stick had parallel, carved handles on each side, both of which were marked with a ζ. Shiloh stared at the symbol, trying to remember where he had seen it before.

When nothing came to mind, Shiloh reached for the wood to retrieve the flame. A loud, grinding noise startled him before he could reach the closest handle. Frozen, he watched as the bases of the four Kirin statues rotated inward toward the Flame. His eyes widened as the statues came to life, yawning and stretching as if waking from a long slumber.

The figures focused toward the center of the patio, and Shiloh could have sworn the beasts were smiling at him. He shuddered, wondering if he were about to be attacked, but the creatures suddenly burst into flames and ran away in opposite directions. Letting out a sigh of relief, he returned his attention to the Flame.

When another scream came from the forest, Shiloh

grabbed the burning stick and stood up, scanning for an escape route. He soon realized without Bud to carry him, there was no way to go down. Each direction off the patio seemed worse than the last. Two sides had steep vertical drops into the dark valley. Another dropped off toward the incline between Haines' home and the forest. The last side was blocked by a wire wall from Haines' strange, metal structure. The only option was a ladder attached to the wall of the metal building.

Shiloh paced back and forth, staring off into the dark woods, hoping to find Bud levitating toward him. Eventually, a shape rose up out of the woods, but it was not the silhouette Shiloh wanted to see. With its rapid ascent and precise movement, Shiloh knew there was no way it could be Bud.

Not knowing what else to do, Shiloh backed away from the patio's edge to the ladder. As the shape flew closer, he turned and carefully began climbing up. At the top, Shiloh found a wide walkway with a railing surrounding the perimeter of the metal edifice. Wire netting covered the inner part of the roof, except for a circular opening at the center, which led down into the metal sphere.

He was curious about the sphere but had no time to investigate, instead moving toward the far side of the walkway. Seeing an opening in the railing directly across from where he climbed up from the patio, Shiloh picked up his pace, hoping there was another ladder to climb down. Before he reached the opening, a figure dressed in a familiar orange and black raincoat climbed up on to the walkway. It was Haines.

Shiloh began to slowly back away and Haines threw off

his hood with a smile. "Good evening, young Williams. Back again, I see."

Shiloh turned, thinking he could retreat to where he climbed up, but before he reached the ladder the Mothman landed on the walkway, blocking his path. "You've nowhere to go, young Williams. Just give me the Flame and we'll see that you get back to your grandfather's safe and sound," Haines sneered.

With both directions blocked, Shiloh took a chance and ducked through the railing to make his way across the wire netting. "Get out of there, you fool!" Haines yelled.

Holding the Flame while trying to maneuver was like trying to balance a full teacup while walking on jelly, but somehow Shiloh managed to navigate to the other side. When he reached the far railing, the Mothman landed on the walkway in front of him and Shiloh let out a sigh of defeat.

As Haines began to move around the walkway, he called out, "You see. You can't get away! Now, give me the Flame!"

"Or what?" Shiloh cried out. "You'll kill me, like you killed my parents?"

Haines stopped and huffed. "What? I did no such thing, you foolish boy! Now, give it to me, before someone gets hurt!"

"No!" Shiloh yelled.

Haines sighed, "Fine." He looked to the Mothman and said, "Take it from him."

The Mothman stepped through the railing and flew straight at Shiloh. Shiloh froze, but jumped out of the way at the last second, causing the Mothman to speed by toward the far side of the walkway. Seeing a chance to escape, Shiloh ran across the netting toward the ladder leading to the patio.

Despite the wobbly footing, he managed to stay upright. He made it through the railing and started down the ladder. When he stepped off the bottom rung, he turned around and recoiled when he found the Mothman waiting for him. The Mothman advanced, but halted when loud growling noises echoed out of nowhere. Shiloh thought of climbing back up the ladder, but hesitated when four massive paws came over the ridge and dug into the patio, cracking the cement with their claws.

Eyes wide and heart pounding, he watched a gray tiger with black stripes and a gray panther claw their way up onto the patio. The massive felines began circling the patio, and Shiloh thought he recognized them. "Cheepie?" Shiloh called to the tiger as it strutted along the far edge of the patio. The tiger bared its teeth in an almost smile, and gave a low growl.

He turned his attention to the panther. "Lovie?" The panther affectionately brushed against him, just like Lovie always did when she saw him. Only now, her loving graze nearly knocked him over.

Shiloh turned his attention back to the Mothman, who was rotating his head trying to keep track of the cats' positions. Lovie continued to pace back and forth between Shiloh and the Mothman, while Cheepie stopped in a corner to stretch out his front paws, again penetrating the cement patio as he extended his claws.

The Mothman backed away from Shiloh toward the edge

Shiloh's True Nature

of the patio between Haines' home and the forest. Out of the corner of his eye, Shiloh saw Cheepie preparing to pounce. The Mothman saw it as well and spread his wings to take flight. As he leapt into the air, Cheepie dove at him and the two went tumbling over the edge of the patio. Lovie jumped over the edge in pursuit.

Shiloh breathed a sigh of a relief and walked to the edge of the patio, looking down into the darkness trying to determine the cats' and the Mothman's whereabouts. "Give me that Flame, boy," a voice called out.

With a flinch, Shiloh turned to look behind him and began to slip. He waved his arms, the Flame still in hand, trying to regain his balance, but it was no use. He fell backward off the patio and landed hard on the ground, dropping the Flame.

Pain filled Shiloh's body. He wheezed and choked as he struggled to breathe, the taste of blood filling his mouth. He stared up at the star-filled sky, his gaze darting around the heavens. He caught a glimpse of Haines looking down at him from the patio. Shiloh raised his hand upward to find the bandage gone and his palm bleeding profusely.

Out of the corner of his eye, Shiloh saw the Eternal Flame flickering and moved his hemorrhaging hand over the top of it. He felt cold and shuddered, watching as the red fluid made the flame disappear. Delirious, Shiloh laughed and choked, "Blood ... blood ... of the innocent."

His coughing continued for a moment, then Shiloh lay still.

August 2nd

As the Stone Balloon struck midnight, Haines made his way down from the patio. When he reached the ground, he started toward Shiloh's broken body, but paused when he heard something in the forest. Realizing the noises were footsteps and voices, he quickly scurried into a shadowy, dark corner to avoid detection. He frowned as Doc, Crow, Luther, Bud, Kaz, and Brinda approached his home from the path in the woods.

"Shiloh?" Doc called.

When no response came, Luther asked Bud, "Where did you say you left him?"

"Up there," Bud answered, pointing to the patio.

Everyone gazed toward the now-darkened patio and Luther asked, "What do you think, Doc? You want me to knock on Haines' door? Get him to let us up there?"

Doc started to answer, but was interrupted by Brinda's gasp.

"What? What is it?" Kaz looked around, eyes wide.

337

Shiloh's True Nature

Brinda pointed at Shiloh on the ground not far from them. Doc broke into a run, again calling out, "Shiloh!"

Everyone followed. Doc stopped and they crowded around Shiloh's motionless body. Doc knelt at Shiloh's side and felt his neck. He looked up with his eyes full of pain and everyone knew Shiloh's condition.

The others could only watch in shocked silence as Doc laid his hands on Shiloh's chest to try to save him. He tensed and strained, pressing his hands hard against Shiloh's chest, but nothing happened. He stopped momentarily, exhaling before trying again.

Sweat dripped down his face as Doc tried with all his might to reanimate his grandson. Again, nothing happened and he fell back into a seated position, panting for breath and completely exhausted.

A moment later, Doc sprang back to his knees and leaned forward, placing his hands on Shiloh's chest. His face contorted and his body shook, but it did no good. Shiloh remained lifeless. Doc fell back once again, gasping for air.

Doc leaned forward to try again, but a hand pulled at his shoulder. He gazed up to find Crow staring down at him, shaking his head.

Doc fell back, placed his head in his hands, and started to cry silently. While the others sniffled and wept, Crow bent down and slid his arms underneath Shiloh. He stood up, cradling Shiloh's body, and began to walk away. The others helped Doc to his feet and followed Crow into the darkness.

Haines watched from the shadows and waited until everyone disappeared down the dark path. When he was sure they were gone, Haines stepped out of the darkness and approached the spot where Shiloh fell. He knelt down to examine the burnt acacia stick, which sat in a small pool of Shiloh's blood.

After a moment, Haines reached for the stick which the Flame had burned upon. Before his hand reached the stick, he winced and recoiled. Fuming, he stood up and backed away, leaving the acacia stick where it had fallen.

The only sounds were footsteps and an occasional sniffle as the somber group made their way back through the forest by the full moon's light. When they arrived at Doc's, Crow carried Shiloh's body toward the backyard, while Doc hurried into the house. Luther rushed to the back porch and began pulling out some Torch-lights from underneath the stairs.

With help from the others, Luther lit and placed the Torch-lights around the yard, while Crow waited in the center of the yard by the rectangular, marble platform. Doc emerged from the back door carrying Shiloh's favorite blanket, which he and Crow wrapped around Shiloh's body. Crow gently laid the body at the base of the platform and stared down at it with a sad sigh.

Everyone stood staring toward the platform when rustling noises sounded from the woods at the rear of the yard. Suddenly, Cheepie and Lovie ran out of the darkness, still in their big-cat forms. Their appearance slowly returned to normal as they approached the platform.

Cheepie jumped up on the platform and walked to the edge, hanging his head and staring down at Shiloh's blanket-covered body. Lovie walked all over the blanket, sniffing it, and looked up at Crow with a sad little meow. "I know," Crow said, tears welling in his eyes.

Doc cleared his throat. "I could use some help. Would someone begin gathering up some acacia?"

Looking at Brinda and Kaz, Bud said, "We'll do it." Kaz and Brinda nodded in agreement.

Doc looked at the three with a nod. "Thank you."

Bud sniffed and choked up a little. "Doc, we're so sorry . . ."

Doc raised his hand, interrupting Bud. "I know it's not your fault."

The kids nodded sadly to Doc and headed off in search of acacia wood.

Doc looked around at the ornate pieces of wood lying in the yard, and turned to Crow and Luther. "Will you help me assemble the Revenant?"

Both men frowned and Crow turned to Doc. "Are you sure? That's our way, but not those of the outside world. What if his parents reappear?"

Doc didn't answer, just glared at Crow with a despondent look. "Okay," Crow said, knowing Doc had made up his mind.

As Doc, Crow, and Luther began assembling the pieces of what was soon to be Shiloh's funeral boat, they noticed a peculiarity in the sky. The full moon seemed to have stopped moving across the heavens, as if it were stuck. No one mentioned the anomaly. They remained focused on the task at hand.

Luther was the first to break the silence as he examined

some carvings on a piece of the Revenant. "You know, this boat was one of my finest creations," he announced in a gloomy voice.

Doc gave him a little smile. "I agree."

Doc thought back to the afternoon a couple of weeks prior when Shiloh had examined the pieces. He wondered if Shiloh ever realized they all fit together. "I know I'm getting up there in years, but, I mean, I never thought I'd see this thing put together," Doc spoke up. "I surely never thought I'd be putting it together." Crow patted Doc on the shoulder.

A short while later, Jace and Martina arrived in the backyard to find the men hard at work on the Revenant. Martina walked straight up to Doc with tears in her eyes and said, "Doc, I'm so sorry. He was . . . he was a wonderful young man."

They hugged for a moment and then Martina patted the bag she carried. "I brought some food. I'm going to make you all something to eat."

Doc managed a little smile as Martina went into the house.

He then turned to Jace, who said, "My condolences, Doc. I really liked Shiloh."

"Thank you," Doc said.

They stared at one another for a moment and then Doc pointed over his shoulder. "We could use an extra hand."

Jace nodded and said, "Of course."

As Doc and Jace turned to work on the Revenant, Regina arrived. Jace went to help Luther and Crow, while Doc approached Regina. "I'm so sorry for your loss, Doc. I regret not getting to know your grandson better. My Kaz spoke

Shiloh's True Nature

highly of him."

"Thank you, Regina," Doc answered.

"If there's anything I can do to help, please let me know," Regina added.

Doc thought for a moment before saying, "You know, there is something."

Regina tilted her head. "Anything. You name it."

Doc sighed. "I'm going to have a Funus for Shiloh in a few hours. Could you let Mina and Maximo know? And Saige too?"

Regina frowned. "In a few hours? In daylight? Wouldn't you prefer to wait until later? After midnight?"

Doc shook his head. "No. My grandson was born at 10:02 A.M. on this day thirteen years ago and I'd like to send off his remains while they are still in the age of innocence."

Regina gave a glum nod of understanding and said, "Okay. So just Mina, Maximo, and Saige?"

Doc nodded in confirmation. "I know many others might want to be there, but I'd like to keep it small."

Turning to do as asked, Regina gave another nod and said, "I'll let them know immediately."

"Thank you, Regina," Doc added, watching her depart.

Just before dawn, Martina opened the porch door and called out, "The food is ready. Get in here and eat something, all of you."

Though the Revenant was nearly complete, the four men didn't bother to argue. They hadn't slept and knew they needed to keep up their energy if they were to finish the task. They dropped what they were doing and headed for the porch.

As the men entered the house, Harmony watched, hidden near the corner of the house by the horses' stalls. Waiting until they were inside, she moved swiftly through the backyard. She headed straight for the path in the rear corner, trying not to look toward the platform. She even closed her eyes for a moment as she passed through the center of the yard to keep herself from looking toward Shiloh's body.

When she reached the path, Harmony paused for a moment to glance back over her shoulder, but then forced herself onto the dark trail. She walked until she reached the intersection and discovered an odd flashing down the path ahead of her. She moved forward to find the fully lit moonflowers behaving strangely. The petals continually pulsed, fading and contracting inward to a close, and then stretching open with a bright burst of white light. She had never seen them do that before, and continued to examine them as she passed.

At the end of the path, Harmony stepped out into the clearing overlooking the small valley and walked to the embankment. She had no blanket this morning, but knelt down on the ground anyway. She gazed across the valley's misty treetops as the sun began to clear the horizon, tears dripping from her eyes. Reaching into her pocket, she removed a multihued friendship bracelet and stared at it for a moment.

As the rising sun illuminated her grayish-silver hair, she tied the bracelet around her wrist. Tears still streaming down her face, Harmony ignored the rising sun and fiddled with the bracelet, thinking about Shiloh. She fidgeted for a mo-

Shiloh's True Nature

ment or two, but then stood up and walked back toward the path, forsaking the sunrise.

Harmony plodded along the trail, ignoring her surroundings to try to cope with the tremendous sorrow filling her. It was only when she reached the end of the path and saw the men unwrapping Shiloh's blanket-encased body that she regained an external focus. She stopped and quietly sighed as the body was placed into the Revenant.

Once the Revenant was closed, Doc threw the blanket across the top of it. A loud grinding sound echoed through the yard, startling everyone, including Cheepie, who jumped down from the stone platform. Crow looked toward the cat and then to the platform's dial. Luther, Jace and Doc walked over and gazed down at the dial. Its fin was now casting its improper shadow past the ζ and clearly on the symbol.

"What do you think it means, Doc?" Luther asked.

Doc shook his head and looked over his shoulder to Crow. Crow's focus, however, was not on the dial, but on the sky above. He was staring up at the full moon, which still appeared to be stuck in the same position it had occupied all night.

When Crow broke his gaze with the heavens, he looked toward Doc with raised eyebrows. Doc shrugged his shoulders and then turned to Luther and Jace. "I want to thank you all for your help with this difficult task, but time is marching on and I need to get ready for the Funus."

Luther nodded at Doc.

"I'll see you all back here shortly then?" Doc asked.

"Of course," Luther answered.

Doc nodded at everyone and then walked into the house.

Harmony watched and waited at the rear of the yard until Crow, Luther, and Jace departed. She passed through the yard, again trying not to look toward the center where the Revenant sat. She continued on to the front of the house and down the dirt road, until she arrived at home.

As she drew near, she found Regina departing and Saige standing despondent on the front porch. Saige noticed Harmony and gazed toward her with a pained look. Harmony stepped up onto the porch as tears streamed from Saige's eyes. The two women held one another for a moment before entering the house.

Doc spent the early part of the morning trying to rest, but it was no use. The hours seemed like days to him as his mind raced with thoughts of his departed grandson. He was almost thankful when the Stone Balloon struck nine, because it meant he could focus on preparing the cart.

When Doc stepped out of the house to the front porch, he discovered everyone had already arrived. His horses had been brought around and the acacia-filled Revenant had been placed in the rear of the cart. He looked over the faces of his friends as they sat waiting for him to lead the way. He wanted to express his appreciation but couldn't find the words, so he gave them all a small smile of thanks, climbed up into the cart, and started off down the road.

Once they were in the air, a general sense of unease swept over everyone. The somber mood of trips to Peas Isle were normally masked by the cover of darkness, but not this time. The moon's eerily fixed position, coupled with the blinding-

Shiloh's True Nature

ly bright morning sun's ascent, gave the flight an unsettling aura.

As the river drew near, Doc's focus shifted from the sky to the tiny isle just offshore of the reed-covered riverbank. He slowly descended and landed in the center of the isle. As the others followed, Doc swung the cart around, bringing it to a stop by the sloping bank facing the heart of the river.

Once the others had arrived and formed a semicircle around the edge of the islet, Crow, Luther, and Maximo came forward to assist Doc in unloading the Revenant. Bud, Brinda, and Kaz gravitated toward one another, standing together in silence. As they watched the men place the Revenant at the mouth of the dirt ramp, Bud nervously rolled something around and around his index fingers.

Noticing the movement out of the corner of her eye, Brinda turned toward Bud. The object seemed familiar to her, but she couldn't clearly distinguish what it was. "What is that?"

"It's Shiloh's friendship bracelet. I found it hanging from a piece of broken glass in the shed the night he . . . borrowed . . . my dad's wings," Bud sniffed with a sad little chuckle.

Kaz fought back a smile and patted Bud on the shoulder.

Brinda gazed over toward Harmony, to find her fiddling with the bracelet around her wrist. Brinda pulled the bracelet from Bud's hand, saying, "Gimme that." She walked over to Harmony and handed her the bracelet. Harmony stared at the bracelet as Brinda sniffled, "I think if that jerk knew what they meant, he would have given them to you."

Harmony's eyes welled up, and Brinda gave her a quick hug before returning to Bud and Kaz.

Once the boat was in place, Crow pulled the blanket from atop the Revenant. Doc stepped forward, clearing his throat and gazing around at everyone with a pained, but grateful smile. He could see from their faces that their hearts were as heavy as his. He cleared his throat once more, but hesitated when he saw something flying toward the isle.

Thinking someone was late to the Funus, Doc made a second pass over the faces before him and found no one missing. He squinted at the object in the distance, but the surroundings began to take on a dark-orange tint. He gazed up over his shoulder to find the morning sun slipping behind the stationary moon. When he turned back toward shore, whatever was approaching the isle had disappeared.

Finally ready to start the proceedings, Doc pointed to the sky, saying, "The Astral oddity notwithstanding, I imagine it was a morning not unlike this thirteen years ago that my grandson, Shiloh, was born."

Doc looked over his shoulder toward the Revenant and continued, "You know, I spent the better part of the morning trying to cherish the memories of the last two weeks with Shiloh, but in the back of my mind there was something bothering me. You see, I've tried to live my life the right way, so I can look back to the past with no regrets. What was bothering me was the realization that I do have regrets. Unfortunately, all those regrets seem to revolve around one person: Shiloh."

He could see the immense sadness amongst his friends, but Doc tried to keep his composure. "I regret not spending more time with him over the last thirteen years. I regret that

Shiloh's True Nature

I won't get to experience his sense of wonder and answer all the little questions that came from it. I regret that I won't get to see him smile or hear his laugh again."

Doc's emotions began to overwhelm him, but he fought back his tears. "And I regret that he died trying to do something for all of us. Something we should've done for ourselves. But mostly . . . mostly I regret that he never got to see his thirteenth birthday."

Unable to go on, Doc turned away from everyone to wipe the tears from his eyes. A faint chiming rang out in the distance, and Doc quickly grabbed a torch from the rear of the cart and lit it. He stepped up to the Revenant and tossed the torch into the mountain of acacia.

As the others came forward, Doc gave the boat a little push. "Good-bye, Shiloh. You will be missed."

Everyone stood around Doc, comforting hands on his arms and shoulders, as the swiftly burning Revenant slid into the river. They watched the bluish-green flames dance around, emitting yellow and red streaks as they consumed the drifting boat. The sun's complete disappearance behind the full moon enhanced the distinct brilliance of the flames.

While the anomalous eclipse banished the dark-orange tint blanketing the surroundings, a new source of illumination replaced it. A stunningly bright white dot appeared in the sky at the center of the now-darkened moon. It was as if a hole had been punched in the center of the moon to let the sun's rays through.

What began as a peculiar speck of light soon grew into a rapidly descending, glowing orb that lit up the sky as brightly as the sun. Everyone shielded their eyes from the blinding light, but the sky suddenly returned to normal, the sun illuminating the world like any other morning. The stationary moon had vanished without a trace, and a giant, shiny, white pearl hung in the air above the burning Revenant.

The pearl hovered above the boat, emitting a pulsing, white glow, as if it were waiting for something. Everyone watched in awe, marveling at the pearl as the tenth and final chime of the Stone Balloon echoed in the distance. The fire from the revenant then began to die, and the pearl of light crashed into the funeral boat with a loud crunch. The remains of the boat disappeared into the water, along with the shiny pearl.

Aghast, everyone took a step back from the sloping incline, looking around at one another for some sort of explanation. When it was clear no one had any answers, everyone's attention returned to the water, which had begun to rapidly ripple and bubble. The disturbance beneath the river's surface extended from the nearby shore to farther than the eye could see.

When the nearby river water began to gush into the air, like a geyser had formed underneath, everyone's awe turned to fear. Breathing was rapid and hearts were pounding as the river suddenly erupted and a giant, unidentified creature began to surface. Those onshore found themselves witnessing the emergence of a beautiful, blue-green sea dragon.

The creature's massive head was complete with rainbow-colored fins and whiskers. Water poured off the sea dragon's brow as it stared down at those gathered on the islet with

Shiloh's True Nature

one blue eye and one brown eye. The creature steadied its emerging torso, which extended nearly halfway across the river, with four gigantic limbs. The surfacing of the creature's tail seemed to go on forever. The tail thinned as it extended out from the body, but it was so long that the onlookers couldn't tell where it ended.

Everyone onshore recoiled at the sea dragon's presence, except for Harmony. While the others drifted back from the river, she stepped closer, staring up, entranced by the creature. As their eyes met, Harmony's hair became a kaleidoscope of colors, matching the blues, greens, and faded highlights of red and yellow in the scales of the creature.

The sea dragon turned its attention to the shoreline just beyond the islet. The creature craned its neck to and fro as if searching for something. Suddenly, it let out a massive roar. Everyone except Harmony huddled together in fear of an |attack, but the creature was not focused on them. The dragon roared again as its incredibly long tail rose into the air behind it.

The dragon continued roaring, until someone peered out from behind the reeds. It was Haines hiding on the riverbank, watching the Funus. When Haines made eye contact with the creature, it appeared to smile at him before turning its head toward the far side of the river. Suddenly, its vast tail began swinging and looping around over and over.

A moment later, a massive, ripping sound echoed from far across the river. Everyone covered their ears, and looked up toward the sea dragon to find it reeling in its tail. The dragon returned its gaze to the shoreline as it swung its mighty tail into view. The appendage was wrapped around a giant building with a protruding, brick smokestack. The creature had torn Haines' factory from the ground.

The dragon looked once more toward the shore and roared. Haines popped up from his hiding spot, a look of horror on his face at the sight of his factory in the creature's clutches. The dragon appeared to smile at him yet again , lifting one of its forelimbs out of the water. Haines watched as the creature wrapped its massive claw around the smokestack and crushed it into dust. Haines panicked and jumped on his Cyclopean Beetle to leave. As he took flight, Haines looked back and saw the mighty dragon wrapping its powerful tail around the factory, completely crushing it into a ball.

The sea dragon returned its focus to the isle, gazing down at everyone with a smile. It then unhinged its jaw and proceeded to stuff the factory into its mouth. It didn't stop at the balled-up factory, but continued stuffing its entire tail into its mouth, until the Dragon itself disappeared in a flash, transforming once again into a shiny, white pearl.

The pearl hovered just offshore, pulsing with a bright, white glow before crashing into the water. Everything went silent, except for the waves lapping against the shore. A moment later, the water began to ripple and bubble again. Only this time, it was a much smaller disturbance under the surface, and it appeared to be moving toward the isle.

Suddenly, Shiloh rose naked from the water, gasping and coughing. As he caught his breath, he wiped his eyes and found everyone staring at him in awe. He looked to Harmony, who was closest, and her hair transformed from the

Shiloh's True Nature

multicolored rainbow to blond before his eyes. "What just happened?" he asked, shivering.

A loud cheer came from the funeral party, and Shiloh flinched in shock and confusion. Crow rushed forward with a smile, throwing Shiloh's favorite blanket around him. Doc smiled at Shiloh with a tear in his eye before giving him a big hug. Crow announced, "I knew it. I knew he was a gift."

Harmony stepped forward, staring into Shiloh's eyes, noticing one of them had changed color. One was now brown, while the other remained blue. An overwhelming sense of relief and contentment swept over Shiloh as he returned her gaze. Harmony smiled and covered her blushing face with shaking hands. Shiloh noticed the familiar friendship bracelet on her wrist, and Harmony opened her other hand to reveal the second bracelet. She then took Shiloh's wrist and tied the bracelet there. Shiloh looked at her with a smile as she kissed the tips of her fingers and placed them to Shiloh's lips, saying, "Happy birthday."

As Harmony backed away, Shiloh found Bud, Kaz, Brinda, and everyone else staring at him with grins of astonishment. Shiloh felt a little awkward and said, "Hey, Bud. What's going on?"

"I have no idea. But I can't wait to see what happens on your next birthday," Bud answered, a huge grin plastered on his face.

Everyone roared with laughter. Doc held up his hand and said, "I hope everyone will join us back at the Deer Park for the celebration of my grandson's thirteenth birthday. Once we get him some clothes to wear, of course."

D.W. Raleigh

Everyone gave a final cheer before disbursing to leave the isle. Shiloh paused and looked around, still unsure how he came to be there. Doc approached Shiloh and asked, "Are you ready to go?"

Shiloh frowned. "Seriously . . . what just happened here?"

Doc grinned from ear to ear and said, "I'm not quite sure. How about we go home and talk about it?"

"Home? To Fair Hill?" Shiloh asked.

"Yes," Doc answered, his grin still firmly in place.

As Doc turned toward the cart, Shiloh asked, "Does this mean I'm a Mover?"

Doc let out a hearty laugh without answering. Shiloh took a quick look out at the river and then followed Doc to the cart.

The End

About D.W. Raleigh

D.W. Raleigh was born in the Delaware Valley and has spent most of his life in that region. He has attended multiple colleges and universities, collecting several degrees, including an M.A. in Philosophy. After toiling away for many years in various unfulfilling jobs, he began to realize that what he really wanted to do was write. Scribbling down ideas and little short stories he eventually came up with something he wanted to share with the world. Thus, *Shiloh's True Nature* was born. D.W. currently resides in Newark, Delaware with his longtime love, Judy, and their two cats, Lovie and Cheepie.

For the latest news about our authors and events, or to learn more about upcoming releases and other projects from Hobbes End Publishing, visit:

www.HobbesEndPublishing.com

Made in the USA
Lexington, KY
21 July 2014